THE
EINSTEIN
CONSPIRACY

Also written by Steve Israel

Big Guns

The Global War on Morris

THE
EINSTEIN
CONSPIRACY

A NOVEL BY

STEVE ISRAEL

The Einstein Conspiracy is a work of historical fiction. References to historical incidents were researched and depicted to the best of the author's ability. The descriptions of real-life characters in the novel reflect faithfulness to historical accuracy. Many characters in the story are products of the author's imagination, and any resemblance to actual people, living or dead, is entirely coincidental.

Copyright © 2025
Steve Israel

Compass Rose Publishing
228 Park Ave S #620056
New York, N.Y 10003-1502

Hardcover ISBN: 979-8-9988995-7-7
Softcover ISBN: 979-8-9988995-6-0
Ebook ISBN: 979-8-9988995-8-4

First edition November 2025

Author Photo
by Steve Israel

Cover Design: Danielle Kane and Thomas Hurd
Interior Design: Diane Kane

Publisher's Note: The publisher's decision to keep the text true to the author's vision of the time period and characters depicted is not meant in any way to endorse offensive cultural representations or language.

To Cara

CONTENTS

PART I

1933–1938

Chapter One

ON OCTOBER 17TH, 1933, THE WORLD'S greatest scientist peered over the rail of the ocean liner as it steamed toward Manhattan and thought about ice cream. Not just any ice cream, but a real American ice cream cone, with two scoops of vanilla. The kind he had had the year before, on some pier in Los Angeles. Thick and creamy, better than even the best he could get in Berlin.

It was all he could look forward to. Everything else about America, looming up before him, felt gray. *Looked* gray. Gray water lapping towards gray buildings, all but their outlines hidden behind a gray, sullen mist.

And this was to be their home now.

He sighed. He had left behind a continent full of elegant palaces and charming villages centuries old; of cities full of quaint, winding streets and snow-capped mountains and color-splashed homes. Now he approached America: charmless and raw. A boring and barren society, consumed with itself. He shook his head despondently, wondering whether he would ever return to Europe.

Aaach.

All around him, his fellow passengers stood pointing their cameras at the skyline and jabbering in different languages: German, Yiddish, Polish, some garbled English. Yes, the skyscrapers were monumental, a symphony in stone and steel. The golden, pyramidal summit of the Woolworth Building, the new Art Deco spires of the Chrysler Building, and the Empire State. Yes, they rose higher, much higher, than any other buildings anywhere in the world—but at their feet were clustered ramshackle tenements and hovels, like children begging on a street by their mothers' skirts. Clusters of grim industrial smokestacks—almost none of them smoking. The piers bristling out from the island of

Manhattan like quills of a porcupine, but few of them unloading ships. Uncollected heaps of garbage piled up everywhere along the waterfront. Each time he had returned to it since the start of the Depression, America seemed shabbier, grimmer, aging before its time.

He knew that the other passengers felt it too, most of them. They sounded elated to be in New York, to be safe anywhere. Yet beneath their squawks of pleasure, he thought he could detect a gnawing unease—a fear of what awaited them in this new world. An undertone of despair over what—and who—they had left behind.

Few, if any, would make a return voyage.

They had been evicted by the Nazis, just as he had been. In the nine months since Hitler had taken power, Germany had descended into a frenzy of hatred. Jews were attacked and humiliated on the street; spat upon, beaten, sometimes even killed. Jewish businesses were boycotted and smashed. Jews were turned away from public schools and banned from the parks. They were thrown out of jobs everywhere, no longer allowed to be civil servants, journalists, judges, artists, actors, farmers. Jewish businesses were boycotted or smashed, Jewish books—*his* books—burned in huge piles at universities throughout Germany. The students' faces glowing like goblins as they carried armfuls of volumes to the bonfire.

How could he go back to such a place, even if it were possible?

Einstein felt a soft hand on his arm and grasped it instinctively. Elsa stood beside him. His constant companion, his protector against the outside world. Just the gleam in her eye and her sly smile steadied him.

"Look, our welcoming committee!" she told him, pointing to the flock of seagulls swooping down around the deck, flapping their wings and cawing their greetings. He grinned at her and whooped "Halloo!" back at the birds.

When they sailed out of Southampton, Elsa had pointed to the seagulls escorting them out to sea. Now they ushered them to their new home. He smiled at her again, buoyed by her unconquerable optimism. Even amused by her charming cloche hat. Yet his thoughts drifted into grayness again. *We are the same. Refugees. Birds of passage for the rest of our lives.*

He spied another, less agreeable, welcoming committee approaching the ship: a launch full of determined-looking men in raincoats and fedoras speeding out toward their ship from the 23rd Street pier. It was his nemesis, he realized with another sigh: the press.

Agent Harry Weiss stood near the prow of the small launch, struggling to maintain the appearance of calm determination. He felt like throwing up. He felt the same way he always did on or around the water: like curling up into a ball and hugging the deck.

He blinked hard and forced himself to concentrate on the job. Not that it was much of a challenge escorting a rabble of newspaper reporters and newsreel boys over to the ocean liner *Westmoreland* to interview Albert Einstein. None of them seemed particularly lethal, though most looked hungover and some were clearly still drunk, even at ten in the morning. *From this, Einstein needed protection?* Still, the Nazis and their sympathizers had tried to kill him in London, and again in Belgium. And there were those letters…

He glanced down at Patrolman Robert Larkins at his side. Bobby grinned back up at him. He was an NYPD rookie, wearing an oversized blue uniform with sleeves to his knuckles. Just six months on the force. This was a lark for him, a day off from being a "squirrel cop," walking a beat in Central Park like all the other rookies.

Weiss had requested Larkins from the NYPD for the assignment. A chance to see Albert Einstein up close. A favor to a special friend: Larkin's uncle Danny.

"Hey, hero. Don't look at me," Weiss tried to tell Bobby gently but firmly, remembering how patient the kid's uncle had been with him. He had practically been Harry's rabbi on the force. "Where are your eyes supposed to be?"

"Right, Har—Yessir!"

Bobby snapped to, switching his gaze immediately to the newsmen, who were now singing an obscene version of "Clementine." Harry hoped to Christ one of them didn't fall over the side. It would be hell pulling a man out of the water in this mist.

"Once you've established where he is, don't look at Einstein, either. Your job is sussing out any threat, not staring at the guy we're protecting."

"Yessir!"

Bobby nodded vigorously, not switching his eyes back to Weiss for so much as a moment. Harry smiled. The kid was going to be all right. Still a string bean, with a row of peach fuzz along his upper lip before his uncle made him shave it. Smart, alert, responsible. Dating the same girl since high school, engaged two weeks ago. *He'd make a good family man*, Weiss thought.

Weiss shifted his gaze to Agent Amos, his partner for this assignment, covering the reporters from the back of the launch. His eyes were where they should be, which didn't surprise Harry. The man was a serious agent, no-nonsense, observant, and...a Negro. When he introduced himself at the pier, Harry had thought for a moment it must be a joke, another hazing ritual by all the friendly *goyim* he worked with. It had never occurred to him that the Bureau even *had* a colored agent. But he seemed every inch a professional: middle-aged, balding, but with a younger man's trim physique. Fastidious and correct down to every last detail—what hair he still had cut Bureau short, shoes polished to a shine, suit and tie spotless under his raincoat. Harry sighed. *Exactly the sort of attention to appearance that Director Hoover demanded—and that Harry was never able to quite get right.* As Harry looked at him now in the launch, Agent Amos caught his eye and made a small sign of acknowledgement: *Everything a-okay.* So far.

It had never occurred to James Amos that the Bureau even *had* a Jewish agent. He thought it was one of the little jokes the white agents liked to play on him. He almost laughed out loud when he saw his look of surprise reflected in the man's eyes. Then Weiss had grinned and stuck out a hand. It was a welcome gesture. Even now, in his mid-fifties, Amos could never get used to how many white men refused to shake hands with him.

The man was nodding back at him from the prow when the launch cut a small wake, and his eyes snapped from Amos to the water's surface. Amos pretended not to notice.

Agent Weiss was a short, compact individual, no more than five and a half feet tall, wearing a trench coat and a Stetson. Amos also pretended—for now—not to notice his sloppily knotted tie, nestled in a wrinkled shirt collar. Weiss had a prominent scar on the right side of his brow and black, combative eyes that seemed to be constantly scanning everything around him, which was all for the best. Amos didn't need his partner to be perfect, or to like him. He just needed to know he could trust his partner with his life.

James had stepped quietly onto the launch behind the reporters, ignoring their gawking and occasional rude questions about just who he was. By now he was accustomed to the ritual: producing his FBI credentials to the widening of eyes, the slow disbelieving shaking of heads, in some cases the heaving of shoulders as if to say, "Now I've seen it all." But today he fought a dry mouth and a constant tensing of his neck muscles.

It had started at breakfast in the sunlit kitchen of his house in Queens. He drummed his knuckles on the table, responded robotically to his wife's early morning chatter, and moved his fork aimlessly around his plate. Finally, Annie said, "Are you here, James?"

Amos sighed. "I have an assignment today. Not looking forward to it."

"Is it the Italians, the Nazis, or the Jewish mob?" she asked.

"None of them. Protective detail. For Albert Einstein."

Annie reached across the table and rested her hand lightly on his. "You'll be fine."

"Will I?"

"It's been over twenty years."

"Sticks with me."

"What happened then wasn't your fault. Stop being so hard on yourself."

Now, standing on the launch as it cut across the harbor, Amos fought the doubts.

This was his first FBI assignment to protect a dignitary since that long ago day in Milwaukee, when he was supposed to guard his boss, Theodore Roosevelt. He'd served Roosevelt first as a White House valet, then in a succession of jobs after his presidency ended. Roosevelt's trust in James was so deep that he'd made him his personal bodyguard. Four years after leaving the presidency, Roosevelt decided to run again. James joined him for a campaign rally in Milwaukee.

Damned Milwaukee—

He forced himself to stop thinking about it. *Anything*, any distraction could be fatal in an assignment like this. After breakfast Annie had straightened his tie and called today a *chance at redemption*. She'd only wanted to see him laugh a little, but maybe she was onto something.

Amos tried to clear his mind, reducing it to a hunter's focus. Looking for anything, anything out of the usual.

Einstein stared balefully at the boat full of reporters, pondering the physics of what it would take to make it sink and pull all of them down to the bottom of the Hudson. He felt a squeeze on his elbow.

"Smile, *Liebchen*. Please. Remember how glad we are to be in America," Elsa said softly. "You are the great man with the funny hair who just wants a place to be let alone to do his work."

It was true enough. That *was* all he wanted. He smiled down at the reporters, gave them a little wave. Her instincts were always so good. They hooted and howled back up at him.

"Hey, Perfessuh! Looking sharp—*relatively* speaking!"

"Perfessuh! You figure out the formula to win at shuffleboard every time?"

"Hey, Perfessuh—is it true the Nazis put a $5,000 bounty on your head?"

He smiled with a tranquility that did not extend beyond his lips.

"I never knew my head was worth so much," he called down to them, which drew a raucous laugh. He thought that he would just as soon swim to shore.

It was the press who had nearly made it impossible for him to return to America at all. At the end of his first trip to the States, departing from this same harbor all the way back in 1921, he had given an interview to an old family friend, a Dutch-American woman married to a New York publisher. He had been exhausted after weeks of giving major new lectures on his general theory of relativity and working ceaselessly to raise money for a Jewish hospital in Palestine. Tired, cranky, he had been dismissive, speaking freely, delivering himself of all sorts of opinions about the United States.

The sciences in America couldn't compare to those in Europe. American men did nothing but work. They let American women treat them like toy dogs and spend all their money. No, he could not understand the interest in him in here, except for the fact that the people must be so bored. Americans were so intellectually impoverished, their culture so dull, that when any sensation appeared they pursued it with a monstrous intensity.

He had thought nothing of it; the reporter was writing for a provincial newspaper back in the Netherlands. But within days her article had been picked up by a big Berlin paper, then translated and reproduced all over the United States.

"But they are just my honest views!" he had protested to Elsa.

"In the future," she had scoffed, "confine your honest views to your diary. You would not accept such superficial observations from the least of your students!"

It took another tour of America—and all sorts of outright lying, at Elsa's insistence, about how he had been misquoted—to put the whole furor to bed. Or so they had hoped.

"Professor!"

A stocky man with a scar above his eye was striding toward them now. He had the commanding air of an official of some sort. Einstein steeled himself for the usual test of strength these Americans called a handshake. Sure enough, the man grabbed Einstein's arm as if he was working a water pump.

"Dr. Einstein, Mrs. Einstein. Welcome back to the United States. I am Agent Weiss from the Federal Bureau of Investigation. I'm here to escort you to Princeton," he told them.

"Thank you. But I don't believe we require such protection," Einstein told him, a little stiffly.

"I don't wish to alarm you, but the Bureau has received a number of threatening letters."

"From Americans?" Einstein asked, genuinely surprised.

"In part," Weiss told him, sounding abashed. "We, uh, intercepted a number of them from the Woman Patriot Corporation—"

"Those lunatics!" Elsa exclaimed. Einstein put his hand on his wife's arm now.

It had been almost a year ago, December 1932. Germany was tumbling into chaos and they were rushing to get out—to get to England, or to America—anywhere he could live and work in peace. A woman with the impossible name of Mrs. Randolph Frothingham, on behalf of the so-called Woman Patriot Corporation, had sent a sixteen-page public letter to the State Department. Einstein, she wrote, was "the acknowledged world leader" of a vast conspiracy, intent on using pacifism to disarm the world's militaries and foment a "people's revolution."

"Not even Stalin himself is affiliated with so many anarcho-communist groups, as ALBERT EINSTEIN," Mrs. Frothingham had frothed.

Einstein had thought it was a joke until Elsa and he were called in to the American Consulate in Berlin for a lengthy questioning. As the questions went on, Einstein could feel his patience slipping away.

"*Are you, or have you ever been, a Communist or an anarchist, Dr. Einstein?*"

"What is this, an inquisition?" Einstein exploded before the pair stomped out.

The affair had nearly cost them their entry. Had they not succeeded in pressuring Hoover's White House through a few strategic wires to the *Times* and the *Herald Tribune*, their visas might not have been issued in time. The Einsteins escaped Germany less than three weeks before Hitler was invited into the government.

They had lingered in Europe for a few more months, as if they couldn't quite bear to go. Even after they had renounced their German citizenship the Nazis had called for Einstein's death, and Belgian police began receiving tips about plans by a Nazi hit squad, the *Fehme*, to assassinate him. The police had asked him to discontinue his daily walks. Einstein refused.

Finally, they had come to America. But it seemed that all the furies had followed.

"The, uh, women patriots," Weiss told them now, "are part of our concern. Others…they just don't seem to like your theories."

Yes, that was part of it, too, Einstein conceded. They hated his theories, even as they didn't understand them. *Relativity*—it was the word that stuck in their craws. It made them think he believed in a universe with no moral center, at a same moment when the world seemed to be falling away.

"There have been some other tips, too," Weiss continued. "About the Friends of the New Germany over here. And then there's Berlin."

That brought Einstein's head up. *What did that mean? The Abwehr? The Gestapo? The SA?* Those people were truly frightening, too vicious to restrain themselves. They had stalked him in Belgium and London, he knew. Could their reach extend this far?

"Is my wife in any danger?" Einstein asked the FBI man. Elsa squeezed his arm in appreciation. "Also, my secretary is with us, Frau Dukas."

"We don't think there's any active danger, but we don't know," Weiss said.

Einstein warmed to the man. *It was so rare that Americans admitted they didn't know something.*

"That's why we're here, just to make sure. But if you'd rather go directly to Princeton…"

He let the question hang. Einstein nodded, looked at Elsa.

"It might be good to answer a few questions, keep them satisfied," she said.

"All right, Agent Weiss," he said. "Let the scoundrels do their worst."

Chapter Two

THE GENTLEMEN OF THE PRESS SURGED the deck of the *Westmoreland* shoving and elbowing and cursing. James Amos thought it was a miracle that none of them ended up in the water. He stood by the gangway and watched them closely as they passed, trying to fix his eyes on each one in turn. Reading the press cards with the names of all the New York papers and news organizations that they kept fixed in their hatbands as proudly as so many escutcheons: the *Times*, the *Herald Tribune*; the *Sun*, the *Daily Mirror*, the *World-Telegram*, the *Journal* and the *American*. The UP, the AP, and the INS. The newsreel boys from Hearst, and Movietone, and Pathé.

Wait. There was one he glimpsed that didn't quite make sense—that was wrong somehow. He looked for it again, found it. On the hat of a reporter near the back of the pack, head bobbing about. Amos moved a little closer, hoping to get a better look. There it was: *Evening Graphic.* He frowned. Could it be an out-of-town paper? Then he remembered: it was the lowest of the tabloids, a raucous scandal sheet that specialized in cosmographs—photos and drawings combined to make up fictional scenes about the rich and mighty. A paper full of lurid gossip and police reports. Annie wouldn't have it in the house, called it "the *Porno*graphic." There was no reason a reporter from the *Graphic* wouldn't be in the interview boat, though. Save for the fact that it had gone belly-up over a year ago.

Amos studied the man closer. He remembered him from the pier. He had seemed a little stiff at first, uncertain of his place, greeted by cries of, "Hey, lookit the rookie!" Now, just a couple hours later, he acted like he had been one of the gang for years: hat tilted back on his head, laughing with the others, swigging from the flask they passed around. Something about how easily he had adjusted didn't seem right.

There was something else, as well. The man was pushing his way forward, looking for openings in the crowd. And while the other reporters all had their little notebooks and pencils or their cameras up and ready, this one's hands were held loosely in his pockets, eyes fixed on where Professor Einstein would speak.

He had seen that before. It had been outside the Hotel Gilpatrick, James remembered, on 3rd Street in Milwaukee. The big crowd, festive, jocular. Clogging the entire route between the hotel and the Milwaukee Auditorium where Roosevelt was to speak. A sea of cheerful faces waiting for a glimpse of the President. *Except for one.* A short, heavyset man, darkly dressed. If he'd been standing still, James never would have noticed him. But he was moving with determination, pushing his way forward through the seams of the crowd, unnoticed.

Like this one.

Just as he remembered this, Amos saw the unknown reporter sneak a quick peek—back at *him*—before looking away. Now he was certain. As a Black man, James Amos had no standing on this boat, or anywhere. A white reporter could stare at him as long as he liked with impunity, for any reason—and many of them had. But this was so quick that Amos would never have caught it if he hadn't been looking right back. The question wasn't why he would look—*but why would he hide it?*

Amos was already moving across the deck of the *Westmoreland,* making his way quietly but directly toward the front of the press pack. Doing his best to play the obliging Negro— a part he hated, but one that had probably saved his life more than once. Nodding, grinning, half-bowing. Nothing but a harmless, oblivious man of color, probably on his way to fetch drinks for everyone. And as he did so, he noticed that the *Graphic* reporter's eyes were on him again. His gaze hard, menacing—though he kept back, fading into the crowd away from James.

Agent Amos reached the front of the interview space and made a little gesture to Larkins to come over to him. He carefully resisted any temptation to touch Larkins' arm. To the outside eye, he was just a Negro asking permission for something.

"Patrolman Larkins," he said as quietly as possible, moving his head so that the kid would be forced to turn his head too, away from the reporters. "I don't want you to show the least sign of alarm. Just smile at me, the way I'm doing now—only not so big. Good. Keep your eyes on me, too. Got it? All right, there's a fella on the edge of the crowd, to the right. Slightly darker raincoat, maybe five-ten, one-sixty, dark hair close cut. Don't look! But whatever you do, don't let him get past you."

"You think he's a threat?" Larkins said, his face lit up by the thought of adventure. "Why, we can—"

"Keep smiling! I'm going back to see Agent Weiss. Just don't let him get past you. I don't care if you have to shoot him. Got it?"

"Yessir," Larkins breathed.

To his relief, the kid didn't seem scared—or overexcited, either.

"One more thing: do *not* look directly at him when I'm gone."

Amos found Weiss and the Einstein party in their stateroom on the main deck. The professor was signing autographs for the *Westmoreland's* captain and some of the ship's officers. James felt the same small shock of recognition he had whenever he saw famous people close up, in the flesh. *Was it the newsreels that made them seem like gods?* He had felt it the first time his father had taken him to meet Teddy Roosevelt. He'd been offered a position caring for the Roosevelt children in the White House. "The hardest job in America," the President had joked, with a clipped laugh that seemed to dance off his teeth.

Amos explained what he had seen out on the deck to Agent Weiss. To his surprise, the man listened to him carefully. *In Milwaukee, the white cops had not even made a pretense of listening, barely able to contain their anger that a colored man should dare to talk to them at all, unbidden. Even when he explained he was Roosevelt's bodyguard, they turned their backs. The crowd cheered wildly as Roosevelt emerged from the Hotel Gilpatrick, climbed into his car and waved his hat. That famous smile, electric white, seemed to ignite the crowd. The whole scene was earsplitting. But James spotted the little man getting closer. Raising a fist—*

"Where is he now?" Weiss asked.

"Back with the reporters. I told your man Larkins to shoot anybody who tries to get past him, if he has to."

"He will, too. He's a brave kid."

Weiss made a small gesture toward the Einsteins. Amos could see that both Elsa and Einstein's assistant, Miss Dukas, had noticed it.

"We should get them off the boat. Now. That way we've got the professor out of danger and our friend trapped on board, whoever he is."

"Is there a quiet way off?" Amos asked.

"The captain said they're expecting a pilot boat. Soon as it gets here we can send the Einsteins back on it. We can get a car to the dock to pick them up."

"That'll work. You get them off, and I'll go see about the reporter from a dead newspaper."

Weiss yearned for nothing more than to get on solid ground again, off this water. But he knew better.

"No," he made himself tell Agent Amos, thinking as clearly as he could, "you should take the Einsteins off the boat and drive them to Princeton. I've worked with Officer Larkins before. I'll tell the Captain not to berth until we deal with our friend."

The thought lay unspoken between them: as a colored man, James Amos would never be able to get the captain of an ocean liner to do what he wanted.

"All right," Amos said, and moved toward the Einstein party, fingering the Colt semi-automatic in his pocket. He'd carefully cleaned and reloaded it the night before. Weiss was already talking urgently to the captain and the chief steward.

"Sir, what is the matter?" Helen Dukas asked him before he could even get to the Einsteins. She was a trim, efficient woman with a beak-like nose.

"Probably nothing, ma'am," Amos told her. "But we don't want to take any chances. We think the professor should forego talking to the press just now and go directly to New Jersey with the pilot."

"But what about our luggage? The professor's personal effects?" she asked, her English accented but precise.

"Is there a problem, Helen?" Einstein asked her, coming up to them, nodding courteously to the agent.

Amos explained the situation quickly, and he nodded.

"In other words, 'Welcome to the land of freedom. Now go hide.' It's all right, officer. Just let me stop back in my stateroom, and we will be right with you."

Amos thought he should refuse the professor's request.

"I'll need to accompany you down there," he said.

Arriving at the stateroom, Einstein stuffed two pipes into his jacket pocket and picked up his battered violin case. Amos tried hard to mask his impatience. Remembering the little man in Milwaukee. *Spotting him suddenly, the pistol already in his hand, pointing at Theodore Roosevelt, not 25 feet away.*

Out on the deck, Harry Weiss tried to keep a look of serene confidence on his face. He strolled slowly over to Bobby Larkins, smiled, said something close by his ear.

"Where is he, hero?"

"Back right now. On the edge. The darker raincoat."

"Yeah, I see him. Perfect position on the outside. He can make his break and fly by the whole pack the minute the flashbulbs start poppin'. All right, keep an eye on him while I make the announcement."

Weiss whistled with his fingers and waved his arms in the air.

"Listen up!" he called out.

"Who're you?" one of the reporters demanded immediately.

"Where the hell's the great man?" another yelled.

Tough crowd, Weiss thought.

"There's been a change of plans. Dr. Einstein is not going to hold a press conference today. He and his wife and assistant have already disembarked."

"Whaddya mean 'disembarked?' We haven't seen a boat."

Harry was in no mood to argue. "You should have looked harder. Now if you'll move back down the deck there—"

The assembled press of New York did no such thing. Instead, they rushed forward, outraged, shouting questions at Harry, a couple of the photographers firing their flashes in his face. Half-blinded, yelling futilely at them all to back off, he turned to Larkins—only to see him blinking rapidly too.

"Harry. Harry!" he said, his voice verging on panic. "I don't see him! Harry, I don't know where he is!"

"I don't see him either," Weiss admitted.

He gripped the .38 Smith & Wesson in his trench coat pocket, then pulled Bobby away from the reportorial scrum.

"I'm going to go back through the cabin, to try to cover the Einsteins on their way out," he told Larkins. "You go the other way, see if you can get behind him."

"Got it," the kid nodded, already starting away. Harry Weiss still grabbed his arm.

"Listen. Chances are our friend is just looking for cover right now. As long as Einstein's off the boat, long as he's safe, we've done our job. Don't shoot some hoity-toity passenger. And for God's sake, don't get *yourself* shot. Do you hear me?"

"Yessir!"

"Good man. Now go!"

Weiss turned to find another reporter in his face, pad and pencil drawn.

"Where is Einstein? Why can't we see him?" he demanded, the combination of scotch and garlic on the man's breath nearly enough to knock Weiss over.

Weiss shoved past him to one side while sticking a knee in between his legs—a little self-defense move he had learned at the Bureau's training courses. The reporter tripped and went sprawling out over the deck. Harry rushed towards the stairs.

Amos and a steward were ushering the Einstein party to a lower deck, where they would meet the pilot boat. Members of the crew and other passengers were trudging up and down the narrow passage, flitting in and out of doors. James forcing himself not to pull out the semi-automatic. *This was a security nightmare— though not as bad as the nightmare in Milwaukee.*

The little man squeezing off a shot directly at Roosevelt. The retort of the gunshot. Roosevelt, flinching, clutching the seat back, straightening himself, then slumping. James hesitated, unsure whether to attack the gunman or aid Roosevelt. He saw someone wrestling the shooter as the revolver rose for another round, and the confused swarm of city policemen. He rushed to the car, where an aide had wrapped his arm around Roosevelt in the back seat and asked if he was alright. Roosevelt pulled himself up and said, "He pinked me."

Finally, they were at an open hatchway on the *Westmoreland*, just above the waterline. More crew members stood there open-mouthed, staring at Einstein. Drops of rain had begun to pelt the harbor, and James heard an approaching rumble. It wasn't thunder, but a bright orange pilot boat belching black smoke from its single funnel, chugging towards them through the whitecaps. A couple of blasé deckhands in their grease-soaked sweaters and pants balanced along the rail, one hand on a lanyard—as if it were every day they sailed right up to the steel wall of an ocean liner. Then they spotted Albert Einstein.

"Hey, Perfessuh! Perfessuh! What I tell ya, it's really him!"

All our love for this man is going to get him killed, James Amos thought.

"Welcome to America, Perfessuh Einstein!" They were still

calling to him as the bright red tug came alongside. "Say, can I getta autograph?"

Einstein, amused, saw the anxiety in Amos' eyes, and guided his wife and assistant up to the hatchway.

"I believe our ride is here," he told them.

Chapter Three

AGENT WEISS RACED DOWN THE STAIRS, elbowing, pushing, grunting at anyone in his way. He kept the S&W in his pocket but slid the safety off. He was not going to be outdrawn, no matter what the risk. He wondered how well their mysterious reporter friend knew the boat, knew where they were headed. He worried about Bobby.

The lad had already distinguished himself on the force. It had been all over the tabloids: a pair of little boys had managed to hide out in the Central Park Zoo after closing time and climbed into the polar bear's enclosure. Someone had told them that polar bears couldn't swim, and when it had dived in and gone after them they had panicked and run into its cave. The bear had followed them in. Bobby had just swung by on his rounds. The old rummy that Tammany had hired to be the night watchman thrust an ancient double-barreled shotgun into his hands and advised him to say a Hail Mary. Bobby Larkins had put the gun down and picked up a big slab of fetid seal meat—the bear's supper. He walked into the cave with it, and two minutes later emerged with the little boys, one in each arm and both clinging for dear life to his neck.

Weiss had never seen Danny Larkins so furious. He would not stop laying into his nephew during the raucous celebration up at Rosenhain's.

"Ya went in there with nothin' but your revolver? In its holster? Against a *bear*?" he asked his nephew, incredulous.

"That old blunderbuss he gave me would've liked to take my hand off quicker'n the damned bear," Bobby told him. "Supper come, and what could a couple of little runts and a beanpole like me compare to a nice, rancid slab of seal meat? Jesus, but it stank to high heaven!"

It was hard for Danny to hide his pride, Harry knew, but he tried to get his point across.

"Don't ever do that again."

"What?"

"Don't ever go into a situation where you don't know what yer up against, an' not even a pop gun in yer hand. D'ya hear me?"

"I thought I would need my hands for the kids, Uncle Dan. I figured I might get us all killed, swinging around that shotgun I didn't know from a cannon."

They had gone on fighting half the night about it, but Danny had finally got his point across—he'd always been able to, with Harry. Would the boy remember it, though? He was a natural-born hero, much as Weiss teased him about it, and heroes didn't think enough about their own asses.

Harry charged down another flight, then stopped. He was sure that he had heard something: steps almost exactly echoing his own, coming down the stairs after him. He flattened himself against the wall and looked back up. Did he see something? The hint of hat brim, perhaps? At least if he had, the man was caught. There was no way he'd get past Harry.

Weiss pulled out his Smith & Wesson, while still making his way down the stairs. Keeping close to the wall, so his unknown pursuer would have to show himself if he wanted to get a good shot in. He expected to see him at any moment.

But there was nothing. Harry made his way down the very last flight of stairs, to where the hatch was just closing. No one here but a couple of *Westmoreland* crew members, babbling excitedly to each other about having seen Einstein.

Thank God, Harry thought to himself. Their charge was off the boat, headed to New Jersey in the capable hands of Agent Amos. Now they could concentrate exclusively on whoever had pursued him down the steps. Taking a deep breath, Harry Weiss raced as loudly as he could back up the first four steps, gun in hand—then stopped. Sure enough, he heard footfalls, and staring up saw a flash of movement, a suggestion of a figure bolting off into a deck far above him.

Now we got him, Harry thought, running back up the ship.

Chapter Four

EINSTEIN STOOD IN THE CABIN of the tugboat. He would have just as soon been back out on the deck, even in the growing rain, but he had yielded to the heartfelt entreaties of the colored FBI man. *Pursued even here.* The Nazis had been hounding him even before he'd won the 1921 Nobel Prize for his work—even before anybody knew about Nazis, or Einstein. *In retrospect, it was a good thing*, he thought, *how he had known to leave Germany before they took power.* Nonetheless, he was vilified in the press, renounced by his former colleagues. Lenard, that bombastic old idiot, and the unspeakable Stark. No retaliation, no action was too petty for them.

That was how dictatorships intimidated people, he knew. After Einstein had denounced the Nazis and repudiated his German citizenship, they had seized his beloved summer retreat on the lake at Caputh. He had known it would happen—the last time they were there, he had told Elsa to say goodbye to his beloved little house. The reason the Reich gave out was that he was storing a cache of guns and ammunition there. All nonsense, of course. What they were really looking for were his papers, he knew, to find any secret breakthroughs that they might use. They didn't find anything. He had been able to rely on the husband of his dear stepdaughter, poor Ilse, to smuggle out everything that might be useful to him and burn the rest. But the Nazis had confiscated their cottage anyway, turned it into part of a Hitler Youth camp. They had even seized the *Tümmler*, his thick sailing boat, and sold it off.

They could have it, as much as it stung. All he wanted now was enough time and distance from those jackals to do something useful.

"It's the work, isn't it?" Elsa asked, next to him now in her wool coat on the tug. "As much as anything?"

As usual, she had read his mind. *Lieben und arbeiten.* Love and work. That was all a man needed, Freud had said. The love, Einstein had. It was the work that worried him. It had been a long time since he had burst on the international scene and won the Nobel—longer still since his *annus mirabilis* in 1905, when he published four groundbreaking papers that revolutionized physics. He was just twenty-six. He was more than twice that now, and the years had fled while he was tempted by one idea or another. Coming up with—then rejecting—a steady state model of the universe. Delving into the mysteries of black holes and superconductivity, of lasers and maser and transverse mass. All fascinating fields of study. But nothing that led back to what he was really after: his unified field theory, or his "theory of everything," as he and his colleagues joked.

There were so many distractions. The Zionists who wanted his help to build a Jewish community in Palestine. The pacifists, all those idealistic young people looking for him to lead them through a world that somehow seemed to be drifting back toward war. The refugees, like so many of his fellow passengers on the *Westmoreland*, pleading with him for help. Distinguished men and women of science, who had held teaching positions in major universities, now without a job, without a country.

Meanwhile, he knew, he was drifting further and further away from the latest debates and discoveries in physics. He felt alienated from Heisenberg's quantum mechanics, now sweeping the field. Einstein acknowledged the man's genius, but he found the theories inelegant, unsatisfying. "God does not play dice," he had told Elsa.

Or was the problem him? Hadn't they always told each other back at university, laughing up their sleeves at their doddering professors, that physics is a young man's game?

"Here, you will be able to work," Elsa told him. "Helen and I will guard the door. We will be your Scylla and Charybdis. And here, the police want to protect you."

Einstein smiled at her. Outside, their tug swung past the cheery French Renaissance towers of Ellis Island, and the rain had started to lighten. *It might be a bright day after all*, he thought.

The man moved swiftly up through the decks of the *Westmoreland*, discarding parts of himself as he rose. First went the hat card for his newspaper, slid under the door of a locked maid's closet. Next went the hat itself, folded up and stuffed into an inner pocket of his trench coat. A walking stick unfolded in sections from another pocket. A lit Rothman's materialized in his mouth, heavy puffs of smoke partially obscuring his face.

Yet these were superficialities. Props. The man himself had changed. The reporter's swagger gone, replaced by an aristocratic saunter. The eyes now bored, mouth turned down in a faint, mocking smile. He had the mien of a man who had seen it all, knew it all, owned it all.

No one would have guessed that Anton Gunther was seething inside.

Was zur Hölle ist passiert? he asked himself. *What in hell went wrong?*

He had penetrated the press corps without the slightest problem, made it on board the ship. Made it to within a few yards of the target. All he had to do was shoot Einstein when he emerged, then all hell would have broken loose. He had had a smoke bomb in another pocket, just in case. Then he would have vanished into the interior of the ship, just as he had done now. *Pandemonium. Terror. Fear.* And the message put across that there was no escape for the enemies of the Reich, anywhere.

But somehow, something had tipped off the Americans' Keystone Kops of a security force. Could it be the *Schwarze* who had spotted him? His meticulous plan and clever disguise disrupted by a fleeting glance? He felt the *Westmoreland* moving again. *As soon as he got off this boat, he could make it to Princeton and finish the mission.*

Meanwhile, he recalled his training in Berlin. *Evade. Confuse. Blend in.*

His best way off the *Westmoreland* was with the disembarking first class passengers, who'd be politely, expeditiously ushered to a hatch when the *Westmoreland* slipped into Pier 88.

He emerged back on deck, now crowded with passengers gawking at the skyline.

A police officer, barely old enough to fire a gun, was heading towards him, eyes wide. To his shock, Gunther recognized the skinny young officer who had boarded with them. Gunther ducked back inside, returned to the steps. Waited.

The young policeman swung open a door, coming face to face with Gunther. He spread his legs in textbook shooting position. Both hands cradling a police revolver, carefully aimed at his chest. A *Kleinkind*, a baby.

"Am I in the wrong class, officer?" he asked in his accented English, trying to affect startled amusement. "I see they are very strict about such things in America."

"Put your face on the floor, sir, and put your hands behind your back," the policeman told him, his voice anything but beseeching.

"Here, you can see my passport," Gunther told him, putting a hand inside his jacket.

"*Don't* reach in—" the young policeman told him, pulling back the hammer on his revolver.

Just then, Gunther got a break. The *Westmoreland* bumped into its berth—not hard, but enough to throw the cop a little off balance, his gun jerking to the right. A cheer went up throughout the ship at their landing—and at that moment, Gunther did indeed throw out his passport, to his left side, several feet in the air. The young cop reflexively looked at it just for a moment—but that was enough. Gunther traversed the few feet between them in two long strides, eight-inch folding knife in his hand already. He hit the skinny cop before he could get a shot off, knocking him over, hand across his mouth. The blade plunging deep and ripping upwards, its corrugated edge doing untold damage. When he finally pulled it out, the cop could only gasp. Gunther pushed a knee onto the boy's chest and steadied his lolling head with his free hand.

"*Shhh,*" he said, eyes fixed. "Look at me, *Kleinkind.* Just look right here." He brought the blade to the policeman's throat. There was little time. "I'm afraid I must confess—"

Anton Gunther stopped, listening. There were footsteps. Pounding up the steps below. *Someone running.* He took his knee off the cop and darted back towards the deck, pausing only to snatch up the passport he had flipped up in the air, disappearing around a corner.

A few seconds later, Harry Weiss came upon his best friend's nephew, bleeding his life out. He dropped down to his knees.

"Ah, hell."

Bobby Larkins was trying to say something, pointing vaguely with one arm.

"That way…to the right," he rasped.

"They'll get him, all right," Harry tried to reassure him. "Time to take care of you, first."

But the moment he pulled Bobby's coat away from the terrible wound, he could see that it was hopeless. He tried to keep the realization off his face, even as he felt Bobby's left hand tugging weakly at his coat.

"Tell Uncle Danny…had my gun out," he breathed. "Bear got me anyway."

"Hang on, hero, they'll patch you up good," Harry told him, but the lad was already gone.

Chapter Five

THEY DISEMBARKED AT SOMEPLACE called Elizabeth. Einstein signed his name for the entire awestruck crew of the pilot boat before they would let him leave. Agent Amos had ushered the three of them and their luggage into an immense black Cadillac touring car. The interior was warm and redolent of new leather.

"Courtesy of Princeton University," Amos told them, the vehicle having been hurried over the great steel bridge just completed up the Hudson. The white, uniformed chauffeur from the university sat in the front passenger's seat and seemed to expect James to do the driving, which was just as well to him.

They sped down into New Jersey, leaving behind Germany, Belgium, and England. Moving through a fantastic tangle of factories, boxcars, rusting metal barrels, pipeline, and gas tanks, all leaching oil and chemical into the wetlands and the blackened water around them. Amos doing all he could to keep from rocketing over the Pulaski Skyway.

The trip in the car, too, reminded him of that night—of what had happened after they had finally wrestled the little man away from the crowd. Roosevelt insisting that they drive straight to his speech at the Milwaukee Auditorium, despite the blood pooling outside a hole in the breast of his jacket. He took the stage and announced to the audience of 15,000 that he'd been shot.

"But it takes more than that to kill a bull moose!" he proclaimed.

He reached into his breast pocket for the folded thirty-page speech, noticing a bullet hole perforating every sheet, telling the crowd, "It probably saved the bullet from going into my heart. The bullet is in me now, so I cannot make a very long speech. But I will try my best."

Fifty minutes later, James and Roosevelt were back in a car, racing to a hospital through the dark streets of Milwaukee. Roosevelt, wheezing in the rear seat. James, next to him, demanding that the driver move faster. Praying that it wasn't too late.

They arrived safely at the hospital. Surgery to remove the bullet was deemed too risky.

Roosevelt would live with the bullet inside his chest for the rest of his life.

James would live with the guilt for the rest of his.

If only he'd forced someone to listen.

Chapter Six

IT WAS THE ONLY TIME HE HAD SEEN a man stand up so well to such a thing—until Albert Einstein today. The scientist sat drowsily in the back seat now, next to his wife, his eyes barely open, surveying the New Jersey countryside as they sped out of the industrial wastelands and into a bucolic landscape. To think that he had met such men: Theodore Roosevelt, and now Einstein. And that it was his duty to protect him. He was more resolved than ever not to let Einstein down. Checking his rearview and side mirrors for about the five hundredth time since they had left Elizabeth. Foot on the pedal, semi-automatic on the seat next to him. Across from him, the Princeton chauffeur snored.

It took them just over an hour to reach Princeton. The rain had stopped, and the gray stone buildings of the university glistened in the sun. They drove down Nassau Street, which was lined with small shops, restaurants, a movie theater. Einstein sat in the rear seat with Elsa.

"Quaint," he commented, "like a yet unsmoked pipe, fresh and young."

He craned his neck as they passed an ice cream parlor.

They pulled into the Peacock Inn, an eighteenth-century brown clapboard structure three stories high. The Einsteins would be in a suite, Miss Dukas in the room next to them, until the house that had been arranged for them was ready. Elsa and Helen cooed over how comfortable the rooms were—tastefully appointed with colonial-era paintings, a sofa positioned near a Zenith radio. Einstein stepped into a bedroom to quickly change his clothes, then lit a pipe and sat down in front of the radio. It hummed as he turned the dial. Out poured the staccato voice of a news announcer recapping the news: Winston Churchill had given a radio address the day before urging both Britain and the United States to arm themselves against Nazi Germans. Four Germans were arrested as spies at the Panama Canal when they were caught taking photographs of Fort Randolph. And a mystery! The renowned Professor Albert Einstein had been scheduled to arrive in New York this morning aboard the *Westmoreland*. But local dignitaries who gathered to greet him were surprised to learn he had left the ship earlier. Even now, his whereabouts were unknown.

Einstein giggled like a child. Miss Dukas had already retired to her room. Now Elsa smiled and kissed him on the cheek, and went in to take a nap. James Amos had returned to New York City after receiving assurances from the local police that they'd look after the Professor.

Einstein had pulled on his battered leather jacket and slipped out the back servants' entrance to their suite. He wrestled a fedora over his unmanageable white hair, and walked over to Nassau Street, unnoticed. There he saw what he wanted: a sign reading "Baltimore Ice Cream." Inside was a small parlor, with a few scattered chairs and tables. He walked in, removing his hat. By the soda fountain stood a tall, slender, sepulchral young man dressed almost all in black and eating a vanilla ice cream cone thick with chocolate sprinkles. He stopped eating and stared at Einstein as if he had seen a vision. Einstein smiled and pointed a thumb first at the young man's cone, then pointed it back at himself. The young man, who looked like a church deacon, kept staring at him.

A friendly looking blonde waitress, maybe in her mid-thirties, came bustling out from the kitchen.

"Yes, sir, what I can do—" she started to say, and stopped dead, looking at Einstein. "Aren't you—"

He brought his index finger to his lips, signaling for her to remain quiet, then shot a glance at the young man's cone, now untended to, the vanilla running over the top of the cone and down his hand. He still did not move.

"This one goes in my memory book," she whispered, and went

jittering about nervously scraping the ice cream out and handing it over to him.

Einstein paid, smiled, bent his head in thanks, and stabbed his cone into a dish of sprinkles out on the counter. He nodded back to the waitress and the young theologian, then stepped outside again, resuming his walk. He savored the cone, gazing at the imposing university buildings, occasionally catching the surprised glance of a student—unaware that an older man in a dark raincoat had fallen into his pace not far behind him, jotting down something with a pencil in a little notebook.

Einstein then veered onto Mercer, where comfortable homes graced the curbs, and walked down to a department store. There he poked about aimlessly until he spotted a comb—a good, plastic comb for five cents. He could not resist buying it, even as the man in the raincoat behind him stared and jotted down something more. The professor turned back up Nassau Street, circling back to the Peacock Inn.

He smiled. In Germany, the streets had become too dangerous for his daily walks. In Belgium and England, he was accompanied by bodyguards.

Now he walked freely, exulting in the crisp, rain-freshened air of America.

For the first time in a long time, he felt safe.

Chapter Seven

ANTON GUNTHER GOT BACK TO Manhattan by helping a longshoreman crew wrestle ashore a Mercedes Benz 770. Then he simply walked away in his workingman's overalls, pretending to wipe grease off his hands with a convenient rag. Sirens blared behind him as police cars and an ambulance raced up to the ship, but they would be looking for a trenchcoated aristocrat, or perhaps a rookie reporter. Gunther did not so much as turn around, wandering down the docks as if he had nothing more on his mind than deciding which saloon to step into.

His anger had ebbed a little, but he was still trying to puzzle it out. The young cop back on the ship had confirmed it—something had given Gunther away. *But what?*

It hadn't been a total waste. The young cop was surely dead by now, even if Gunther hadn't been able to watch the end. But he hadn't traversed an ocean to knife some no-name from the NYPD. Einstein had vanished again, for no clear reason. Slipping through their grasp just as easily as he had done in Berlin and Belgium and London. It was as if the great man were himself Schrödinger's cat, neither here nor there at any given moment, bending the rays of the sun itself to evade their surveillance.

The elusive genius would be on his way to Princeton, and Gunther needed a plan.

But first…

He had been strolling down the docks for half a mile when he came across a little brick Romanesque church, all but pushed up against a roaring, elevated freight railroad line. It looked like something that might have been sitting in the fields of Tuscany for the past three hundred years, but on closer inspection it appeared to be brand new. It was the sort of thing he liked about America, and particularly New York. Everything was crazy, and out of order, and unexpected. Ancient churches shoved up against elevated freight rails, next to the docks. Cars everywhere, roaring about much too fast, honking at the pedestrians who took crazy risks, shouting and cursing back as they barely missed being hit. It was a country out of control. It couldn't last, of course. But while it did, you could feel free to do anything, anything at all.

Gunther glanced up at the clockface near the steeple. *No sense rushing*, he thought. *Princeton isn't going anywhere.*

He stepped inside the church, removing his cap and crossing himself as he did. To his fortune, he found the confessional flickering with soft candlelight and moved toward it. *Just one more rouster, come to make amends for getting drunk last Friday night and slapping the wife around.* It wouldn't be Gunther's regular ritual, but it might scratch the itch.

There was almost no one in the sanctuary, he saw at a glance—just two women, all in black, kneeling up at the rail. The church was agreeably dark and cool in the afternoon. He stepped into the booth and knelt.

"Bless me, Father, for I have sinned."

A gravelly, older voice with an Italian accent asked, "How long since your last confession, my son?"

He started into it slowly, much preferring to confess to his victims before they died. Growing up in their little hamlet near Salzburg, his mother had always impressed upon him the importance of confession. "There is nothing so terrible you can't confess, Anton," she would say, smiling down at him in her warm kitchen. "You say your confession and you make your penance, and then your sin goes away."

"Why does it go away?" he had asked once.

"Because God forgives you," she said.

"What if there is no God?"

She smiled and leaned down to him. "If there's no God, *mein Liebchen*," she said, chucking him softly on the chin, "then who will have mercy?"

Now, realizing that Gunther had gone silent, the priest asked, "Is that everything, my son?"

"Father, I've killed a man. Killed him in cold blood."

"What?" The priest believed him, all right, his voice suddenly alert, even indignant. "When was this?"

"Nearby. Not long ago," he said. "I had to kill him to get away. But only because I was trying to kill another man."

"Are you one of King Joe Ryan's thugs?" the priest asked sharply, words that meant nothing to Anton. "Coming in here, trying to get absolution after another of your filthy murders of good working men? Shame on you! It won't be that easy for you here!"

Anton was surprised—and amused—at the old man's vigor.

"What penance will you give me?" he asked.

"Only that you turn yourself over to the police. That's the only way you can start to repent—that, and a long prison term. Or maybe they will roast you. I promise I will come up to Sing Sing to hear your confession and give you absolution then."

"Certainly, Father," he said, and crossed himself again. He stood and turned to leave, but the priest's voice stopped him.

"Don't think you can just walk out of here and say a *novena* somewhere. I will go to the police!"

Anton whirled and rammed a fist through the confessional screen, the aluminum latticework giving way like so many matchsticks. The priest cried out, startled, but he did not move. Gunther thrust an arm through, grabbing the man by his withered neck, thinking that he would kill him right here. He had to. *It would be the worst, greatest thing he had ever done.* The cleric's face ancient and stubbled, like that of a saint in an ancient fresco. His hands grabbed weakly at Gunther's arm, unable to dislodge it.

"Do your worst," the man hissed at him with his waning breath. "I'm in a state of grace. Are you?"

"*Shhh,*" Gunther said. "Just look here, Father... I said *look at me.*"

Then he saw it: the priest's milky eyes, rolling sightlessly back in his head. *He's blind,* Gunther realized, almost laughing out loud. *No danger here.*

His enthusiasm drained. He released the old man's neck and stumbled out of the church, holding his cap up to one side to keep the old women up front, alarmed by the ruckus, from seeing his face. The priest coughing and barking after him.

"You can't run! Your sins will follow you everywhere!"

A freight train passing overhead drowned out the maledictions the priest was raining down on him. Forcing himself to walk at the same pace as the people on the sidewalks around him, Anton reached his seamen's lodging—little more than a flophouse—in a few minutes, and threw the few items he had in his duffel bag. He headed back out at once, stopping only to pay his bill at the front desk.

"Gotta ship?" the wizened clerk there asked, though he could not have cared less.

Anton grinned and nodded at him, and flipped him a quarter tip.

"For luck," he said.

The clerk's eyes widened, one hand grabbing the coin out of midair like a lizard snatching a fly.

"You got it," the desk clerk said, as though he were in charge of dispensing all luck in the universe, but Gunther was already gone.

Time for a change of lodgings, he thought.

Within a few minutes he was at the subway, where he took the C train down into Brooklyn. Then a walk up to the Navy Yard, and back up to Manhattan on the F. Along the way, Gunther the roustabout was discarded in various vacant lots, and subway restrooms. Another change of trains and he emerged just outside a modest hotel on the Upper West Side, wearing a worn suit and squinting through a pair of eyeglasses, a small, battered salesman's valise in tow. He thought the clerk in his new hotel was about to cry, he seemed so grateful for the business.

Up in his room, the bed beckoned, but instead he dutifully

made his preparations. He bolted the door to his room and slid a doorstop underneath it for good measure. As he had requested, the rooms next to his were empty, but had connecting doors. These were locked, but it took him only a moment to pick both of them. He went into each room in turn and unlocked the hallway doors. If anyone came for him, he could be out of his room and into the hall in a moment.

He looked back at the bed, still longing for sleep. Instead, he sat up in an uncomfortable straight-backed chair by a scratched-up table and tried to think how they had spotted him. Back in Germany, they called him *Das Chameleon* for his ability to change his appearance so utterly and so fast. But his abilities had been pushed to their limit today—and at least twice, he hadn't fooled anybody.

His appearance, he was sure, was good enough. He had looked just like the other reporters. He hadn't talked too much, was prepared in any case to explain his accent by saying he worked for one of the foreign-language presses in the city. He stopped—*maybe that was it.* His credentials? Curious, he called down to the front desk and ordered several of the day's tabloids: the *Daily News,* the *Mirror,* the *Post.* The *Evening Graphic.* When he mentioned the last, the desk clerk chuckled.

"You haven't been in New York for a while, have you?" he asked. "*Evening Graphic* been gone for a year, year and a half. But I can get you the others, sir."

Was that it? he wondered. *Was that what they spotted?*

His handlers, he now realized, had blundered in choosing his cover.

Still, he'd learned that the men protecting Einstein were attentive, intelligent, quick to act on what they saw. Not men to trifle with. He would have to be careful down in Princeton, he realized, but at the same time he welcomed the challenge. They would be angry after he had killed their boy, too. *Well, let them stew.* First, he would give it a few days before he even began to look over the terrain down there. Let them grow lax, convinced that no one was coming. Or they would drive themselves crazy looking around the immense rabbit warren of a city for him.

They won't find me, he thought as he opened the drapes. Just outside he could see the crazy ziggurats of colossal new apartment buildings running up and down Central Park West. Not five blocks away, he knew, was what they called Riverside Park. It was not much of a park at all but an open rail line, besieged by overflowing hobo encampments. This was America too, unable to make anything run well. A country run by the *Mischling,* for the *Mischling,* and dedicated to the proposition that all half-breeds and subhumans were created equal. An outlaw land, like the Karl May westerns he loved to read as a boy—that and the other adventures set all over the world, where strong Aryan men brought order to African natives, or the wild Indians.

In such places, there were no rules. You could do *anything.*

Gunther knew he should report to his American contact, who was so far only a voice over the phone. But he was still angry over their careless preparation. And his visit to the old priest hadn't been the release he had hoped.

He had, however, been told about a brothel not far away from where he was staying, one run by a Jewess in a new building called The Majestic—in New York, much to Gunther's amusement, all the buildings, from the highest to the lowliest, had pretentious names. Despite his exhaustion, he locked up his room and headed for the street. *What else does one do in Babylon?*

This Majestic was nothing much to look at on the outside, but the apartment the doorman directed him to opened into what looked like a Chinese palace from the Forbidden City. If, that was, such a palace also had a bar that might have been excavated out of King Tut's tomb, and what looked like a real Gobelin tapestry on one wall. It was all too much, this crazy quilt of luxuries, but spectacularly, sensationally too much. *American* too much.

A woman with black curled hair and a face like fine porcelain came up to him. She was wearing a red silk vest, a pair of high heels, a garter belt, and fishnet stockings—and nothing else. He wondered if she was the Jewess who ran the place. But before he could ask anything, she slid an arm through his and asked in a lush voice, "What is your pleasure?"

What isn't? he thought.

He let himself sleep late the next morning, then went out to a nearby diner to have an immense breakfast in the American fashion: fried eggs, sausage, toast. Bad reheated coffee that the waitress constantly refilled his cup with, whether he wanted it or not.

Gunther worked his way through it, using the time to study another sheaf of newspapers like the ones he had gazed at the day before. All sorts of stories dominated the front pages: another state had voted to get rid of America's absurd ban on alcohol, a squat little man who yelled at everyone was running for mayor, the new jobs report was good. But two of the tabs did have what he was looking for:

HERO COP STABBED BY DRUG SMUGGLERS

Scanning the articles quickly, he noticed that the official police story, at least, had moved the stabbing off the *Westmoreland.* Now the policeman he'd stabbed had been part of a special unit, trying to break up a drug smuggling ring. There was nothing about the man's death. All the papers said he'd been hospitalized, with details withheld until his family could be notified.

But Gunther had no doubts. The policeman could not have survived the way he had ripped him.

The *Daily News*—"New York's Picture Newspaper!"—had run a grainy photograph of the victim. *Robert Larkins.* Gunther read the name silently. The face was still that of a boy. It seemed he was a heroic young man, who had rescued some boys from a cage in the zoo.

Well, heroes die quickest, Gunther thought. *And they are asking for it.* When his time came, he was certain, he wouldn't ask anyone for mercy.

It occurred to him that he should probably get out of the city after all, just to be on the safe side. He was gratified to see that there had been no description of the hero cop's killer, no artist's sketch of the perpetrator, no matter how crude or misleading that might be.

Still, like Polizei everywhere, they wouldn't like the killing of one of their own. They would be searching everywhere—certainly the hotels—looking for anyone with a funny accent.

Gunther decided it would be best to head over to New Jersey after all—if that was where Einstein really was. Still thinking, he flipped another page, and to his delight saw an article on the great scientist's arrival. It seemed that a wire service reporter had staked out Princeton, hoping to get whatever crumbs of news might be left after the big reception at the dock, and happened upon Albert Einstein eating an ice cream cone—and another scoop as well.

EINSTEIN BUYS COMB! read the headline. Complete with the inn he and his wife and assistant were staying in, and even the room number. *The press in America were invaluable,* Gunther thought, not for the first time. *It was like having a private spy service to report on everyone.*

He tossed some coins down on the diner counter, folded the paper under one arm, and strolled out. He stepped into a drugstore just down the block and called the number he had memorized, finally condescending to make his report. To his surprise, this time the voice of a young woman answered.

"This is the New Europe," she said. The voice softly seductive in that peculiar American way, but with an edge of something else—something dangerous—just below the surface. He was intrigued.

"Yes, I'd like to know if your next newsreel will be about climbing the Grossglockner," he said, the famous Alpine peak serving as the code word.

"Unfortunately, that newsreel will not be playing here. In fact, I understand that the expedition was not completed, and the entire production has been canceled," her voice came back, harder now and even accusatory.

Gunther was stunned, and indignant.

"Yes, certain failures in preparation made it impossible to complete that expedition. But you may be assured that it will be completed shortly."

"You may leave off speaking in riddles," the woman said bluntly, her tone hard and sharp as a blade. "This is not like some country on the Continent. They are innocent as children. The only people whose wires they tap are communists or gangsters."

"All right," Gunther told her, trying to picture her face. "Our target is down in Princeton now. Give me two days to go down there, survey the situation, and finish the job."

"Please…with cops and federal agents on high alert?" she said. "You've had your chance. And believe me, we're all as disappointed as you. I have orders for your new assignment."

His hand tightened around the receiver. No woman had ever spoken to him in such a way.

"Listen, *Amerikanerin,* I will let you know when—"

"*Ich bin genauso deutsch wie Sie,* I assure you," she said. *I am just as German as you.* "And these orders come from H himself."

Her mother tongue was perfect, but that wasn't what had silenced him. An order from Reinhard Heydrich commanded his respect.

"Good," she said, like a fine lady on the Unter den Linden congratulating a recalcitrant dog. "It is an urgent matter on behalf of a personage at the highest levels of The Party. You are to leave immediately for Palestine."

"Palestine!" he said, letting his surprise leach into his voice despite himself. The Holy Land. *How exotic would that be,* he wondered.

"Your ship leaves tonight, from Pier 32 with the late tide," she continued smugly, having firmly established who was in command. *For now,* he thought. "You will come here, to the New Europe Movie Palace, to receive your briefing papers, your steamship ticket, and your visa."

"Who shall I ask for?"

"Hans," she said, the voice cold now. "I will not be there to meet you. Even children sometimes stumble upon things they shouldn't see."

PART II

NOV 1938–APR 1939

Chapter Eight

FIVE YEARS AFTER ARRIVING in New York, Albert Einstein was drifting.

It was November 1938. Einstein had stretched himself snuggly along the bottom of his seventeen-foot sailboat, elbows splayed so that he could rest his head in his clasped hands. It was to be his last sail before winter. A sharp wind roiled the surface of Lake Carnegie, in Princeton, and he let his senses take in the beat of waves against the boat, the fast approach of charcoal clouds, the choppy currents pushing the boat further from land.

Drifting. My own state of uncertainty.

Ever since stepping off the *Westmoreland*, Einstein had often wondered when he'd find his footing. He'd occasionally peer into a mirror at his house on Mercer Street and conclude that Heisenberg's theoretical law of observation had been severely unkind to him. A celebrity stared back. A curiosity. An imitation. Like in the Hollywood movies he so enjoyed, a man playing a role.

It wasn't all bad. He acknowledged that he enjoyed his celebrity status, at times even playing up his image as the kind, befuddled, bare-ankled oddity. But hadn't he capitalized on the fame to speak out against Hitler and raise money for German Jewish refugees? Hadn't it resulted in an invitation by Franklin Roosevelt, only two years after arriving in America, to sleep at the White House, where they spoke late into the night about Hitler's designs on Europe?

If celebrity was what it took to influence presidents and the American public, perhaps he shouldn't mind playing the part of the slovenly, sockless, absent-minded genius.

Genius.

In the intervening years, he'd been too busy signing autographs and attending charity dinners to focus on his real work. He had been unable to produce in America a major scientific breakthrough on par with his relativity theory, now decades behind him. His research on a unified theory, linking the tiniest of particles to the infinite scale of the cosmos, was in its own state of inertia. He was aware of the whispered criticism of his colleagues that he'd grown old, stubborn, uninspired.

America will do that, he often thought. Pull you into complacency. Numb you with its shiny distractions, its hall of mirrors, stretching from coast to coast. Safely nestled between two oceans. Isolated from distant threats, and therefore self-absorbed and naïve.

The truth was, he hardly recognized himself. Even his lifelong commitment to pacifism had dissipated. He'd witnessed, close up, the evil Hitler was capable of; and not just Hitler, but civilized Germans. Now he spoke of resistance. Arming the democracies of Europe. If there was to be a war, the civilized world must be ready for the fight.

Ach.

The current carried him faster away from land. The clouds grew darker, like curtains closing in over the secrets of the universe behind.

Drifting, especially without Elsa.

It had started with a swollen eye. Then a battery of medical tests, promptly followed by a diagnosis of heart and kidney problems. He realized all over again how much he'd loved her, but it was too late. She died in December 1936.

They'd been a perfect match. Where Einstein was prone to invite almost anyone into their home, Elsa had guarded the door. Where he was trusting, she'd always been suspicious. Elsa had protected her husband from the charlatans and con artists, the flimflammers and grifters, scammers, swindlers, spongers…

Assassins.

Oh, how angry she could get!

He thought about their time in Bermuda. They'd travelled to

the island in 1935. At the time, it had a large German émigré community. He'd befriended a German who'd invited him for a sail, and for seven hours they'd explored the coast. When he finally returned to their rented cottage, he found her standing in the front door, arms folded, eyes dark and unforgiving. "I was convinced that the Nazis had kidnapped you," she had snapped.

"Elsa," he insisted, "how preposterous."

"To you, perhaps, but not to the Nazis. Where there are Germans, you must take precautions."

Now he felt alone. Vulnerable.

Adrift.

Einstein closed his eyes. Shutting out the images of Elsa, the barbs of his critics, the distractions, the carnival-mirror reflections that wavered between reality and perception. Retreating deeper and deeper into the one place where he worked best: the dark. Peering into the infinite blackness of the universe, or the wide black slate of a chalkboard, or the luminescent equations dancing across the insides of his eyelids.

Minutes passed. How many, he didn't know. Until a chuckle bubbled deep in his throat, and he found himself reciting "An object will remain still or continue on a straight line until impacted by an external force."

The First Law of Motion. *And where would this damned inertia carry him?*

Einstein's meditation was interrupted by a blast of thunder. A scream.

His eyes flickered open.

He poked his head just above the gray metal railing.

Not thunder, he realized, but the rapid approach of a motorboat from the Princeton Yacht Club. Two men were at the helm, waving and shouting.

"You're out too far, Professor!"

"We'll tow you back!"

This had happened before. Einstein considered himself an able sailor. Never had he experienced a serious problem on the

Wannsee in Berlin, or the lakes near Caputh. But the men at the Princeton Yacht Club considered him a hazard—to himself and to them as well. Their concerns may have been justified by the apparent lack of seaworthiness of his boat. He'd called it *Tinef*: Yiddish for "old piece of junk." It was a decrepit, fourteen-foot sailboat, used and badly used, that he had overpaid for at $130. He'd sawed off half the centerboard—the plank of wood extending beneath the hull that provided additional stability when tacking into the wind—to better navigate the shallows of Lake Carnegie. In fact, this had the opposite effect, rendering the sailboat as agile as a log on windy days. On several occasions the dock-master had dispatched a rescue boat to chase after Einstein. The drowning of the smartest man in the world would certainly be a black eye for the blue-blooded Princetonians.

Einstein thought the rescues an overreaction. And once again, the facts became a projection of themselves, and a new reality formed. Everyone in Princeton had a story about their rescue of Einstein. Mathematically it was impossible. There were about 10,000 people in Princeton, and not 10,000 rescues of Albert Einstein.

Still, he sat up, waved to his rescuers and followed them back to the dock.

Wondering where these Americans might lead him.

Chapter Nine

WEEKS LATER, ON A BITTERLY cold day just after Thanksgiving, Einstein awoke to the patter of an early morning sleet against the window of his second-story home on Mercer Street in Princeton. He groaned, swung his feet from the mattress, wrestled himself up. He trudged across his modest bedroom, the cold wooden floor planks squeaking with each step. He peered into his adjoining office. The room smelled of sweet pipe tobacco. Bookshelves lined two walls. Everywhere else, he'd tacked up portraits of his heroes: Isaac Newton, Gandhi, and the nineteenth-century scientists Michael Faraday and James Clerk Maxwell.

He paused for a moment in front of his favorite photograph, taken at the 1927 Solvay Conference on Electrons and Photons in Brussels, now framed on his desk. Over two-dozen scientists in dour attire and even more dour mien sat for the camera. Here were Schrodinger, Pauli, Heisenberg, Bohr, and Planck. In the front row was Marie Curie, the lone woman in a small sea of men. And at the very center sat Einstein. His hair had already turned gray, but he still sported a dark mustache. *Ah, to be that young again...*

His eye was drawn to a peculiarity he'd never been able to explain to himself. While his distinguished colleagues all rested their hands comfortably on their laps or at their sides, Einstein's right hand was clenched around the side of his seat. As if he were holding on against...what, exactly? Had he been the only one who could sense what was coming?

He sighed anxiously, shifting his gaze to a round table he kept near a window, one where he always kept half a dozen pipes and a glass jar filled with shredded tobacco. Plus reams of correspondence, lapping each other like frothing waves—and these were only the ones that got past Helen Dukas. There were invitations to speak at academic conferences, at banquets and ribbon cuttings. Letters urging him to endorse kitchen appliances, radios, automobiles, polygraphs, tabulating machines, and "space rockets." Solicitations to raise money for countless charities, in a world now full of beseeching, desperate people. Helen always put aside requests to aid Jewish refugees from Germany, as he instructed. That was his priority.

After all, he was one. For all the celebrity, the fame, the constant flash of cameras and demands for autographs, he was stateless. A citizen of the world, denied a country. *A wandering Jew.*

Einstein shuffled down the back stairs, clutching the banister with one hand. The large white-clapboard house on Mercer Street was handsome but lonely. Radiators banged and hissed under windows in every room. One of the new electric refrigerators rattled in the kitchen. A wall clock ticked loudly, approaching 8:15. He walked through a long front hall, observing the glow of early morning through the transom above the front door. He opened the door and a frigid blast of air swept through him.

The morning newspaper had been tossed over the low front hedges, across a patch of brown grass to the porch steps. He hitched up his striped pajamas and stepped out, still barefoot. The gray wood porch was peeling, and paint chips stuck to the bottom of his feet.

"Good morning, professor!"

A group of students waved, smiling and giggling as they headed towards the Princeton campus a few blocks away, delighting to see him living up to his reputation as the absent-minded, eccentric genius. He offered a friendly wag of his fingers, stooped for the paper, and returned inside, padding down the hall to the kitchen—a cheery room with its yellow-painted cabinets, and a huge white refrigerator the size of a bank vault. Americans never did anything in a small way, and they liked to store food as if they were preparing for a ten-year siege. Elsewhere in this house there were not one but two food pantries, a bread box, a root cellar, and a freezer for enormous slabs of meat he would never eat.

He started his morning tea, then sat down at a large oak table and opened the newspaper. The headline caught his eye immediately:

GERMAN POLICE ORDER JEWS' EXPULSION

The Berlin police were now ordering the Jewish community to produce the names of one hundred Jews per day, who would then be given notice to leave Germany within two weeks. It was another of the atrocities they were now continuously perpetrating, all over the Reich, in the wake of *Kristallnacht.* Seizing on the shooting of a consulate official by a Jewish-Polish refugee maddened by his family's mistreatment in Germany, they had launched a new orgy of beatings, arrests, expulsions—and worse. Hundreds, even thousands, of Jews murdered. Thousands tossed into concentration camps, released only on their promise to leave the country immediately.

Almost as vicious was the wholesale ransacking of Jewish homes; the burning of beautiful, centuries-old synagogues; the destruction of what Jewish schools and shops still remained after almost six years of Nazi rule. There was an account of some SS bullyboys who had wrestled a grand piano through a window at Wertheim's, the great Jewish department store in Berlin, just to watch it smash in the street six stories below.

What kind of mind was it that wanted to watch a beautiful instrument smash in the street? But Albert already knew the answer. *The kind of mind that wanted to smash anything and everything, no matter how beautiful.*

This world was a dark place, he admitted to himself. Even darker without Elsa.

He regretted that he had not better appreciated her efforts to protect him. Now with darkness creeping slowly, inexorably across Europe, she was gone. *And things were going to get darker still*, he knew.

He heard a sudden rattling of the front door. It opened, then closed rapidly. Footsteps clattered down the hall, in his direction.

Helen Dukas appeared. Dark hair and intense eyes, and that proud beak of a nose. Usually an ironic smile played around her lips but today she looked angry, which he knew was for his benefit. She plunked a worn leather satchel on the table and launched into a rebuke.

"I walked right in, Doctor. I keep reminding you: you must lock and bolt the doors. At all times."

Einstein kept his eyes down on the newspaper and forced himself not to laugh. Because she lived in the house, he knew the rumor around Princeton was that they slept together, but he could not see it. It would be like sleeping with the sternest teacher from his grammar school.

Helen gave a heartfelt tsk-tsk-tsk, then pulled a ream of loose papers from the satchel. "The latest edits on your essay for the *Annals of Mathematics*."

Einstein glanced at the heading of the typed manuscript: *Stationary System with Spherical Symmetry Consisting of Many Gravitating Masses.* He pulled the stack towards him and began leafing through it. Then he heard the rear door open, followed by heavy footsteps.

"*Both* doors unlocked?" Helen asked, incredulous.

"It's only Mrs. Ochs," he replied.

"*Ja*, but it could have been anyone. You must be more careful."

"Now you sound like my Elsa."

There was an uncomfortable quiet.

"We have been in America for years now," he tried remonstrating with her. "And none of those threats have ever materialized."

"Except the first one."

"He never got close to me."

Besides, he thought, *what would be the point of killing an old has-been like me now?*

"He killed a policeman," Helen reminded him. "And he was

never caught."

"That was more than five years ago!"

They both went silent as Einstein's cook and housekeeper entered, clutching a brown bag filled with groceries. She grunted "Good morning" and deposited the bag on a counter. Mrs. Ochs was bulky and even more businesslike than Helen Dukas, with wide hips, a permanent frown, and a complexion like red sandpaper. She wrestled off her oversized brown wool coat, huffing through the effort.

Einstein requested his usual: fried eggs and mushrooms. Mrs. Ochs responded with a few exasperated phrases in German, as though she had already been working for hours. The kitchen erupted in a clamor of pans, plates, utensils, and the hiss of the gas range. Einstein had to smile. Just these two women fussing over him had already lightened his mood—until Helen took a seat at the table and produced a large red leather book, its cover stamped in gold foil: 1939. She opened it to a narrow red ribbon between two pages.

"Shall we review the scheduling changes for next week?"

Einstein glanced at the book despondently. The pages were filled with penciled-in additions.

"Why would you ruin my day by discussing my week, Helen?"

"Mr. Winchell requests an interview for his radio show on Sunday. About the situation in Germany."

He nodded—yes.

"The Hebrew Immigrant Aid Society requests a meeting to discuss plans to build an orphanage for German Jewish children."

"*Aber natürlich—*" *Well, of course.* "I cannot say no to that."

"The American Association of Political Scientists invites you to speak at their annual—"

"*Nein. Mein Gott, nein.*"

"And," she concluded, "Professor Leo Szilard will be at your office at two this afternoon."

Einstein brought a hand to his forehead and grumbled. "No, Helen. Not Szilard."

"You agreed to this meeting months ago."

"*Ja,* but I was betting that he'd forget."

"Be kind, Dr. Einstein. He's your friend. And a former student."

"Who always behaves as if he knows more than anyone else in the room. Including me. He is always trying to convince me of something. This time it's his new discovery about a chain reaction."

Helen narrowed her eyes. "It sounds like the two of you are equally stubborn."

"It's the science that is stubborn. A hypothesis is proven by—"

"*By repeated experiments arriving at identical outcomes,*" Helen and Mrs. Ochs recited with him. Einstein ignored them.

"It leaves no room for ideology, personal opinion, or hysteria! Physics has enough crackpot theories as it is—especially over in Germany."

He fell silent. His mind drifting back to the same debate he'd waged with his colleagues for nearly a decade, one that threatened his friendships. It was the whole principle of wave function collapse again, which argued that matter was not here or there, but formed in relation to the observer. Not actuality but probability. Not real, but random.

Foolishness, he'd thought.

Helen noted Einstein's agitation. Szilard had that effect on him. *In fact,* she thought, *Szilard had a knack for getting under the skin and inflaming the blood pressure of many of his colleagues.* It was time to change the subject.

"I have good news."

She fished through a leather satchel and produced several crisp black and white photographs with a stapled document, then slid them toward Einstein. As soon as he saw it his fingers relaxed and his eyes beamed.

"You've found my vacation home?"

"I believe it's perfect."

He studied the photographs. A small but comfortable cottage, nestled on a bluff in the woods. A quiet cove bordered by thin strip of white sand, and beyond, an ample bay dotted with sailboats.

"Where is it?"

"It's called Little Hog Neck. On the north fork of Long Island."

"Secluded?"

"Ninety miles from Manhattan. Mostly farms and a few quaint, downtown villages."

He nodded, pleased, and thumbed through the images again.

Albert Einstein spent every spring and summer at such remote waterside locations, far from the usual clamor of meetings, appearances, autographs, photographs, interviews, lectures. He'd take his boat out alone on long sails, play his cherished violin, smoke his pipe without frequent interruption…

Helen continued, "Surrounded by water. You can sail your boat on The Long Island Sound. The Peconic Bay. Gardiner's Bay. All within a walk, or a short drive."

"Do the neighbors know I am coming?"

"It's a small town, Doctor. It was impossible to keep this a secret. But I am sure they will respect your privacy. The families there are old, insular. Some have lived in the area since the 1600s. They dislike commotion."

"Well… when do we go?"

"May 1st. All you have to do is sign the lease."

Einstein took a pen and carefully applied his signature. "You have just made my meeting with Szilard tolerable, Helen."

She gathered the papers and stood.

"Two o'clock, Doctor."

A few hours later, Einstein was enjoying a moment of peace in his corner office at Princeton's Institute of Advanced Studies. Outside his window, the normally pastoral campus had withered into swaths of yellow-brown grass and forlorn, barren trees. The room, though, was warm and redolent of his pipe smoke. Over the years he had turned what was once a sterile, institutional space into his burrow. One wall was dominated by a blackboard, cluttered with chalk equations and erasure streaks, like a storm-tossed sea. Mozart's Symphony No. 29 played on a small but very stable phonograph. He leaned back in his creaky office chair, eyes closed. His index finger wagged in sync with the blending of winds and violins, his head bobbed gently.

This room had been his refuge when Elsa was dying, and remained so now. Here he could seal himself away from the trivial events of the day and contemplate the furthest reaches of the universe. Here he could play his records, close his eyes, connect with God.

He heard a violent sneeze from the corridor outside.

Then another.

A plague descends upon this house, Einstein thought.

The door creaked open, and in walked Leo Szilard, bundled in a thick wool coat, lugging along a battered satchel. He looked, as usual, like the very stereotype of a Hungarian: stocky and bull-chested, with his sweep of coarse black hair streaked with white down the middle. His eyes were ominous, two dark pools set against pallid flesh. He had thick cheeks, and a pronounced lower lip that gave him a stubborn look Einstein considered all too appropriate.

Szilard wiped a band of sweat from his high forehead. He looked feverish to Einstein, who offered a courteous *Guten Tag*, then a reproach. "You should not have come in such a state."

"I'm quite fine, Professor Einstein. Merely allergies." Szilard sneezed once more into a sodden handkerchief.

"Allergies?" Einstein waved a hand at the chilly winter landscape just outside his window. "There isn't a leaf or a bud growing in all of New Jersey."

"Perhaps I am allergic to willful ignorance," Szilard told him.

Einstein sighed. He rose from his chair and turned off the phonograph, then called in a graduate assistant to help get Szilard settled in his own chair with some strong tea and a box of the paper tissues that Americans seemed to have everywhere. *You sneezed or coughed into them, then threw them away. Ingenious!*

"You took the train from New York?" he asked politely.

"Yes. I have a vital matter, Doctor Einstein. We are in great danger."

"Of course, Szilard. I've never known you to make a social call. What is it this time?"

The Hungarian rifled through his satchel until he found an article that appeared only weeks before in a German scientific journal.

"Just a few weeks ago, Otto Hahn successfully split an atom in Germany, at the Kaiser Wilhelm."

"Yes, Leo," Einstein nodded, already annoyed. "I still keep up."

"Fritz Strassmann was with him. Neither one of them quite know what they have done, but Lise Meitner does. She did the calculations. Albert, they have achieved fission."

"I know. But Hahn is no Nazi."

"And yet he experiments on their behalf with the ultimate weapon of mass destruction: an atom bomb."

"An overstatement, Szilard."

"By bombarding uranium, Hahn discovered that it breaks into two parts when it absorbs a neutron. If the fragments then emit enough neutrons, they could generate enough energy to—"

"Barely illuminate a lightbulb. The energy released by one atom is too small to have any practical use," Einstein cut him off. "Besides, hitting an atom by bombardment is like shooting birds in the dark. And even if you can do such a thing, there is only the remote possibility of causing a chain reaction, which you and I both know is the only way you could release enough energy for...an explosion."

The word on the tip of his tongue had been "bomb." Why didn't he want to say it?

"What do you mean by 'remote possibility?'"

"Perhaps ten percent," Einstein said with a shrug. Szilard gave a sharp, sarcastic guffaw.

"If I have a disease, Professor Einstein, and the doctor tells me there is a ten percent chance of death, I get worried about it."

"Unless, of course, it is merely an allergy."

Szilard failed to see the humor. He raked through the satchel again, this time pulling out a tattered ream of documents and littering Einstein's desk with them.

"Here are my own equations. I have also included those of Meitner and Otto Frisch, who is up in Sweden with her right now. They all concur."

Einstein pressed his fingertips hard into his brow.

"Leo, *bitte—" Please.* "I don't have the time."

"Time may be running out, Professor. You must warn President Roosevelt! War is coming. If Hitler has a bomb before us—before anyone—think of the consequences!"

Einstein thumbed through a few pages from Szilard's satchel, barely glancing at them.

"If you believe in your theory, why don't *you* warn the President?"

"You and I both know the answer. I'm a nobody. He has heard of you—everyone knows about the great Albert Einstein! Me? Everyone thinks I'm a kook."

It was probably all too true, Einstein reflected, a little sadly. Szilard was probably the most selfless man of science he knew—and it had cost him. Sometimes he thought the stocky little man's mind raced ahead of all of them. He might have won the Nobel several times over for the particle accelerator, the cyclotron, the electron microscope. Together, back in the 1920s, he and Einstein had amused themselves inventing a refrigerator that had no moving parts. The last time they had spoken, Szilard has gone on about his ideas for finding a way to clone human cells.

Yet if his mind was in constant motion, so was his body. Szilard never settled into a long-term professorship anywhere, rarely published or patented ideas that might have made him millions. Such recognition never seemed to mean much to him. He lived off nothing, in cheap hotels and boardinghouses. Never married, never started a family. He lived lightly in the world, perhaps on purpose. His farsightedness wasn't restricted to science. He had seen the threat the Nazis posed almost as soon as Einstein himself had. The same day Hitler joined the cabinet in 1933, Szilard was urging everyone he knew to get out of Germany, to get out of Europe. Within a few months he had cleared out his bank account and gone to England. There he lived on five pounds a week, room and board, while he raised money to get every scholar he knew out of the hands of the Fascists.

Meanwhile nuclear fission, and the energy that a chain reaction might release, had become something of an obsession with him. The patent he filed for a neutron-induced nuclear chain reactor he had assigned to the British Admiralty, so it would remain secret under the Brits' Patents and Designs Act.

Szilard continued, "You must tell the President to convene America's scientists to build a bomb!"

Einstein fought the urge to scold Szilard for the casual way he'd framed his proposal. Just traipse into the White House and tell the President of the United States to build a super-weapon that could incinerate entire cities. Based on unproven theories and one lab experiment in Germany. And if the science was wrong and an atomic bomb impossible? Well then, it was only money.

"Even if I arranged to meet with Roosevelt, I lack confidence in your theory. Atomic power cannot be weaponized. It is that simple. I cannot ask the president to accept a scientific principle which I reject."

"But you must understand!"

"I understand many things, Szilard," Einstein said, coolly.

"Yes, natural science. The nature of matter and energy. But I'm talking about human nature! You can't see the dark impulses of humankind. Your old pacifism blinds you—"

"Aach." Einstein waved off the onslaught and rose, moving again toward the window.

"—blinds you to the true nature of this threat. What if you're wrong, Professor? What if Hitler's scientists see what you don't? Don't forget how we first became friends—back when you could admit that even the great Einstein could be wrong!"

"Did you come here to patronize me, Szilard?" Einstein turned and snapped at him, despite himself.

He remembered the day well enough. It was back at the Friedrich Wilhelm University, one of those high-tiered classrooms in the European tradition that made you feel as though you were fighting for truth in the arena. By the end of the lecture, he knew that most of the students weren't awed by *his* lecture so much as *the* lecture, but one had rushed down to him and, dispensing with any pleasantries, launched into a description of an experiment he had conducted. Einstein, already piqued by the indifference of his class, had informed him:

"That's impossible. This is something that cannot be done."

"Well, yes, but I did it," Szilard had shot back. "Let me show you."

He proceeded to erase a corner of Einstein's chalkboard with his jacket sleeve, picked up a piece of chalk and showed him what he meant. It had taken a good ten minutes for Einstein to concede that he was wrong. They had indeed become friends. But now here Szilard was, treating him like a dull schoolboy up before the headmaster.

"I'm fully aware of the darkest capacities of man." Einstein's voice was low now, each word deliberate. "I, like you, have been driven from my country. Forced to run for my life—"

"Exactly," Szilard replied. "And now we are to sit back and watch those bastards build a bomb like no one's ever seen. You must stop being so stubborn!"

He shook his head slightly and looked absently toward Einstein's blackboard of equations. Einstein could see that his old student was no longer beseeching. Now he was...disappointed. He pushed Szilard's papers to the side of his desk. "Prove it to me, Szilard. Not simply with equations, but in the lab. Do what Otto Hahn did. Then come back."

Szilard began sputtering. "That could take months. I'll have to rent at least one gram of radium. That will cost hundreds of dollars.

And I will need permissions. Meanwhile Hitler has an entire government doing the work!"

Einstein held up his hand. "Who's stubborn now, Szilard? I've given you a path. Take it instead of stomping your feet."

Szilard zipped up his satchel and suppressed another sneeze. Then he offered his hand across the desk and Einstein shook it.

"May I at least leave my equations with you? Just in case—"

Einstein nodded stiffly and sucked at his unlit pipe. With a slight bow, the mad Hungarian moved to exit the office.

"Szilard"—Einstein stopped him—"one thing."

Szilard paused in the doorway.

"Yes?"

"This chain reaction you are talking about trying to start—what if it doesn't stop?"

"Professor?"

"What if you're right—and you start a chain reaction, and it rips apart every particle of matter in the universe? What are the odds of that?"

Szilard grinned unexpectedly at him.

"Well, they are a lot less than ten percent," he said, and left.

Einstein lit up a new pipe, letting the crinkling, burning tobacco, the lazy coiling of smoke to a high ceiling soothe him. He leaned back in his chair again and stared up into the sullen, gray-white sky of the dying day.

He thought about his grand unified theory and wondered if it too was coiling away, dissipating, only to be replaced by weaponized atoms. *Was this the final legacy he would leave?* He wanted no part of it.

He drew again on his pipe, watched the glow of hungry heat spread over the surface of the bowl.

"Your old pacifism blinds you," Szilard had said.

Einstein had continued to shed his old pacifism—much to the praise of people all around the world—ever since Hitler had come to power. To do so ate at his most fundamental instincts, but he realized that like any scientist, he had to accept the hard reality.

The Nazis, the fascists in Italy and Japan, even the communists in the Soviet Union, changed everything. They were an ancient barbarity come back to life again, an enemy pursuing the destruction of life as an end in itself.

He rolled the draw of sweet smoke over his tongue and released it again, watching it rise. *Perhaps no grand theory would ever explain what was truly in a man.*

He remembered another of his old Nobel-Prize winning colleagues back in Berlin. Fritz Haber, who had invented chlorine gas for the *Wehrmacht* in the Great War. A brilliant mind, surely convinced its cause was noble. And what had Haber gotten for it? His wife Clara had shot herself in their garden with his service revolver. Their twelve-year-old son had found her dying there. And a few years ago Faber had been forced to leave the Germany he had so served, wandering across Europe, dying from a heart condition.

No. Einstein wanted no part whatsoever in science that turned laboratories into armories. *Unless...the Nazis might get the bomb first...*

His thoughts were overwhelmed by a terrible heaviness.

The autumn days were growing short, and it was already dark when Mrs. Ochs sat down to a dinner of knockwurst and potatoes with her husband, Alfried. He was a truck driver, delivering fresh fish from the Philadelphia docks to restaurants up and down the coast of New Jersey. He was glad whenever he ran into another driver from his same company, a guy named Ralph Krieger driving the opposite route from Long Island to New York, and then down into Jersey. He was big bruiser, Krieger, who didn't say too much, but sometimes at the end of a shift they liked to stop and have a meal at one of the greasy spoons littered across all the truck stops in the area. Like him, Kreiger had come over from Germany a few years before the Great War, and sometimes it was just good to sit and smoke and drink a couple beers and hear a little of the mother tongue again.

Krieger might not have had much to say, but he always gave Alfried the impression that he had things going on, secret connections that he couldn't talk about too much. When he bothered to consider it, Ochs thought he might be running drugs for the mob, maybe carting hot goods. There was nothing exciting he could think to say or even imply about his own life, except for the job his wife had. Sometimes he let Ralph know that she was housekeeper for the great Einstein, and he seemed impressed, at least a little, so he would talk about it a little more. And Ralph would nod and raise his eyebrows, listen attentively, and then when they had used their bread to rub the last of the gravy off their plates and finished their last cigarette, they would shake hands and drive back to their homes. Ochs to his wife in Princeton, New Jersey, and Kreiger to his home in a little village called Yaphank in Long Island. Which was how the *Abwehr* learned all about Albert Einstein's coming vacation in Little Hog Neck.

Chapter Ten

EVEN IN A FRIGID DECEMBER, the old chicken farm had the stink of death.

They moved slowly across the moonscape before them, leading a group of state troopers and local cops. Each man held his gun drawn in one hand and a flashlight in the other, but the searching beams of light just made the whole scene more macabre. The ground beneath them was frozen but unstable, the surface crust suddenly giving way under the next step forward. Harry Weiss dreaded to think what was under their feet.

The stench was bad enough. The hundreds of chickens they found massacred in their coops, each with their throats individually cut, a big screw you to the raid, he understood. It must have taken hours. Blood and guts everywhere, decapitated chicken heads lying all around. A gory mess cooked up to mask something much worse, he knew.

"Over there," the small colored boy clutching Agent Amos' hand said, pointing to a distant section of the yard. James Amos nodded and signaled with his flashlight for them to follow.

For over six years now, Amos and Weiss had been partnered on nearly every case. Ostensibly, this was because they had worked so well together on the *Westmoreland* back in '33. When the office had applauded James for spotting the would-be assassin, he had demurred and credited Harry with the quick plan to disembark the Einsteins. But they both knew why they were really paired off—the Bureau didn't know what to do with either one of them.

The boy's steps slowed a little, and Amos gave him a reassuring glance.

At least one advantage of being a Negro FBI agent was that people would tell him things they wouldn't tell other agents. Colored people often bore witness because white people didn't even think of them being there when they did monstrous things—didn't think of them as real people at all.

The boy with them now, just eight and small for his age, was thin with a little, piping boy's voice. He had been sent to hang around the Ferraco chicken farm by his mother, hoping to beg some spare chicken parts for their half-starved family. It got so he was almost a fixture out here, on this little patch of hell by the Passaic River, as unnoticed as the junkyard dogs that he had to dodge every day. When Agent Amos came poking around the shantytown on the edges of the farm, the boy told him what he knew.

The crisp dollar bill offered by Amos helped.

Now he led them to a stretch of the yard that looked visibly indented, almost sunken. James nodded at Harry, then took the boy back. Harry signaled for the steam shovel. Its ignition stuttered then caught, the machine revving up like some primeval monster in the still of the night. Nobody said a thing. Harry waved to the steam shovel operator, then pointed to the spot where the ground slumped lowest. James came back to stand at his side, everyone watching as the driver banged the shovel to break the ice, then started to chip and scoop at the earth.

"You know, James," Harry Weiss said, four hours and seven bodies later. "I was starting to worry the Bureau didn't give a damn about you and me."

"With royal treatment like this?" Amos answered.

They sat wearily on the running board of the car Harry had signed out of the office that afternoon, sharing a thermos of coffee and watching their crew—scant and spent—load one sack after another into the ambulance. What was in those burlap sacks seemed scarcely human anymore. Pathetically shrunken, eaten away by the quicklime the bravos of Murder Inc. poured in to make identification as hard as possible. Still, Harry knew from experience by now, there was always something: a telltale gold tooth, a watch fob, a mended bone broken years before. A human body was very hard to reduce to nothing at all.

Harry Weiss felt like crying, he was so exhausted. They'd been investigating mob violence—particularly the Jewish network run by Meyer Lansky, Harry Rothman, and Bugsy Siegel—off and on for two years, and always felt the resistance of the Bureau, the reluctance to allocate any more men or dollars to their effort.

It hadn't evaded his attention that this was probably why he and James Amos had been assigned to the case in the first place—the odd fellows of the FBI, Jewish and Negro. Mr. Hoover, he knew, never liked to get the Bureau involved in mob cases. It wasn't like tracking down bank robbers out in the Midwest, dramatic scenes that drew weeks of headlines and ended with the bad guys incontrovertibly dead, or in prison. No, the mob was like roaches: they kept crawling back in, no matter how many times you tried to stamp them out. There was a considerable risk of losing cases and getting embarrassed. *And if there was one thing Mr. Hoover didn't like, it was risk.*

"All right, that's the lot," the ambulance driver told him, slamming the back doors shut. "You want 'em all at the morgue?"

Harry rose, feeling his bones creak like so many icicles in the wind.

"Uh-huh. That's right,"

The ambulance driver nodded and smiled, then drove his meat truck off Jimmy Ferraco's stinking chicken farm. Harry Weiss watched him go and thought *What does it all amount to?* The men in that ambulance, reduced to those crude remains, had been the best of the best. Longshoremen who never had two nickels to rub together in their lives, but were willing to stand up to bosses who ran the waterfront, and their thugs along the wharves. And what had it got them, being the best and the bravest? Maybe there would be justice, a couple of cretins erased for their murders, though it was just as likely the men they had worked with all their lives on the docks would go D & D—deaf and dumb—when the FBI next came around trying to find witnesses.

It made him think of Bobby Larkins again, even after all this time. *He was the bravest too. And what did we do for him?* His killing, still unsolved, had all but broken his Uncle Dan, Harry's old mentor. It made Harry want to beat the hell out of the next lowlife he collared, to shoot the next swaggering gangster he encountered. Instead he plopped back down next to James on the running board, unable to do anything else.

"Sometimes I hate this fucking job," he muttered to Amos, sitting down next to him again.

"Don't blaspheme. Especially in the presence of the dead."

Harry rolled his eyes. He could barely find a way to vent his anger without profanity, while James' tongue was as clean as a whistle.

"Yeah, I don't think they can hear me," Harry responded. "In any case, I'm going to go home and sleep for about a week. Or a few hours, anyway."

Amos, who looked as weary as Harry felt, only shook his head.

"Nope," he said softly. "We got new orders."

"Orders?" Weiss tried to sound dismayed, knowing it wasn't right, that they should stay with the mob case until it was done. But the idea of doing anything else… "When were you planning on telling me?"

"I thought you might crack if I told you sooner," Amos said. "You've been mumbling about a nap since lunch."

He has a point, Harry thought.

"What're we doing, any idea?" he asked. James Amos nodded stoically.

"Oh, yes," he said. "Nazis."

Harry Weiss shook his head and gave a low whistle.

"Straight from the top," James added. "Apparently, President Roosevelt met with Mr. Hoover and asked him whether the headlines about Nazi spy activity in the region were accurate. You can fill in the blanks: Hoover says yes, Roosevelt tells him to shut it down. Hoover says he needs more money, Roosevelt agrees. And now you and I get day-to-day responsibility for tracking down leads."

"Do we get any of that money? Assistants? Secretaries, maybe?"

James responded with a smirk that told Harry he knew better.

"And just how many anonymous tips and leads to nowhere will we be chasing every day?"

"As many as come in."

Harry motioned out at the nightmarish landscape before them, where a machine was still digging into the earth, searching for the bodies of union men murdered by gangsters.

"Shit, anything's gotta be better than this."

"I said don't blaspheme."

Chapter Eleven

ON A SNOWY EVENING IN EARLY February 1939, Professor Gerhardt Zwick and his wife, Helga, finished dinner in their home at Wilhelmstrasse 25, in the fashionable Berlin neighborhood of Mitte, between the Spree River and Tiergarten Park. It was an ample meal—a rarer and rarer occurrence these days, considering what was available in the markets. They were joined by their usual Sunday night guest, the Professor's young office assistant, Max Goldschmidt. Goldschmidt sat at the far end of the table, voraciously scraping the last of Fraulein Zwick's Black Forest cake into his mouth, as if it was the last dessert of his life.

"Careful Max," the Professor warned with a playful smile. "You'll choke."

Max looked up, smiling gently. "My apologies, Herr Professor. But what a way to die! Will you be playing tonight?"

"Patience," Zwick said. "First let's help Helga clean up."

Helga eyed Goldschmidt, masking her annoyance. Some husbands collected abandoned animals—the emaciated cats and dogs roaming Berlin in search of a morsel of food at a time when most Germans could barely afford a tin of milk. Instead, Gerhardt had rescued Max, a stray Jew who'd been attacked during the November pogrom four months earlier. Helga was morally opposed to the savagery, but as a practical matter she wondered whether Gerhardt was acting recklessly by hiring Goldschmidt as an office assistant at the University and inviting him every Sunday to dinner. On the two occasions when she'd suggested to her husband that Max would only bring trouble to them, he had simply sighed and mumbled about refusing to lose his humanity even as all of Germany had abandoned its own.

And so Max Goldschmidt continued to arrive at precisely six o'clock on most Sundays to devour roasted meats, potatoes, pickled vegetables, and his favorite, Helga's home baked Black Forest cake—all followed by a brief music recital from his hosts.

Finally, when the dishes were cleaned and returned to their cabinets, Zwick ushered Helga and Max into the library. It was a large and dimly lit room. A sharp wind whistled through the corners of double windows, occasionally stirring the lazy fire that flickered in a stone fireplace. The library's mahogany, wall-to-wall bookshelves were wedged full of hundreds of titles, mostly devoted to physics, music, and history, but in no particular order. Two violins were perched in stands. Max took a seat on a couch near the drafty windows.

"Let's play, Helga," the Professor said.

At eighty-six, Zwick was in conspicuous physical decline, although his reputation in German scientific circles as a peerless quantum physicist remained unsullied. Tufts of white hair sprung randomly from an otherwise bald and mottled scalp. His chapped, swollen lips concealed a set of yellow, crooked, increasingly loose teeth.

I am falling apart, he thought sometimes, taking stock of his creaking body. And yet, somehow, he did not much mind it. It made him all the less conspicuous, he knew.

His hand trembled as he reached for his violin and nestled it on his shoulder. It was his most cherished possession: an elaborate, 1790 Hornsteiner with grained spruce in the front and a wide-flamed maple back. Helga tucked her own instrument, an inexpensive model, mass produced in the 1920s, under her chin and waited for him. Zwick looked at her for a moment, and his eyes watered. To an outside observer, he was aware, she probably looked as worn and crooked with age as he was. But to him, she remained a beauty.

The duet began.

Zwick began a brief solo in dark, gloomy tones. Helga's response was brighter, happier. The violins parlayed, a musical point-counterpoint that filled the library and echoed through the rooms of the drafty mansion. This continued for eleven minutes before coming to a dead stop.

It was a piece called *Two Scientists Debate*, an unfinished composition by Zwick and Albert Einstein. The collaboration had started just over a decade earlier, at the fifth Solvay Conference on Physics. There, the world's greatest scientists had gathered to argue the very nature of reality. By day, they waged intellectual battle. Late at night, to ease the tension, Einstein and Zwick took their violins, pencils, and sheet music to a quiet room and composed their musical interpretation of the debates.

Zwick's notations were ominous, reflecting the dark potential of science and technology in the modern world. It had been less than ten years since all the wonders of modern science had been loosed upon the battlefields of Europe: poison gas and bombs dropped from the sky, torpedoes fired under the surface of the sea. Machine guns and tanks and rail guns that could lob a shell five miles into the heart of city. Those who wandered in from the conference sat listening somberly, in mourning for how science had been enchained to such ends. Einstein countered with tones reflecting the greater beauty of the universe, trying to rally and invigorate them again—implying there was some greater, better world that awaited them if they could just pull man through the violent ignorance of his adolescence. Their duet had stirred all who heard it. In the decade since, the composition had gone through multiple drafts, each man revising, deleting, adding. Sometimes it ignited stubborn though creative arguments—arguments not fully resolved when, in December 1932, Einstein visited Zwick in his office late one evening to tell him that he could not remain in Germany.

They began exchanging drafts of the composition via airmail. Zwick's drafts would follow Einstein to America. Einstein sent revisions back to Zwick in Berlin. As a composition, it was nothing special: conventional tonality, pleasant to the ear, the work of talented amateurs. As a bond between the two men and an expression of the great scientific debates of the early twentieth century, it was a masterpiece. One that grew steadily more complex, more uncertain on both ends, even to its present incarnation.

Zwick and Helga finished and placed the violins almost reverently on their stands.

Zwick asked, "What do you think?"

Helga smiled weakly, suppressing a cough. For months she'd struggled with tuberculosis, and now Zwick wondered whether the recital had been too much of a strain.

"Your revisions are perfect," she answered. "But you know Einstein. He will continue to change it. Always trying to top you."

They squeezed hands affectionately.

Zwick turned to Max and said, "I have a few more changes to make. You can mail them to Einstein later this week."

"Of course, Herr Professor!" Max Goldschmidt beamed brightly, his full brown lips spreading across the thick and dark stubble of his cheeks. *What luck! Almost beaten to death in front of the Neu Synagogue on Oranienburger Strasse months earlier, now in charge of mailing packages from one great scientist to another.*

Chapter Twelve

A COLD SLEET FELL ACROSS BERLIN the next morning, collecting in slushy gray puddles across the cobblestoned courtyard of the Friedrich Wilhelm University. Professor Zwick shuffled into his office in the Physics Building at ten, his usual hour, weighed down by an oversized wool overcoat. He was greeted by his secretary, Gerta Lange, a perky young woman with blond hair that splashed at her shoulders. She sat behind a rosewood desk in a small anteroom, adorned with a vase of silken edelweiss flowers. Zwick often reflected that she was the perfect covering for him: the very model of a healthy young Reichsmädchen, swept into a fanatical adoration of the strong and pure young men of the Reich who would breed a master race. It often challenged his trust in her, and he exercised greater caution when she was nearby.

"Max is in your office, Professor. Getting things ready."

Zwick rolled his eyes exaggeratedly. She smiled back.

Inside, Goldschmidt was tidying the office. He turned around, hoisted up his ill-fitting pants, and grinned shyly at Zwick.

"Guten Morgen, Herr Professor!" he said, his usual greeting.

Zwick smiled back and scanned his room. The great mess of papers that he'd left before the weekend were now in orderly piles. His discarded scratchings, crumpled like so many snowballs in the general vicinity of the waste basket, had been scooped up, the basket itself emptied. The opened books had been returned to the floor-to-ceiling bookshelves, a marker carefully inserted just where Zwick had left off. Fresh sticks of chalk now sat like a ridge under the blackboard, and a row of sharpened Farber Castell pencils was spread out at the side of his desk. Zwick frowned. *How was a man supposed to work with such neatness and order?*

"Thank you, Max. Now I must get to work," he said tightly.

"Of course, Professor. I'll be right outside if you need anything."

Zwick sat, and his swivel chair groaned loudly in protest. The sleet rapped against the window behind him, triggering a shiver. He took a moment to study the only two personal possessions on his desk. There was a portrait of Helga, and his photograph from the Solvay Conference. The last time that he and so many of his companions had been together. The greatest minds in the universe, posing for the camera. Heisenberg, smiling coyly. Pauli, distracted, face turned away from the camera. The goateed Schrodinger, staring ambivalently. The balding Plank, forlornly gripping his hat like a country squire hauled to church by his wife. Madame Curie, staring straight ahead: a prophet who had just had a terrifying vision.

Einstein, sitting at the center, seemingly uncomfortable. One hand clutching his chair.

And Zwick, his frail arms crossed over his gaunt chest— ancient even then.

He began shuffling through the neat tacks of paper, quickly returning them to the state he preferred: chaotic, but matching the way his aged mind worked. Each page was filled with his hand-scrawled mathematical symbols. Symbols for mass and time, length and distance, vector and velocity; integers, parentheses, brackets, their formulas sloping up and down in ridges across the edges of each page.

He found the formula he'd been struggling with and tapped the point of his pencil against it, as if that would somehow jar a solution loose. He knew the answer was there, somewhere. It was just a matter of time.

The universe held secrets and, sometimes, it allowed him a glimpse. It would open a door a crack, or whisper a hint in the wind, which was all Zwick needed. A helping hand.

"But the universe is also a flirt," he had told Einstein at Solvay. "It reveals just enough before shutting me out."

His friend had nodded.

"Winking, only to mock," he replied.

This particular equation had challenged him for months.

He tapped his pencil some more and stared at the paper in front of him. Closed his eyes and let the figures materialize in the dark.

Zwick fell into a nap, snoring loudly.

He was awakened thirty minutes later by an insistent rapping on his office door.

"*Eintreten*," he groaned as his eyes blinked open.

Gerta stepped in. Max was directly behind her, grinning excitedly.

"Professor Diebner just telephoned," Miss Lange announced. "The committee is to meet later this afternoon. With Reinhard Heydrich himself!"

Her bright blue eyes looked excited, though he doubted if she knew why. The mere mention of the Gestapo director seemed to awe her. The excitement had been building all over the Reich for almost a year now—people barking orders and convening emergency meetings. Men in uniform everywhere, marching double-time down the avenues, wheeling about in trucks. *Things were happening.* It was how the Nazis worked, Zwick had come to realize. A frenzy of activity, then long periods of slough, lulling the people back into thinking that everything was normal. Then, another burst of activity. Like solar flares, or lightning strikes.

Where it was all heading, Zwick could not say. He could not bear to imagine.

"You are to be at the New Reich Chancellery by four o'clock, Herr Professor," Gerta was saying. Then her mouth twisted into a judgmental scrunch. "You have plenty of time to stop home and change your clothing. Shouldn't you look your best for Heydrich?"

Zwick looked down. His shabby, oversized charcoal vest was splotched with the evidence of that morning's breakfast. Above it, his old-fashioned, detachable shirt collar seemed to be taking flight from his neck

"Thank you, Gerta, I'll let you know when I'm ready to leave."

"Professor, may I drive you to the Chancellery?" asked Max.

Zwick couldn't mask a grimace. "I don't think it would be best, Max."

Max's eyes looked resolute. "Please, Professor. I really don't mind. Besides—pulling up to the Chancellery in a taxi? I will drive your car."

Zwick sighed. "Very well. But don't linger. The guards will harass you."

They closed the door, leaving Zwick to himself. He sat back in the squeaky chair and massaged his chin.

A meeting called with Heydrich. Something is happening.

At 3:40, Zwick was crossing Berlin in the passenger seat of a blue Opel coup. The sleet had turned into a pelting rain, and the windshield wipers thumped and squealed. Max was behind the wheel, smiling like a fool. He was always smiling, it seemed, and Zwick wondered how it was possible—particularly at this moment, driving to the physical manifestation of Adolf Hitler's power.

Max Goldschmidt was a Jew, driving to the very heart of Nazi Germany.

Max had come to be Zwick's assistant at Friedrich Wilhelm University even though Jews had been officially expelled from academia years earlier. The purge was intended for faculty and students, but many of Zwick's colleagues in the Department of Physics argued that the ban should apply to everyone. Even Max, the lowly office assistant who emptied Zwick's trash bin, cleaned the blackboard, ran his errands, and retrieved books from the university library.

Zwick did not have the heart to dismiss him. Instead, he used what pull he had to keep him on. He was opposed to the Nazis' treatment of Jews in principle and sickened watching it in practice, though he kept his opinions to himself; nowhere in all of Germany did feeling for the Nazis run hotter than in the Reich's great universities. The risk notwithstanding, Zwick felt a genuine affection for the young man. Max was in his early thirties, though he often seemed younger. Perhaps it was the perpetual smile. He had bright eyes and a tassel of black hair that fell boyishly, endearingly, across his brow, and a dark complexion that made everyone who encountered him in the race-obsessed Reich think immediately: *Jew.*

Zwick could not help but feel protective, even if Max could, at times, test his kindness. He peppered the professor with questions about physics, events going on around the world, and politics inside the Reich. There could not have been more dangerous topics for a Jewish office assistant to broach—especially out loud and in public. But there was a naiveté to the lad. A lovable quality that made Zwick fear for Max's life.

Zwick would suppress his exasperation and answer Max's questions, hoping mostly to get him to be quiet before he attracted more attention. Unless the questions came too close to his most closely guarded secrets, the ones hidden in plain sight in his scribbled equations, or in the locked bottom drawer of his desk at the University. Then the Professor would simply say, "Another time, Max," and Max would look hurt but seem to understand, nodding and quieting.

Now Zwick looked at his watch and said, "If you like, you can drop me off a few blocks away, Max. The walk will do me good."

"In this weather? You'll freeze. Besides, you don't even have an umbrella. You can't appear at your meeting looking like a drowned rat."

"But what goes on inside that building…I would understand if you preferred not to come so close to it."

"It's fine, Professor. I've wanted to see what the New Chancellery looks like close up."

So did everyone in Germany. The story was that the Fuhrer had given his favorite architect, Albert Speer, an unlimited budget and all the manpower he needed, as long as he swore to finish it within a year. *And why that time limit?* Zwick wondered. Whatever the reason, Speer had crews working night and day and even on most holidays, thousands of men, the racket echoing all around the Wilhelmplatz. The immense, forbidding structure had just been completed—on time. Three vaulted stories of yellow stucco and gray stone, its austere neoclassical façade looming right over the street. The pinnacle of Nazi architecture: perfectly symmetrical, monotonous arrays of windows. Almost devoid of decoration, smartly modern and sleek—and overwhelming.

As the complex came into sight, Max asked, "Is this your first meeting with Heydrich?" His voice had become somber. *It was as though,* Zwick thought, *he had been straining to appear cheerful in this awful errand all along.*

Zwick smiled sadly at him and shrugged.

"We've met."

"He knows you personally?" Max said.

"By reputation. And I know him the same way."

"What do you think of him?"

Zwick looked at the young man for a long moment, frankly incredulous. *Of course,* he thought. *The boy must be terrified.* Then he noted, not for the first time, how shabby Max's clothes were. The pants that wouldn't stay up as he lost more weight. A shapeless sweater with a moth hole here and there, a tie with more soup stains than Zwick's own vest, a raggedy excuse for a jacket. At that moment, he regretted all the doubts he'd ever had about his assistant.

"I don't think about politics, Max," he said as gently as he could. "I think about other things. Far more important things."

They pulled up before the main public entrance, on the Voss Strasse. The towering set of doors had been punched through the Weimar extension to the Old Chancellery. Hitler had happily vandalized it, dismissing it as "fit for a soap company," just like the rest of Germany's brief fling with democracy under the Treaty of Versailles. Zwick opened his door, looking up apprehensively at the huge towers and the staircase in front of him.

"What time should I pick you up, Professor?" Max asked from

behind the wheel.

"I can't possibly say," he told Max, shivering already in the cold rain. "Please—take the car back to the institute. I can surely find a taxi."

Zwick gave the car a sharp pat, and Max pulled away with a wave, tires splashing through a puddle. Zwick gave a sigh of relief and turned toward the steps, squinting through the soft rain, even as something else troubled him deep in his remarkable brain.

All such concerns were absorbed in his struggle to penetrate the heart of the Reich. Behind the giant street doors, there were more doors, across an endless courtyard that waited just inside. It felt like entering the mouth of a terrible beast. Zwick had never known a building to exude such menace. Standing guard by the second set of doors was a pair of those dreadful life-sized Arno Breker statues that had come to pock Reich museums like an infectious disease. Ridiculously muscled nude figures with the faces of furies. Exactly the same save for what they were holding: one, a torch; the other, a sword. *Die Partie* and *Die Wehrmacht.* As he went past them, he couldn't help but notice how proportionately smaller their penises looked. *And were they...circumcised?*

Once inside he stumbled through a confusing series of rooms, past bombastic portals of gilded stone, with bronze eagles clutching swastikas overhead. Then—to his dismay—the longest hallway he had ever seen, one that looked to be at least five hundred feet. Already exhausted, mopping at his neck with his handkerchief, Zwick made his way slowly along the corridor. Its marble flooring was polished until it gleamed, and it was all he could do to keep his balance. Others moved past him, he noticed, civilian or military or SS, dressed in dark civilian suits, or in black and gray uniforms. Underlings trailed the most important ones closely, like so many suckerfish sticking to sharks. Zwick noticed that they had already developed what was almost a skating motion to traverse the endless marble hall.

Huge swastika banners hung from the walls, over vacant

upholstered chairs, and untended wooden tables. He could not imagine that any hall in the entire world could be so vast—nor so empty. It was a labyrinth, he realized, like something out of Greek mythology.

And what would he find at its heart? *A modern minotaur—the monster beyond imagining?*

At the end of the hall, he walked through a reception room so large it might have passed for a football stadium—but Zwick was no longer surprised by the scale. He opened a door into still another room that was almost as large. It was stunning in its luxury, the polished wooden walls and furniture glowing in the soft lamplight, enormous hand-knotted rugs covering the floor. At its center was a table wide enough for a tall man to lie across it, and long enough to fit eleven elegant chairs on each side. There were paintings by the masters on each wall, more Nazi regalia, and another immense tapestry—*something from the Middle Ages*, he thought, though his glasses were clouded with sweat from his exertion and he was too tired to figure out what allegory or Biblical scene it was depicting. Instead he flopped into the first open chair before him, too exhausted even to be embarrassed that all of his colleagues were already seated and staring at him.

Chapter Thirteen

THEY WERE, OFFICIALLY, CONSULTANTS to the Reich Research Council at the Ministry of Culture. That bland title, which wouldn't raise an eyebrow to anyone scanning the reports of the Reich bureaucracy, didn't tell the real story, of course. This was a meeting of the Reich's most celebrated scientists—those who were left, anyway—as selected by Kurt Diebner: Otto Hahn and Werner Heisenberg; Erich Schumann and Walther Koch. The two fanatics, Phillip Lenard and Johannes Stark, were sitting up closest to the head of the table, as usual. Across from them, their intellectual opponent, the physicist Carl Ritter. Unlike the others, Ritter had not only opposed the Nazis but remained unguarded in expressing his opinions. And while his research on atomic physics had been valuable enough to shield him from the Gestapo's wrath, Zwick admonished Ritter privately to stop tempting them. They were more valuable alive than dead, and that meant remaining inconspicuous.

Zwick and Ritter were here for two reasons. First, the invitation to serve on the Research Council wasn't an invitation, but a summons—and one did not decline a summons from Reinhard Heydrich. More important was their second reason: the summons had given them, together with a covert network of scientists, an opportunity to observe what these madmen were doing in order to thwart them. Some might call it sabotage. Zwick called it salvation. He'd dedicated his life to physics, and he wasn't going to sit idly by and watch it exploited by anyone, especially the madman Hitler.

Some three seats at the head of the wide table remained empty, but then a door opened on the far end of the room and Diebner walked in. He was short and thin, with a receding hairline and round, comically oversized spectacles that slipped constantly down his nose. A sycophant who spoke in a hesitant cadence, measuring every word like the bureaucrat he was. Right behind him came another figure: General Becker, in his army dress uniform. To Zwick's disgust, the men around the table immediately stood as one, except for Ritter, who rose half-heartedly. Becker waved them down, his uniform immaculate but his thick face looking haggard.

"If I might commence the meeting, Herr General..." Diebner oozed at Becker, who nodded his permission.

Becker was not a thinker at the level of the others assembled around the table, but he was a genuine man of science, with a doctorate in engineering and a deep interest in ballistics. After the Great War, it was Becker who had found a loophole in the Versailles Treaty that allowed Germany to start experimenting with missiles. His presence at the Research Council meeting was another confirmation to Zwick that things were happening. Usually, Becker relied on Diebner to report their deliberations to him. Becker had many other responsibilities—he was in charge of munitions production for the entire army—and the rumors were that he was being flayed by Hitler and Heydrich for not producing more. *And why was that? Why were they so concerned just now?*

One chair at the head of the table remained empty, Zwick noticed. He saw that the door Diebner and Becker had entered through was left slightly ajar. *Who was that for?* he wondered. *Who was listening?*

There was a feeling of ebullience around the table today, he realized. Zwick looked across the table at Otto Hahn, his old friend and fellow pacifist. Soft-spoken and kindly. Opposed to all the brutalities of the Nazis. And yet he had gone ahead and made his great breakthrough, splitting an atom in his laboratory. *Opening another door—this one to Armageddon.* Now the man who'd stared into the deepest and most minute particles of the universe couldn't bring himself to look Zwick in the eyes.

He glanced down at the rest of the table. Learned men.

Civilized men. The cream of the scientific establishment, in what had long been the most advanced scientific nation on earth. Yet they would go right on keeping their heads down and focusing on their experiments, their obsessions. Willing to find and turn over a force of unimaginable power to a maniac, entrenched in their little corner of the apocalypse.

How can they be so foolish? Working to destroy the very planet, Zwick thought. More than almost anyone alive, he had a very good idea of what a series of atomic explosions might do. *What took billions of years to evolve, they would find a way to annihilate in a matter of days.*

In the weeks since Hahn's discovery, the committee had intensified its research to liberate atomic energy on a massive scale and weaponize it—to find a way to start a chain reaction. Initially, Zwick had thought it was poppycock. But they'd marched closer. Researched, theorized, and calculated. Chalk on blackboards, pencils on notepaper. *Tap-tap-tap.* Diebner reviewing all the progress they had made, enthusing over what this might mean for the war effort.

Diebner was droning at General Becker. "Professor Hahn has made a brilliant discovery. Historic. You see, when uranium absorbs a neutron, the neutron breaks into two parts. This is called fission. Now, if enough neutrons are emitted in this process, it should be possible to sustain a chain reaction and, potentially, yield massive amounts of energy. Energy that might be adapted into a weapon—"

Fortunately, Zwick knew how to divert their attention. He made a very loud old man's grumble, more like an explosion, and waited until he had drawn their attention.

"Excuse me, gentlemen, but isn't this what the Leader warned us against? Aren't we delving into the realms of *Einstein's* theories, with their discredited, *Jüden Physik* ideas? Didn't the Fuhrer himself charge us with building a new *Deutsche Physik,* which our own esteemed colleagues, Lenard and Stark, have discovered?"

Just as he had hoped, Lenard had gone off like a giant firecracker, leaping to his feet and wagging his fingers at his colleagues.

"Zwick speaks the truth!" squawked Lenard. "We must have a *German* physics! It is our duty as Aryans!"

Zwick contained a smile at how easy it was to ignite the man. He looked like someone's ordinary grandfather, with a gray beard, a few thin strands of hair combed over a balding scalp, and a proper black bow tie wrapped around a high collared shirt. Beneath it all, however, was a rabid anti-Semite. He'd spent the past two decades crusading to purge German science of Jewish influences and discredit Albert Einstein. Now his eyes raked the table, seeking a target. "Some of these charlatans should not even be sitting in on our councils—certainly not a white Jew like Heisenberg!"

Heisenberg, the youngest in the group, only slouched back in his elegant cabinet chair, a smile playing around his thin lips, looking on with his usual, friendly condescension.

Now it was Ritter who popped up. "There you go again, Lenard! Contaminating our research with your ravings. Ideology has no business in this room!"

Lenard glared at Ritter. "And yet, here you are, Ritter. If you are so disturbed by ideology, why do you participate at all?"

Around the table, pencils scratched insensibly on paper, and papers were folded and refolded anxiously. "We all know the answer, Lenard. To decline an invitation here is to accept one to Dachau."

Sit down, Ritter, Zwick thought. *It's too much!*

"One would think your sense of honor would accept such consequences." Lenard snapped at Ritter.

"I'm also practical, Lenard. I know that science will long outlive the politicians who rise and fall with the winds. Mark my words, gentleman: Hitler's thousand-year Reich will crumble under its own calumnies. I'm here in the interest of science. Nothing more."

The room fell to a perturbed silence. It reminded Zwick of one his lecture halls—schoolboys slumping in their seats, hoping not to be called on. He was satisfied that nothing would move forward today. Still, Hahn's discovery of fission meant that it wouldn't be long before Hitler had a bomb. He'd need to warn his contact in America.

His thoughts were interrupted by the sly smile spreading across Lenard's face. Zwick wondered whether this time Ritter had simply gone too far.

General Becker slapped his hand on the table.

"Be careful, Ritter. No one is immune to Party discipline—"

The door at the back of the room opened wider, and a man in a black SS uniform walked in. He had the face of a whippet hound, and he moved with casual, deliberate menace. The room fell silent, though he never said a word. He sat in the last empty chair at the head of the table, between General Becker and Kurt Diebner. No one introduced him. They didn't have to. Everyone knew who Reinhard Heydrich was.

"I heard only a portion of your discussion," Heydrich said. His cold eyes scanned the table, landing on Ritter before moving on. "What I have not heard is when we will have an atomic weapon."

Kurt Diebner cleared his throat nervously. "Well, of course this is all very preliminary. We must continue testing. There are numerous—"

Heydrich leaned forward, as if inspecting a rabbit he'd just cornered before tearing its throat out.

"*How long?*"

Diebner's face tightened, as if he were in physical pain.

"I...would say at least...I'm estimating...two or three years. Perhaps more."

Heydrich's gaze swept around the table once more, as if inviting any of them to contradict Diebner. No one dared to say a thing.

"Three years is unacceptable," Heydrich stated plainly. "The Fuhrer must have this weapon much sooner. One year at the most."

He leaned back again in his chair. It seemed to Zwick that the men around him became statues: marble, gleaming, and still, staring vacantly at their papers. From a tradition willing to challenge the assumptions of Aristotle, Galileo, Newton, Descartes, they were now rendered mute in the presence of the monster who sat among them.

"Does any other country have the ability to achieve such a weapon?" he asked.

The discomfort around the table felt almost palpable to Zwick. The long, painful silence continued.

"We have no specific intelligence on the matter," General Becker admitted. "Perhaps the English, though we doubt it. Certainly not the Russians."

He hesitated, and Heydrich looked at him, his gaze alone compelling Becker to answer.

"Perhaps America."

"Are their scientists as good as ours?"

There was a sneer in the question. Becker nodded glumly.

"Well... they now have many who have left, uh, *Europe.*"

Left? Zwick thought. *You expelled them from our universities. Confiscated their bank accounts, even their homes. Hounded them until they had no choice but to flee the country they loved. Nobel laureates. The greatest professors of theoretical physics the world has ever known. Your insanity has set our very best minds against one another—*

Philipp Lenard joined in as if on cue.

"And good riddance to them! Their degenerate dark arts contaminated the purity of Aryan physics! Science, like all other human activities, is racial and conditioned by blood—"

Heydrich turned his head, just an inch or two, in Lenard's direction. The old man stopped talking. Diebner began listing names—making sure to include as many as possible who had not gone to America from Germany.

"There are, uh, Szilard, Wigner, and Teller, from Hungary. Fermi from Italy. Rabi, Bethe, Einstein, a number of others—"

"All capable of telling Roosevelt how to build an American

bomb, while you debate and dither," Heydrich interrupted. "That is why the Fuhrer himself has made a decision."

The pronouncement landed like a death sentence.

"We are bringing in a new man. He will join you within the next two months. In the meantime, we have secured rooms for you at the Luftwaffe Airfield, so your work will be undistracted. You will report next week. I apologize in advance for the less than gracious accommodations."

Diebner began stammering. Heydrich silenced him with another look, then without speaking, stood and left the room. The entire table seemed to let out its collective breath, though they soon noticed that he had left the door ajar again.

The meeting adjourned shortly thereafter.

As Zwick left the room, he felt Ritter's sudden tug at his shoulder. "Not here!" Zwick whispered and pulled away. Moments later, he came upon Lenard, standing in front of the Breker statues near the building entrance.

"One moment, Zwick," Lenard called out. "I wanted to thank you for your comments. Some in that room cannot be trusted."

Zwick nodded, masking his pity for Lenard. So jealous of Einstein, so vulnerable. Always trying to prove himself by spouting off about who and what he knew.

So easy to exploit, Zwick knew.

"What did Heydrich mean, bringing in a new man?" Zwick asked.

Lenard smiled, "Come to a quieter place."

They found a small reception room off the lobby and closed the door behind them. It was windowless, lit by a single crystal chandelier. Dark paneled walls exhibited photographs of the Fuhrer and foreign heads of state, notably Chamberlain, Mussolini, and Daladier. *The men who'd recently taken out their carving knives and cut Czechoslovakia to pieces*, thought Zwick, *in a dangerously naïve attempt to appease the Fuhrer and avoid war.*

Lenard leaned towards Zwick, whispering "Do I have your solemn oath of confidentiality?"

"As always."

"I have friends at the Abwehr. It's just chatter, of course, and almost unbelievable, but they tell me of the most audacious plan."

"Go on."

"They're going to drag the old Jew back to Germany!"

"The old Jew—"

"Einstein!"

Zwick scowled. "It *is* unbelievable, Lenard."

Lenard placed his hands on Zwick's shoulders and brought his voice even lower. "They're sending in an agent, posing as a Jewish refugee to get close to him. What's the English proverb? *Birds of a feather flock together*? I must admit I have conflicting feelings. I thought we were finally rid of him. But forcing him back, to sit in Dachau where his secrets will be beaten out of him—well, that's a thought I could get used to."

Zwick nodded. "Yes, it would be quite a trophy for the Fuhrer, wouldn't it?"

Zwick exited the massive doors, reprimanding himself for forgetting his umbrella. He hurried through the cold drizzle to a line of black taxis on Voss Strasse, wondering whether the Gestapo was testing his loyalty by planting an absurd secret; or whether Lenard was actually privy to an operation to target Einstein. State secrets were often leaked by weak men with fragile egos.

Chapter Fourteen

ZWICK RETURNED TO THE KAISER Wilhelm Institute, gazing out the taxi's rain-streaked window. The streets bustled with happy shoppers as dusk settled across the city. They clutched packages, popped umbrellas, skipped around puddles, darted in and out of shops and cafes, streamed to and from the outdoor market in the dark gray mist.

Slow down, my friends, he thought to himself. *I have just left a short meeting that may end time itself.*

The taxi pulled up to the Institute just before 4:30. He trudged up a dimly lit flight of steps to the long wood-paneled corridor of offices—quietly thanking God it was nowhere near as long as the Olympian distances at the New Reich Chancellery.

Max was already inside his office, of course, tidying up. *Always tidying something.* He looked up, surprised—back to his usual cheer.

"Professor! Back so soon?"

Zwick mustered a smile. "Yes Max. Now please allow me to get to work."

The Professor shooed Max away with a brisk wave of his hands, regretting his impatience even as he did so.

He waited for the door to snap closed behind Max, then sat behind his desk. From his pants pocket he fished a small metal key, inserted it in a lower desk drawer, and carefully pulled the drawer open. Almost immediately he noticed that the small coin he'd positioned atop the jumble of papers inside had been moved. He'd instructed Gerta Lange to leave his desk alone. Now he cursed to himself, more disappointed than angry.

Zwick rifled through the pile until he found a particular

document scrawled with equations. He dragged his fingers down the page until he landed on a string of digits. He picked up the receiver of the black rotary phone on his desk, dialed the numbers he had just looked at—but in reverse order.

"Yes."

The voice on the other end of the line was neutral, almost ethereal.

"I'm calling to inquire about my family's hotel reservations. We met today and they are worried about the weather. Thunderstorms are coming."

"Thank you," the detached voice replied. "We will look at the weather advisory and call you regarding those dates."

Zwick plopped back in his chair and exhaled a labored breath. For several months, he'd been conveying messages about the status of the Reich Research Council through a trusted contact in Berlin to Professor Leo Szilard, at Columbia University. He trusted that Szilard would deliver his latest warning about Germany's atomic bomb program to the U.S. government. He'd often wondered whether Washington's lethargy in developing its own research was the result of willful ignorance, political cowardice, or naïve indifference of a nation buffered by two oceans.

Or all three.

He considered his next step: how to warn Albert Einstein of what he'd learned from Philipp Lenard at the Chancellery. The very idea was pure insanity. Preposterous!

Yes, but hasn't simple insanity been the most effective strategy for the Reich so far? Doing exactly what most rational thinkers considered simply impossible? The execution of hundreds of its own paramilitary in 1934, the organizing of the murderous anti-Jewish pogroms last November, the filling of concentration camps, the annexation of Austria, the occupation of Czechoslovakia, the demand for lebensraum, living space, for Aryan expansion across Europe.

The building of an atomic bomb, so that no nation on Earth could defy Hitler.

He wrestled with various methods to alert Einstein. He couldn't pick up a phone to warn his friend—not with German military intelligence listening in. A cable was just as likely to be intercepted. And in the cipher of imaginable contingencies related to the Nazi bomb program, no one had thought to add *a German spy, posing as a Jewish refugee, is coming to America to snatch and return Albert Einstein to Germany.*

No, he'd need to find a different way; create a new cryptogram that only Albert Einstein would understand.

Cradled in his top drawer was a large envelope containing the manuscript of *Two Scientists Debate*, played the night before with Helga and Max.

He smiled gently.

It was no coincidence that so many great physicists had an abiding love of music. Music and physics were two parallel measures of the universe, each based on time, measurement, and frequency. Vibrations and waves, depth and layers. Musical structure was an expression of quantum mechanics: symphonies constructed of movements, movements made up of stanzas, stanzas of notes, half-notes, quarter notes down to barely perceptible beats in a majestic, complex whole.

Music was mathematics and mathematics was the basis of all code. One day, Zwick had theorized, the simple binary of 0 and 1 would be the foundation of great advances in computational science.

He scanned the top page, smiling again at his own cleverness. He and Einstein had always assumed that the SS had intercepted and scrutinized their work. But really, it was only the work of two amateur musicians. Nothing more.

Until now.

He looked at a wall clock: 4:45. He calculated he could alter the manuscript and embed a cipher key in less than an hour. Then he'd have Max drive him to the *Reichspost*, before it closed at six.

He'd have to work fast.

He positioned the eraser of a Faber-Castell pencil against a note at the bottom of the first page—changed the duration of a note.

Then flipped a page in search of another discreet location.

So intense was his concentration that he didn't hear the sudden rumble of tires on the cobblestone outside or, moments later, the clatter of boots charging through the hallway.

He changed a second note and flipped to a new page, his pencil hovering over a new section, seeking just the precise place for a third change.

Gerta Lange's scream finally caught his attention.

He looked up just as his office door flung open.

Mein Gott!

Two burly men in gray overcoats and homburgs burst in, followed by a short man with flabby jowls and a flat nose. Zwick tried to look surprised and indignant.

"What is the meaning of this? Who are you?"

"I am *Kriminaldirektor* Bartels," growled the short man, his voice like a saw slicing into wood. It was the voice of a man who liked to hurt people, and break things.

"How dare you intrude like this! As if I am a common criminal! I am—"

"We know exactly what you are, Professor Zwick. You are under arrest."

"That's impossible—"

"You tried to leak state secrets to your spy ring. Thunderstorms, indeed."

Bartels turned to the guards and barked, "Search him."

The guards yanked Zwick from his chair, pinned his arms behind his back, and roughly worked their hands across his body, plunging their fists into his pockets, slapping and poking at his frail body, ignoring his whimpers and grunts. Satisfied that the old man was carrying nothing more than old business cards, notes, mint candies, and keys, they stood back, awaiting further orders.

Zwick stood, wheezing heavily, arms braced on the desk for

support. "This is a mistake. I am Gerhard Zwick! Nominated for a Nobel Prize—"

"Silence!" Bartels screeched.

"Past President of the Kaiser Wilhelm Society—"

"I warn you."

"Recipient of the Barnard Medal for Meritorious Service to Science—"

"Shut him up!" Bartels ordered the guards.

One of the men forced Zwick into his chair. The other wrapped his hand around the back of his neck and forced his head to the desk, like a hammer to an anvil. Zwick's cheek landed on the portrait of Helga, shattering the glass. His ears rang and the pain felt as if lightning itself had ripped across his face. Zwick tasted hot, thick blood; it flowed across the shards of glass, staining two errant pages of his unfinished warning to Einstein. He struggled to focus on Helga's portrait, crinkled behind the shattered glass. He closed his eyes, concentrating on the memory of her image. Ready to die.

"Stop!" a voice bellowed. It sounded vaguely familiar.

Zwick reopened his eyes. Bartels had moved quickly aside as someone entered his office.

"Move away from him, goddamn you!" the voice commanded the SS guards.

The figure rushed to the desk. Zwick struggled to lift his head.

"We need this piece, and you've ruined it!" Two hands fumbled under Zwick's face, sweeping away the bloody page.

Zwick managed to turn his face to the figure with the familiar voice.

Max Goldschmidt towered over him, studying the blood-streaked pages.

Searing pain and heavy confusion enveloped Zwick.

Darkness came.

Chapter Fifteen

LESS THAN AN HOUR LATER, Gerhard Zwick's eyes fluttered open to a small cell in the basement SS headquarters on Prinze-Albrecht-Strasse. It was damp, dimly lit, and reeked of sweat and blood and piss. His open cheek burned beneath a sloppily affixed bandage. He'd been plunked into a straight-backed wooden chair; across a table from him sat an SS guard, leafing through *Der Angriff*, the newspaper founded by Joseph Goebbels to attack political opponents and Jews. A semi-conscious moan from the Professor caught the guard's attention, sending him in a quick march from the room.

The hall outside resounded with urgent chatter, followed by the approach of footsteps. The door to the cell creaked loudly as it swung open.

The man Zwick once knew as Max Goldschmidt stood over him. Other than the shabby black suit, everything about him had changed. The warm eyes had disappeared entirely, replaced with a cold, clinical glare. He studied Zwick as if he was an experiment, and Max the scientist now.

"Who are you?" croaked Zwick.

"Oh, Herr Professor. I am whoever the Reich needs."

"I don't understand. I demand an explanation."

"Actually, I am owed one. Why have you betrayed us?"

"I don't know what you're talking about—"

"Come, Professor. You and your associates have been leaking secrets to set back our ability to acquire an atomic weapon. No more charades, shall we?" He circled the table and took a chair opposite Zwick. He pulled a thin Sturm cigarette from the pocket of the same moth-eaten shirt that had once been worn by Max, the meek Jewish assistant. "We have just arrested Professors Ritter, Vogel, and Birken. Have we missed anyone?"

Zwick closed his eyes, fighting back the sudden urge to vomit.

Goldschmidt shrugged. "Actually, I happen to be more interested in your American contacts. Szilard, we already know. Who else? Bohr?"

"You're wasting your time," Zwick croaked.

"Wigner, perhaps?"

Silence.

"Teller? Von Neumann? Einstein himself?"

"Go to hell."

Goldschmidt slipped the cigarette into a glass tray and stood from his chair. "Surely a great scientist like yourself doesn't believe concepts like heaven or hell. Or perhaps the past hour has brought you some religious enlightenment? As for me, my relationship with religion is quite complicated. But I will save that for later."

He gave a deep, gravelly chuckle, circled the table, and positioned himself directly behind Zwick.

He leaned forward and wrapped an arm around the old man's throat, squeezing just enough against the larynx to reduce the passage of air without causing him to black out. A steady hand; a well-practiced technique.

"Interrogations of the elderly can be challenging. You see, I cannot kill you before you have told me what I need to know. In most cases, it is a matter of hours. Once, the beatings lasted two days. It would be less painful for you and less work for me if you gave me the names now. Please. Bohr?"

The pressure tightened.

"Fermi?"

The room spun in gray and black. But Zwick remained silent, welcoming his own death.

Goldschmidt released his grip. Zwick wheezed. "Kill me."

Goldschmidt returned to his chair, smiling as if enjoying the spectacle of the old, half-dead man gagging. "We certainly will.

But then we must decide…what shall we do with your beloved wife?"

Zwick closed his eyes in defeat. He could endure his own suffering. But not the suffering of Helga. "Please. My wife knows nothing."

Max shrugged. "Perhaps not. But if you do not provide the names, we will be forced to arrest and interrogate her. She seemed so frail last night."

The old man felt something rolling deep in his chest, a wave that rose to the back of his mouth and emerged as a defeated sob. Tears flowed down his bloody face. Stinging.

"Here, I will make it easy for you, Herr Professor. You say the names and I will write them for you. *Ja?*"

"You will leave her alone?"

"Of course…if your names check out. A few harmless questions and then she will be returned home safely. She will be told that you have been sent to Dachau for political crimes. She will never know the truth. I am quite good at hiding truths, as you now know. Shall we begin?"

"Szilard…Wigner…Fermi…Franck…"

The names continued to ride out of his mouth, each with the weight of a death sentence.

An hour. Hours. Days. Zwick had lost track. From a ratty mattress in his dank cell, he'd been in and out of dreams: floating above a cavernous, sun-streamed lecture hall; walking through the Tiergarten with Helga; driving to the Chancellery with Max.

He found himself playing violin with Einstein at the *Institut International de Physique Solvay* when he was wrenched away and dragged to the small table. Goldschmidt was already seated. He wore a black wool turtleneck and black slacks and was smoking the usual Sturm cigarette.

Zwick noticed the pages of *Two Scientists Debate* set in a neat pile.

Goldschmidt smiled as if they were friends about to enjoy a

beer. "Shall we discuss your composition, Professor?"

Zwick wanted to return to his dreams.

Goldschmidt continued. "Now that we can be completely honest, I must tell you something. I have often thought of your recitals as worse torture than anything we do here. Like a hammer to my skull. Chaotic structure. Overuse of motifs. Absolutely no sense of progression or climax. And, my god, how poorly notated! Inconsistent markings, riddled with errors."

Where is this leading, Zwick wondered.

"And due to the carelessness of our guards, ruined." He held up two pages, stained thickly with Zwick's dried blood.

Zwick mumbled, "I don't understand."

"You will rewrite these pages." He slid them across the table, followed by a sheaf of clean sheet music and one of Zwick's dull pencils. "So that the composition is presentable to your collaborator. And recognizable as written by you."

Even in his half-sleep state, the plan dawned suddenly on Zwick. He recalled Lennard's tip that Einstein would be abducted by someone posing as a refugee. Now Max—or whoever he was— was in possession of a document that would help gain access to Einstein. He needed time.

"He'll see through you in a matter of minutes."

Goldschmidt smiled. "You didn't, did you? You let me into your house. With your wife, no less! You protected me from your colleagues. Einstein has the same fatal affection for such poor, oppressed Jews. Now please be careful rewriting. I'll be watching."

Zwick examined his own dried blood, which blotted out entire sections of the pages. A thousand possibilities ran through his broken mind. When he'd first attempted to code a warning to his friend, in his office, it was vague. Now…

"Of course, Professor, we will check every detail. You have fifteen minutes."

Zwick picked up the pencil. Shut his eyes, conjuring ideas. He began transcribing onto the fresh pages, slowly, methodically, as if the universe itself was dictating.

The sloppy work of amateurs.

He slid it back.

"Very good, Professor," Goldschmidt said. "Very good. Now, our work is finished."

"Now you kill me, Max." Zwick said, matter-of-factly.

"Actually, if you will indulge me, I would like to come clean myself. *Clear the table*, yes? On the possibility of my going to hell, will you hear my confession?" He rose from the chair and pulled an SS "honor dagger" from a scabbard at his hip—black handle, inlaid with the silver Parteiadler eagle and SS symbol. He seemed to be humming as he approached the Professor.

Zwick shut his eyes and imagined the universe stretching before him.

"I'll need you to look at me, Zwick. I won't ask you again." He crouched at eye level with Zwick, positioned the blade in the usual spot.

"My name is Anton Gunther. I work for the Abwehr, the Reich's intelligence agency. I operate undercover to root out and disrupt enemies of the state. Most recently, I have been posing as Max Goldschmidt. My mission was to penetrate a suspected network of scientists." 'Gunther' held Zwick's gaze intently, his tone incredulous and mocking. "Scientists who were betraying our development of super-weapons."

The universe is also a flirt, thought Zwick.

"There." Gunther smiled coldly. "Now I have confessed. I must say, you do not appear so surprised."

Revealing just enough before shutting me out...

"It is a pity, Professor. I rather liked you. But now..."

Winking, only to mock.

Zwick closed his eyes again, thinking of the preparations he had made. Thinking of Helga, who he prayed might live—or die quickly.

Thinking of the other thing he had done, that even this devil could not know.

"How does it feel, being this close to death?"

Zwick opened his eyes to a new face on Max Goldschmidt: cheeks flushed, eyes widening, tongue brushing against thick lips. Exhilaration, he thought. No—*lust*.

Zwick said, "You're sick. I pity you."

Pain ripped across his opened neck, consuming his breaths, unleashing a final torrent of blood. The universe ignited, an explosion of fire and ice, blinding streaks of light against the blackest black. Burning, freezing, drowning him at the same time. The breaking apart of infinite atoms, a final burst of energy that claimed his flesh, bone, and blood. The thunder of countless long-gone voices: students, colleagues, Helga.

Einstein.

He slipped from the chair, a barely perceptible, defiant smile of triumph on his face.

In his final moment, he heard music.

Chapter Sixteen

"THE SMARTEST MEN ARE OFTEN the most careless," Anton Gunther proclaimed, then released a stream of cigarette smoke and watched how it rose to the high-coffered ceiling. "For all his genius, despite running his own network of traitors, Professor Zwick had no idea that his office, even his home, had been penetrated."

He was in Heydrich's office in the Reich Security headquarters, on an infinitely nicer floor of the same building where Gerhardt Zwick had died with such disappointing suddenness just a few hours before. The room had once been a library, and it reflected the Deputy Reichsfuhrer's refined tastes: Bauhaus furniture in simple, sleek lines. Nineteenth-century German landscapes by the Romantic painter, Caspar David Friedrich, on the walls. Bookshelves stocked with Goethe, Nietzsche, Hölderlin, Rilke, and von Kleist, along with music portfolios. Like so many of the physicists under his supervision, Heydrich was known to be an outstanding violinist and pianist.

Gunther knew he was walking on a razor's edge even smoking in the man's office, much less pontificating aloud. He could not help himself. After laboring as Max Goldschmidt for so many months, after finally breaking Zwick, he felt satiated, omnipotent, capable of anything.

Heydrich kept his head down, writing at something on his desk.

"And at the end, Gunther, you performed your little ritual, didn't you?"

Gunther smiled at the slight.

"My confession, you mean? Of course. How else could I have killed him?"

"One day, that habit is going to get you in trouble," he said instead, lifting his head to look at Gunther.

Heydrich's eyes seemed to stare right through him—another of the disconcerting tricks he had, Gunther knew. Nonetheless, he was disconcerted.

"It is superstitious. Beneath you," Heydrich went on lecturing. "And it makes you predictable. A National Socialist should be free from such compulsions."

Anton forced himself to be as serious as he could, despite his post-kill jubilation.

"More importantly, your obsession has cost us dearly. Your assignment was to keep Zwick alive as long as possible, breaking him down slowly, so that we might extract more information from him about an atomic bomb. What use is he to us now? His secrets are in his grave."

Gunther knew better than to say anything more. Despite the dressing down, he felt privileged to be in the man's confidence. Everyone in Berlin knew Heydrich was the future. Not quite thirty-five but already gathering all of the Reich's security forces in his long, tapered white fingers. Deputy to Himmler and director of SS security. Director of the Gestapo, of the SiPo—the security police—of the *Kriminalpolizei*, member of the Prussian State Council. It was rumored that Himmler hated him. Those who didn't hate him feared him.

But hate him or fear him, they could not do without him. It was Heydrich who had arranged everything, planned everything, from the great triumph of the Reich Olympics in 1936, to the planned orgy of violence that was *Kristallnacht.* Heydrich, the model Aryan, tall and lean and accomplished and fearless. Heydrich, with his love of German music and German poetry, who would not flinch from putting a bullet in any man's head. Heydrich, who had first brought Gunther into the party and had given him all of his assignments for years now. Who had ordered him to become Max Goldschmidt. And long before that—

"I gave you an assignment to do once in America, Gunther."

Heydrich's voice broke in on his thoughts. "I'm sure you recall?"

"Yes. You sent me to kill Albert Einstein."

"And instead you murdered a hero policeman."

"My handlers botched it. Choosing a failed newspaper as my cover. Even so, I could have completed my assignment," Anton protested a little heatedly. "Just a few more days! But you sent me to Palestine instead of Princeton—"

How well he remembered that job. Posing as a tour-guide for the ravishing woman from the British government, ushering her down the narrow streets and stairways of Jerusalem for weeks. Slipping, the final day, down an alley behind the Church of the Holy Sepulcher, allowing her to kiss him, pulling her in. His fingers probing her breasts, up her neck, to a milky white throat. Whispering his sins in the original site of expiation. Watching the life fade from her eyes. Experiencing his own rapture in that holy place.

"Yes," Heydrich was saying. "Palestine. Spain, Italy, and here in Berlin. So many complex identities. Work that no other agent could do. You have grown, and now I must know that you have learned from your failures and are ready for a final mission."

"*Jawohl, Direktor!*"

"Good."

Heydrich pulled a fine cigar out of a fine leather box on his desk and lit it, making no move to offer Anton one. "We are living in momentous times, Gunther. Have you noticed? World war, depression, the rise and fall of great empires. The emergence of the Fuhrer alone is a world-shattering event. He has rebuilt the Reich in less than six years, unshackled us from the abasement of Versailles, made our military the strongest in the world. And now he will fulfill his destiny."

"So war is coming," Anton said aloud, though he hadn't meant to.

"Yes."

"Where?"

"We are going to move east. That is what the Fuhrer has always promised—that is Germany's destiny," Heydrich told him. "One Reich, spreading all the way to the Urals—a natural defensive barrier, holding back the hordes of Asia. It is a great vision."

It was dazzling. Anton Gunther could see the tidy, bounteous homesteads of the *Volk* spreading out across the steppes of Russia, in farms of plenty. The destiny of the German people that they had always dreamed of—the dream the Leader had awakened in them again.

"Which is why we need a super-weapon," Heydrich was saying. "Even with that bungler, Becker, the *Wehrmacht* can sweep aside any army on this Earth. But as Napoleon discovered, it is a question of numbers. All those subhumans to the east, they will drown us in numbers—especially if the Jews get them an atomic weapon before we have one."

Anton Gunther understood immediately, enjoying his own cleverness. "Einstein."

Heydrich removed his cigar from an ashtray and studied the smoldering tip. "I argued, privately of course, that we had to be strategic in the expulsion of Jews from the Reich. No one listened. We were in such haste to get rid of them that we let them take their secrets with them. So back they come. Or, at least, the smartest of the bunch. We need Einstein's brain. Then we will dispose of his body."

Heydrich said this as casually as if he had been telling a family retainer to dispatch an old, sick dog. Once again, Anton saw why even Hitler—admiringly—called him "the man with the iron heart."

"You want me to kidnap him?" Gunther asked incredulously.

"I don't believe he's going to come voluntarily," Heydrich said, venturing as close to a joke as he ever did. "He will be staying at a remote location on eastern Long Island. Surrounded by water. You will bring him back, to correct a mistake that even the Fuhrer himself now understands."

Heydrich continued. "Golschmidt will have made a miraculous escape from Berlin with the assistance of the Jewish underground.

And you will bring this with you." He opened his top desk drawer and produced the clean copy of *Two Scientists Debate.*

"Your passkey to the old Jew's sympathies. But of course, you've figured it all out already. Always steps ahead."

Gunther knew that he should have accepted the compliment gracefully. But he stared forward, swallowing his unease.

Heydrich read his discomfort. "I realize the danger, Gunther. I wouldn't send you if I wasn't confident in your success. That is why I have personally supervised the planning. Every contingency is covered. You will have our best team behind you. I assure you: you will return safely."

"That's not it," said Gunther.

"What, then?"

"May I speak freely?"

Heydrich nodded.

"I'd rather hoped that the role of Goldschmidt had died with Zwick. I'm tired living the life of a mongrel Jew. I want to serve my country as a proud Aryan. Like you."

Heydrich's whippet face suddenly beamed, the thin lips broadening into a smile.

"My friend, after this mission, you won't simply be a proud Aryan, but a hero to the Reich. Like a phoenix, rising from the ashes of the Jew, Goldschmidt, to national glory."

The possibility brought a smile to Gunther as well.

"You are returning to America, Anton. This time, you will not fail."

"No, *Direktor!*"

"Good."

"When do I leave?"

"Our sources tell us that Einstein won't be on location until the first of May. You will leave once he is settled."

"And what am I to do in the meantime?"

"Take a nice break from Goldschmidt. Go to your farm in Juterborg. Then report to the Abwehr training facility at Lake Quenzsee on the first day of spring. Six to seven weeks of training should be sufficient—"

"I can manage it in two."

Heydrich bestowed a courteous smile. "Not for this assignment."

Gunther rose, thrust his arm in a formal salute, and turned towards the door. Then asked, "Who will be running the operation in America?"

"Our top asset in the U.S." Heydrich replied.

"Tell me about him."

"*Him?*" Heydrich smirked.

Chapter Seventeen

THE WOMAN DROVE HERSELF sixty miles from her home in rural Long Island to Madison Square Garden in New York City. Several neighbors had offered to ride with her, but she firmly declined. That night, February 20th to be exact, she had work to do, and therefore needed to be unaccompanied.

She pushed her Willys-Overland west toward Manhattan, keeping her eyes on the road except for periodic glances at her wristwatch, a cheap model purchased intentionality for its plainness at Woolworth's. She'd been looking forward to the event at the arena since it had been announced months earlier. But it had taken on new urgency that very morning, when a ticket was left unexpectedly in her mailbox:

Section 105. Row D. Seat 2.

Pleasure was to be mixed with business.

She was troubled by the decision to rendezvous in such a large gathering. Over twenty thousand people were expected. Mostly good and decent Americans, she recognized. Patriots. But any one of them could witness an interaction and unwittingly compromise her. Plus, the arena would be crawling with both uniform and plainclothes police. To avoid scrutiny she'd have to blend in, which was uniquely challenging for her.

Maria Voigt was a strikingly beautiful woman, the kind that turned heads: blond and blue-eyed, creamy complexion, athletic. In Germany she could have been a film actress, maybe one of the "German sweethearts" promoted by Propaganda Minister Goebbels.

However, she was born in America. *Her original sin*, she

thought.

The Queensborough Bridge deposited Voigt in Manhattan by six o'clock. She plied across town, past Bloomingdales Department Store, the brick and granite canyons of apartment and office buildings; through the glare of the theater district where, that very evening, Ethel Merman and Lillian Helman would captivate audiences. To her great disgust, an African American musical revue called Blackbirds was being staged there too. In her new America, she thought, such a grotesque display would surely be banned.

At 6th Avenue, still blocks away from the Garden, traffic came to an agonizing crawl. In front of her, an endless trail of red blinking taillights. Blaring horns and the cries of protestors as they swept towards the arena enveloped her.

"BE AMERICAN! STAY HOME!"
"BE AMERICAN! STAY HOME!"
"BE AMERICAN! STAY HOME!"
"BE AMERICAN! STAY HOME!"

The speeches wouldn't start for at least an hour, but she needed to park the car, navigate through the thick crowd, and find her designated seat.

She spotted a neon white sign, flashing "GARAGE" nearby, and pulled in minutes later.

An attendant, neatly dressed in a white uniform and black bowtie, informed her that the facility was full. Maria pressed a dollar into his hand as inducement, allowing her fingertips to linger in his fleshy palm.

He smiled. "You goin' to the rally, Miss?"

Maria nodded politely.

"Which side you on? Pro-Nazi or anti-Nazi?"

Before she could respond, he said, "Not that it matters to me. For or against, everyone needs a parking spot tonight. Good for business."

She made her way down 49th Street, managing her cadence to make decent time without attracting attention. But as she approached the massive structure on 8th Avenue, she was stopped by a wall of humanity. The entire building was engulfed by the protestors, thundering their opposition to that night's program. Waves pressing behind waves, close to breaching a solid line of mounted police. Shrieking, imploring, demanding. Heckling and shaming ticketholders as they pressed through the gauntlet and under the glow of the marquis:

PRO AMERICAN RALLY
HOCKEY TUESDAY
RANGERS VS. DETROIT

God bless America, she thought.

The chanting of protesters around Madison Square Garden pounded into Harry Weiss' brain. Even though he agreed with the sentiments, the clamor was giving him a headache, just where the scar stretched along his brow. He wished that the protesters had followed their own advice and just stayed home.

He and James were crowded into a makeshift office on the fourth floor of the arena, overlooking 8th Avenue, barely large enough to fit a portable table and folding chairs. Around the table sat two weary assistant Chiefs of the NYPD, a deputy mayor with a trim moustache and a habit of tapping his manicured fingernails on the table surface, and a variety of other state and local police agencies assigned to keep the peace at Madison Square Garden that evening. Fluorescent lights buzzed from the ceiling. The room reeked of cigar smoke, stale beer, and sweat. A window was cracked open to provide some relief, increasing the volume of the chants.

"Mayor LaGuardia has deployed the entire force to keep the peace," the Deputy Mayor proclaimed, to the drumming of his own fingers.

"A tinderbox," Harry mumbled to James.

"Madness," James muttered back.

Harry thought back to the marquis he'd seen when he arrived. Hockey Tuesday. *What's tonight? Nazi Monday?*

One of the Assistant Chiefs stabbed the soggy end of a cigar in an overfilled ashtray and declared "Anyone lookin' for trouble here, they'll find it sure enough—in the new jail on Rikers Island."

A murmur of agreement rippled around the table. Beers were quaffed, cigars puffed. The chants from the sidewalk and the screams of police whistles on the street sharpened the pain just above Harry's eyes.

"I need fresh air," Harry told James. "Gonna inspect the arena."

"Be careful. You don't exactly blend in."

"Look who's talking."

The men around the table didn't find the banter at all funny.

Over three months now into their joint investigation of Nazi activity, the partners' relationship with local law enforcement hadn't exactly thawed. The NYPD was suspicious of Hoover's Bureau, and defensive over its autonomy. There were arguments about approach, territorial grumblings about jurisdiction, and no shortage of snide comments about Amos and Weiss themselves. Many officers, they knew, still blamed the pair for Bobby Larkins' death.

Harry stepped onto a gray concourse surrounding the arena. By now most of the crowd had found their seats inside: forty cents for the balcony, a buck-ten to get on the floor, right up close to all the Nazi action. In concession booths where popcorn and hot dogs were usually sold, vendors were hawking copies of *Mein Kampf* and other Nazi literature. Swastika lapel pins and pennants. Portraits of Hitler. Harry was only surprised they weren't selling programs.

He made his way down a series of ramps to the arena floor, wishing away his headache. He emerged to a scene even more surreal than the one outside. Twenty thousand Americans, jamming every aisle to celebrate Nazi Germany. From the rafters, blinding spotlights were trained on a thirty-foot banner of George Washington flanked by equally enormous banners of an American flag and a swastika. Across the stage stood a long palisade of American flags, with still more being hauled up and down the aisles of the Garden by uniformed marching bands, uniformed Hitler Youth, and a battalion of the Ornungsdienst—the security force of the German American Bund—dressed as Nazi stormtroopers in their black pants, brown shirts, and Sam Browne belts.

The whole spectacle was deafening, blinding, overwhelming. A thunderous roll of drums startled Harry, then another phalanx of stormtroopers swept down the main aisle, trumpets blaring, swastika and American flags hoisted high, singing and chanting something in German. The crowd was instantly on its feet, roaring its approval, arms thrusting out and up, over and over, in the Nazi salute.

"Sieg Heil! Sieg Heil!" they kept chanting.

The stormtrooper marching band lined up along the stage and fell silent. A glamorous raven-haired young woman stepped up to the microphone, and began to sing.

Oh say can you see…

Bemused, Harry snatched his hat off his head and stood at attention, staring at all the committed Bundists all around him singing with an unfeigned fervor.

Do they actually love America? Harry wondered. *Or just their idea of an America that looks and thinks like them?*

When the anthem ended, the long speeches began. Harry Weiss sighed. They loved to talk, these fascists. In the few short weeks since he and James Amos had been reassigned to the fledgling Nazi Squad, he had already become utterly sick of Bund speeches. James had too, telling him once he didn't know how every fascist in the world had not already died of boredom.

Now, on the stage, some short, bespectacled, would-be American Fuhrer was going on about how "everyone" knew there were "boatloads of illegal Jew immigrants, just out past the Verrazano Narrows, who come in every night and kick good, native-born Americans out of their jobs."

Sometimes Harry thought every gentile in New York did indeed know this, judging by the number of people—including well-educated, respectable people—who repeated such things to him. Not long ago, the Labor Department had even had to put out a disclaimer, telling the American people there were no boats full of Jews fresh over from Europe about to take their jobs. He wasn't sure if anyone was listening.

"The Jews and foreigners are poisoning the good Aryan blood of America!" the speaker was droning on. "They are planning to bring millions of dirty Mexicans, even Africans, in with their lot soon."

Harry scanned the seats—the faces of men and women who, on other days and nights, cleaned other people's houses, drove trucks, repaired cars, butchered meat, served meals, delivered milk, tabulated accounting books, taught in classrooms, voted and paid taxes. People with dirt under their fingernails, who had pounded the sidewalks during the worst of the Depression, and took any WPA job they could get, just like the rest of America. Everyday Americans, salute-the-flag Americans.

Americans who, he knew, hated people like him just because someone had convinced them to do so.

The final speaker was announced. The crowd erupted, spilling out of their seats and into the aisles in ecstasy. The Bund's grand pooh-bah emerged: Fritz Julius Kuhn.

Harry had read through his extensive Bureau file. A joke of a man. A two-bit con-artist. He'd emigrated from Germany, become a naturalized American citizen, and now beat the drum for closed borders. Trading in his overalls as a Detroit autoworker for a pseudo-Hitler uniform and finding his way to glory selling venomous snake oil to Americans robbed of hope by the Great Depression.

"American patriots," he began. He was a heavy, jowly man

with a receding hairline, thick glasses and a faintly worried look. If you hadn't known he was the representative of the world's most dangerous dictator, Harry thought, you would have taken him for a used-car salesman anywhere in America.

"American patriots! I am sure I don't come before you as a complete stranger. You will have heard of me through the Jewish controlled press as a creature with horns, a cloven hoof, and a long tail."

This passed for an opening joke at Nazi Night at the Garden.

Harry had had enough. *Time to get back to Amos.*

He slipped into the narrow passageway connecting to the concourse and noticed a woman walking briskly towards him. Beautiful, he thought. All-American, with shimmering blonde hair to her shoulders, striking blue eyes, and the kind of sculpted calves he'd seen so often in the movies. It wasn't unusual to see an attractive woman in New York City. What stood out about her for Harry was how she seemed to want to avoid being seen, wearing a nondescript dark housedress, flats, and cheap costume jewelry.

She clutched her pocketbook suddenly, as if fearful that Harry would snatch it away. He'd seen the model before—widely available in department stores and Montgomery Ward catalogues. The kind even his mother carried.

She stood warily, and Harry rolled his eyes. *As if his proximity might somehow infect her.* He debated flashing his badge to demonstrate his authority over her. Perhaps get close enough to frisk her—just for fun.

Instead, he said, "S'cuse me, ma'am," as he backed up to a wall.

She studied him for just a moment, then brushed past him wordlessly, leaving Harry with a faint whiff of floral perfume.

Such beauty, he thought, *caught up here in all this ugliness.*

Harry began to resume his walk when he heard a disruption.

Kuhn had been cut off.

Someone was shrieking, "Down with Hitler!"

The crowd roared angrily. Harry raced back to the arena floor, almost shoving the woman out of the way.

On stage, a man was charging at Kuhn. The Bund leader looked horrified. He stepped out of the way, but the man—skinny as a rail— managed to knock down his microphone before going down in a scrum of Nazi security guards. The open, downed mic amplified the sound of fists and boots hitting flesh and bone, as if a particularly action-filled fight was going on at the Garden that night. Fritz Kuhn stood at the side as his thugs pounded at the man, looking amused, then soaking in the roar of the crowd.

There were warning cries of "Police! Police!" and then Harry Weiss and a stampede of cops were in the melee, pulling the skinny assailant out of the grasp of the Nazi thugs and off the stage.

When they had him back in the makeshift security office, Harry let go of the man and shouted at him. "What's your name?"

"Isador Greenbaum," the young man told him.

Izzy Greenbaum had a big *Ashkenazi* honker that was now busted, a black eye, and pants that had somehow been mostly torn off. But he seemed ebullient.

"I didn't mean to do anything," he told Harry. "Honest! I just thought I'd go down here and hear 'em talk. But then after I heard everything they had to say against my people, I just had to do something."

"Don't you know you coulda been killed?" Harry asked him.

"Don't you know a whole lot of Jewish people could be killed, from what they were saying up there?" Greenbaum answered him, looking him in the eye. *As if to say what're you doing?* Harry thought.

Several cops ushered him away.

Exhausted, Harry lit his own cigar and peered out the window. Most of the protesters had dispersed, and now the crowds spilled out from the Garden and into the cold night, as if they'd just seen a hockey game or a boxing match. Harry thought about how they'd get in their cars or take the subways and return to their homes and apartments. How they'd kiss each other goodnight and sleep soundly, satiated by the hate they'd ingested at the Garden.

"This can't go on," said Harry.

"What do you mean?" Amos asked him in his puzzled church deacon's voice, which Weiss knew from experience he used mostly on those occasions when he feared Harry might be crazy.

Harry continued staring outside. "What kind of country is this? Letting fascists parade around like this. Using their freedoms to create a place that will squash everyone else's?"

"You got a better option?"

"Yeah, Izzy Greenbaum. I mean, maybe we should just go and get us as many Nazis as we can, just like him. Instead of pussyfooting around, trying to investigate them like they're normal, peace-loving citizens?"

"I hate to give you a news bulletin, Harry, but do you know how many normal American citizens there are, peace-loving or not, who'd just as soon kill both of us as look at us?"

Harry thought of the woman in the tunnel. The way she'd recoiled and clutched her pocketbook. Not even trying to hide her disgust at seeing him there.

He shook his head. "Too many to kill, that's for sure."

"Exactly," James said slowly. "We got to do this by the book, just like anything else, no matter how damned slow it seems. Besides, we don't want to be like them. We're the good guys. We play by the rules."

"Sure, until they manage to change 'em. Then it's over for guys like me and you."

Chapter Eighteen

MARIA VOIGT PUSHED THE WILLYS overland as hard as it would go, back over the lumpy local highways of central Long Island, which was not very fast at all. Maria loved driving, just as she loved doing anything that did not require relying upon anyone else. Just not in the aging Willys, an uninspiring car off the assembly line that was a good five years old and approaching the end of its useful life. Still, she felt exhilarated.

At first she had warned her contact at the German Consulate that the Bund rally was the most foolish place possible to receive a packet. But the courier had insisted upon it as the only place he felt safe. And once she'd taken her seat inside the Garden, the sheer spectacle of the rally had swept away her inhibitions. The adrenaline rush of being in the arena with so many of *her* people. The true believers, able to sing and shout out loud what they believed in, their love for the Leader, and their faith in the new day that was coming. The Jew mob they could hear baying outside, the rings of police everywhere, only made it all the more exciting.

Let them just try it, she had thought. *Let the Jews come into the arena and see who prevails.*

She shifted gears, placed a cigarette in her mouth, ignited it with her lighter, and floored the gas pedal all in one continuous motion, pushing the obdurate car dangerously close to the guardrails of the narrow, badly lit highway. She didn't care. The sense of danger made her feel alive, let her concentrate better, just as it always did. She lived so much of her life in disguise—her life in Yaphank, her work at the movie theatre, the clunky old Willys itself. It was good to step out whenever she could, to take a risk.

Her only chastening thought was the brief exchange in the

narrow arena tunnel. As soon as she saw the man, she knew he was a cop. And a Jew. The cheap, rumpled suit, the beady eyes scanning her, the pronounced nose. And the skin—not the pale red of the Irish cops, or the pure olive of the Italians. Jewish skin, mottled from impure streams in Russia, Palestine, Africa, and America. *Mischling* skin, contaminated, infected, soiled by mixed blood.

Scarred, as well. A gash above his eye, probably from some fight in which he'd been unable to handle himself.

Still, she thought it impressive that he'd spotted her, and she knew now she'd tried too hard to blend in. A needle in a haystack, just one that shined a bit too bright. But that wasn't her real mistake...

The courier had arrived just as the crowd rose for the Star-Spangled Banner, taking the seat next to her; slipping the document into her pocketbook as the anthem ended, then disappearing. Maria remained at her seat impatiently, waiting for the right moment to slip away and open the message. Just before Fritz Kuhn emerged, she headed for a ladies' room in the concourse. Tucked into a stall. Decoded the dispatch.

The four points in the notification electrified her.

Heydrich himself had approved final plans for an operation against Albert Einstein.

An Abwehr agent would arrive in New York in the middle of May.

Voigt was to prepare accordingly, and increase surveillance of Einstein's movements.

She was to confirm receipt directly with Berlin by radio, at exactly 01:00 hours.

This was it—the biggest assignment she had ever had, one that actually might make a difference. Might make her whole life of subterfuge worthwhile. She tucked the document into her purse and hurried back towards her seat to watch the Bund leader's address.

Then the Jew was eyeing her in the tunnel, and she reflexively clutched her bag—an error, she'd realized immediately, suggesting it contained something of value. It was foolish. Impulsive.

But she had been lucky. The cop had let her pass, with a Jew-accented "S'cuse me, ma'am." The proximity had made her cringe.

Still, she thought, he'd ended up where he belonged.

Against a wall.

Maria Voigt was born in America. *But conceived in the Fatherland*, she liked to assure herself. Her father, Dieter, had worked as an instructor in chemistry up at City College. Her mother worked ceaselessly at cooking and cleaning their big comfortable apartment on St. Nicholas Avenue, grumbling about it all the while. Maria adored her father, who was witty and affectionate and liked to sing Schubert lieders in his wobbly but charming voice—her mother, less so. They all spoke German at home, though she took the language when she got to junior high, too. In those days, before the war, her parents and all their friends and even many of her schoolteachers agreed that Germany was the country of the future, and that America should be its ally.

When the Great War broke out, Dieter organized clandestine meetings in the family's comfortable apartment. Men would come, report observations of various military installations in and around Manhattan, drink schnapps, and leave. During those late-night meetings, Dieter would spot his little girl hovering in a dark foyer nearby and flash a private smile, as if letting her in on his secrets.

It was the summer of '16—on a sweltering hot night near the end of July—when she lay in bed unable to sleep and felt the ground tremble, heard a distant eruption that did not quite sound like thunder. She put on her robe and went into the parlor of their apartment, where she saw her father looking out the window. When she came in he turned around, grinning broadly, and to her astonishment danced a small jig.

"What is going on?" she asked, afraid that the war had somehow come to New York. But her father wouldn't say anything, only poured himself a glass of schnapps and told her with his usual gentleness to go back to bed.

The next day, the news was all over the papers: a big explosion at a munitions depot in New Jersey called the Black Tom—an explosion so great it had killed four people, broken windows all over Lower Manhattan, and riddled the Statue of Liberty with shrapnel. Maria didn't think anything of it, simply assuming that her father was glad it meant more arms could not go to Germany's enemies in Europe.

But the next year, when the U.S. entered the war, everything was different. Many of her family friends began to tell people they were Swiss, not German, and even changed their names. Her father refused to let them do anything of the sort. He continued to speak German on the street, and talk of how Germany was in the right, and that soon enough the American government would understand how duplicitous the Allies were. Her mother, almost frantic, begged him to be quiet, but Maria was secretly proud of him for standing firm.

Then one Sunday, when a war bond parade swept past their home, Dieter Voigt, who was enjoying one beer too many at an outdoor café, insisted on toasting the German people. Before she knew it, a small mob of men—some of them in American army uniforms—had grabbed her father by the arms, lifting him up and dragging him into St. Nicholas Park. There they smashed his straw boater down around his head, slapped his face, and smashed his spectacles. They told him they would hang him if he did not kiss the American flag they were holding and swear his allegiance to the United States. Maria could hear a woman screaming, and she realized it was her mother. But she herself said nothing, refusing to show any emotion at all. Dieter Voigt refused to kiss the flag, and they rubbed his face in a patch of mud. Someone produced a makeshift noose and put it around his neck, and only then did her father agree to kiss the flag. As he did Maria could not hold it in anymore, and she burst into sobs as she ran back to their apartment.

She swore to herself that she would never let anyone see her cry like that again.

The war ended, and it was if the world had defeated Dieter Voigt. He'd sit at the window of the apartment, staring blankly at the street below, waiting for a victory parade that would never come. Meanwhile, Maria had blossomed into his Nordic beauty, as her father called her—the very ideal of German womanhood, with her fair skin, radiant blue eyes, and golden hair. He was delighted by her—and worried.

"You must be careful," he would warn her, gripping her hand. "These *Schweine,* these degenerate races we must live with, all around us! Latins and greasy Italians, and Negroes, and worse— Jews! You must be careful. You are the flower of German womanhood—you must not give yourself to anyone."

"I am your girl only, Papi," she would smile at him, and that seemed to calm him.

When Dieter was diagnosed with lung cancer in 1929, he began spending as much time as possible instructing Maria in German literature and history, reminding his Flower of her true roots. He spoke only *die Muttersprache*—the mother tongue—to her, and together they began reading the local German-language papers, finding out about what was going on back "home." Her father was always hopeful that the kaiser would come back and sweep away the miserable little politicians of the Weimar Republic, which he loathed. He was always clipping little articles for her about the various nationalist parties. One of them began to pique his interest above all, the *Nationalsozialistche* party, with its leader who people called mad, but whose speeches he admired for their honesty.

"He speaks the truth, where the others are just trying to find the best way to lie," he would tell his daughter, tapping the paper with his pipe, a shawl she had knitted for him over his lap. "He is not afraid to say anything!"

On Christmas Eve, just a month before Hitler became Chancellor, Dieter called her into his bedroom. By then, the cancer had ravaged his entire body, turning his skin chalk white, drawing his eyes into his skull, reducing him to an emaciated heap wrapped in sweat-soaked sheets. *Almost subhuman*, she thought. Repulsed, she froze at the foot of the bed, far from the putrid breaths rattling from his corroded lungs. He pointed a skeletal finger at a large envelope on his bedstand.

She opened it and removed the contents: a type-written, properly notarized Last Will and Testament, a bank check made out to her for seventy-five thousand dollars, and a business card:

HERMANN GANS

German-American Chamber of Commerce,

New York

"Who is Gans?" she asked, keeping her distance.

"Your guardian angel," he wheezed.

He died that night.

Ever since, Maria regretted that her father hadn't lived to see Hitler ascend to power and restore Germany's greatness; and punished herself for freezing at the foot of her father's bed, denying them both a final embrace.

At midnight, she pulled the Willys into her driveway in an orderly neighborhood called German Gardens. The house was empty; it had been since Gans's brusk farewell.

After her father's death, Gans had taken Maria in like an uncle, or a godfather: he put her up in a spare room in his small home, sent her to summer camps in Pennsylvania to develop certain skills, shielded her from the advances of older boys. He'd owned several businesses, including a German-language cinema in Manhattan called "The New Europe," where he hired her as a ticket-taker on busy Friday and Saturday nights.

But one morning, a few years later, he'd informed her that he had to leave immediately. *Called back to Germany*, he'd explained. *On business*. Maria was clever enough to understand that his real business involved the passing of certain secrets from Long Island's concentration of defense plants to Berlin; that he'd likely been exposed to American authorities and would be smuggled out on a ship bound for Germany.

He'd asked her to see after the house, and she was grateful for it. But with Gans away she preferred staying in Manhattan to living alone in this enclave in the middle of nowhere. Many nights she'd lock up the theatre, then sleep in the small upstairs flat to avoid the long drive. But tonight, there was procedure to follow. She was expected to make contact right away. She grabbed her pocketbook and killed the engine.

Maria dropped her pocketbook on the kitchen table and went next to the small closet in her bedroom. She removed a nearly invisible panel in the back wall and pulled out a bulky black suitcase. Next, she opened the drawer to her nightstand and withdrew several handwritten postcards from Germany, and a stack of letters from a childhood friend and Yorkville neighbor named Gretel. She lugged all of this to the table back in the kitchen without turning the light back on, knowing every inch of the room. She slid a step ladder almost silently over to the counter, climbed to the top step, and felt along the top of the kitchen cabinets until she grasped a small key. Maria returned to the table with it, and unlocked the case of her Afus, her agent radio, provided by Gans as a parting present.

It was a hand-keyed Morse instrument, tuned to a unique preset frequency: ten watts powered by a battery. The message would go out to one of the German U-boats routinely trawling the local waters, surfacing at a set time every night, which would then pass it on all the way to the Reich. She thumbed through Gretel's letters and postcards for her call signs and her cipher keys, working only by the lights of the Afus.

She began with "Briar Rose," her agent handle, after the Grimm fairy tale character also known as "Sleeping Beauty," cursed to sleep for a hundred years until awakened by a handsome prince. Next, she tapped out as succinct a coded message as she could manage:

BEFEHL ERHALTEN UNTERSTÜTZE.
(ORDER RECEIVED WILL SUPPORT.)

She waited, just in case there was a response, though she knew it was still early in Berlin, and did not expect to hear anything until at least this time the following evening.

All around her, the night was silent—as silent as it always was in the winter. The quiet irked her, having grown up in the city. Much as she knew that all the noises in the night were the indications of a disordered, mongrel, crime-ridden society, she still had trouble sleeping without them. She padded to the windows, as though she shouldn't disturb the house's slumber, and peered outside through a small crack between the shutters. All of the neat little German homes were dark and bolted against the night, she saw. Much as she imagined they might be one day along the steppes of Russia, when all the present inhabitants had been removed, and the greater German Reich had fulfilled its destiny and spread across that land.

She was interrupted by a sudden clatter from the Afus. Much to her surprise, the answer must have been transmitted almost instantly. She jotted it down and decoded it hungrily:

BESTÄTIGUNG ERHALTEN. ERWARTE ANWEISUNG.
(CONFIRMATION RECEIVED. AWAIT ORDERS.)

She read the words over and over again, her body tingling. She had known it since hurriedly deciphering the briefing at the arena, but the direct contact made it all the more concrete: This was far and away the most important mission her unit had ever been asked to assist on—maybe the most important espionage mission any Reich operative had been ordered to take part in. Once she had read the dispatch through twice more, she carefully locked her radio away again in the closet and hid the message in plain sight amidst Gretel's correspondence, just as she had also been taught.

She was too excited to sleep, but she took out a silk nightgown all the same. She was beyond ready to shed the plain housedress she had chosen for the rally, but just when she pulled it off she thought she heard something near the window—a rustle against the thick winter silence blanketing the house. Quickly, she slipped on the nightgown and listened.

Eyes everywhere, she thought. But she heard nothing further.

As she stretched in bed, her mind flooded with the echoes from the rally: the martial music, the resolute chants of "Sieg Heil! Sieg Heil!"

For a moment her thoughts were disturbed by the image of the stocky man with the scar across his forehead, who'd studied her in the tunnel then stepped aside. She'd watched him leap on the stage and drag the skinny Jew, Greenbaum, to safety.

Birds of a feather…

She soon fell asleep.

Chapter Nineteen

"ANOTHER COLD, PROFESSOR?"

Leo Szilard honked into a crumpled handkerchief and stuffed it back into his pocket. "If I didn't know any better, I'd swear I am allergic to America."

His assistant, a young blond-haired Columbia University doctoral candidate named Jaworski, smiled politely. "Did you suffer like this in Europe?"

Annoyed, Szilard shook his head. "In Europe the malady is fascism, Jaworski. Here it is only the weather. Pay attention to the experiment."

The news of the Nazi rally at Madison Square Garden, weeks earlier, had given new urgency to Szilard's research. They were huddled in his small seventh-floor laboratory in Pupin Hall near the northern end of the Columbia University campus. The fifteen-story building featured an elegant green crown, an observatory hood that could be opened and rotated so that the university's outstanding astronomers, could scan the stars with a state-of-the-art thirty-centimeter refractory telescope. Unfortunately, nobody had thought about the ambient light that a great, modern, electrified city like New York generated. Or the smoke constantly pouring out of its countless factories and the thousands of apartment house incinerators, each burning their own trash. By the time it was finished, it was clear that the observatory could be used only for the most rudimentary teaching purposes, allowing undergrads to study the one or two stars that might be visible on a good night.

However, though the immensity of outer space was not available to those gazing from the top of Pupin Hall, a few floors below Leo Szilard was studying the smallest quanta known: the atom.

The lab was closet-sized, windowless, with just enough room for a cluttered workbench and two chairs. It connected to a larger outer office containing two desks, crowded bookshelves, and a blackboard that stretched across an entire wall, covered with chalked equations and the wispy white streaks of an eraser. Szilard kept the door to the lab locked at all times. There he conducted his most sensitive research.

Szilard was in a private race. A race against scientists an ocean away. A race to split an atom and generate a chain reaction powerful enough to destroy an entire city.

He recognized the irony: in order to save the world, he had to prove that it could be destroyed.

He craned his neck and tinkered with final adjustments to an oscilloscope.

His experiment to replicate Hahn's findings was simple enough, if one understood the cutting edge of modern physics. They would bombard the radium with a shiny, steel-gray block of beryllium. If it produced a chain reaction and fissured the uranium, the escaping "fast neutrons" would show up on an oscilloscope screen. Szilard carefully connected the ionization chamber to the screen, making sure everything was in place, and checked his connections over as well. He instructed Jaworsky to turn off the light, threw the master switch, and held his breath.

Nothing happened.

No streams or flashes of light. Nothing on the screen at all. He sat staring at the machinery, uncomprehending, for a few long minutes. Then he stood up, turned on the light, and checked the wall socket.

"Sure enough—unplugged," he said, sinking his head into his hands.

After Jaworski connected the machine, Szilard tried again.

He took a long breath.

Threw the master switch.

Watched as tiny green flashes of light shot across the screen, like shooting stars appearing and vanishing in the night sky. He and Jaworski watched, mesmerized, for a good ten minutes as they moved across the screen.

The tiny little flares. Like the striking of a match. The quavering embryonic flame that could ignite consuming fires.

"Now what, Professor?" asked Jaworski.

Szilard said nothing.

Lost in thought, he bundled himself in a jacket and shuffled from the office.

A walk always provided the answers.

Szilard had always prided himself, both as a man of science and a Jew, on his ability to look reality in the face. To see which way the wind was blowing and move ahead of events. His stimulating walks put ideas in his head, his epic morning baths let him put them in order. On the day that Hitler took power, he was having a long, hot soak in the tub of his faculty apartment at the Kaiser Wilhelm Institute. He closed his eyes and let the lukewarm water wash over him. The slow drip of the bath faucet became louder, more urgent, as if beating out a warning. Pinpricks of light danced on the back of his eyelids, red, yellow, orange.

Flames, he thought.

That same day, he packed two suitcases and propped them by the door, where he might grab them up at a moment's notice. The next weeks he spent transferring his bank accounts to London, soliciting job offers, warning friends. Three months later, the Reichstag burned. The Nazis blamed the Communists, but Szilard figured it was just a matter of time before the flames consumed the Jews. He and both bags disappeared the next day.

Now he trudged up W. 116th Street, the bitter March wind from the Hudson at his back, and turned down Broadway. At least the sun was out. And, as always, New York was an explosion of sound, color, action. Big yellow Checker cabs, trucks, and buses battled for space along the avenue. The subway pounded under the grates beneath his feet. The little shops along Broadway still looked festive with their Christmas lights and even a few Christmas trees. The stoplights blinked green, yellow, red—

It had been at a stoplight that Leo Szilard had first realized atomic power might be possible. It was not long after he had fled Germany for London in September of 1933. His mind had felt especially stimulated by his freedom in England, blissfully away from the cloud of the Nazis that had spread over everything back in Berlin. Reinvigorated by a new city, a new land, a new language. It had happened that fall, standing on a curb on Southampton Row. He'd looked up at the changing lights and it had come to him, almost like a revelation from the sky. How, once an atom could be split, it might cause a chain reaction.

And release...what? All the power in the world.

Like all ideas, it was just an idea. It was what theoretical physicists loved about their calling. All ideas, up in the air. Ideas that might explain everything that was. No chemical reactions burning a hole in your coat, no mining machines tearing into the bowels of the earth. It was pure science, which Szilard loved.

Back on Broadway he crossed against the light, in the middle of the street—the local custom he had taken to heart. A fish truck blared its horn at him, and then the driver hurriedly rolled down his window just to curse at him for good measure. Szilard sneezed and kept walking, oblivious, then crossed back the same way. More horns—but also the chimes of a church bell. Peering back uptown, he saw the new, gleaming white towers of Riverside Church. The highest church in the United States, he had read—*a skyscraper church to match a skyscraper city.* It stood proud and tall against the clear, cerulean sky.

Poof.

One atom bomb, he thought—*perhaps not even a large one—could level it.* Could level everything around him, all this glorious, bright, cacophonous life, for at least ten kilometers.

He could see it. The great fireball vaporizing steel and glass, water and soil. *Flesh and bone!* The massive cloud rising over the city, consuming the sky. The spread of radioactive fallout, attacking and poisoning organs. The untold generations of sick, dying people.

Yes, he could see it, but the Americans and their politicians were willfully blind. Coddled between two oceans, their soil untouched by the machines that burned, bombed, gassed, and mauled so much of Europe in the Great War, turning it into a vast chain of cemeteries. So naïve about man's worst impulses. So damned *American* in their optimism about human nature.

Hitler and his men were indeed dark enough to build the bomb. America preferred to stay safely in the dark.

He kept walking. Kept searching for answers. They were there, somewhere, he knew. Shrouded by the universe. Enfolded somewhere in time and space. Vibrating, perhaps, in a quantum particle. Waiting for him to drift into that special place, where the bands of light danced against the blackest black and the answers revealed themselves. He just had to keep walking towards it.

Warmth emanated from a bar, along with raucous voices and loud music from one of the jukeboxes Americans seemed to love. He was in no shape for that, he knew. He crossed over at 113th Street, to a coffee shop called the College Inn. He loved places like this, what New Yorkers called a diner, with a counter and booths and almost anything you could imagine, for any meal, on the menu. That and the soda fountains they seemed to have in every pharmacy. They called to him. This was his private idea of paradise: cheap, sumptuous food, served up in a flash.

He sat at the counter and ordered all the things his doctor was always telling him to avoid: a fatty hamburger sandwich on toast, grilled medium rare. A slice of apple pie with a scoop of ice cream on top. Restored, he began to think again.

He thought of his old friend, Reinhard Zwick, whose last report was that the Nazis were accelerating research to build an atomic bomb. *Why would they not, after Hahn's breakthrough?* And putting Heydrich—the only truly competent man in the party hierarchy—in charge of the project....

The idea sickened him.

He was worried about Zwick. It had been many weeks since he had checked in, and now the communications network seemed to be out of order, disrupted.

Not a good sign. Hitler's army of scientists were advancing steadily, while it had taken him three months to raise the money, procure radium and beryllium, navigate the bureaucracy, and receive the approvals for his laboratory experiment.

But he'd just done it. Einstein had told him to prove his theory in the lab; those flashes of light represented his vindication. For the second time in his career, he would be able to show the old man the light.

Now all he had to do was present his findings to Einstein, he thought, who would then share them with President Roosevelt. He would then convene a meeting of the best minds in America to authorize the spending necessary for a crash project to leapfrog Hitler in the building of an atom bomb.

The empirical proof was now irrefutable, the urgency undeniable.

It shouldn't take long at all, he reasoned.

He returned to his office and dialed Einstein in Princeton. "It's Szilard!" he announced to Helen Dukas, before she could finish saying hello.

"I must speak to Einstein, immediately!"

"I am very sorry, Professor, but he's lecturing at the moment."

"Please tell him to contact me. At once."

Chapter Twenty

IT WAS THE MIDDLE OF MARCH, but to Harry Weiss, driving through the Yorkville section of Manhattan, the world was entering a dark winter.

No part of the city was more hateful to Weiss than Yorkville. Not the docks, where his loathing of the water had soured him even before they saw the latest mob victim. Not poor, shabby Brownsville, where they had tailed the contract killers of Murder, Inc. as best they could. Yorkville, which styled itself as a cosmopolitan neighborhood of Berlin: newsstands cluttered with German newspapers trumpeting Hitler's latest diatribe, the guttural barking of German everywhere, even the marquis of the New Europe Theater proclaiming:

FUHRER TAKES PRAGUE!

He sat slumped in the passenger seat as James Amos wheeled their dark blue Oldsmobile 60 through the streets.

They must have seen half a dozen such movie houses in the half hour they had spent cruising the neighborhood. All with huge letters advertising the new German-language newsreels about the Leader's latest bloodless triumph. There was a festive air in the neighborhood, the restaurants and shops all decked out with the German colors, or even little swastika flags. As usual, there was a parade going across 86th Street, all the marchers dressed in Nazi or Hitler Youth uniforms of one sort or another, banging out some martial air. The headlines on the German-language papers on the newsstands echoing the Fuhrer's triumph, and how good life in the Fatherland was.

It all gave him the willies. So did the attitude of the people here, so friendly on the surface but very different once they suspected you were not simply a tourist. James—who did most of the driving because Harry was known to exhibit an occasional flash of road rage—had suggested that Weiss ride in the back, so the locals would at least think he was some bigshot in a chauffeured car. He could see the necks of all these loyal citizens craning to look into their car, faces closing up like steel traps once they confirmed what they had seen. *A colored man and a white riding side-by-side?*

"The hell with them," Harry told his partner. "Let 'em stare, so they remember what country they're living in."

"Not exactly the philosophy behind surveillance work," James replied, giving him one of his telling sidelong glances.

It was true, they hadn't had much success. It was over three weeks now since they'd been assigned the investigation of Nazi activities, and they'd uncovered exactly nothing by way of a crime. Except for Isadore Greenbaum, whose protest at the Bund rally resulted in a sentence of ten days in jail or a $25 fine. It still irked Harry: Greenbaum convicted and punished for his crime that night, while the men and women saluting swastika flags and chanting "Heil Hitler" went scot-free. *What was that new Kate Smith song? God Bless America.*

Amos dropped Harry off a couple blocks from their subject, according to procedure. Weiss ducked into and out of a couple stores, making sure no one was following. It was quiet though, and most of those who were out were at the Nazi youth parade. Harry pretended to stare into a window at E. 84th Street and Madison, Schaefer's Fine Tobacco Shop, then strolled inside, trying to act like a man who was just out of smokes.

Behind the counter was Walther Schaefer. He was entirely bald, with a full-moon head and a slightly crooked smile revealing small, tobacco-yellowed teeth. A full barrel chest bulged against an expensive suit adorned with a carnation in the lapel of his jacket. *More like a banker*, Harry thought, *than a cigar proprietor.*

"How may I help you, sir?" he asked in steeply accented

English.

"Do you have any La Palinas?" Harry said, trying to ape his accent, though his guttural New York enunciation snuck through instead.

"La Palina?" Walther Schaefer said, sounding impressed but dubious. "A premium cigar, though…above your price range, no?"

"Oh, price is no object," Harry told him. "If what you're purchasing is worthwhile."

Schaefer crouched behind the counter, slid open a glass door, and brought up an exquisitely illustrated cigar box. He pulled out a single La Palina and placed it on the countertop as if he were a clerk at Tiffany's, laying out a dazzling diamond necklace.

"I think you will find this as advertised," he said.

Harry picked up the cigar and turned it under his nose, just to watch the man squirm. The smell of the shop itself was heady. Weiss had been trying to quit smoking for some time. This would not be the day.

"Will there be anything else?" Schaefer asked.

"There certainly will be."

Schaefer seemed to suddenly lose his nerve, darting a glance through his window, consulting his watch.

"This might not be the best time to discuss that. We get very busy—"

Harry Weiss snorted and looked all around the empty shop.

"Yeah, quite a crowd in here. Like Times Square on New Year's Eve," he said drily, pretending to take out his wallet to pay for the cigar. "Don't waste my time. What are you hearing?"

The man almost dropped behind the counter, in his anxiety to be rid of Harry.

"All right, all right!" he said hurriedly.

He bent his head forward, gesturing for Weiss to do the same. Whispering, even in the vacant shop.

Ten minutes later, Weiss pushed back through the door of the tobacco shop, looking considerably more somber. He lifted the collar of his coat to his jaw, against the wind. The only person on the street was a shivering newsie, no more than ten years old from what Weiss could judge, hawking the day's *Herald Tribune* from a wind-whipped stack. Harry glanced at the headlines: Britain and France were talking about a pact to defend Poland if Hitler went after it next. He bought a copy, flipped a quarter to the newsie, tucked the paper under an arm and walked briskly east on 84th Street, where James and the Oldsmobile sat waiting.

"Did he produce anything useful?" James asked.

Weiss pulled the cigar from his shirt pocket. "A La Palina. Cost me half a buck."

"Seriously? For a cigar?" James Amos shook his head. "Nothing else?"

"Just that he heard from his brother-in-law, guy named Kimmler, who lives out in that Nazi town in Long Island. You know, the one in Yaphank?"

James blew a troubled breath. "I've seen the reports. German Gardens. Also known as Camp Siegfried. A Gestapo paradise smack in the middle of Long Island that makes Yorkville look tame."

"Why do we allow it?" asked Harry.

James shrugged. "It's America."

Harry studied the cigar and sighed. "For now, it is."

Both men gazed quietly out the front windshield. A Checker cab stopped next to them. A pretty young woman scurried across the middle of the street, clutching her hat against the wind. Traffic lights blinked red, yellow, green.

Harry broke the silence. "Anyway, *something's* going on. No details, but lots of chatter. Orders coming straight from Berlin. Something having to do with Albert Einstein, believe it or not."

"Albert Einstein, the scientist?"

"No, Albert Einstein, the plumber."

Amos frowned, the usual signal to Harry that he was bordering on insubordination. "How reliable is Schaefer?" he asked.

"I had a hunch about him, back when I was NYPD. One of his customers refused to pay his bill and ended up in Bellevue with two broken legs and a fractured skull. When I went to arrest Schaefer, he offered a deal: information about the Dutch Schutz mob, plus two boxes of Cuban cigars. I didn't take the cigars, but the rest of the deal paid off. Now he keeps tabs on local Nazis. But he's like all the rest: expedient. The second he thinks he's compromised he'll hightail it back to the Nazis."

"And the brother-in-law, Kimmler?" asked James.

"Won't know till we pay him a visit."

James shook his head. "We need authorization for that. There are forms."

"I'm not letting the bureaucracy slow us down."

"That's not how I do business, Harry. I cut one corner, I'm fired. You know how it is."

"James—"

"We follow the rules," Amos said as he pulled away from the curb.

"Fuck the rules," Harry said, thinking again of that day, so long ago now, when Bobby Larkins, working under his guidance, hadn't made it off the goddamned boat.

Harry Weiss knew the very day he decided to become a cop— if not an FBI agent. It was July 8th, 1923. He was eighteen and had decided to see one of the newest attractions in New York City: the brand new Riegelmann boardwalk at Coney Island.

It was the kind of day the developers must have had in mind when they built the massive amusement complex: a hot sun beat down on the boardwalk, practically steering crowds to find refuge in bars, food stands, and thrill rides. They spilled from the boardwalk onto stretches of glinting white sand, and clung to the foamy waves splashing at their ankles. Harry leaned against a rail and gazed at the behemoth ocean liners tracing the distant horizon, back and forth to the rest of the world. He took it all in, fully aware that he'd be late for dinner, where there'd be yet another argument with his family about their plans for Harry to take over his father's butcher shop and live out his whole life trimming briskets.

His thoughts were interrupted by a cry under the boardwalk, then an eruption of cackling laughter.

"Kike!" someone laughed.

Another cry.

"Yid!"

Harry swung himself over the railing and jumped, landing on the spongy white sand.

Under the boardwalk, beneath the pilings, he saw four older boys kicking and stomping at something. *Such a strange game*, he thought. He caught a glimpse of what seemed to be a giant rag doll on the sand, the kind they gave away at the arcade games along the Boardwalk.

Then he saw what it really was.

Soaked in his own blood, a battered boy about Harry's age lay sprawled in the sand. Moaning incoherently when he was able to make any sounds at all. Harry could have easily turned and run away. The thought never entered his head.

"Leave him alone!" Harry screamed and rushed toward the boy.

One of the downed boy's assailants heard and turned to study him for a moment. He was tall, much taller than Harry, and not really a boy at all anymore, muscles rippling from under a filthy undershirt.

"Another little kike!" he whooped, and the group turned their attention to Harry.

He charged anyway, too enraged to stop himself. He landed some punches, smashed his head into some boy's nose, and reveled in how it felt crumpling beneath the blow. But then two of them pinned his arms back, and fists began to pummel his defenseless stomach. He felt a razor tear at his forehead, ripping wildly just over his eye.

"Kike! Kike! Kike!" they were chanting at him. Then somebody kicked him in the balls.

He gasped for air, blood spilling into his eyes from a gash across his forehead. The humiliation stabbed at him as much as the pain. It occurred to him, in some little part of his brain that was still functioning, that he could die here, just as that boy on the ground seemed to be dying.

Then the boys grabbed him and the other boy and dragged them from under the boardwalks, across the sand, and through the crowds, which parted and watched in curiosity.

"Drown the kikes," they said.

Harry waited for someone to intervene. But the crowds simply watched. No one willing to stop them before they plunked the two Jews into the ocean to be claimed by the waves. Only a few yelling at them to quit "roughhousing."

It was too late to make a difference, he was sure. But it was then that Harry heard the shrill sound of a police whistle.

He looked up to see a tall, lean cop—a single Irish cop—hurrying toward the boys, kicking up sand. A couple of them fled, but the others stood their ground, grinning at the prospect.

"We beat up coppers before. We'll be wearin' your hat an' badge around the neighborhood!" the thug who had first spotted Harry crowed.

"You talk a lot, laddie," the cop said, advancing upon them, "but I know your problem: too many teeth."

He took the rest of the distance between them in one sudden, impossible stride, his nightstick lashing out as he did. From what he could see, staring up from the ground with his swelling eyes, Harry thought the officer moved with incredible speed and certainty, the nightstick lashing out at one tormentor after another. His free hand, augmented with a set of brass knuckles, struck out just as fast.

Harry tried to get up, but his legs gave out from under him. Instead he crawled to the boy, the pain rippling across his back and ribs, and deep in his stomach and crotch. He noticed the boy's eyes rolled back in his eyes, leaving slivers of white. With terrible effort he managed to get up to a sitting position, and cradled the boy's motionless head on his lap, looking to defend him, somehow, against whatever might come.

The fight was almost over, though. Harry could see that three of his attackers lay smashed and witless on the pavement. A couple more, seeing how the battle had turned, ran hobble-legged away, dodging down the narrow ways of the courtyard. Only the big, mouthy thug in the filthy tee shirt was left, but he was on his knees, his mouth filled with blood and many of his teeth now missing. He gurgled hatred at the cop, trying to get to his feet again.

"See? What I tell ya, lad?" the cop said. "Always listen to your betters."

With that he jabbed the end of his nightstick into the base of the boy's throat, right where it met his chest. The young tough made some more indistinguishable noises and keeled over. The cop walked to where Harry was sitting with the unconscious boy's head in his lap, stooped down to take a look, then stood up again and raised his head to the gawking, silent faces in fifty windows.

"You're a fine lot! Send someone out to get an ambulance here, on the double!"

He sat down next to them on the beach, and only then did Harry notice the cop studying him with real concern. Taking in the despair on Harry's swollen face.

"You did good, son," he tried to comfort him. "Taking 'em all on and tryin' to protect your friend here. You have a cop's heart."

Harry had all he could do to whisper encouragement to the boy whose head lolled in his lap, listening to his breathing become shallower and shallower before the ambulance arrived. Two days later the cop showed up at Harry's apartment, carrying a small cake for Harry's mother and delivering the news that the boy had died in the hospital without ever regaining consciousness. He let Harry absorb the news in the dimly lit parlor and said, "You're healin' up well, boy-o. Flesh like leather, which is a good thing in this city. How are the eyes? All right? And nothing broken, which is almost a miracle. That cut on your forehead will stay with ya' though. Mark of honor, I'd say."

He had stayed and chatted with the family for a little while, charming Harry's mother despite herself, acting almost as though he were apologizing for the city, for what her son had been through. His name was Daniel Larkins, and Harry soon discovered that everyone in three precincts around seemed to know who he was—the parents respected him, the young men idolized him, the gang boys feared him—and it occurred to Harry that he wouldn't mind that himself.

Before Larkins left that evening, Harry asked him about his administration of justice in the ally. "Didn't you break the rules? Beating them up like that?"

Larkins smiled, and his blue eyes beamed above leathery cheeks. "This is America, lad. Sometimes, you have to bend the rules 'till you get justice."

It was a lesson Harry wouldn't forget.

Soon, most of his wounds had healed, save for a three-inch scar on his forehead that he rather liked, and an aversion to beaches.

He didn't announce it to his family just yet, but he had decided to become a cop.

James Amos had their Oldsmobile back to the Federal Courthouse in Foley Square before midday. It always made James feel proud, coming back to the Bureau offices in the courthouse, a sparkling new Classical Revival building, rising thirty-seven stories to its gold-leaf, pyramidal peak. They strode across the green-and black-veined, white marble floors of the lobby—James never failing to point out to Harry the walls and ceilings shimmering with all sorts of colorful ornamentation. Dolphins to represent freedom. Owls for wisdom. Oak leaves for strength and endurance. The Greek word *meta*: *change*. He loved that such an edifice could be built for the people, even if his partner was more cynical.

"Look at it down here," James said as they went in, waving an arm at the array of formidable government buildings that ringed the square. "Can you believe this used to be the Five Points, the worst slum in America? Full of street toughs and thieves."

"Still is, only they're politicians wearing nicer suits," Harry joked.

It was a cheap punchline, Harry knew, and he didn't quite believe it. The lobby was filled with the usual bustle of lawyers, judges, court officers. Harry liked seeing them a lot more than all the doodads on the wall. Here were some of the greatest legal minds in the country and regular New Yorkers of all kinds, colored and white, men and women, Jews and gentiles. He was soaking in the scene until a couple of their fellow agents hailed them.

"Hey, look, it's the Bobbsey Twins!" They knew this was their nickname in the Bureau.

James and Harry both waved and grinned back—with their teeth only.

"Stupid sons-a-bitches," Harry muttered when they got on the elevator.

"I've been called a lot worse," James said.

The two of them went back to the large office they had been sharing since J. Edgar Hoover had ordered additional manpower devoted to Nazi spy rings in New York. It was a depressing sight—wall-to-wall gray metal cabinets, each containing hundreds of files spilling with tips, leads, suspicions, and conspiracy theories about possible Nazi spies. The waiter at the Saint Moritz Hotel with an uncanny resemblance to Joseph Goebbels himself, the drunken dockworker who'd wagged his tongue about his connections with senior Reich officers. It turned out he had a distant cousin who worked as a clerk in the Office of Jewish Emigration in Vienna.

"You check to see if headquarters has anything on Kimmler," James instructed, "while I get approval for a trip to Long Island."

Harry plunked himself on his swivel oak chair and pulled it to his desk. The desk was disorganized with files lapping around an Underwood typewriter, a black rotary Bell telephone, and an ashtray coated with the detritus of cigars smoked long ago. He pulled from his top drawer a directory of offices within the NY Bureau, found the specific contact he needed, and dialed.

Moments later, a woman's voice snapped, "Records Office."

Harry introduced himself. "I need you to check a name against our file indices."

"Go ahead."

"Name is Viktor Kimmler."

"Spell it."

The fastidious collection and compilation of records in FBI bureaus in Washington and across the country had been a priority for J. Edgar Hoover. Thousands of file cards, neatly typed with the intricate details of shadowy lives: people arrested, prosecuted, found guilty (or innocent—it didn't matter), people associating with unsavory organizations and causes, communists, Bolsheviks, fascists. The suspicious and seditious. Every cross-referenceable white card a potential red flag.

"Do you want me to check it with D.C. as well?" the woman said.

Harry said yes and plunked down the phone.

Still, it took only a few minutes for the clerk to call Harry back with the news that there was no record of Viktor Kimmler in the indices, either in New York or Washington.

Harry said, "There is now."

James returned ten minutes later with a travel authorization signed by the Special Agent in Charge of the New York Bureau. "How fast can you arrange an interview with Kimmler and Schaefer?" he asked. "The brass doesn't want anything slipping through the cracks. Not this time."

Harry knew exactly what James meant. A year earlier, a German immigrant named Guenther Rumrich had been arrested by New York police for a brazen plot to forge passports, steal U.S. military plans, and assassinate an Army General. He confessed and revealed the names, identities, codes, and procedures of an elaborate Nazi spy operation across the city. Additional arrests were made. Grand juries impaneled. Indictments prepared. But most of the spies had fled before they could be arrested. The affair was a stunning embarrassment to the Bureau, and Hoover directed his ire at the New York Field Office for the bungling.

Harry picked up the phone, dialed, and waited to connect.

"Meet us tomorrow. Pick a place convenient to Kimmler. And bring a La Palina," he told Walther Schaefer.

Chapter Twenty-One

HARRY WEISS WAS UNCOMFORTABLE on bridges. As James piloted the Oldsmobile across the enormous new Triboro Bridge complex spanning the wide East River, he noticed his partner clenching his fingers around the armrest and fixing his eyes forward, avoiding any view of the water 135 feet below. It wasn't until they were on terra firma that Harry released his grip.

It had always been that way, thought James. Harry tensing up near water, refusing to tell him why.

It was two days after the visit to Yorkville. They were heading for a distant waterfront village called Port Jefferson, a drive two hours from Manhattan and a good half hour past Yaphank. Harry noticed that construction was going on everywhere. Bob Moses' crews were at work blasting out a massive new highway project they were calling the Long Island Expressway, a road that was supposed to run all the way down the middle of the Island. For the time being, though, they were stuck maneuvering their way around Flushing, their progress halted by a sudden snarl of traffic.

A large sign proclaimed:

NEW YORK WORLD'S FAIR
The World of Tomorrow
OPENING APRIL 30

They crawled along, a miasma of construction dust enveloping the car. Harry craned his neck at the expanse of nearly completed buildings, pavilions, plazas, and exhibitions taking shape across the 1200-acre construction site. The finishing touches were being made to those monuments to modernity that would define the fair: the Tyron and Perisphere, a 610-foot obelisk towering over a 180-

foot diameter orb, that everyone kind of liked even if they didn't understand what the hell they meant.

"Gonna be something to see, when it opens," said Harry.

"Fifty million people, they're expecting."

"Quite a party. What's that lake supposed to be?"

"I think it's called the 'Lagoon of Nations,'" Amos told him.

"More like a swamp these days."

James Amos sighed, putting the Olds in gear, and motored past the wonderful World of Tomorrow.

Harry alternated between navigating and reviewing the material for their meeting as they plunged into Long Island.

"Camp Siegfried," he said, shaking his head. "How the hell did that get started in Yaphank?"

"Yaphank—wasn't that where Irving Berlin set that show?" James asked.

"He was stationed there, in the army during the war. It had that great song— 'Oh, how I hate to get up in the morning!'"

They sang a couple lines of it alone in the car, because neither one of them could sing much and for once there was no one around to tell them so:

"Oh! how I hate to get up in the morning! / Oh, how I'd love to remain in bed!..."

They sang until they broke up laughing themselves at how bad they were. But afterwards, James still wanted to know, "So how *did* a Nazi youth camp end up in Yaphank?"

"Seems this German American Settlement League just came in one day and bought up a bunch of land."

"Where did they get the money?"

"Where do you think?" Harry asked, still poring over their briefing materials. "James, you know how many of these Nazi youth camps and German Bund communities there are in the U.S. now?"

"No, what does it say?"

"Nearly fifty, from my count."

"Dear Lord."

"Yeah, they're all over, too. Texas, Wisconsin, Indiana, Ohio. They got eight in California alone."

"How many in New York State?"

"Six, I think," Harry said, counting again. "All over the place. Same procedure. They get a hundred, two hundred acres and fill 'em up with little Nazis."

"They stopped 'em in Connecticut a couple years ago," James remembered. "A little farming town called Southbury."

"Oh, yeah? How'd they do it?"

"Local preacher led the fight, I think. No youth camps allowed. No restricted communities."

"Stopping fascism through zoning," Harry chortled. "Hey, whatever works."

"Yeah. For now."

They skirted the great estates of Long Island's Gold Coast, traveling instead through the stamp-sized villages that had been settled before the Revolutionary War. Each marked by a Presbyterian church steeple, standing like a sentry, plus a modest brick post office the WPA had just put up, a village green, and — in a grudging concession to the modern age—a gas station. At noon they pulled into a dirt parking lot, at something in Port Jefferson called The Mermaid Inn. A slumping clapboard building, once the home of a whaling captain, it sat on a craggy bluff high above the Long Island Sound. A cold wind snapped off the white-capped waters and Harry could make out the coastline of Connecticut some fifteen miles away. He suddenly froze, the color draining from his face.

"Let's go inside," Amos said, ignoring Harry's condition.

The restaurant was drab and dimly lit and reeked of the years of cooking grease baked into its dark paneled walls and scarred wood plank floors. Harry counted about twenty tables, draped with red-and-white checkered tablecloths, looking old and threadbare but spotlessly clean. Patrons slurped soup and chomped on the chowder and gnawed at the lunch special: a steak sandwich smothered in mushroom gravy, with French-fried potatoes. Swing music scratched out of a staticky Philco radio.

Harry noticed Walther Schaefer, the tobacconist, sitting at a rear table. His companion had closely cropped silver hair, as if a light snow clung to his scalp, and piercing blue eyes set in a pasty white complexion. His expression was sober. *More the look of a condemned man*, Harry thought. Both men had dressed for the occasion: stiff Montgomery Ward suits and dark vertically striped ties, precisely knotted.

A harried waitress wearing a polka dot dress and soiled apron scribbled their orders: four lunch specials, beers all around.

Harry dispensed with any pleasantries. He fished from his pocket a pad and pencil that had been ground to a stub and launched into an interrogation. "Your brother-in-law tells us you have information to share. Concerning a foreign power operating on U.S. soil."

Kimmler's thin lips clamped shut; his eyes froze disdainfully on James Amos. He muttered to Becker: "Er ist schwartz."

He is black.

"*Ich wusste nicht!*" Schaefer whispered back. *I did not know.*

"English, if you please!" Harry snapped.

"Forgive my brother-in-law," said the tobacconist. "He is nervous about meeting. It could place us in great danger with certain people."

"What people?" Harry asked.

The front door opened. A couple of sailors stepped in—and right behind them, Harry noticed, two large, brooding men. They weren't dressed at all like sailors, but looked around the room, then settled into a table not far from them. They ordered coffee and soon were enmeshed in what looked like a very serious, whispered conversation.

Kimmler looked them over. Schaefer fidgeted nervously with his napkin, then muttered, "*Lass uns gehen.*"

"What's he saying?" Harry asked Schaefer.

"He's saying he wants to leave," Amos cut in. He smiled at

their shocked guests. "I speak three languages, if you include English. Don't know why that surprises everyone."

Schaefer and Kimmler exchanged awkward glances. Harry gave a gleeful little chuckle.

"Now," Amos continued, "why don't we just have a friendly lunch. No sense wasting a nice meal, right?"

"We have information," Schaefer told him in what was barely a mutter, after a couple more attempts to pry some steak from his sandwich. "But the risk to us is very high. There is the matter of a reward."

Harry glowered across the table at them.

"You'll be lucky if we don't make you pay for our lunch. Enough already. What's going on?"

"Why don't we discuss a reward later," Amos cut in. "Tell us a little about yourselves, please, gentlemen. What brought you to America?"

The tobacconist cast a wounded glance at Harry.

"The hunger pains in our bellies. In the Great War, Viktor and I served with the Engineers, Battalion 9, in Finland and France. After we got home, he married my sister, and we were going to go into business together. But the war destroyed everything. *Kaput*. I sold single cigarettes to whores on the streets of Hamburg. Viktor is an educated man, an engineer. He couldn't get work. Then we read that America was closing immigration to anyone but Nordics. Viktor and my sister came over in '25. Me, a year later."

"Viktor, what do you do for a living?" James asked calmly, putting them both at ease.

"I am an engineer at the Seversky Aircraft Corporation," Kimmler said proudly. "Over in Farmingdale."

"Aircraft!" Harry exclaimed, despite himself. "Commercial or military?"

"Military. Mostly. There will be another war. America must be prepared."

"You see, we are good Americans," Schaefer insisted. "Patriots! That is why I wanted to provide information to you, when I heard from Viktor."

Harry rolled his eyes. *What the hell was wrong with Army Intelligence, letting a German national from Camp Siegfried work on their latest avionics?* They'd be lucky if complete plans for all the newest Seversky planes weren't sitting back in Berlin already.

"You don't want to provide information," Harry said, "you want to sell it. For a price."

"In America, doesn't everything have a price?" Schaefer replied.

They stopped talking for a moment as the waitress brought another round of beers, Harry and James pretending to drink from theirs while they let the brothers-in-law imbibe. After a long swallow, Schaefer wiped the foam from his lips and continued.

"My brother-in-law lives in German Gardens. In Yaphank."

"You told us. You mean Camp Siegfried," said Harry, angrier than he wanted to be. "German Gardens" sounded like something from *Town & Country.*

Schaefer shook his head. "*Nein.* The camp is for parades. Children. The community around it…is something else. Viktor is involved in the Neighborhood Association. He has learned that it is not…what it appears to be."

"Meaning?"

"It supports certain…activities."

"Like what?" asked Amos.

"Mostly reporting to Berlin on certain observations," Schaefer answered. "Military installations, ports—"

"Defense plants," Harry interjected.

"—and sometimes, moving freight."

"Freight?"

"It's what they call special visitors coming in from Germany. Pick-ups and deliveries."

"And who runs this association?"

Kimmler pushed his plate away. "This is a mistake," he muttered, then whispered fiercely to Schaefer, "I have told you too much, now you are telling them too much. Let's go home."

His brother-in-law rested a hand on his wrist.

"Her name is Voigt. Maria Voigt," Schaefer told them. "She communicates directly with Berlin."

Harry scribbled the name in his pad.

"And who does she talk to in Berlin?"

"It could be anybody," Kimmler spoke for himself now. "The *Abwehr*, Gestapo, SiPo. There are so many security services back home now."

"She isn't just a ham radio nut, is she?" Harry asked.

"No, no. It was nothing like that. This was…a sophisticated machine. Of a kind I've never seen before. It had its own antenna."

"And what has she been talking about?"

Kimmler took another swig of beer, then clenched his lips.

Schaefer said, "They are preparing for a new visitor. Unlike any other. Very high level."

"How do you know?" asked Harry.

"Viktor is on the Executive Committee of the Association. It's a very small group that handles certain logistics."

"Logistics, meaning espionage against the government of the United States, your adopted country," Weiss said, his voice slamming down like a hammer.

"Take it easy, Harry," James urged.

Kimmler seemed completely rattled now. His hands shook as he brought his glass to his mouth, so that the beer churned inside. Schaefer noticed the big brooding men at the next table turn around, and he put a hand on his brother-in-law's shoulder. "Tell them."

Kimmler set down his glass, and brought his hand to his chin, rubbing as if to coax out the words. James noticed the spidery fingers, neatly manicured. *An engineer's hands*, he thought, *the delicate fingers of a man who didn't enjoy getting his hands dirty.*

"We know this is hard," James said gently. "Tell us—who's coming?"

"You won't believe me," Kimmler murmured.

"These days, I'll believe almost anything," Harry said.

Kimmler pitched forward and whispered, "An agent. From Berlin. Very high up."

"For what purpose?" James asked.

Kimmler's lips opened, then closed again, as if fighting his words.

Schaefer whispered, "To kidnap Albert Einstein. And return him to Germany."

In their careers, both James Amos and Harry Weiss had listened to countless tips, leads, hints, and clues. They'd sifted through conspiracy theories, suspicions, hunches, inklings, intuitions, innuendo, fiction and nonfiction, threats real and imagined. If they had heard this tip without having been through what they had over five years before, Weiss thought, they would have considered it a crackpot conspiracy, not much different from the tips that inundated the office about Martians landing in New Jersey.

"Where?" Amos asked.

Kimmler continued. "Einstein is planning to vacation here. He is renting a cottage on Little Hog Neck."

"Where's that?"

"It is a very remote area. On the Peconic Bay. Difficult to find. The perfect place…" Kimmler trailed off, his eyes finding a sudden interest in the empty glass in front of him.

"How much do you know about the agent? Military? Gestapo? An intelligence agency?"

Viktor rubbed his chin again. James noticed beads of sweat breaking out on his ashen forehead.

"I know very little. Only that he has been in America before."

Harry and James exchanged an uneasy glance.

"When?" Harry snapped. "When is he arriving?"

Kimmler answered. "We don't know for certain. Only that Einstein is arriving on the last day of April."

"How do you know all of this?" Harry asked Kimmler. "The radio, the planning?"

"I…observe things," Kimmler stammered.

Schaefer cut in. "I swear, we have told you everything we know. We can learn more. But what about the reward? That has always been our understanding, Agent Weiss."

Harry sighed angrily. "If you're playing us, wasting our time for a goddam reward, I'll personally guarantee that you spend the rest of your lives in solitary at Sing Sing. If it checks out, we'll arrange a goddam tickertape parade down Broadway."

"We'll need to speak to this Maria Voigt," James said.

Kimmler turned towards him, eyes widened anxiously.

"*Nein!* You would be sentencing us to death..." His words trailed off, swallowed by a clatter of dishes.

Amos cleared his throat softly. "Let's get a game plan together first. We'll run a check on Voigt. Maybe she can lead us to a bigger fish. We'll protect you. I promise."

Kimmler leaned into Schaefer, whispering in animated German. Schaefer rubbed his round jaw, as if calculating the risks and rewards of this deal.

James translated. "He's saying we can't protect them from this Voigt woman. Says she's connected everywhere."

"You have a personal guarantee from J. Edgar Hoover himself," Harry lied. "Now what's her address?"

"80 Adolph Hitler Road," Kimmler answered.

The two agents exchanged glances.

"Do I look like I'm in the mood for jokes?" said Harry.

Kimmler shrugged.

"See for yourself."

Chapter Twenty-Two

OUTSIDE IT HAD TURNED COLDER. The agents turned up their collars against the wind starting to whip off the ocean. Harry felt sick again, but not just because of the water. Neither of them said anything until they were both out of Port Jefferson, headed east for Yaphank.

"Do you think it's him?" Harry asked James.

"Hmm?" James asked, then understood what he meant. "We can't know," he told Harry, sensibly enough. "We can't know if it's him at all."

Bobby Larkins, gurgling his life up on the deck of that boat. The image had haunted Weiss ever since.

"I hope it's him. I hope to God that son of a bitch sets foot here again."

"Don't blaspheme," said James.

Harry had started out with the NYPD to be just like Dan Larkins. Larkins treated him like a son, introducing him around the precinct, dropping in from time to time to see how he was doing. He didn't flinch when Larkins took him to the NYPD Pistol Range, along the southern tip of Ann Hook's Neck. He made himself into a decent shot, though it didn't come naturally to him.

Harry had been thrilled when he was officially named to the force. His mother had cried when she saw him in his new blue uniform—at least a little out of pride, not just despair, he convinced himself—and he became a cop on the beat.

He expected it to be a hard adjustment, and it was. There was barely another Jew on the force anywhere, and the hazing and the insults came fast and furious. But Harry could endure the attacks.

What he wasn't prepared for was the pervasive corruption he encountered. If he wanted to advance, even a little, it was made known that he would have to pay off to make sergeant, captain, detective, commander—each step along the way, the bribes getting larger and larger, funded by shaking down the bootleggers, bookies, streetwalkers, and pimps.

After just three years, despite how much he revered Officer Larkins, Harry had decided to leave the force. He'd begun to hear about the new federal law enforcement department, the Bureau of Investigation. At the time, it was still something of a joke, a sleazy backwater of the Harding Administration. But it had been taken over by J. Edgar Hoover, a young man who was trying to modernize it, making it scientific and professional, all of which appealed to Harry Weiss. He had started going to City College at night—much to the relief of his family—after having heard that Hoover wanted only college men and lawyers. He worked his shift on the force while getting an undergraduate degree in criminology.

It was the hardest Harry had ever worked in his life, but he took a certain satisfaction in it. He never felt quite right if he *wasn't* working as hard as he could, wasn't filling up every free moment doing something that mattered.

It was time for Jews to step forward, he told himself. Looking on with satisfaction as more and more forced their way into the government, into the best colleges and universities, into the elite professions where they had been banned—openly or covertly—for so long. *Time to stop acting like we can survive living apart, manning the ghetto walls.*

He had seen how that had worked out under a boardwalk in Coney Island. The bright, glittering amusements above, the dark dangerous shadows below.

On the day Bobby Larkins was killed, Harry thought it his responsibility to break the news to the man who had saved his own life. It was the most terrible thing he had ever had to do.

The old man nodded, and thanked Harry for coming himself, but he could see the older man almost shrivel with the news.

"Are ye all right?" he had asked Harry Weiss as he went to leave, nothing more left to say. The simple decency of that question was so overwhelming that Harry had had all he could do to nod and turn wordlessly, and hurry out into the street before he burst into sobs.

They had scoured the docks for hours after the killing, looking for a man they could barely even describe. *A phantom.* Harry had gone to the funeral, of course, and since it was the nephew of Danny Larkins, half the force had turned out. It was a big, full-dress affair, with the pipers and the white gloves and all the police medals on. The mayor, the police commissioner, and all the politicians had made speeches. Harry had stayed through every minute of it, even though he could almost feel the waves of hatred emanating off the uniformed ranks. All directed at him: the man who had got Danny Larkins' nephew killed, who had quit the force and taken some cushy job with the feds, and then come back as some big deal and got one of them killed. The college boy, the interloper. *The Jew.*

Dan had pushed his way through the crowd to go over and shake Harry's hand and hug him in front of the whole force. He had leaned in while the organ was still playing and the bagpipes blaring, and told him outright.

"This isn't your fault. The boy knew what he was doing. Don't let this end our friendship. Come around and see me sometime."

Harry had wanted to weep all over again, had held on to Dan's hand and told him he surely would. He had tried to be true to his word, had gone back up and visited with him at his home. He could no longer bear the looks he got at the precinct house—or how much he believed he deserved them. Bobby's mother had passed away by then, which Dan insisted was a blessing. But he seemed so lonely, batting around the house with no one there. They tried talking about this and that—talking about Bobby or not about Bobby—but either way, it didn't go well. Inevitably they brought out the Jameson's, and they both ended up drunk and sadder than ever. Then, a few years later, there had been the first lump in Dan

Larkins' armpit, and then one in his neck. He had survived the operations, was still hanging on in his fine empty home up on Silver Street near Morris Park, but he was just a wreck of his former self, the cancer eating him up.

Harry could hardly stand it, seeing how Dan looked at him, imagining him thinking, *if only I hadn't heard the fight. If only I hadn't stopped and helped him, then my nephew would still be alive.* Dan, nonetheless, had told him again the last time he had seen him, six months ago:

"You know, it's not your fault, boy-o," though he could barely rasp out the words. "It's the world, and it's not your fault."

They reached German Gardens by three, and though the afternoon light was beginning to fade a little in the late winter day it all looked very pretty. Harry and James pulled up to a large sign, planted in a flowerbed still barren from the winter.

German American Settlement League
PRIVATE COMMUNITY
MEMBERS & GUESTS ONLY

"We're guests of Uncle Sam," Harry quipped.

It all looked much like any other model development going up in Queens, or out on the Island. Neater, better maintained than most. The roads freshly paved, lined with modest bungalows on small plots.

The houses did look a little different, like something they'd be more likely to find in Bavaria than in Yaphank. And there were the street signs.

"German Boulevard," Amos read out, as they drove down the main drag of the community.

"Hitler Street. Goebbels Street. Goering Street—boy, you'd think that one would be wider," Harry tried to joke again. But neither of them was laughing.

The village was almost unnervingly quiet, with lights on in only a few windows.

"Everyone's still at school," James surmised. "Or buying dinner down at the market, or at work."

"Yes, hard at work passing on plans at the aircraft factory," Harry said.

They passed Kimmler's home, at 3 Goebbels Street. It had brown painted shingles, two front windows without shutters, and a tiny stoop covered by a small gable roof. Floral curtains were tied neatly behind the windows. The house next to it looked identical. So did the next one, and the one after that.

"Look at the flags," James said.

Harry did. Several of the residents of German Gardens had run the Stars and Stripes up their lawn flagpoles—with big, red, Nazi swastika flags right underneath them. Or above them.

They drove German Boulevard. They could see a pine barren across the lake, the melancholy scene of a children's summer camp in the winter. Locked up bunkhouses and chained up canoes and gymnastics equipment.

"That's where they're growing a new generation of Nazis," Harry said.

They drove past all the swastika flags, half entangled with Old Glory, and Harry shook his head again, trying to get over where he was—over what America had turned into. *Fifty of these camps? These little German states within a state? All teaching Nazi racial doctrines, Nazi ways of thinking and doing, blunt power over everything?*

"I've seen enough," Harry said. "This place gives me the willies. Let's get back to the office and find our suspect."

James pressed on the gas pedal. As soon as they'd exited the development, it was as if they'd returned to America from another planet. A stretch of pavement through welcoming small towns where the only flags flying were red, white, and blue. Brick schools which taught math and language and nothing about a master race. Church steeples full of welcoming faces and flying American flags.

Before long they approached the World's Fair construction

site. Even in the late afternoon, bulldozers rumbled across the grounds. *Like the armored tanks of the Great War,* James thought, *trampling barren fields, kicking up enough dirt and dust to turn the air gritty and gray.* Again, traffic slowed to a crawl.

"There's no way he could snatch Einstein at the Fair," Amos said. "It's preposterous."

"But he could kill him easily enough," Harry interrupted. "Take his shot from the crowd."

Like Milwaukee, thought Amos. Then shook his head. "They wouldn't need to bring an operative from Germany for that. Any decent marksman could do it."

They fell silent, each man mulling over the range of possibilities.

Minutes later, after they cleared the fairgrounds and the road opened, Amos said, "We have to cover every contingency. I'll call Einstein and ask him to stay away from the Fair. Meanwhile, we do some basic shoe-leathering, Keep our eyes on Maria Voigt."

"What about the possibility of a German agent coming in?"

"Judging by past practices, which is all we have to go by, German intelligence will bring an agent in by a German ocean liner. The name of every passenger appears on the ship's manifest. Along with ages, spoken languages, addresses. We start going through every manifest."

"Dozens of ships, each with thousands of passengers. It's a goddam needle in a haystack, James. Worse, it's a bunch of haystacks, going back and forth across the ocean."

"We start with a small window. Ships that arrived or will arrive before the World's Fair. Then expand the search if necessary."

"The passenger manifests won't tell us anything," Harry interrupted. "Our man will come in undercover."

"So we'll look for a red flag. Something unusual that stands out in a manifest. I'll put Eddie Crowley on it." James was referring to one of the young recruits who'd joined the Bureau as part of Hoover's recent surge in recruitment, to aid in the deepening war against Nazis, mobsters, tax evaders, union thugs, kidnappers, swindlers, communists, and other public enemies.

"Let's keep tabs on Kimmler too," Harry added, "and German Gardens. For all we know, the agent is already there. Living in plain sight."

The rest of the ride back to Manhattan was spent quietly, each agent processing what they'd learned, churning in their minds how a Nazi agent would abduct Albert Einstein from the safety of the United States. The silence was broken when they reached the World's Fair construction site.

"My God!" James blurted.

"Now who's blaspheming?" Harry joked.

"The World's Fair!"

"What about it?"

"I read in the Daily News last week," James answered. "They announced the opening night speaker."

"Who is it?"

"Albert Einstein."

Chapter Twenty-Three

IT WAS THE FIRST DAY OF SPRING, when the wind still snapped off the lake in Seekirchen, and the snow remained like lace atop the distant hills. At five o'clock in the morning, Anton Gunther arose in his farmhouse and proceeded directly to the bathroom. The bathroom walls were wood plank and drafty, with just barely enough room for shelf toilet and pedestal sink. Gunther turned the faucet and waited for a trickle of yellow-brown water. He inspected himself in a tarnished mirror. He'd put on a few pounds since the Zwick operation, which he knew he could take off easily. It was his eyes that concerned him: no longer the dark, innocent eyes of Max Goldschmidt, but pale and cold, even in their sleepiness. His eyes revealed hidden truths, he knew, especially as the life ebbed from his targets.

It was time to go to the training camp at Quenszee, to shake off the identity of Anton Gunther and become Max Goldschmidt all over again.

Which was the point of it all, of course—to change, and change again.

His farm was near the town of Jüterbog. Row after row of simple homes, each with their burnt-orange roofs and slots of well-tended lawns and gardens stretching out behind them. *The very essence of Germany*, he'd always thought, *bustling and prosperous since the Fuhrer had come to power.*

There, he lived by himself. A prosperous businessman, the real estate agent told the neighbors, who'd acquired the old farm on the outskirts of town to find refuge from the pressures of his hectic life in Berlin. To be left alone.

That morning he dressed in his sleek black trousers and

cashmere sweater, and combed his back hair straight back. In the kitchen he found his lambskin driving gloves and sunglasses. He turned out the lights, locked the front door. Headed for the bright red Mercedes Roadster waiting for him.

Late winter had hardly given way, and the morning was so cold that his breath made white puffs of smoke in the air. Still, he drove with the top of the Mercedes down, taking a leg of the *Reichsautobahn* for much of the fifty-five miles to the Quenzsee, enjoying how fast his beast of a car could handle it. There was barely another car on the broad new highway the Fuhrer had built, and he could push the Mercedes up to ninety or one hundred, afraid only of a blowout. Thinking about the mission ahead, becoming someone else again.

In a more placid time, Anton Gunther often thought, he might have been an actor. As it happened, he was the best undercover agent in the Reich, already a legend in the ever-multiplying intelligence services, one that others barely dared to whisper about.

He'd been raised near Salzburg. His father owned a factory; his mother worked in it. There would be rumors, later, that his father was Jewish—rumors that would plague Anton, with his dark complexion, throughout his young life. But he never could find out, despite searching the records for years.

All he knew was that one warm morning when he was an infant, he was unceremoniously brought to an orphanage tucked discreetly between the city and the mountains, like a delivery of warm bread. In a small office with a desk and two chairs, he was exchanged for an envelope containing a significant monetary contribution, pursuant to already agreed-upon terms.

Anton had been abandoned. Growing up, he rather liked it.

Even before the rise of the Nazis, Anton's Jewish features worked against his adoption. Prospective parents would wrinkle their noses, as if he carried the stink of impure blood, then choose a child who seemed more physically suitable. The orphanage staff, feeling sorry for him, was kind and generous. When young Anton went to the kitchen, the cook let him stand there and learn how to make food. The gardener let him trail after him and learn how to take care of the trees and the flowers on the grounds, the mechanic taught him how the machinery around the place worked. He read every book in the orphanage library—history, science, art, music—sometimes falling asleep late at night with the book open on his lap. Anton had particularly enjoyed reading about America, a vast and wild place an ocean away.

There was nothing Anton couldn't learn quickly. Absorbing. Storing. Emulating.

It wasn't until age twelve that Anton was adopted by Martin and Eva Gunther, a couple from a little farming village outside the city, who'd finally given up on having a child of their own after too many miscarriages had nearly killed Eva. At first, Anton felt that his life had been shattered. But both of his new parents loved the boy. Martin cradled him on his lap and held his hand on daily walks through nearby meadows. He patiently taught him how to fish from the stream that cut through their property. At night, when animals howled from a nearby forest, he lulled Anton to sleep with stories of great German heroes and legends: of Tannhäuser, the knight-poet; and Theodoric the Great; and Frederick Barbarossa, the King under the Mountain, who would emerge someday and redeem all the German *volk*.

His mother, Eva, made him wonderful gingerbread cookies and pinched his cheeks, and held him in her arms by the fire. A devout Catholic, it was she who took him to mass every Sunday and introduced him to the communion, the ceremony of blood, the ritual of confession. When he asked whether he had any sins to confess, his mother laughed sweetly and told him he could not have any very bad thoughts to confess at all; that if he ever did, God would forgive him.

Two years after he was adopted, Archduke Franz Ferdinand was assassinated, igniting the Great War. Martin's unit was sent to stop the Russians in the foothills of the Carpathians. He returned, but not as the same man. His eyes stared vacantly through Anton, who was a teenager now, as if he didn't recognize his son. When the boy touched him he recoiled, then pushed him away. He drank heavily, broke out in tears for no reason.

Austria was a rump state, a once-proud fragment of its former Hapsburg greatness. The disintegrating economy drove the once-proud Martin deeper and deeper into his despair. He'd mutter about the Bolsheviks, bankers, communists, and Jews—the evil powers that he believed had brought Germany to its knees. One night, Anton heard his father whisper in protest, "For all we know, our son may be the issue of a Jew."

"We have raised him our own way," his mother argued back.

"But his blood, Eva. His *blood*."

The news itself confused him; his father's rejection seared him. It was as if he'd swallowed something that should be purged, or sprouted a growth that needed to be cut away.

All he wanted to do was fix what had broken his father. To return to the time before everything had fallen apart. But one warm summer morning Anton was reading a book of poetry near the fishing stream when he heard an explosion, followed by his mother's screams. He raced to the house and saw his father sprawled on the wood plank floor, bleeding from the head with his service revolver in his hand.

Martin had blown himself apart—and nothing could ever be put together again.

Anton had been abandoned by his adopted father, just as he had been by his birth father. Soon after, his mother sold the farm and moved with Anton into the village. Times were no better there, his mother doing needlework to help them survive, weeping in her room when she thought she was alone. Worse yet was the new school, where there was one boy in particular, a lanky older boy with a perpetual smirk on his face, named Alois. The boy was constantly going on about how "Anton must be a Jew." Pointing out how dark his hair and his complexion were. Insisting that his nose, which was not very big at all, was long and crooked like a Jew's. Alois had an effeminate way about him, thought Anton.

Maybe he was trying to deflect attention.

Whatever his reason, it seemed to Anton that his tormentor would come to school every day with a new taunt about how Jewish he seemed. Before long, all the other boys had joined in. Pushing him away, refusing to include him in their games, sometimes even pelting him with rocks. They wrote crude things about him on village walls and sang stupid rhyming chants at him about Jews.

One Sunday early in the summer, when he was seventeen, Anton had gone back to the fishing stream on the farm they had once owned. He went to get away from his schoolmates, who loitered around the village square after church with nothing to do but torture whoever came by. He sat by the stream and thought of his father and cried a little. He tried to read a new book of poetry he had brought but fell into a light sleep. When he awoke it was the height of the afternoon. He took off his clothes and went for a swim, remembering the way he had done that before everything had gone wrong.

A small stone skimmed along the water near his head. Startled, he looked around—only to see Alois, his constant tormentor.

"Jew, Jew, what are you doing there? Poisoning all our water?" Alois had jeered at him. He was fresh from church, dressed in a nice Sunday suit his parents had bought him, with a pocketful of stones he had gathered to wing at Anton.

"But you don't really think I'm a Jew. Do you?" Gunther asked him.

Alois had shrugged and looked away for a moment, as if embarrassed. Anton swam toward him, a sudden clarity filling him.

"No. I don't know. I suppose," the boy had mumbled. "Why aren't you in church, if you're not a Jew?"

"Why do you say it, then? If you don't really believe it?"

Alois shrugged again and took a couple steps back, now that Anton had swum up to where he was standing along the banks of the stream.

"I can say anything I want. Don't tell me what to say, Jew!"

He is afraid of me, Anton thought.

He stepped out of the stream, still naked, and walked toward the boy. He saw it then, the fear in Alois' eyes, but there was something else as well: the glance darting to Anton's groin, the unmistakable frisson. As Anton came closer the boy twitched softly, his lips parted. Anton grabbed him by the waist, pulled him against his wet flesh, listened to the pounding of his breaths. He pressed his mouth down by the boy's neck and heard a primal moan. Anton realized that the boy needed something from Anton, and that now he was in control. He nuzzled Alois' ear and whispered, "Say I'm not a Jew."

Alois tried to push him away. But Anton quickly moved his hands around the boy's neck, squeezing harder. Alois, realizing he was trapped, could only make little desperate gasping sounds as he tried to wriggle free.

"*Say it!*" He tightened his grip.

"You're not a Jew!" Alois gasped. "Please, let me go."

Anton enjoyed the dominance over the boy, and the stirring in his groin unlike anything he'd felt before. "I will let you go. But first…"

He thrust a knee into the boy's groin, sending him to the ground, then straddled him. Reaching around blindly, he found a large rock. He brought it down hard on Alois' head. The boy cried out in pain.

"*Say it!*"

"You're not a Jew!" Alois sobbed beneath him. "Don't kill me! Please don't kill me."

It was not an idea that had quite formed in Anton's mind before. But now that he heard it, he knew that that was exactly what he was going to do. He brought the rock down again. Alois screamed, but Anton only stuffed the boy's mouth into the dirt. He brought the rock down again—the cry muffled this time. *That was better.* He brought it down again and again, harder, faster, working to a state of ecstasy. When he'd finished, he saw that Alois' head had broken, and blood and other things oozed out of it.

Still, he saw life in the boy's eyes. He gripped the boy's throat with his bloodstained fingers. "Now that I know what *you* are, I will tell you what I am." He tightened his grip. "I was born a Jew. Adopted by a father who blew his brains out, ashamed of my blood. But it wasn't my fault, was it? It was all the other Jews, who drove him to his death."

Hot tears streamed down Anton's face, cleansing the dirt and blood. Tears of release.

Anton dressed hurriedly, then dragged the body deep into the woods and hid it well, jamming it down deep in a small cave of rocks he had found years before. He covered it with fallen branches and old leaves, but not before he had stripped off the boy's suit, folded it up, and taken it back to the village with him. There he hid it away, in a spot beneath his mattress he knew even his mother wouldn't find it.

The next day, Alois was reported missing. No one could imagine what had happened to him. Soon after, all the boys in the school scoured the woods along with the police, looking for him. Anton was proud that he could search as diligently as any of them, shouting out Alois' name as if the dead boy could hear him.

They never came close to the stashed body, and soon talk around the village had begun to speculate that maybe Alois had gone off to Vienna with the school's music teacher, who had quit just a few weeks before and who everyone thought was *that way.*

Anton himself left before the next school year started, going very early one morning. He wrote a note for his mother about how he was off to Munich to try to find work, and that when he did he would send for her. He thought that it was as nice a lie to leave as any he could think of. And he made sure to take Alois' nice Sunday suit with him.

It wasn't difficult finding his way to Munich. Making any kind of living, even for himself, was another story. Runaway inflation was sweeping the country, making everyone's savings worthless overnight. Families lugged wheelbarrows full of paper money to the market—something that people said was the evil doing of the Jews, too. Anton noticed the offended glances, as if he'd done something wrong—no different than the couples who'd rejected him at the orphanage. So he disguised his features, cropping and lightening his hair with various dyes, adopting the mannerisms, dialects, and features of the proud Aryans around him. Immersing himself in gatherings where he could perfect his mimicry.

Soon he was confident enough to join The National Socialist German Workers Party, where he could wrap himself in the authenticity of a crisp uniform, collar patches, and shoulder boards, and pledge a war to defend the master race.

The party ignited the war in the slums of two dozen German cities, battling the Communists in the back alleys. The two groups were more like each other than anyone else, which was why their fights were so merciless: outcasts against outcasts, two street gangs battling each other for the bragging rights to hell.

Anton excelled at street fighting. The more ruthlessly he fought, the more his peers seemed to overlook his Jewish features. He found his way into communist hideouts and clandestine meetings. He stalked the Party's enemies, the men and women responsible for the crushing depression that had forced Germany to its knees and exacted the Party's vengeance. Proving that he was a pure Aryan, willing to do anything to dispel the whispers that he may have carried Jewish blood.

At a Party rally, Reinhard Heydrich took an empty seat next to Anton and struck up a conversation. Heads turned; conversations fell to whispers as the aristocratic Party leader conversed with the ruffian from Austria.

Over the next several weeks, Heydrich continued talking to Anton over beers and hearty meals across Munich. Finding out all sorts of things, seeming to sense Anton's abilities and inclinations. Heydrich got him off the street gangs and set him up in a Party training program where he learned marksmanship and the basics of spycraft, where his body was molded into a condition he'd never achieved before.

One day Heydrich showed up unexpectedly to check on his progress, inviting him to the *Burgerbraulkeller*, one of the Nazi's preferred beer halls in Munich. In a private room on the second floor, Heydrich inspected his protégé admiringly. "They have done a fine job," he said. "You have developed perfectly."

"I hear the whispers," Anton responded. "There are still some who believe I'm a Jew."

Heydrich grinned. "Why, yes, that's exactly the point. Are you ready for your first mission?"

Gunther's first *Yiddishe* role was posing as Samuel Rossman, a busboy in a kosher restaurant in *Spandauer Vorstadt*, a neighborhood with a large Jewish population. There the Communists, the KPD, met secretly to plan assaults on National Socialists. Gunther had managed to draw the eye of Rebecca Schoenwald, a rare woman leader in the group. Rebecca was beautiful—sharp, brown eyes, a lush body, and the sort of proletarian beliefs that would never allow her to look down on a mere busboy. Particularly one so eager to learn about the workers' paradise. It was only days before they slept together, and the romance soon became torrid. Gunther would remain awake and move stealthily through the darkened apartment, photographing documents stashed in cabinets and drawers, with an ingenious little camera the Party had provided.

When he'd extracted every bit of valuable information, Heydrich congratulated him and told him it was time for another assignment.

Anton made a final visit, lulling Rebecca into bed. After a full hour of lovemaking she moaned, exhausted, "No more today." She began rolling away.

He pulled her shoulders back to the pillows. She protested, "I said enough."

Anton swung himself on top of her and pinned her arms to the mattress. She moved her hips under him, not in arousal, he realized, but a futile effort to move him off. He lowered his face close to hers, studying as her eyes cycled from annoyance to anger to confusion to fear.

He smiled, and as he did, he felt the deadening mask of the busboy fall away and the brute strength return to his muscles. A rebirth. Resurrection.

"I am not Samuel Rossman" he blurted out. Then reached for the kitchen knife he'd hidden under the mattress.

But why tell her this? he asked himself silently.

Her hips slackened. Her eyes seemed to roll back, and a small tear dribbled down her ghostly white cheek. "Please…"

"My mission is to stop your conspiracy against my party. Even now, your comrades are being arrested. Murdered."

"Shema Y'Israel…" she began praying.

With one hand he raised the blade against her full left breast, tracing her nipple, fighting his own arousal. With the other he held her chin steady, then skimmed the knife along her chest, to her neck, recalling his training, probing for that exact target. When he found it, he locked his eyes on hers. Silently revealing everything he needed her to know.

Say no more. Kill her. Now.

He positioned the tip of the blade, adjusted his grip.

"My name is Anton Gunther," he said, then sliced cleanly across her neck.

As he washed the bloodstained sheets and pillows in her kitchen sink, he felt a cleansing himself. It was the confession, he'd told himself. He'd discovered that the ancient ritual had nothing to do with God; it was simply a way of returning from one personality to another. Confession didn't relieve a man of guilt, but of his false identity.

He was born again.

Once the party had come to power, he became Heydrich's personal operative, his troubleshooter. Moving all across the Reich and then beyond. Sniffing out threats, penetrating suspect organizations, reporting, disrupting, killing. Spreading lies like poison. Undetectable, invisible. A legend in the intelligence community, his real identity so secret that he was known only as *das Chameleon.* A cold-blooded killer with a three-hundred-sixty-degree arc of awareness.

A man so swift and efficient in his ability to identify and kill his prey that few could believe he even existed.

Few except for his victims, who heard, in the final seconds of their lives, his confession.

Less than hour after leaving his home, Gunther pulled his car into a long cobblestone driveway that was flanked by barren maple trees standing against the bitter winter cold like sentries. He soon came upon a lakefront mansion of gray stone with a pitched roof of red clay tile. It was built in 1888 as a country house for a prosperous Berlin family. Now it had become a modern, pitiless enterprise. It was the Reich's covert training facility for espionage missions: a commando college. The graceful old drawing rooms had been converted to classrooms. Agents selected to infiltrate a target learned the local language, dialect, geography, customs, dress, and culture. Plus marksmanship, knife work, abduction techniques, hand-to-hand combat, long-distance swimming, wilderness survival. They learned how to forge signatures, doctor photographs, sever arteries, administer lethal injections, pick locks, plant explosives, derail trains.

He pulled to the front entrance, pulled his luggage from the car, and marched up the middle steps and through the elegant old doors.

Here, the transformation back to Max Goldschmidt would occur.

Only then would he travel to America.

Chapter Twenty-Four

ALBERT EINSTEIN SAT IN HIS OFFICE in Fuld Hall at the Institute of Advanced Science, in Princeton, holding a phone receiver some six inches away from his ear. Even at that distance, he heard every frantic word in Leo Szilard's rambling. Once again, the student was lecturing the professor in that heavy Hungarian accent, the words spewing from the lips before being filtered in the brain.

Despite receiving almost daily messages from Szilard about his supposed breakthrough in his lab, Einstein had put off a conversation. It wasn't necessarily procrastination but other, more pressing business. He'd been concentrating on his submission to Annals of Mathematics. Plus there was the major address he'd written and delivered at a mid-March fundraising dinner for the American Committee for Jewish Refugees at the Waldorf Astoria in Manhattan. Still, he'd realized that at some point he'd have to accommodate Szilard's incessant demands to speak. After all, he'd followed Einstein's instructions from the previous December to conduct laboratory experiments on the feasibility of an atomic weapon, and there were reports that other scientists—namely Enrico Fermi and Eugene Wigner—had conducted their own corroborating research.

Could it be true? The splitting of an atom leading to a superweapon?

Now, nearly fifteen minutes into Szilard's diatribe, Einstein's doubts mounted again. It wasn't that Szilard was unconvincing, it was that he was so damned condescending.

"As I've already stated, Einstein, it can no longer be disputed: I have liberated a neutron in the disintegration of uranium, and if more than one neutron is liberated, a chain reaction is possible.

Which of course could, in certain circumstances, lead to the construction of bombs. Which would be an existential threat in the hands of the madman, Hitler."

"Szilard—" Einstein interjected.

Szilard spoke over him. "The question, of course, is how many neutrons can be emitted to create the chain reactions. I have cut down all extra laboratory activities and tried to get more information about this, which is the most important point at present. Though this number seems to be above one, I am still not certain about it. Fermi agrees. Accordingly, we are preparing an experiment on a semi-large scale, using five hundred pounds of uranium oxide. We will have to borrow the sample, because I have no money for a purchase."

"Szilard—" Einstein raised his voice.

"Meanwhile, we must take immediate steps to stop Hitler from procuring a reliable supply of uranium. My God, with enough of it, he could have a bomb in no time. We must notify the Queen of Belgium to secure her uranium mines in the Congo against attack by Hitler. No, we should not do that until after we contact Mr. Roosevelt. Perhaps the State Department as well. I believe you know the Queen? Of Belgium?"

"*Szilard*," Einstein snapped. "Two parties are typically required for a conversation. Won't you allow me to say something?"

"Well," Szilard said after a brief silence, "why have you been so quiet all this time?"

Einstein took a deep breath. "You have proven the ability to liberate a neutron. But still, you have not shown that even a possible chain reaction is, as you say, an existential threat. Indeed, you have not proven that it would generate enough energy to power a small flashlight."

"But—"

"Before we warn Presidents and Queens, there are other offices that may be more appropriate. The military, for example. Perhaps they will fund further research. Why not—"

Now Szilard interrupted. "Hah! You are as naïve as I was!"

"Meaning?"

"When you didn't return my calls, Fermi decided to go to Washington himself and brief a committee of the Navy. Fermi! Who fled the Italian fascists to protect his Jewish wife!"

"I know the story, Szilard."

"He explained the science in detail. And do you know what the gentlemen of the Navy asked? They wanted to know if *he* was a Fascist. They dropped everything else entirely!"

The story stung at Einstein, triggering an unpleasant memory. "Well, then, what about publishing your results in a scientific journal? As a basis for additional research?"

"Are you crazy, Einstein? This must remain top secret. We cannot allow it to fall into the hands of our former colleagues in Berlin: Diebner, Heisenberg, Lenard, Stark—"

"I know the names," he sighed woefully. *How had such brilliant men fallen so willingly into Hitler's grasp? Had their rational thought processes been devoured by sheer ego? Does the will to survive override decades of scientific facts? Freud would have had a field day analyzing his old colleagues,* Einstein thought, *had he not had to flee to London himself.*

"In any case," Szilard was droning, "we must assume that Germany is already ahead of us, and organize a program under the direction of President Roosevelt, himself!"

Before Einstein could respond, there was a knock on his office door. A young student assistant poked his head in, and announced, "You have visitors. Important ones."

Einstein welcomed the excuse to end his conversation. "Szilard, I have unexpected guests. Please continue with the next phase of your experiments and keep me informed. How long will you need to show the possibility of a chain reaction?"

"Well, again, I have to procure the necessary supplies, get the approvals—"

"As fast as you can, Szilard. And get some help. Fermi, Wigner. There is strength in numbers. Then we will see about calling the President and the Queen."

"Yes, but—"

Einstein terminated the call.

"Now," he said, turning to his assistant, "who is it who wants to see me without an appointment?"

The assistant widened his eyes and whispered, "The FBI."

Chapter Twenty-Five

EINSTEIN SAT BACK IN HIS CHAIR, considering the statistical probability of two miserable conversations arriving only minutes apart. He wondered what false allegation, anonymous tip, or rumor about him had reached J. Edgar Hoover, requiring the dispatch of an agent.

"The agent claims he knows you," his assistant had said sheepishly.

"The FBI claims to know everything about everybody," Einstein had replied. "Alright then. Show the agent in."

But when his office door opened again the professor's face brightened, and he let out a loud "Halloooo! I do remember you!"

James Amos returned the smile. "The day you arrived to take up permanent residence."

Einstein thought back to that strange, unsettled day, when Elsa and he had been whisked off the boat. The gracious colored FBI man, driving them down through New Jersey, making sure that everything was all right.

"Ah, yes, Agent Amos! How are you? I must thank you again for all your help and courtesy that day."

"It was my pleasure, sir. And thank you for the very nice letter to Director Hoover about that," Amos told him—refraining from adding how, after he had called in to the Bureau and gone back to the Einsteins' hotel rooms, he had almost had a heart attack when he discovered that the great man had gone out for his little jaunt to have his ice cream and buy a comb. He'd had a hell of a time explaining to the Director how, unbeknownst to the reporter, Amos had been carefully shadowing him the whole time.

Einstein waggled his fingers towards a chair, which Amos

took. "How may I help you, Agent?"

"I understand you are planning a vacation on Long Island this spring," Amos continued.

"This is against the law?" Einstein asked, immediately suspicious.

"No, sir. Not at all, sir. But I did want to advise you about our concern for your safety."

Aaach.

"Agent Amos, I am not nearly as bad a sailor as the newspapers would have you believe," he tried to joke.

"It's not that, sir. We've received a confidential tip that the German government may be organizing...well...they may be a threat to you."

Einstein shrugged. "This is old news, Agent Amos. Certainly Mr. Hoover has more serious things to worry about these days."

"You're aware of the threat?"

"Of course. Herr Hitler wishes me dead. Fortunately for me, the Nazis have demonstrated their total incompetence in achieving the objective. In London, in Belgium. As you can deduce, I remain very much alive." He chuckled softly.

"We're treating this threat seriously, Professor."

"Forgive me, but you must know that I have not been an admirer of your employer's notion of what a threat is. When Elsa and I first sought refuge in America, Hoover did everything possible to prevent it on the grounds of our being communist sympathizers."

"I have heard that story, sir."

"I have never been a communist, Agent Amos. I am merely a citizen of the world who believes we should live in peace. The only threat I have ever presented to the United States is my offensive sense of fashion."

"Be that as it may, Professor, I strongly advise you not to travel to Long Island. The threats that existed when you entered the country have only grown more persistent. The Nazis are operating aggressively on U.S. soil."

"Hitler is a bully, Agent Amos. He doesn't pick on countries his own size, or more powerful. He would not dare the possibility of war with America."

"Please, sir. Just as a precaution."

"I appreciate your concern, Agent Amos," Einstein said. "But of course, the day we met, that was supposed to be a very serious threat, too. And what happened? You drove us to Princeton, where the threat was only a high calorie ice cream."

"Something...*did* happen, Professor. I didn't want to mention this to you, and please do not repeat it to anyone else," Amos told him. "But there *was* a trained, professional assassin on the boat that day—from the best we can tell, someone sent from a German security agency."

"Well, if that is so, he seems to have been equally incomp—"

"He was very competent, Professor. So much so that he stabbed a young, armed officer to death, then escaped the boat uncaptured. If you had still been aboard, he may have killed you as well."

Einstein's eyes fluttered shut. "My God. That poor boy."

"We kept it quiet at the time, because we didn't want to let the Germans know how close they'd come," Amos explained. "We attributed his death to another incident on the dock."

"I see."

"All we're asking you to do for now is to cancel your appearance at the World's Fair and remain out of harm's way while we investigate the newest threat."

Einstein traced a ring on the wooden table with his fingertips, lost in thought. After a long moment, he said, "You are asking for much more. You're asking that I allow fear to control me. That I remain a prisoner."

"Professor—"

"Thank you for your concern, Agent Amos, but I must return to my work."

Amos stood and shook hands with Einstein, their palms lingering for a moment.

After Amos departed, Einstein turned towards the window. A grassy common area was coming to life after the long winter. A straight line of trees stretched to the distance.

The Nazis are an ocean away. Can't I stop running?

Perhaps it is time to make them run.

Chapter Twenty-Six

VIKTOR KIMMLER KNEW THE HAPPINESS that only satiety—satiety from some of the best food from your native land, excellently prepared—can bring. His wife, Margarite, had just treated him to a meal of roast beef stew and potato dumplings. She was no beauty, but at least he ate well. After eating his fill, he pulled on his leather jacket, plopped a gray wool cap on his head, and started off for the regularly scheduled meeting of the Executive Committee of the German Gardens Neighborhood Association.

He'd walked to Maria Voigt's home many times, mostly for a quick peek at Maria through her bedroom window, just above a low line of juniper shrubs. But tonight his mind was otherwise occupied on the short walk down Goebbels Street to Goering, then over to Hitler. It was chilly outside, but a nice evening in early April, the pink halo of a full moon quivering in the sky. The streets were quiet. The only sound was the clicking of his heels on the pavement. Lights glowed from inside tightly drawn curtains. Every so often, as a precaution, he turned his head to ensure he wasn't being followed. The FBI. The Gestapo.

What have I gotten myself into?

Kimmler turned onto Hitler Steet and crossed to number 80. He knocked on a metal storm door, monogrammed with a large aluminum letter *G*. Things were simpler, Kimmler thought, when Gans was still here. It was easier to keep his head on straight before Maria Voigt had been left in charge.

Maria opened the door, and Kimmler's eyes reflexively raked up and down her lush Aryan figure.

She scowled back at him.

"You're late," she snapped coldly.

Kimmler mumbled an apology.

She whirled around and headed back to the meeting. Kimmler followed her avidly. She looked like quite the modern American housewife, he thought, wearing blue gabardine slacks crimped at her small waist, then draping to wide cuffs at her ankles. The scent of her lavender perfume was positively heady.

His Margarite was a wonderful cook and a loving wife. But after all, a man has needs.

The meeting was in Maria's living room—what all of them would have called a parlor growing up—but was now a fine new creation of suburban America. The room was crowded with local residents, filling up every available seat and any number of bridge chairs they had hauled over from their own homes. A folding table featured heaping plates of food brought by several neighbors. Stuffed as he was, Kimmler helped himself to a plate of strudel and *schneewittchenkuchen* and slumped down against a wall near the back. As the meeting droned on—discussing what sorts of flowers should adorn the street corner boxes, the planned community dances and picnics, the celebration of the Fuhrer's birthday later that month—Kimmler found himself getting drowsy, barely able to keep his eyes open in the warm, comfortable room.

"Thank you all for coming. I hope we will continue to stand together as a German American community in these perilous times," Maria Voigt was purring now, as Kimmler fantasized happily about doing obscene things with her. "The executive committee will now go into session in the kitchen, please. *Danke schön,* and please return safely to your homes."

After an extended flurry of cheek-kissing and hand-shaking and chair-folding, the vast majority of the German Gardens Neighborhood Association made its way out into the night. That left only Kimmler, Voigt, and the four other members of the executive committee: Krieger, a fish deliveryman; Haiden, a butcher; Lutz, a court clerk; and Kuhn, a banker. *Good, upstanding Americans, productive Americans, hardworking Americans.* Yet in the kitchen, Kimmler knew, there would be no maps of playgrounds or sidewalk verges on the table. The community they were interested in was the Aryan race, and the neighborhood they intended to run was the United States.

Kimmler sloughed along into the Voigts' modest but spotlessly clean kitchen. Just as they walked in, the dark wooden cuckoo burst forth from the clock on the wall, distracting him from the two men who were already seated around the kitchen table. It took him an additional few seconds to focus on them—and by that time the others were behind him, blocking any possible bolt for the front door.

Only then did he really see the men at the table, large and broad-shouldered, with their hats and coats still on. He blinked once, then he recognized them.

The two, big brooding men who had walked into the Mermaid Inn. When he was with—

Kimmler immediately turned, as if to go.

"Pardon me—the bathroom—"

Maria stood in the doorway, the others right behind her. Unmoving.

"How was the steak?" one of the seated men asked, moving a toothpick about in the mouth. An unmistakably German accent in his voice.

Kimmler's eyes widened in panic. He knew he should say something, making some clever excuse. But all he could do was to emit a soft whimper, like a wounded animal. The men rose from their chairs, their shoulders looking broader than ever. Behind him, he could hear Maria lighting a cigarette.

"Kimmler, don't be so worried," *Frau* Voigt told him after she exhaled, the tendrils of smoke playing around his neck. "Nothing will happen to you. We simply need to know what you told those two American agents. Then everything will be fine, I assure you."

Kimmler summoned all the courage he had remaining, which was not much, to turn back to Maria, expecting to be blackjacked at any moment.

"*Es tut mir leid,*" was all he could think of to say. *I'm sorry.*

"What do they know about the operation?" repeated Maria.

"Nothing. I swear! It was my brother-in-law, Schaefer, that scoundrel. But I never told them anything! Just where I work."

"Who did those men work for, Kimmler? Was it the FBI?"

Viktor Kimmler began trembling, his eyes watering.

"Do they know that Einstein is coming to Long Island?"

"I never mentioned such a thing! I am a loyal German. I would never—"

"Do they know that an agent is coming from Berlin?"

"Please, I keep telling you—"

Maria rested a hand on his shoulder, caressing the leather of his jacket.

"Make it easy on yourself, Viktor. Tell us and we will protect you."

His desperation deepening, Viktor Kimmler found his tongue at last, continuing in a tremulous voice.

"I told Schaefer things. That's all! I would never tell anything to an American agent! It was Schaefer who told them I knew something. He was the one who set up the meeting—"

"We know you were at the meeting," Maria said, her voice like an ice dagger. "What did you say there?"

"Nothing! I—I was just trying to draw the agents out. Trying to find out what they knew, to see if I could send them off on the wrong track. I was using them. To learn about the FBI, don't you see—"

"Ah. So it *was* the FBI. Go on—what did you tell them?"

"*Nothing!* Yes, they suspect that we pass information...back home. But they already knew that. He knows nothing about Einstein. I was only being...clever. Or I thought I was."

Kimmler trailed off miserably, squeezing both hands together in front of his chest, almost in a sort of supplication.

"Wait here," Maria ordered abruptly, and led the "executive committee" back into the living room, where they spoke in whispers—leaving Kimmler's lunch companions to guard him.

"We have to inform Berlin," she told them, seething with

anger. "The operation will be cancelled. Kimmler has ruined us."

Lutz, the court clerk shook his head.

"Don't be hasty," he argued. "We don't know what, if anything, was revealed. Besides, Kimmler has no operational knowledge of the plan."

"Neither do we," the banker, Kuhn, noted.

"But the threat itself is enough to increase security around Einstein," Maria argued.

"Perhaps," Haiden nodded. "But we must trust our agent to find a way."

"Do not let the traitor win, Maria," Krieger pleaded. "This is our moment! Let us show them what we can do."

Maria paused, an idea forming in her head. She nodded and led them back into her kitchen.

"Let's go for a walk," she told Kimmler.

"*Please, Maria!*"

The curtains and shutters of the little community were all closed. German Gardens was not the sort of place where people poked their noses into official business.

The walk was brisk, with Viktor shuffling between Krieger and Hayden, an arm in each of their powerful, meaty paws. Kuhn and Lutz walked several paces behind. Maria marched ahead of them all, shining a flashlight carefully pointed down. There was little need for it. The recreational lake of Camp Siegfried shimmered black in the light of the full moon, its reflection bright enough to make their way along the shore.

Kimmler's panic only grew as they neared the lake.

"*Please* give me another chance," he continued to beg in a whisper, feeling his shoes sinking into the soft, wet sand landscaped around the edge of the lake. "Let me prove myself!"

"You have already proven yourself sufficiently, Viktor," Maria said calmly.

"I can help you. I know these FBI men. How they behave. I can provide important information—" he began to babble more loudly.

"Keep your voice down!"

"I will redeem myself! I will kill these FBI men. I'll—"

The shot rang across the lake. Kimmler's body fell back into the water with a splash.

At 8:57, the German Gardens Neighborhood Association meeting was officially adjourned.

Chapter Twenty-Seven

HARRY WEISS GLANCED AT THE PILES of passenger manifests in his office and wondered how it was possible that they were growing higher. For over a week he, Amos, and the rookie agent, Crowly, had combed through lists from every German ship that had arrived in New York, and they weren't making a dent.

In fact, the spring of 1939 had been a busy time for German passenger ships to America. The Norddeuttscher Lloyd Company dominated the trade. Harry and James had prioritized passenger lists from ships arriving from a German port in the past several weeks- there were eight in total: the *Hamburg, Bremen, Europa, Hansa, Columbus, Deutschland, Berlin* and *New York*. Tens of thousands of names had been reduced to just under ten thousand. It was a laborious, time-consuming process.

At exactly nine o'clock, Agent Edward Crowley knocked lightly on the open door and stepped in. Tucked under his arm was a thick manila folder.

Crowley was right out of Columbia University, and looked more like a first-year accounting clerk than federal agent. Slim, with a smooth pink face and blond hair slicked back on his scalp, and thick, black-framed eyeglasses that seemed to rest halfway down his nose. He looked nothing like Harry or James had looked when they joined the Bureau. Harry studied his eyes, earnest and wide. *Eyes that hadn't yet seen bodies dug up at chicken farms*, he thought, *or a man with his tongue cut out and a sign draped around his corpse*.

"How are you doing on the manifests?" James asked, nodding to the piles.

"So far, nothing stands out. No red flags. But I thought you should see this." He handed the file to James.

Inside was a dossier on Viktor Kimmler, compiled with the help of field office and the headquarters in Washington. His immigration permits—properly signed and stamped by the U.S. Consulate in Berlin on February 7, 1925—and Department of Labor work permits; copies of his New York State drivers and marriage licenses; records of his current and prior addresses; and a copy of his original job application at Seversky Aircraft Corporation, filled out in the labored cursive of a man uncomfortable with English. James flipped through it and shrugged. "Everything looks in order."

Crowley smiled coyly. "I got his job application from one of our agents watching the defense industry. He called a source at Seversky. Evidently, Kimmler quit."

James Amos felt a chill beginning to creep up his spine.

"Quit Seversky?"

"Yessir. He hasn't been in all week."

James Amos pushed the Oldsmobile down E. 84th Street toward Madison, with no time now to scout the location according to procedure. Harry noticed the same chilly-looking young newsie, in a thin sweater near the street corner, but there was no one else around. This time James parked, and they both sprang out of the Olds and headed directly for Schaefer's Fine Tobacco.

CLOSED

The sign had been hastily scrawled and taped with un-German crookedness to the closed front door of the shop. James banged on the door, while Harry cupped his hands against the plateglass window and peered inside. The room inside was dark and empty at midday, with no indication of where its proprietor was, or when he might be back. Fine cigars remained neatly aligned and wrapped inside the glass display counters, a row of foreign cigarette packages arrayed near the cash register. But no Schaefer.

"God *dammit*!" Harry cursed, then glanced reflexively in

James' direction, expecting the usual reprimand. But Amos looked even angrier than him—as if he might explode.

"Son of a bitch," was all he said.

Trying to contain himself, Weiss went over to the newsie. He fished a quarter out of his pocket and pressed it into the boy's hand. The boy's eyes went as wide as if it had been a diamond.

"You here every day, kid?"

The boy's lips parted, revealing a skinny discolored tongue and several missing teeth.

"Uh-huh."

Another quarter found its way into his palm.

"How long has the cigar store been shut?"

The boy shrugged, his eyes suspicious now, but genuinely trying to remember.

"I dunno. I guess all week."

A third quarter.

"You want to earn more?"

The boy nodded dumbly while Harry scribbled a phone number on a small, blank card and handed it over to him.

"You see anyone inside that store, anyone at all, you call me from the payphone. You understand me?"

The kid nodded again, and Harry forked over a fourth quarter,

"If I'm not there, you tell whoever picks up the phone what you've seen. You got it?"

The boy nodded again. Resisting the urge to tousle his hair or pinch his ear in the manner that so many adults loved to torture kids, Harry spit into his palm and solemnly shook hands with the boy, who had done the same. *It was now a contract among men.*

For good measure, he bought a copy of the *Herald-Tribune* from the boy and automatically glanced at the front page—the habit of a lifetime. Then he stopped, rooted to the sidewalk. The main headline was about how the Chamberlain government had announced military conscription for all English males aged twenty and twenty-one.

Back in the car, cruising slowly downtown, Harry and James

tried to dissect the situation.

"Looks like your Herr Schaefer's got the Catskill creeps," Amos said.

"Kimmler, too."

It wasn't uncommon for informants to vanish, temporarily. They would grow a conscience, or at least a healthy sense of fear about ratting out their associates, and disappear into the mountain resorts of the Catskills, or the Adirondacks. Often it was just their own paranoia. Sometimes it was a death threat that did the trick. Usually they would reappear on their own—though if they didn't, Harry and James might have to go pull them out of their upstate bungalow.

This was something different. Now they had two informants in the wind, who had vanished without a trace. It didn't look good.

"Now what?" Weiss asked bleakly.

James had no answer.

Chapter Twenty-Eight

ALL ROADS LED TO opening night at the World's Fair on April 30th.

On the new Grand Central Parkway, Maria Voigt inched forward in bumper-to-bumper traffic. She calculated at least another hour before she arrived at the fairgrounds. The news had reported that over five-hundred-thousand people were expected by the end of opening day. President Roosevelt had spoken earlier. At seven, Albert Einstein would commence the evening's festivities.

Maria studied the leaden sky. The weather forecast had called for thunderstorms, and she wondered whether Einstein's speech would be called off. In that case, it would be a wasted trip. She couldn't even visit the German Pavillion, which had been cancelled due to opposition to Hitler's invasion of Czechoslovakia. *No matter. What's an acre in Flushing when we're swallowing entire nations in Europe?*

On the seat next to her she'd tucked a Kodak Brownie camera.

Maria would be in the crowd, just another tourist. She'd take in the sites, shop for souvenirs, and, if Einstein's speech went ahead, record the size and strength of his security, the weapons they carried, signs of vulnerability, carelessness.

The Abwehr craved such details, after all.

On Route 1 in New Jersey, approaching the Holland Tunnel, Albert Einstein sat in the front seat of his 1937 Buick Century Sedan. He was running late for his own speech.

This was due mostly to his own frantic, last-minute packing of various necessities: clothing, books, journals, toothpaste for his extended vacation on Long Island. Plus his violin, sheet music, pipes, and tobacco. After everything was packed, he'd had the nagging feeling that he'd left something behind. Something important.

Einstein had wanted to do the driving, but Helen forbade it. The professor was still unpracticed on American roads, and his mind was prone to drift from a car in front of him to the far reaches of the universe. "With you behind the wheel, the Big Bang will be a collision at the next intersection," she told him.

For most of the ride they'd driven in silence, their mood seeming to fit the day, which was increasingly overcast. The rain clouds stretched ominously out ahead of them, like a distant range of hills. Only the rise of the Manhattan skyline lifted their spirits, the sight of such beautiful, monumental buildings always reminding Einstein of the possibilities of human endeavor.

"Have you practiced your speech?"

"What speech? More like a telegram, Mrs. Dukas."

Einstein shook his head in frustration. Grover Whalen, president of the Fair, had invited him to open the first night with a talk on cosmic rays. A talk that was to be limited to five minutes— hardly enough time to so much as scratch the surface of so complex a topic. His demands for additional time were declined, and he soon learned why. His brief comments were to be no more than the overture to a cheap publicity stunt. When he concluded, ten cosmic rays would be "captured" by the Hayden Planetarium in Manhattan. The arrival of each ray would trigger the ringing of a bell and the appearance of a band of light on the Trylon, the towering obelisk at the center of the fairground. When ten layers of light reached their apex, Einstein would press a button and the entire fairgrounds would illuminate in the world's first public demonstration of fluorescent lighting.

At least, that was the plan.

The sedan plunged into the darkness of the Holland Tunnel.

Harry Weiss and James Amos were riding a Greyhound tram across the fairgrounds to the Court of Peace, a seven-hundred-foot-long open-air plaza ringed with pavilions from over thirty countries. On one side, northeast, stood the imposing Federal Building, immediately behind the stage where Einstein would speak at seven. On the opposite end was a man-made lagoon and, beyond, the Trylon and Perisphere. The tram deposited them near the stage which, at the moment, was vacant.

They wandered, occasionally stopping to chat with several World's Fair police officers in uniforms festooned with bright orange Bakelite buttons. Everything was quiet, they were told. Too quiet, actually: damned weather had scared away the crowds.

They approached the stage where Einstein would speak in just over two hours.

"Damn. He'll be a sitting duck up there," said Harry.

"Hard to protect a man who doesn't want protection," James replied.

On Rodman Street in Flushing, a man stood in an endless line, waiting to pass through the Flushing Gate and pay seventy-five cents for admission to the Fair. He wore a bulky tan gabardine trench coat with wide lapels, deep pockets, and a belt cinched at the waist, and a brown fedora which he'd pulled low on his forehead. While the flood of visitors surged toward the ticket booths with giddy anticipation, he steeled himself—grim with determination.

He had work to do.

Just over an hour after leaving bucolic Princeton, The World of Tomorrow rose before Einstein and Dukas. A line of Art Deco and Art Moderne shapes stretched for miles across the flat horizon. Predominantly white, almost translucent, almost a mirage wavering along the skyline. Above it a swirl of thick charcoal clouds made it look all the more dramatic, and ominous. Despite themselves, it took their breath away.

"It appears that the World of Tomorrow is very gloomy," Einstein tried to joke.

As they approached, the two rather crazy thematic objects of the fair emerged, dominating the landscape. The towering obelisk that was the Trylon, with the low globe of the Perisphere beside it, both so dazzling white it was hard to look at them.

"Poor Freud! He would be amused to see this—a gigantic phallic symbol next to a woman's breast!" Einstein tried to jest again, but Mrs. Dukas only gave him a baleful look.

"The Trylon and the Perisphere are a reference to the American Crystal Palace, and the Latting Observatory tower, from the 1850s," she said primly. "If you insisted on delivering your speech, you might as well have read up about the Fair."

"Reading for the fair, reading for my citizenship exams. So much studying there is to do in America!" he told her with a smile, but Helen was lost in the darkening sky.

Maria had been careful to keep her distance from the site of Einstein's speech for as long as possible. She knew it would be crowded with police and undercover agents, just like Madison Square Garden back in February. Forty-five minutes before the scheduled start of the program, she stationed herself at the Schlitz Palm Garden, a large open-air restaurant and beer hall near Constitution Mall, where she nursed a Riesling. On the chair next to her she'd plunked her camera and a bag filled with souvenirs that fit into her cover as an enthusiastic fairgoer. It included, among other trinkets, a carefully studied official World's Fair Map, a blue and orange World's Fair silk scarf, a World's Fair souvenir pocket knife, and— from the Kodak exhibition—a set of official World's Fair binoculars. The binoculars had been particularly useful, allowing her to scan the stage where Einstein would deliver his address. Sure enough, it swarmed with security personnel.

A soft rumble of thunder sounded.

At 6:40, the man in the bulky trench coat began a slow walk across the grounds, conscious of the thunder. He pulled his collar up, plunged his hands into his deep pockets, and headed toward the stage.

James Amos heard the thunder as well, lifting his eyes to the clouds then quickly returning them to the long rows of empty seats where an audience was just beginning to gather. Thirty seats in each row, he counted, stretching to the distant lagoon.

He searched for someone with the right profile: lone male, Aryan features, occupying a seat that gave him the advantage of a clear shot and fast escape. Perhaps that young man thumbing through his guidebook; or the one sitting off to the side, hunched forward, eyes darting constantly. But when the man with the guidebook was joined by his souvenir-laden family and the one on the bench scampered after an attractive woman—who instantly rebuffed him—Amos realized the search was futile. The best he could do was protect Einstein from a threat by staying as close to him as possible.

"Gonna pour," Harry said, standing next to him.

"Maybe that's good," James replied. "Weather is keeping people away. Any assassin is going to want crowd cover."

All around Harry and James, there were posters with pictures of Einstein on them looking his very goofiest, along with huge letters promising,

"THE WORLD'S GREATEST SCIENTIST!
COSMIC RAYS! SILENT FIREWORKS!"

Somehow, it hadn't attracted a mob.

"I'll take the other side of the stage," Harry said, and walked away.

Maria found a seat where she could mix with the crowd while maintaining a clear view of the stage. She raised her camera and snapped photographs of the uniformed NYPD and World's Fair Police, the plainclothes detectives, and the FBI, rather easily identified by their cheap suits and distrustful eyes.

Except for the Negro she spotted just to the side of the stage. He was impeccably dressed and stood ramrod straight, like a soldier, she thought. She peered through her souvenir binoculars, bringing his face into view: midnight black eyes sweeping across each row, occasionally stopping, narrowing, before resuming their movement. She wondered what J. Edgar Hoover was thinking allowing Blacks and Jews into his ranks. There couldn't be many.

Maria swung the binoculars across the stage, skipping past the dignitaries and police until she found another second agent. She adjusted the focus dial, sharpening the image. A sharp nose, a shadow of stubble across his face, a short, stocky body in a rumpled suit and sloppily knotted tie.

A scar.

Is it possible? she whispered to herself, still peering through the binoculars.

An image flashed in her mind: The same man, standing in front of her in the ramp at Madison Square Garden. Rushing into the melee on the stage, dragging Isidore Greenbaum to safety.

She lowered the binoculars and aimed the camera. The shutter clicked loudly, punctuating the soft whine of approaching sirens.

It was the kind of fanfare Einstein disliked—a police motorcade escorting him into the fair. The Buick was surrounded by six motorcycles, lights flashing and sirens wailing as they crawled through the thick crowds. Helen leaned forward, locking her fingers around the steering wheel and occasionally blowing a nervous breath.

As they inched towards the stage, Einstein turned towards her and said, "It's a long drive to Long Island, Helen. The moment I finish, we will leave for the cottage. No photographs. No autographs. I want to be on my way."

Just as the motorcade approached the stage, James' heart began racing uncontrollably. The sirens wailed against his skull, forcing his eyes shut. His steely composure seemed as if it was washed away by a powerful wave of dread, coursing through his entire body.

It's happening again, he told himself. *Milwaukee. Theodore Roosevelt's car enveloped by the huge, cheering crowd. James, unable to move, while he had to watch that little man push forward and raise his gun—*

He managed several deep breaths, each one restoring his focus on the present moment. He decided to leave his position and check on Einstein's arrival behind the stage. The motorcycle police had dismounted and stood near the passenger door of the Buick as it opened. James saw the unmistakable halo of white hair, the compact body wrapped in an overcoat.

Einstein cocked his head at the sky and said, "The storm is coming."

As the professor was escorted up a set of improvised steps, James hurried back to his position.

Maria fixed the binoculars on Einstein as he appeared on the stage. The most important target in Germany jittered in the tiny lenses. Squinting at the blazing spotlights. Trying to smile as officials reached out to shake his hand and pound his shoulders and tug him to his chair. She scanned the stage, then the audience itself, until she noticed a lone figure standing at the edge of the crowd, wrapped in trench coat.

She quickly adjusted the focus. His face sharpened into view. *It's impossible*, she told herself as the shock set in. She left her seat.

A light drizzle began to fall just as Whalen, the fair's president, introduced Einstein. To James' relief some of the spectators began scrambling for shelter. Einstein stood at the microphone with a bemused smile, then began in his thick, almost indecipherable accent.

"If science, like art, is to perform its mission truly and fully, its achievements must enter not only superficiality, but with their inner meaning, into the consciousness of people...."

It began to drizzle harder and—as if on cue—a sudden wave of newspapers and guidebooks unfolded over people's heads as improvised umbrellas. James' chest tightened as he wondered just which one might conceal a weapon. Einstein's speech was droning on, almost incomprehensible.

Focus. Be alert.

Another peal of thunder.

The metallic echo of Einstein's voice through the loudspeakers.

James' eyes swept back and forth. Perhaps only Einstein himself could explain how five minutes might stretch and morph into an eternity.

He noticed Harry, on the other side of the stage, one foot thumping uneasily.

When Einstein finally concluded, the audience applauded lightly and Grover Whalen announced "a very special treat."

A voice boomed from public address system, "Give us ten cosmic rays."

Then: "Here comes the first ray!"

The first band of light hugged the base of the distant Trylon, behind the audience. They turned away from the stage to watch the spectacle.

"Two cosmic rays!"

A bell began to peal as additional tiers of light rose towards the apex of the Trylon.

"Three cosmic rays!" the loudspeakers blared.

The man dug his hand into his pocket and fingered the 45 caliber Colt. He knew nothing of cosmic rays or the inner meaning of science. *What difference did it make?* He was there not to learn but teach a lesson. To prove and redeem himself at the same time.

"Five...Six..."

He took the Colt out of his pocket. Held it in his right hand. Just then, out of the corner of his eye, he caught a figure rushing towards him like a coming wind, almost invisible.

"What are you doing here?" the wind whispered.

"Seven...Eight..."

The man gasped at the site of Maria Voigt, blocking his view of the stage. *How could she have known he'd be there? Did she have spies everywhere?*

"Move away. Let me prove myself!" he hissed.

"Nine...Ten!"

Einstein placed a hand on the switch that would ignite the nighttime lighting across the fair.

He threw the switch.

Amos was jolted by a roar of static from the loudspeakers. It lowered to a dying hiss, then silence. The fairgrounds plunged into complete darkness. Not even the flicker of a single light.

A blackout.

Einstein's flick of the switch had overloaded the electrical system.

Whalen turned frantically to his aides while Einstein chuckled at the confusion.

Then, a sudden ear-piercing whistle followed by an explosion thundering across the plaza.

"Gun!" James heard himself shout. He wrenched his revolver from his pocket and pointed it forward.

The audience rose, as one.

The sky ignited in fireworks of red, white, blue, illuminating the crowd. Like the flashbulb of a camera, revealing but blinding at the same time. James spotted a figure dropping like lead to the ground as a second figure dashed away. He rushed forward, gun in one hand, finally reaching the lifeless body. He discovered a gash in the man's neck, oozing warm blood down the wide collars of his trench coat. The Colt lay at his side.

James stared at the ash white face.

"Jesus Christ," he blasphemed.

Harry was now crouching at his side. "You okay?"

James looked up at him. "Jesus Christ," he repeated. "Look who it is."

Harry stared at the face. "Awwww, hell," he groaned. "Call an ambulance!"

Walther Schaefer's eyes remained open to the fireworks still lighting the sky.

The tobacconist Schaefer had been on the run since learning from his sister of the death of her husband, Viktor Kimmler. Viktor, she'd sobbed, had gone to a meeting of the German Gardens Neighborhood Association the night before. When he didn't return, she called Maria Voigt, who reported that Viktor hadn't shown up for the meeting. Voigt counseled her not to call the police ("It's always best for us to keep these things inside the community"), and promised that the Association would find out what happened. ("We have our own ways.") The next day, Maria called with tragic news: Viktor, it turned out, had been collaborating with the FBI. Evidently, wracked with guilt, he'd shot himself at the Upper Lake. ("No one need know the details. Haven't you been through enough already?") Of course, the German Gardens Emergency Fund would take good care of her.

("And one thing more—have you heard from your brother, Walther?")

Schaefer wasted no time. He grabbed the contents of the cash register, the gun he kept nearby, and a fistful of La Palina cigars. He instructed his wife to pack enough food and clothing for several weeks. When she asked why, he was forced to respond honestly.

"They killed Viktor and will come hunting for me."

She packed quickly.

They spent the first week in a motor lodge in upstate New York, near Bear Mountain. Schaefer paid up front, using an alias. He didn't leave the dingy room until it was time to relocate, always trying to remain a step ahead of the hunting party.

Lake George. Rochester. The Finger Lakes. Always under a different name, always locked and bolted inside, with the Colt in his pocket. Hardly sleeping, convinced that at any moment Maria Voigt herself would barge through the door and slaughter his wife and him. Descending deeper and deeper into an almost feral state.

One morning, at the Iroquois Motor Lodge on the outskirts of Utica, he heard on the bedside radio the news that the World's Fair was opening later that week, with President Roosevelt and Albert Einstein as speakers. He growled like a bear.

His mistake in the first place, he realized, was cooperating with the FBI agent, Weiss. Providing an occasional tip about a rumor heard in Yorkville. Or Yaphank. Then, allowing Weiss to convince him to bring Viktor to a meeting at the Mermaid Inn. With the Negro, Amos.

They'd promised to protect them! To pay a major reward! And what did he get? Viktor was dead and Walther was sharing a decrepit motel room with scampering cockroaches.

Scheiß auf sie!

Fuck them!

They'd tangled with the wrong man. Now the price must be paid.

If Einstein was speaking at the World's Fair, there was a good chance Amos and Weiss would be with him.

He would kill Einstein right in front of them. In front of the entire world!

Perhaps then Maria would forgive him. Even reward him. Smuggle him back to Germany!

And if he failed? If the police shot him dead before he killed the agents?

What's the difference? I am a dead man anyway.

Schaefer made out the vague forms of the two FBI agents hovering over him. He struggled to open his mouth, despite the fire raging beneath the opened skin of his neck.

Voigt, he wanted to say.

But the word was consumed by the fire, and the sky grew dark, and the World of Tomorrow came to an end.

Maria Voigt raced to the parking lot on Flushing Bay, taking one of several routes she'd memorized on her creased souvenir map. She drove the Willys carefully, observing every traffic rule to ensure she wasn't stopped. Only when she crossed into Suffolk County, nearly an hour later, did she relax her muscles, flooring the engine.

In her mind, she ran through each of the decisions she'd made at the Fair. Confronting Schaefer was an instant calculation. Her timing, she smiled, was a stroke of brilliance. The fireworks show was widely advertised and would easily divert the crowd as she approached him. The blackout? Pure luck. She'd used the cover of dark to thrust the penknife into Schaefer's throat, then removed it and fled. No evidence, no fingerprints.

As she neared Yaphank, she continued to grapple with Schaefer's motives. Einstein's assassination would have foiled the cat and the mouse at the same time: ending Berlin's operation to abduct the scientist and exacting revenge against the FBI that was supposed to protect Schaefer. She wondered whether she was giving him too much credit. It was either an act of strategic genius or primal madness.

Either way, he needed to be terminated.

She continued down a secluded road, past a neon sign that blinked "Yaphank Motor Court" against a scattering of darkened cottages. She was almost home.

For the second time, these two men—Schaefer and his brother-in-law Kimmler—had come close to ending her mission. And not just the mission, but her career. Had they succeeded, her reputation would have been sullied forever. Berlin would have relegated her to administering payroll for its network in New York while she sold tickets to propaganda flicks at the New Europe.

Now her superiors would know what she'd always known.

When pushed to her limits, Maria broke through. Like her car, now racing home at over eighty miles an hour.

Papa would be proud.

The rush was exhilarating,

Like the wind.

Chapter Twenty-Nine

ALBERT EINSTEIN WAS SO TRANSFIXED by the fireworks in the sky that he'd missed the scene that had erupted on the ground. When power was restored, the fluorescent lights bathed the fair in a garish, ghostly white.

James Amos had grabbed him by the arm and yanked him offstage. It wasn't until he was back in the passenger seat that Amos told him: a man, believed to be carrying a gun, had been killed only fifty feet from Einstein. A search was underway for the assailant.

"And you believe he was targeting me?" Einstein had asked.

"I do, Professor. I warned you about possible attempts on your life."

"The attempt failed. Again."

"All they need is one success."

"I'm on my way to the end of Long Island, Agent Amos. It will be hard for anyone to find me there."

"Don't go—"

Einstein rolled up the window. The motorcade raced away.

Three hours later, he was dreaming in the passenger seat of the Buick. *He was at his old job at the Swiss Patent Office in Bern, nearly thirty years earlier. Somehow Elsa was there, trying to capture his attention—trying, he sensed, to warn him—but the piles of applications, equations, and notes was an impenetrable wall between them. Then, outside the window, the sky erupted in fireworks, and thunder rolled.*

He was forced awake by the rumble of the Buick on a lonely, pitch-dark road that twisted along the shoreline of Little Hog Neck.

He blinked his eyes open.

From behind the wheel, Helen Dukas said, "You've been asleep most of the ride."

"Did I miss much?" Einstein asked, staring out the passenger seat window.

"Nothing at all."

The fragments of the dream gnawed at Einstein as they passed black marshes and an occasional cottage, barely discernible in a moonless field. The road curved around a narrow beach along a large black bay. The gears of the vehicle suddenly groaned and whined as it ascended a steep dirt road surrounded by thick foliage.

They finally pulled up to an isolated bluff overlooking a dark harbor, along Grove Road. Einstein exited the vehicle and stretched. In front of him was a lonely seaside bungalow with a modest veranda. A dormered window peeked from the center of a gray shingle roof. The property was heavily screened with maple trees and overgrown bushes. A dilapidated black jeep, streaked with dried mud, was parked at the side of the house. Einstein's eyes suddenly caught a few pinpricks of light twinkling in a great expanse of black below the bluff. He realized the lights came from boats rocking in the harbor, like a few flickering stars peeking through a cloudy black sky.

He inspected the house, shuffling barefoot from room to room. The home was rustic, musty. The wood floors were creaky. The plumbing old but seemingly functional. There were several bedrooms, a decently stocked library, a parlor furnished with shabby, upholstered furniture that looked twenty years old, and an office where he would work. The kitchen was spacious—faded yellow linoleum floors, faded yellow daffodil wallpaper, faded yellow-painted cabinets and countertops.

It was everything he could have dreamed of. Even more exciting: there, by the side of the house, was the *Tinef,* still secured to its boat trailer, delivered just as Helen had arranged.

"We are in the middle of nowhere," Helen remarked unhappily as she unpacked in the kitchen.

"It is exactly where I want to be," he responded. "Peace and quiet. At last."

The next morning, Albert Einstein's tranquility was interrupted by a stark realization.

He'd worn his dress shoes to the speech at the Fair, and left his sandals in Princeton.

"Can I go barefoot for the entire summer?" he asked Dukas at the breakfast table.

The thought appealed to Einstein. He hadn't come to Little Hog Neck to wear suits with neckties and Oxford shoes. He had come to walk around as he pleased. To feel the tickle of grass between his toes, the cool waves swashing around his ankles, the press of pebbles and shells against his soles.

To feel freedom.

Helen Dukas sighed at him.

"I believe you would strut around naked all day if nobody objected."

"And what is wrong with that? Especially when I am so irresistible!" he blinked at her, teasing. "Come, Helen, we'll take the jeep."

"I forbid you to get into that jalopy. We will take the Buick. And I'll drive."

Soon Helen Dukas was guiding the Buick Century sedan down into the town of Southold, on the North Fork, where she was looking to do some shopping for herself. She dropped Einstein off at something called Rothman's Department Store, which was more like what had always been called a general store, only with big aspirations.

Most of those came from David Rothman, the proprietor. Rothman was smiling, which he did constantly, but that morning he had reason: all the summer homes and beach cottages were opening up as city dwellers began their summer migration to their second homes and rented beach cottages. It looked to be the best season in years, since the start of the Depression. He expected the customers to start piling in any minute now. He placed an album on their wobbly old phonograph: Mozart's "Jupiter" Symphony. The record crackled for a moment, then the first exhilarating bars reverberated across the store, to the accompanying hum of three fans spinning from a tin ceiling.

The bell above the front door jangled. David looked to the customer. And froze.

Their first patron of the day was unmistakable. He wore wrinkled beige pants that were tied around his waist with a rope, a baggy, moth-bitten gray sweater, and black dress shoes on sockless feet. There was also that instantly recognizable snarl of white hair.

"Albert Einstein! In my store!" David gushed. "I heard you were staying here for the summer! Welcome, welcome!"

"Yes, I am told I am in Doc Moore's cottage," he replied.

Rothman rushed to turn off the phonograph. But Einstein insisted, "Please do not touch it. Leave it. Let it play. It is beautiful!" The professor closed his eyes and swayed rhythmically to the music. Then his eyes fluttered open, returning him to his present task. "Have you any sandals?"

Minutes later, Rothman rang up $1.50 for women's sandals—the only pair he had in Einstein's size. But the professor didn't seem to mind. He was already distracted by a display of musical instruments.

"Do you play?" asked Rothman.

"*Ja,* I play the fiddle, but I am only an amateur."

"Well so am I."

"One day we must play together."

"It would be a great honor, Professor."

"Ach, I have my fiddle. But no music."

"I will bring a selection, Professor."

Einstein turned towards the door, then hesitated.

"Do you sell lifejackets? For my sailboat?"

"What kind of boat do you have?"

"According to anyone who has ever sailed with me, the kind that needs a lifejacket."

PART III

MAY–JUL 1939

Chapter Thirty

EVEN IN SPRING, LAKE QUENZSEE remained frigid and gray as Gunther took his morning run on the footpath surrounding the water. The linden trees stood like shivering sentries. He enjoyed the bracing cold against his face, the burning in his lungs, the crunch of his Dassler running shoes against the hardened dirt path. It was May 1st, four days before Anton Gunther's departure for New York.

Every other element of his tactical training had focused on maintaining his cover, resisting interrogation, protecting his lie. Only the daily runs allowed him to be himself. Three loops around the frigid lake: ten kilometers. No false identity, no alternate personality. Just Gunther, alone on the quiet path, testing the limits of mind, muscles, heart. Since reporting to Quenzsee five weeks earlier, he'd improved his pace to a blistering forty minutes.

He charged forward.

After another kilometer and a half, his solitude was broken by the sudden *meep-meep* of a Volkswagen Beetle. He swung his head over his shoulder, maintaining pace, as the black vehicle rumbled from behind.

The driver bellowed, "Sir, please stop!"

Gunther slowed, giving up enough of the dirt path for the driver to pull next to him.

"Sir, I have orders to take you back."

Still jogging, face forward, Gunther panted, "Why?"

"An urgent briefing. I'm to drive you back immediately."

"I'll run."

Twenty minutes later Gunther entered a library, still in his gray sweatsuit. The small windowless room occupied a quiet wing of the villa, making it perfect for sensitive meetings. Floor-to-ceiling shelves displayed the frayed spines of books, some dating back a century. Faded rugs were strewn atop a dark parquet floor. An oil-painted portrait of the Fuhrer had been positioned above a fireplace.

At a small round table sat a man in a drab civilian suit. As soon as he saw him, Gunther knew there'd been a significant development. Helmut Swan was assigned operational management of Gunther's mission, reporting directly to Heinrich himself. And while Gunther regarded him as just another bureaucrat with no field experience, Swan was at least judicious in his planning, always craning his neck around curves that others missed. He was short and round, with bushy white hair and overgrown white eyebrows. *A snowball of a man,* Gunther thought.

"What's so important to interrupt my run?" Gunther asked as he sat.

"Your target," Swan said. "He was nearly killed yesterday."

Swan delivered a detailed account of the attempted assassination of Albert Einstein at the World's Fair a day earlier, highlighting how an astute field agent had neutralized the threat by a German emigrant named Walther Schaefer.

"What do we know about Schaefer?" Gunther asked.

"Left Germany for America in 1926. Never a cause for concern. Until recently, when he became an FBI informant." Swan ran his tongue across his upper lip, as if washing away the bitter revelation.

"Makes no sense," Gunther said. "If he was working with the FBI, why would he try to kill Einstein?"

"Just before our agent inserted a knife through his jugular, Schaefer mentioned that he was trying to prove himself. Perhaps he wanted to atone for his crimes. Regain our favor. More likely, the FBI cheated him out of whatever payment they promised for information."

"Have we assessed what information he might have passed on about my mission?"

"He could not have known much. But—" Swan removed a brown folder from a black leather attaché case, produced three freshly developed black and white photographs, and slid them across the table. "Our agent took these at the World's Fair, just before observing Schaefer."

Gunther studied the images. The first was instantly recognizable: Einstein at the microphone. The others were vaguely familiar: a black man, and a white man with inescapably Jewish features. "Who are they?" he asked.

Swan continued. "The two FBI agents were seen with Schaefer and his brother-in-law, Viktor Kimmler, weeks before the Fair. They have been turning up frequently at events. A source inside the FBI has told us that they have been assigned to investigate Party activities in New York. If you see them, if you believe at any point your mission is compromised, you are to notify your handler immediately."

Gunther focused on the images. So familiar. But where—

Christ. On the Westmoreland! The day Einstein arrived in America.

The scene replayed in his mind. The suspicious glance by the Negro. The young cop confronting him. The hurried knife plunged into his chest.

He placed the photos in the envelope and left Swan alone in the library.

He went to his small room on the third floor. It had been comfortable enough, drafty though it was. There was an unusable fireplace, two large windows overlooking the lake, a small wooden table for meals, a writing desk and a large four-poster bed. It didn't matter. Gunther made it a rule never to complain. That was, after all, part of the job—dealing with whatever came his way.

Bookshelves spanned the wall opposite his four-poster bed. They were crammed with volumes and bound newspaper clippings on Leo Szilard, I.I. Rabi, Gerhardt Zwick, Enrico Fermi. There were two entire shelves with titles on Albert Einstein, including his best-known works: *Relativity: The Special and the General Theory* and *The World as I See It*. There were also Yiddish- and English-language books. Cipher books. Operating manuals for the new Leica cameras, for tape recorders, and for the weapons he would require. There were routes to safe houses; stacks of roadmaps for New Jersey, New York, and Long Island; railroad and subway schedules; and maritime maps of the bays and harbors across Long Island.

Most importantly there was a biography of Max Goldschmidt, to remind him of the most granular details of his own self. It was a fictional masterpiece.

He placed the photos from the World's Fair on the desk, stripped off his jogging suit, and stepped into the bathroom, studying himself in a full-length mirror. He was satisfied with how his cheeks were hollowing out, and how his neck was thinning again. When he inhaled, he could see the faint outline of his ribs. But the sleek muscle tone in his upper arms remained a problem. He would have to be sure to keep them covered in America—or to make up a good story.

He entered the shower and turned the faucet, lifted his head towards the spigot, let the water splash against his face. Gunther enjoyed showers. He strongly believed in the Aryan imperative of racial hygiene. But, he wondered, as a poor refugee, would baths and showers be a luxury in America? He couldn't appear too well groomed, after all.

He stepped out of the shower, briskly dried himself off, and dressed: black wool pants and a cashmere black turtleneck sweater. He left his hair wet and uncombed— slovenly, like Max. Slowly, he felt his old tormentor possessing his body again. Things like the cashmere sweater were much too good for his alter ego, he knew. Like the showers, he enjoyed them while he could.

Gunther seated himself on a chair, looked out the window, then closed his eyes and let the image in view gradually solidify in his mind, like the deliberate development of a photographic print. He visualized the high stone wall surrounding the villa, the trees hugging the lake, the flat farms stretching to Brandenburg, only three miles away.

Since arriving at Quenzsee he'd recorded the image in his mind every morning, noting how each unique sunrise changed the landscape, producing near-infinite variations: the stone wall pink or orange or flat white, the icy lake blue, gray, or black. Compartmentalizing every image in that vast photographic memory. Once on the mission, consumed by his new identity, he would summon these images, like a slide show, as a reminder of the country that awaited his return.

His revelries were cut short by a knock on his door.

Another tedious briefing.

It takes a chameleon about twenty seconds, depending on a variety of factors, to reflect wavelengths of light through their skin and change colors. Anton Gunther's metamorphosis was taking longer.

His first psychological briefing by Dr. Kurt Kemper, only a week after arriving, had truly tested Gunther's patience. Today was no different. *Every minute detail,* insisted the young doctor, *had to be unquestionable.*

Kemper was young, with thick brown hair brushed back above a high forehead, boyish eyes, and a polite smile. He was in charge of a little known *Abwehr* unit that composed psychological profiles of foreign leaders and other persons of interest to the Reich. For Gunther, this was almost worse than useless. To think that you knew someone before you met them was merely to influence yourself in one way or another. The trick was to read those you encountered. To work your way into their minds and pick up on every unconscious cue: the twitch of a muscle, the intonation of language, the shape and direction of the eyes.

But Kemper carried on, reading party propaganda at Gunther from a thin report he pulled out of a sleek, black briefcase.

"The subject, Einstein, exhibits deviant behavior in a number of areas and may have been born with neurological disorders. As a child his language skill development was slow—"

"Please, Doctor, shall we skip to more recent analyses?" Gunther interrupted him.

"Of course." Kemper flipped through the report, looking rather nettled.

"Einstein seals his emotions in two activities in particular: music and sailing. He even has a name for his violin, Lila. Quite abnormal, I would say. As for sailing, it is where he retreats when he needs solitude and comfort. This is important. These are his sanctuaries. If you can find a way to share them, you will have achieved an intimate bond. Any doubts he may have had will vanish."

"According to what I have read, his sailing skills are considered to be rather poor."

"As long as your skills are better, you will be in no danger," affirmed Kemper.

"Anything else?"

"Einstein has several vulnerabilities which may be exploited. He is drawn to the weaker among us. A compulsion, actually, to assist those he believes are powerless. He spends much of his time advocating on behalf of Jewish refugees. Pressuring the American government to liberalize their immigration policies."

Gunther had grasped it immediately: "He is vulnerable to the vulnerable." *To someone like Max Goldschmidt.*

"I will leave you with the written evaluation. If there are any questions—"

"I will contact you. Thank you."

The psychologist offered his polite smile and rose from his chair. He took a few steps towards the door, then turned.

"May I ask a question?"

Gunther nodded.

"I don't know the details of your mission. But, if you are being sent to kill Einstein…well, this is rather crude, I suppose. But it would be fascinating to study."

"You're not making sense, Doctor."

"His brain. Some believe that Einstein's brain is considerably larger than a normal human brain. It would be a major contribution to the advancement of science if we could…examine it. Again, only in the event you kill him."

"*Guten Tag, Herr Doktor*," Max sighed.

The practice interrogations were just as annoying.

It was late in Gunther's final week now, and the interrogator had still begun by asking his name, as he did in every session.

"This is a waste of time," replied Gunther. "All very basic. Let's move on."

"Name," the man repeated.

Gunther sighed, annoyed. "Very well. Max Goldschmidt."

"Born where?"

"Salzburg."

"When?"

"Twenty-one February, 1905."

The interrogation trainer kept his eyes glued to Anton Gunther, who sneered back at him. He had the dull, glazed eyes and slumped spine of a bureaucrat, with unkept gray hair and a cockeyed bow tie above his dowdy brown vest. Eyes a little red from a few too many nights enlivened by schnapps or wine.

They were seated across from each other at the small table in Gunther's room. Whatever the man ate for lunch—herring and onion, Anton assumed—was rank in the still air. His eyes strayed out the window at the Quenzsee Lake. He should be there, he knew, getting in some more sailing practice before he began his mission. The details of Max Goldschmidt he already knew by heart.

"What synagogue did you attend?"

"In Austria or Germany?"

"Both."

Anton sighed again. "I did not attend synagogue in Salzburg. In Berlin, I went to the Neue Synagogue. But only on the Holy Days."

"On Friedland Strasse?"

"Everyone knows the Neue Synagogue is on Oranienburger Strasse."

"What was your most recent employ?"

"I was the office boy—uh, office *assistant*—for Professor Gerhard Zwick. At the Friedrich Wilhelm University." Despite the tedium, he enjoyed this pathetic little improvisation. They would hear him trying to give his title more dignity and pity and underestimate him all the more. *Just what he needed.* Gunther began to relax his resistance, to assume Max Goldschmidt's voice and cadence.

"In the atomic physics building?"

"There was no atomic physics building. It was simply the physics building."

"Yes, on the north side of the courtyard."

"Correct."

"And how did you, a Jew, get such a job?"

"I had a friend. A university student. He took pity on me and recommended me to Dr. Zwick. Of course, it was very menial work."

"So menial that Zwick entrusted you with the delivery of a musical composition to the United States? How exactly did that happen?" The trainer's voice was full of disbelief, working to project authority and skepticism as Anton Gunther melted into Max Goldschmidt before him.

"The night of the arrest, the Professor asked me to take it to the *Reichspost*. He said it was urgent that it be sent to Professor Szilard, in New York. But I arrived late. It had closed. So I returned to the University…"

"And?"

"The Professor's office was empty. A security guard told me that that the Gestapo had taken him away…"

Tears stung his eyes.

"Why are you crying?"

"I panicked. I thought they were going to arrest me next. I have a friend who had certain contacts in the Jewish underground. They arranged my escape and insisted that I deliver the music."

He shook his head, wiped his runny nose.

"I stayed in cellars, traveled by night. They got me to Hamburg, where I was smuggled out in the hold of a ship. God, the smell of it—I was seasick for days!"

"And then?"

"The boat got me to Helsinki. Then there was another one to Norway, then England. Then, here."

"And you expect me to believe that this whole time, you never looked in the envelope with Zwick's message?"

"Quite the contrary! I looked at it many times. I'd played it several times with the Professor."

Abruptly, the interrogator changed the subject.

"Do you like to sail, Mr. Goldschmidt?"

"Yes, I used to sail on the Scharfe Lanke."

"Where did you learn?"

"At the Westphal Marina."

"When?"

"In 1935."

The trainer looked up from his notes. "You are sure?"

"Max" glared at his interrogator, while the gears in his mind clicked back over the response. Westphal Marina. At the northwest corner of the Lake. He'd been there many times, though not in the past several years. *Another trick question, designed to pierce his cover.* He was losing his patience again.

"No, no," he said, careful to stay in Max's persona, humble and cur-ish. "I remember I took sailing lessons at the Westphal Marina. In 1935. Yes. I have sailed Scharfenberg Lanke many times!"

"But—"

They were interrupted by the sudden, uninvited opening of the door.

"*Guten Tag*," declared Reinhard Heydrich as he entered the room.

Gunther stood and issued a reflexive Hitler salute. Heydrich waved it away. He was wearing an immaculate, black SS uniform, the cap with its death's-head insignia worn at a rakish angle. Tucked under one arm was a violin case, and from his tunic he pulled a copy of *Two Scientists Debate*.

"I wasn't told you were coming," Gunther said.

"I find that surprise visits are the most fruitful," Heydrich responded. "How are you getting on?"

"If I may be honest, I'd like to get out of here and to America. I'm ready."

"Soon enough," Heydrich replied. "In the meantime, let's see how much progress you've made." He waved the manuscript at Gunther. "It's a most curious piece."

Gunther picked up his own violin case—or rather Max's case—scarred leather with a threadbare handle and two latches on opposite corners. He pulled out the cheap, battered instrument he dutifully lugged along whenever Professor Zwick wanted to play, and which he had practice enough on to even become surprisingly proficient.

"Of course, I had the best decoders from the *Abwehr* inspect it for any possibility of a message," Heydrich told him as they tuned and plucked at their strings. "They came up with nothing, other than the usual amateur mistakes. A complete lack of form. Imagination over technicality. A clear example of why we have forbidden such cultural impurity. Shall we suffer together?"

They played the latest version of the scientists' correspondence together again, over the next half-hour. It was a difficult piece—daunting, obscure, amateurish, but strangely complex. Gunther had long ago given up on trying to figure it out. Now he just tried to keep up with Heydrich on Max's vastly inferior instrument—and was pleased to see that he could.

"Curious," the master repeated when they were done. "Perhaps it is just the senile ramblings of two old men. Or perhaps we should not be surprised that not even two of the greatest Jewish minds could fool the *Abwehr*, hmm? Well, with any luck, we shall soon have *Herr Dokter* Einstein at closer quarters to ask him. Or perhaps the secret will die with him."

Heydrich turned a rare, beneficent smile on his pupil.

"Thank God for you, Chameleon. There aren't many of us who can pass as a Jew and also play the violin."

Gunther knew it was meant as a compliment, but it annoyed him. "Remember our conversation, *Reichsfuhrer,* in your office? I told you how tired I am of playing these Jewish roles. When I return home, I will be finished with Max Goldschmidt, yes?"

Heydrich nodded slowly. "The war will be here by the fall, at the latest. The Fuhrer will wipe Poland from the map. Whether that leads to a bigger war...the democracies all screeched like old women when he scooped up what was left of Czechoslovakia, but they did nothing. In any case, come what will, your mission, Anton, may well decide everything. As I said, you go to America as a Jew, you return a hero."

"I will do my best for Germany, and for the Fuhrer, *mein Herr.*"

"I have no doubts, Anton."

Later that night, after another long day studying maps and transportation routes and Yiddish and English and physics, Gunther returned to his room. He'd already worked through most of the books about Einstein on the shelves. He was reminded of the distant days in the orphanage, when he'd be found asleep in a chair in the early mornings, a book opened on his lap. He chose one now and sat to read through it once again, committing every detail to memory, forming an intimacy with his target.

The predator, studying, stalking his unsuspecting prey. Registering its behaviors, movements, and vulnerabilities. The prey that had been so close, over five years before, without even realizing he was there.

He studied the photographs from the World's Fair.

Einstein. Harry Weiss. James Amos.

"I'm coming," he whispered.

Chapter Thirty-One

THREE DAYS AFTER THE INCIDENT at the World's Fair, Weiss and Amos were at their desks in Foley Square. A gloomy gray drizzle had descended outside. It seemed just as gloomy inside.

There'd been occasions in both of their careers when leads had dried up and shriveled, and the case had turned cold. But this one was different: an informant had been killed right in front of them, the killer unidentified. And then there was Albert Einstein, still entirely unwilling to cooperate, even after an attempt on his life.

James rubbed his chin and ran through it again.

One informant was missing—Viktor Kimmler—and likely dead, Amos thought. The other—Schaefer—dead for sure. No one apprehended it. Not a single red flag suggesting the possibility of a German agent from their scouring of thousands of names on passenger manifests.

Across the room, Harry was absorbed in the official police report on Walther Schaefer's death.

Fifty-two-year-old male...five feet, ten inches...Naturalized American...no prior record...observed drawing a weapon and aiming at Einstein before the blackout... killed by an unknown assailant...penknife to the neck, wound diameter of 1.5cm...carotid artery severed...victim dead in minutes. Harry flipped the report on his desk and broke the silence.

"This much is clear: someone wanted to keep both Kimmler and Schaefer quiet. Whoever it is, they have shown their capabilities. This isn't that radio show, *Amateur Hour*."

"But we still don't know whether the agent is here, in Germany, or somewhere in-between," James replied. "Or, for that matter, whether there *is* an agent. We shouldn't be ruling out the possibility that this entire operation is a misdirection, planted with Kimmler and Schaefer to test our reaction, or distract us from something else. We're still dealing with more questions than answers."

"We have a pretty clear idea of who might have some answers. Let's get search warrants and start kicking in doors on Hitler Street, starting with Maria Voigt's. We have probable cause."

"Maybe," said James. "But we'd need approvals and then approvals of the approvals before we even get near the right judge."

"James, I'm glad you're finally understanding how the bureaucracy works."

James smiled vaguely before resuming the rubbing of his chin. "Schaefer told us Voigt uses a radio to receive instructions from Berlin. If that's true, she could lead us to some bigger fish."

"Hoover would just love that."

"But we need a smart strategy. We don't want to spook her. I say we test her and see how she reacts. Knock politely on her door for a chat."

"I'd rather smash it in," Harry joked.

"One more thing," James said. "The only thing we do know for sure is that Einstein is sitting on a bluff over the bay, like a duck oblivious to its hunter."

"We'll get him a local security detail."

"He won't like it. The Nazis tried to kill him in Belgium. The Queen herself put twenty-four-hour guards around him. And he gave them the slip to take his cherished walks."

James pressed the button on the intercom that sat on his desk and called for Agent Crowley. He appeared a minute later, beaming at the summons.

"Get me a file on the Chief of Police where Einstein is staying," Amos ordered. "And call him. Tell him we need to see him. Today."

"Yessir."

They left before ten o'clock. James carried a manila folder with the Bureau's records on Southold Police Chief Phineas Murphy.

The Oldsmobile lumbered east, wipers squawking against the rain-splattered front windshield, past the Perisphere and Tyron—which were shrouded in a thick, gray mist—past the great estates of the north shore owned by Vanderbilts and Pratts and Fields and Whitneys. They spent the time chatting about the news that Lou Gehrig's major league record for consecutive games played had ended; the speech by Hitler, days earlier, claiming that an "international clique of war agitators" was encircling Germany; the newspaper article, that very morning, about a Gallup Poll that found that 84 percent of Americans believed the United States should stay out of a European war.

And as they drove past a sign pointing to a place called Oyster Bay, Harry noticed his partner fall suddenly silent, his fingers tightening around the steering wheel.

"You alright?" asked Harry.

James forced a smile. "Of course."

"You know, I'm a pretty good agent, James. I can tell when someone's stonewalling."

James decided not to point out the same about Harry bottling up his anxiety whenever they neared a body of water. He sighed loudly. "Oyster Bay is where President Roosevelt lived. Place called Sagamore Hill. Last time I visited was the night he died. I was with him."

"Jeez."

James sighed deeply. "After he was shot, in Milwaukee, he ordered us to take him to his speech. The minute it ended, I insisted that we go to the hospital. X-Ray showed a 32-caliber bullet lodged in his chest, close to the pleura. Doctors said it'd be less dangerous to leave it in place than attempt to remove it. He carried that damned bullet with him for the rest of his life."

"Nothing you could have done—"

"Seven years later, around Christmas, Mrs. Roosevelt called me. Told me the president was ill, and he'd asked that I care for him. So I packed a grip and rushed to Oyster Bay. As soon as I saw him, I knew he was dying. As if the light had gone out of his life. He wasn't the same man. That night I gave him a bath, and I could feel his pain. Then I took him upstairs, to bed." Amos's voice tightened.

"I lifted him into that bed like he was a child. He asked me to turn out the light. I did, but something told me, 'Don't leave him alone. You stay close—not like in Milwaukee.'"

James paused, took a hand off the steering wheel and rubbed his wet eyes.

"So, I stayed put. Guarding him. A while later, I heard his breathing change. Like no breathing I've ever heard. Whistling, gasping. Fast, then slow. Like he was fighting death. All I could do was stand by him. Then, nothing. Lungs stopped working. Roosevelt died with that bullet still in his chest. To this day, I wonder if it weakened him, had anything to do with his lungs, at the very end."

Harry glanced at James. He wanted to tell James that he was being foolish, that there was no connection between the assassination attempt in Milwaukee and the death of Theodore Roosevelt, that he couldn't allow something that occurred so long ago to affect him now. But he thought better of it. After all, there was that scar above his eye.

"Don't worry, James. We'll get the son of a bitch. Before he can do any harm to Einstein."

The rest of the ride was silent.

Chapter Thirty-Two

MARIA VOIGT KNEW THAT Walther Schaefer's death would invite unwelcome attention from the police. But America was a free country, after all. There were rules, principles, procedures that ensured that the government acted fairly. One's property was protected from searches and seizures. One couldn't simply be plucked off the street, beaten in an interrogation room, and thrown into a prison cell for the rest of one's life.

Not yet, at least.

In the aftermath of her visit to the World's Fair, she sanitized her home for any hint of her mission. The Afus radio in her closet was placed in a wooden crate and packed into Krieger's fish truck, which traveled across Long Island to New Jersey every day. Her ciphers and code books were temporarily hidden among the books at the clubhouse library near the lake, ready to be relocated at a moment's notice. Any police search of her home would reveal that Maria Voigt was simply a good American, living quietly in a good American town, harboring only one secret: the pistol she kept in her pocketbook. It could be easily explained as an excessive precaution—and her constitutional right. A beautiful woman alone in the house required such safeguards.

Her instincts were confirmed when she heard a car pull up to her curb, footsteps up the drive, a businesslike knock on her front door. She glanced at the bathroom mirror and took a deep breath. She purged the details of her conversations with Berlin and the meticulous plans that crowded her mind, replaced them with the lessons she'd learned from Mr. Gans about encounters with law enforcement. She wore a bright smile as she opened the door, and there they were: the two FBI agents from her photographs at the fair now standing on her front lawn.

She greeted them, wondering whether the Jew with the scar would recognize her. If he did, he gave no sign of it. He was either clever or not entirely perceptive. She couldn't know.

She allowed the agents to identify themselves—Agents James Amos and Harry Weiss—flashing their badges as if to intimidate her, she thought.

"Have I done something wrong?" she asked innocently.

"We just have a few questions," said the Negro agent. "Might be better if we came inside."

She ushered them to the kitchen table and politely offered them water, which they just as politely declined. She noticed how Agent Amos's eyes bored into her, while the Jew's seemed to dart frenetically around the kitchen.

She silently recited what she'd learned from training with Gans. *Show them confidence. Control the time. Make them work. And don't overexplain—that's what liars do.*

"May I have a cigarette?" she asked.

Amos nodded.

Maria retrieved her pocketbook from the kitchen counter and brought it to the table with a small glass ashtray. The agents watched as she fished for a packet of Lucky Strikes, unaware as her fingers encountered the grip of the Lugar. She pulled out a cigarette, lit it, and blew out a ring of smoke. "I am happy to answer your questions, however, I do have an appointment at the clubhouse. At 12:30."

"What's on the agenda?" Harry asked snidely.

"Our Decoration Day Planning Committee is organizing a patriotic ceremony."

"I can tell from all the swastika flags," Harry snapped.

She was pleased. His emotions were controlling him.

James interceded. "Ms. Voigt, I'd like to ask you about your neighbor, Viktor Kimmler."

Maria sat, perfectly still, looking back at him.

"The Suffolk County police have been here several times. I

answered all of their questions."

"Answer ours," said Harry.

She shrugged. "Of course I knew Kimmler. Everyone in our community knew him. As I told the police, he was quite troubled."

"Troubled in what way?"

Maria tapped some ashes from the cigarette into the glass tray. "He invented stories. Exaggerated. Would you believe he was working directly for the Fuhrer himself, in America? Passing military secrets to him? While at the same time working secretly for Mr. Hoover?"

"He told you this?"

"Particularly when he drank. And he spoke often of the profits he made by convincing others that his absurd secrets were true. And you might ask the neighbors about his little perversion. Peeking through my window late at night. I hope you didn't fall for his stories and spend any of our taxpayers' money on such an uncredible source."

James continued. "What about Walther Schaefer? You know him?"

"Only by name. He's Viktor's brother-in-law. The two wives are sisters, no?"

"Where is he now?" asked Harry.

"As I said, I know him only by name."

Such ridiculous tactics, she thought. Maybe there was nothing to worry about—surely the FBI could have spared someone competent if they thought there was a threat.

Amos leaned forward and cupped his hands on the table. "Are you in regular contact with Berlin?"

"Of course."

"Can you describe the nature of those contacts?"

She took another languid drag on the cigarette. "My aunt and her family. Is that illegal?"

"How do you communicate?"

"Correspondence."

"Never by radio," Harry asked. "To your dear aunt?"

Maria blinked at him, pretending to be perplexed. "How would I do that?"

"You tell us."

"You're free to look around. For a radio, or anything else Viktor Kimmler's imagination concocted."

James smiled. "We may take you up on that."

Harry asked, "Do you consider yourself a patriotic American?"

"Red, white, and blue."

"Funny kind of patriotism. You want an America with no one but your kind. No one but Nordics or Aryans. Everyone else—out."

"My beliefs are not a secret, Agent Weiss. Is my patriotism to be impugned, just because I believe in white supremacy? You know, the race laws in Germany are much less strict than in the American South. Down there, just one drop makes you a Negro!" She stared at James, evaluating whether she'd found a way to rattle him. But he sat, fingers laced, emotionless.

Harry continued. "You remember me, don't you Mrs. Voigt? From that Nazi rally at Madison Square Garden? In the tunnel." He couldn't resist a slight smile.

"I don't recall," she lied, masking any sign of being impressed.

"That was quite a show," Harry continued. "The Jew bashing. The attacks on the President. Who are you more loyal to, Ms. Voigt? Germany or America?"

"What a question! I am a loyal American citizen, Agent. I support close ties between the United States and my country of national origin, just like countless Anglo- or Irish-Americans. Do Jews feel the same way about *their* countries of origin, Agent Weiss? But maybe that's what really leads to all the unnecessary strife in the world today—a lack of national pride." She looked at the cuckoo-clock on the wall, ticking back and forth. "Now, as I said, I do have an appointment. Decoration Day—"

"Then let's be a little more direct with each other," Amos said. "Is it true that you and others in German Gardens are conspiring with a foreign government? To threaten a leading scientist here in the United States?"

She cackled. "Absurd. Also, not true."

Maria stabbed the cigarette in the tray. "But since we're being direct, I have a question for you. You come to the home of a law-abiding citizen. You practically accuse me of a crime, interrogate me in my own kitchen. Would it be fair to say these were what people like you call might call Gestapo tactics?"

Harry leaned back in his chair and hissed, "Cute."

"I am going to exercise my rights now and ask you to leave my home. Unless you'd like to look around. I have nothing to hide."

"As soon I saw her, I remembered her from Madison Square Garden," Harry reported when they returned to the car. "Back then, she looked insulted to be so close to a Jew. Today, though, she was cool as a cucumber."

"Still, she got the message. Now it's just a matter of watching her next steps. Let's go see the police chief. Murphy."

"Yeah, first we need to make a stop."

"Where?"

Harry grinned. "You gotta know how to handle these local police yokels. Let's find a liquor store."

Chapter Thirty-Three

SOUTHOLD POLICE HEADQUARTERS was thirty miles east of German Gardens, which, to Harry Weiss' mind, was the best thing that could be said for it. The one-story brick building consisted of three rooms and two jail cells and didn't seem particularly overtaxed by crime. When he and James walked in, they found a constable leaning back in a chair, feet propped on his desk, engrossed in the April edition of *Dime Store Detective.* A ceiling fan spun lazily from a tin ceiling.

Harry nestled a crinkled brown paper bag against his chest. James asked to see Chief Murphy, adding that his office, the FBI, had called earlier.

The constable whisked his feet from the desk and sprang up like a jack-in-the-box.

He introduced himself as Constable Krupski. His hair was a tangled mane of copper red. Light freckles seemed splattered across his cheeks and the bridge of his nose. "Right this way," he declared, escorting them down a narrow hall as if leading dignitaries in a town parade.

They found Chief Phineas Murphy in his office. It was disordered, as if a hurricane had swept through. A file cabinet stood against a wall, drawers yawning open. Rifles leaned haphazardly in a wall rack. An oak-framed notice board displayed several "Wanted" posters, including John Dillinger, who'd been killed in a shootout five years earlier. The only hint of organization was a line of fishing poles, propped upright near a window.

Murphy was leaning back behind a desk that seemed too small for his considerable girth. He was heavy-set, with a barrel chest, silver hair, a silver walrus mustache that drooped slightly over his top lip, and a bulbous red nose. He stared curiously at James.

"No one said anything about a Negro agent. How 'bout that!"

Amos smiled politely. It was his universal language.

Harry removed a bottle of scotch from the bag and placed it on the desk.

"What's that?" Murphy asked in a low rasp.

"Oh, I just wanted you to have this as a token of our appreciation—"

Murphy's eyes seemed to burn. "I don't know what you think about how we do business out here. God knows, you're probably right about how it is in some places. But I don't take payoffs—not even penny-ante, small-timer payoffs like that."

Harry felt like an idiot. James contained a smile.

"I'm sorry, Chief, I—"

Murphy held up a hand; wagged a thick finger, silencing Harry. He rose from his chair and limped to the file cabinet. James remembered reading in his file how he'd been shot through the hip during the War. He made it to a large cabinet, rummaged through a drawer, and produced a bottle of Jameson's.

"Nothin' wrong with a drink, so long as it's honest. How many glasses?"

"I don't touch the stuff." James added.

Murphy asked Harry, "You want ice? Because if you want ice, you ain't getting fucking good Irish whiskey. You can use it with that scotch you brought along."

"I don't want ice."

"Good," he said, pouring out two healthy shots. "Because this is a good sipping whiskey, and we're going to sit here and sip it like goddamned gentlemen. Here's to crime."

They clinked glasses.

Harry felt fortified.

"Now what do our fine federal partners need?" Murphy asked.

Amos stepped in. "We could use assistance in keeping an eye on Albert Einstein. He's staying—"

"Doc Moore's Cottage on Little Hog Neck. No one gets in or

out of this town without me knowing."

"We have information that the German Gardens community, over in Yaphank—well, maybe some elements of that community—may be planning to…"

Chief Murphy's countenance darkened like a storm cloud rolling off the Long Island Sound.

"Those folks—I don't like what they got going over there. Especially with that Camp Siegfried."

"The kids' summer camp?" Harry asked.

Murphy nodded.

"It's more than kid stuff they get up to. Every weekend in the summer is a big beer party over there, with all those people they bring out there drivin' drunk, gettin' into brawls. Marchin' around saluting that asshole over in Germany. But as you might've surmised, I got nothin' against a man havin' a drink, *per se*."

"It's more than that?" James raised an eyebrow.

Phineas Murphy moved a little closer to him over the desk and nodded.

"You should see the things that go on out there. They're encouragin' all the teenagers out at that camp to go ahead and copulate, so they can make more little Aryans," Murphy said, his voice quietly furious. "And if they won't do it, they make 'em do it! Hell, at least two, three times a weekend in the summer, there's a coupla girls comin' all this way lookin' for help. They call it 'physical culture' over there—physical culture my ass, it sounds like rape to me."

"Me too," Harry said, his lip curling back.

"Look, it's not just because I got this back at the Argonne," the chief said, slapping his hip. "I got nothing against Germans—good, decent German Americans. But these people."

He shook his head.

"We had two sources tell us that individuals based in German Gardens may be planning some kind of attack on Einstein," James reported.

"Wouldn't surprise me in the least. I'll post Constable Krupski on Einstein's front porch."

"We'd be grateful," said James.

Harry asked, "Chief, you ever hear the name, Maria Voigt? Lives in German Gardens?"

"Can't say that I have," Murphy said, shaking his head. "They keep the women in the background, like they're the damned Mennonites or somethin'."

"Our sources told us that she may be involved in the plot. We're putting her under surveillance."

"Good luck with that!" Murphy chortled. "You'll stick out like a sore thumb, and if you try to use the local cops in Yaphank, they won't lift a finger. Worse, they'll tip her off."

"Why?" Harry asked.

"You're talking about a different jurisdiction. The Brookhaven Town Police. They're under orders from the local politicians: *When it comes to German Gardens, look the other way.* Let 'em clean up their own mess."

Harry repeated, "Why?"

The Chief narrowed his eyes at Weiss while shaking his head. "Turns out G-Men ain't that smart after all…you know how many votes come outta that community? Enough to sway a town election. Christ, you can't trust anyone near that place. Don't matter what kind of uniform they're wearin'—stormtrooper or town police, the only people they're protectin' are each other."

Harry drained his glass. "We appreciate your assistance, Chief."

Murphy shrugged. "Before you go…" he said, staring into his glass and pondering his next words. "You guys ever get reports of German subs off the coast of Long Island?"

Harry and James shook their heads simultaneously.

"Everyone once in a while, we get a call from some residents. Nuthin' ever pans out. People do some drinkin', get paranoid. You want me to let you know when the next report comes in?"

"By all means," Amos responded.

Chapter Thirty-Four

"HERE IS HOW WE ARE GETTING you in and out of America, with Albert Einstein," announced Helmut Swan.

Gunther sat at a conference table that had been dragged into the villa library. At the head of the room, Swan stood between two easels displaying various maps of the New York region. He held a wooden pointer against his shoulder like a rifle. The table was crowded with the representatives of various intelligence and military agencies.

The Chameleon would depart for America the next day.

Gunther lit a Neue Front cigarette—expensive at six pfennigs, but a perk provided by his hosts at the Abwehr. He smoked three more of them as he listened to the plans, tapping the ashes into a small gold tray at his elbow. Swan poked his wooden pointer at the maps and recited plans for infiltration, penetration, abduction, exfiltration. On paper, at least, the plans were cleverly and carefully designed; rigorously evaluated and tested. A masterpiece by the men and women who sat safely behind desks and imagined scenarios and contingencies and drew up the plans and went home at night and kissed their wives and girlfriends, whose greatest risk was the possibility of a broken pencil while Gunther was thrown into the belly of the beast.

And when Swan finished, returning the pointer to his shoulder and smiling proudly at the genius of it all, Gunther was left only to smile back politely, masking his own sense of futility. For in their intricate, detailed, complex plans, the planners had completely missed the one factor that would determine the success or failure of his mission.

Die Spionagegötter The spy gods.

No matter how precise the planning and meticulous the cover, there was always the matter of whether the spy gods would cooperate.

One needed good fortune, after all.

Swan dismissed everyone from the room and took a seat next to Gunther. He smelled like the sea. "There is one more thing," he whispered. "Directly from Heydrich." He pulled from his jacket a small brown envelope and passed it to Gunther.

"Your handler."

Gunther opened the envelope and pulled out the contents: a single 8 x 10 black and white photograph.

"Is this your idea of a joke?" Anton asked.

Heydrich had hinted there might be a woman involved with his support. But this? The photograph looked more like the publicity photo for a movie starlet: a dazzling young woman with blond hair falling around a sleek neck, ice-blue eyes, and milky, concave cheeks. Her lips were turned down ever so slightly, as if casting judgement on the camera itself.

"Her name is Maria Voigt," Swan told him. "You've worked a mission together before."

"Where?"

"In New York, actually."

Gunther thought back to the voice of the woman on the phone, after he'd failed to kill Einstein. Her tone seductive at first, drawing him in, then turning cold and accusatory. *"You've had your chance, and believe me—we're all as disappointed as you. I have orders for your new assignment."*

"Get me someone else," Gunther demanded.

"She is our most reliable operative in New York. And lives not far from where Einstein is staying, out on Long Island."

"She was difficult."

"So were you. Ms. Voigt has proven herself. She was the one who neutralized Schaefer at the World's Fair. If anyone is equal to your task, she is."

Gunther ran a finger along his chin, thinking in over. He didn't like working with others in a foreign country. Too often, contacts were already compromised, untrustworthy, and uncommitted—not to mention incompetent. But this woman…

He studied her picture again.

"I guarantee you: she is absolutely capable. She will provide you with everything you need."

Would she? wondered Gunther, still staring at the image of Maria Voigt. He still remembered her voice—arrogant, alluring… powerful.

Perhaps she would be worth the risk.

On his final night at Quenzsee, the briefers, planners, and trainers gathered in the ballroom to toast the Fuhrer's fiftieth birthday and the Chameleon's departure. They guzzled champagne and smoked cigars and wished Gunther well. They patted his back and squeezed his shoulder and shook his hands, exhilarated by his celebrity.

Anton returned to his room. On his bed was a tattered old black valise and a violin in its case. Tucked carefully in a false compartment he found a bottle of liquid sedative as well as two Glock pistols, a miniature Leika camera, and a micro-recorder that could fit in the palm of his hand. On his desk were two large envelopes. One contained five doctored visas and passports, an address in New York City, and five hundred dollars in American currency. The other contained Zwick's handwritten score of *Two Scientists Debate* and a tourist-class ticket on the SS *Bremen*, to New York.

In the name of Lev Bronshtein.

He stepped to his window, peeled back the curtain, and took a long last look at the moonlit lake and the surrounding pines, which seemed to be standing straighter for spring.

He was ready.

Almost.

There was only one bit of unfinished business that had nagged him, stored in his limitless memory until resolved. That moment from the mock interrogation that had been interrupted by Heydrich, who'd arrived unannounced with *Two Scientists Debate* and ended the session.

He walked to the reference book on his shelves. Picked out an atlas of Berlin, leafed through the pages until he found it: *Westphal Marina. Scharfe Lanke.*

His response to the interrogator had been accurate. That's where Max Goldschmidt had learned to sail.

Satisfied, he walked into the bathroom, splashed cold water on his face, and stared into the mirror.

Max Goldschmidt smiled back meekly.

Chapter Thirty-Five

HALFWAY THROUGH THE *BREMEN'S* six-day voyage from Hamburg to New York, Lev Bronshtein was finishing the last of his fried chicken with grilled tomatoes in the crowded Tourist Class Restaurant on C Deck. A portrait of Adolf Hitler was displayed high on a wall, as if surveilling the food selections of diners. Musicians played a variety of waltzes, and white-vested waiters scurried around the room, balancing silver platters. When the seating ended, the band began playing the familiar notes of the German national anthem, the *Deutschlandlied*. As on all other nights, Lev dutifully stood with all the passengers and sang:

"Germany, Germany above all,
Above all in the world,
When, for protection and defense,
It always stands brotherly together...."

It was after the song, when the sated passengers left their tables and headed for the exits, that Bronshtein sensed trouble. From the corner of his eye, he caught the glare of a crew member. He was an assistant waiter, but the insignia on his crisp white vest indicated a far more important position, that of the ship's Ortsgruppenleiter, the official who maintained Nazi discipline on ocean liners beyond the reach of the Party apparatus. Most German cruise ships carried one, posing as a steward, waiter, even dishwasher, but possessing extraordinary power, often superseding the authority of the ship captain.

In the past, Ortsgruppenleiters had handled the safe conveyance of spies, secret documents, and covert materials on German flag vessels crossing the Atlantic. They'd usually been briefed on the identity of an undercover agent, so as to facilitate an unmolested rendezvous with the agent's handlers in New York. But the recent spate of arrests of Nazi operatives in America had crimped the practice. FBI agents were boarding German ships in port, questioning the crew, disrupting operations. The scrutiny had forced the Abwehr to cancel assignments, and even yank Ortsgruppenleiters from vessels before they could be interrogated. To safeguard Chameleon's mission, therefore, a decision was made not to reveal the true purpose of his voyage to Ortsgruppenleiter Frederick Frank.

That would become unfortunate.

Frank was short and pudgy, with a stomach that strained against the silver buttons of his vest, a wide pink face, and a double chin that spilled over his tightly buttoned collar. He was known for drunken tirades that terrorized passengers and crew alike. He roamed the *Bremen* freely, armed with a passkey that accessed every part of the ship—including cabins—inspecting for any sign of disloyalty, dissent, or disrespect. His radio reports to Berlin could trigger instant reprimand, dismissal, or arrest.

He was, in short, a loose cannon on the *Bremen*. His very presence in the midst of an important Reich espionage mission was an unforgivable error, one that Bronshtein intended to take up with whoever had blundered when he returned from America... as Anton Gunther.

Until this night, he'd been able to avoid the man as he mostly thundered about, insulting Jews and foreigners and bullying everybody into rising and facing the ubiquitous portraits of the Leader when the *Deutschlandlied* played.

But now, he was approaching with the self-important strut of a lesser man. "You!" he barked.

Bronshtein lowered his eyes.

"You are a Jew."

"Yes, but my papers are in order."

"And where are they?"

"In my cabin."

Frank produced a slim notebook and pen from his vest pocket.

"Name and cabin number," he demanded.

The man was grating on Lev Bronshtein's nerves.

He hurried back to his room, Tourist Class Cabin 373 on D deck. It was more prison cell than cabin, with a single rickety bed and a metal sink jutting from a wall. Windowless, as it was an interior unit. But its complete privacy made it an attractive accommodation when the Abwehr needed to transport its special guests back and forth across the Atlantic.

Lev sat on the edge of his bed, crossed his legs, and waited. He estimated it would be no more than ten minutes.

He heard heavy footsteps in the passageway outside. The rattle of a passkey in the door.

There stood the immense Frank, red-faced, and snorting like a pig after truffles.

There were two types of threats that could blow an operative's cover: the intentional and the accidental. The intentional would come from a sophisticated counter-intelligence program, or a cunning operative who pulled at a loose thread in a story until the story unraveled, or an interrogator trained to inflict certain methods of pain until the truth was extracted. The Chameleon never much worried about intentional threats, because he was sure he was the best in the game, and he always knew what to expect and how to outwit his enemies.

It was happenstance that worried Gunther. The sheer coincidence that no amount of preparation could foretell. And now here he was, confronted with just that at the doorway to his own cabin on the *Bremen*.

"Your papers," Frank ordered.

Gunther pointed to a packet on the small nightstand next to his bed.

"Bring them to me."

"Have I done something wrong, Herr Ortsgruppenleiter? Did I not sing loud enough for you?"

The tone was just enough to darken Frank's jiggly, fat cheeks.

"Very well," Lev sighed. "Why don't we make this easier. My name is not Lev Bronshtein. Nor am I a Jew. I welcome you to search my luggage, but you will almost need a welder's torch to get it open without the key and combination, which I have no intention of providing unless you receive the proper authorizations."

Frank's eyebrows jumped. "I am the leading Reich authority on this ship. I have the power of life and death over everyone on board—including you!"

The Chameleon smiled. "Yes, you've made that quite clear, Herr Ortsgruppenleiter. You're a bit of brute, I think. The way you strut around—"

Frank's face swelled red again, like a mating bullfrog's. "Tell me who you are!"

"As I said, I will make it easy. I am on a mission for German military intelligence. My appearance gives me special access to Jewish enemies of the Reich."

Anton enjoyed watching the conflicting emotions flicker across Freddy Frank's face: from disbelief to confusion to fear. *Yes, you should know fear,* he thought

"But why wasn't I notified?" Frank whined.

"Other than me, only two people are fully aware of this operation."

Frank whipped out his ever-present pad and pencil "Tell me who they are, and I will radio them for verification."

"Of course…Adolf Hitler and Reinhard Heydrich. I assume you know how to reach them?"

He smiled mischievously. Frank stared back blankly now, not sure what to believe.

The Chameleon glanced at his watch: 10:40. *Good. The last promenaders should be going in, lucky or resigned.*

"I can understand your doubts, Ortsgruppenleiter. I will tell you everything. But you must promise not to share it, even with your superiors. Our nation's military capabilities are at stake. Shall we find a quiet place? One never knows who is listening to these cabins, right?" *Or who might overhear them,* he thought, giving Frank a conniving wink.

They strolled along the starboard side toward the stern. The Chameleon noted the low rumble of the engines, the crash of waves falling behind the ship, the whistling of the wind. It really was lovely, out in the middle of the Atlantic, with nothing beyond the ship itself to see. *How bold they must have been, those first European explorers,* he thought idly, *to brave an ocean in their little sailing ships.* He steered Frank to a railing, out of sight of any passengers who might pass by. He quickly scanned the area, then put his mouth close to Frank's ear and whispered,

"You must keep this secret to the grave."

Freddy Frank nodded, wide-eyed, certain that the most exciting thing in his life was about to happen to him. He was right.

"My name is Anton Gunther…"

The Chameleon pulled him closer. In one continuous movement, he wrapped a hand around the man's fleshy neck, the other at his jaw—in neither case an easy task. He felt the sudden panicked breaths of his prey, the reflexive attempt to resist. *Oh, what beauty,* he thought, glancing out again at the wide, still sea. Frank's fingers dug into the railing, desperately trying to take hold. Then—

The clean, sharp snap of bone at the base of the skull.

The splash of a body hitting the frigid black waters, far below. The Chameleon was already gone, chuckling and stumbling along like a man who'd just gotten lucky.

Ortsgruppenleiter Frederick Frank was reported missing when he failed to show up for breakfast service, and his cabin was found empty. A search of the *Bremen* commenced. It was futile. He was presumed to have been lost at sea. The predominant theory of his death centered on the assumption that he'd gotten drunk in his cabin, taken a walk, and managed to fall off the damned ship. The incident was dutifully entered into the captain's log, and a report was radioed to the *Bremen* line offices in Hamburg.

No one suspected that Frederick Frank was murdered and thrown overboard by the Jewish refugee named Bronshtein in tourist class, who spent the final days of his voyage locked in his cabin, practicing his violin.

Chapter Thirty-Six

THE *BREMEN* HAD MADE GOOD TIME, ploughing across the North Atlantic at twenty-seven knots and slipping through the Verrazano Narrows in New York on a balmy day in May. At least half the ship's passengers were out on deck to take photographs or home movies of the big green statue the French had given the Americans to celebrate their liberty. Anton—Lev Bronshtein—shook his head and smiled to himself. He wondered what the Indians thought about their idea of liberty—or all those Negro slaves they had hauled over to do their work for them.

Well, you have to hand it to the Americans, he thought. *They are always innovators worth following.* He knew that Heydrich had plans for all those useless Slavs and Poles and Jews to work the rich farmland in the East until they were no longer needed.

All things considered, it had been a good trip. He had managed to dispose of the unknown threat quite easily. Freddy Frank's disappearance had only seemed to lift the spirits of everyone on board.

The *Bremen* nudged into Manhattan's Pier 92, near Midtown.

The Chameleon remained in his cabin until most of the passengers had disembarked. He was aware that the decks would be crowded. A band would play, and confetti would fly, and passengers would take photographs and home movies of the festivities. No, he could not afford an unwitting appearance that could be viewed by police later. He knew as well that reporters and photographers often gathered on the quay to record the arrival of the occasional First-class celebrity or politician.

He remembered, years ago, the media scrimmage that had nearly helped him catch up with Einstein. He'd replayed the scene over and over. The foolish mistake of using a defunct newspaper as a cover, the eye-contact with the Negro, raising his suspicions. Allowing himself to be caught on the ship's stairwell, so that he had no choice but to plunge his knife into the young policeman's chest.

That had been the worst error of all.

Killing a police officer raised the stakes in America. You got a lot of people hunting for you when you killed a cop.

He wouldn't make that mistake again. He was better now, smarter, more disciplined.

Only when he heard the last notes of the band and sensed that the passageway outside his cabin had quieted did he gather his luggage and violin and leave. He climbed to the main deck as Lev Bronshtein. The last group of passengers was dribbling down the gangway. He closed his mouth at the stink of the port—the putrid, noxious blend of marine life and diesel fuel, the thick gray exhaust that belched from the vehicles clogging Eleventh Avenue. He remembered this place.

His thoughts were interrupted by the quick march of a purser. His uniform was spotless white; he had a sharp nose and blue eyes that cast sharp judgement on the wretch before him.

"Only first and second-class passengers may disembark. Everyone else ferries to Ellis Island. For quarantine."

Lev smiled meekly. "Of course."

Chapter Thirty-Seven

LEV BRONSHTEIN FOUND HIMSELF in a long, bedraggled line in the Great Hall at Ellis Island. Sunlight burst through a towering arched window, just above an American flag stretched between two pillars. The chamber resounded with a multitude of languages, the cries of babies, the commands of military police. Lev choked back the stench of unwashed, perspiring bodies, squeezed like cattle into long pens, trudging forward, inches at a time. He finally presented himself to a black-uniformed physician for a "six second inspection." The physicians had examined so many immigrants that they could almost immediately detect any number of medical conditions that required detention or even return to the country of origin.

Bronshtein was then interviewed in German. Passport, please. Visa. Name of sponsor… Spell it…slowly please…Address of sponsor. Bronshtein maintained a proper, subservient smile as he answered, attested, affirmed.

Three hours after arriving at Ellis Island, Bronshtein boarded a ferry returning to the port, cleared from quarantine. He gazed at the Statue of Liberty, a colossus presiding over the busy harbor. Opening the golden door, as the poem said, to the tired and poor, the huddled masses, the wretched refuse.

Lev Bronshtein had only been in America for a few hours, yet already he couldn't wait to leave.

A bulbous yellow cab took him to Grand Central Station. The driver droned on about the Yankees season, as if Lev Bronshtein had the foggiest sense of how they'd swept the Indians. *That is the central trait of Americans,* he thought. *They never shut up, and they never listen.* Making no effort to even engage politely, Gunther simply stared silently out the window. The city had changed in the almost six years since he had been here last. It was as gargantuan as ever, the great skyscrapers—looming bulwarks of granite, brick, glass and steel—puffing smoke and steam into a cloudless blue sky. Thrust unnaturally from the earth itself and radiating an aura of power. Invincibility.

Turn a corner, and there was an entire new plaza of great stone towers, and the shimmering marquee of a great Art Deco theatre calling itself Radio City Music Hall. *Great art and music, and dancing girls. What more could you need?* Everywhere, there was the noise of construction, of hammering and drilling, as if the city were working frantically to meet some kind of deadline. It was more than just the construction, though—or the smoke in the air, the industrial stench that seemed to be everywhere. *It was the people*, he realized. When he had last been here, just after the nadir of the Depression, they had seemed stunned, reeling, like a valiant army that goes on fighting but knows it is cut off and doomed.

Now their confidence was back. Anton could see it in the way they strode about the streets. Always in their New York hurry, hopping up and down on buses, hustling into their subway holes, shoving one another through the revolving doors of their massive office buildings. Cars and trucks careened through the streets with horns blaring, barely missing the pedestrians who stepped right out in the street in front of them. Ignoring any and all traffic regulations—assuming that there were such things. Everything was filthy, grimy, everyone shouldering for room.

Yet it was, for all that, he realized with a sinking heart, far and away the most modern city in the world. For all of their talk in Germany and Italy of building the fascist future, for all the Soviets talked of a new world, there was nothing like this. Anywhere.

They will be formidable if they enter a war. We must have a weapon that will make them think twice.

Finally, the cab pulled up to the station. Lev paid the fare from the envelope of American currency that had been provided before the trip. He pulled his luggage from the taxi and began a circuitous walk around the block and through the station, stopping, as any tourist would, to gaze at the brilliant blue constellations stretched across the ceiling of the Great Hall. He found the long-distance bag check and deposited his violin, keeping his indispensable valise with him. Then he circled the station for another fifteen minutes and, when he was convinced that he hadn't been followed, ducked into a tiny men's room. He stuck a couple of rubber stoppers under the door and went to work.

Lev Bronshtein went easily. He exchanged the old German suit for the wrinkled, well-used clothes of his next identity: Erich Bauer, film salesman. He dug out his makeup kit and worked a little gray into Erich's hair, combing it back on his scalp. Next, he swallowed a heavy iron supplement, grimacing as he did, anticipating the wave of nausea it would bring on, but pleased to see how haggard it almost instantly made his face look. Then he repacked his valise and walked to the East Side IRT.

As he descended the stairs, he could hear an oncoming train and saw a sign that baffled him at first: HOLD ON TO YOUR HATS. But as he descended the next stair, the blast of wind from the train nearly took Erich Bauer's rumpled fedora off his head, his hand only just fast enough to grab it in time.

And so he should, he thought.

Chapter Thirty-Eight

AT THE NEW EUROPE THEATRE, Maria Voigt was minding the ticket booth out front. In the years since Gans had given her the job, she'd considered promoting herself to theater manager. But the perch had its benefits: observing the movements on the street outside, memorizing the faces and identities of customers, and making direct contact with couriers. She'd been driving in every Thursday and working the weekend shift, but today she'd brought unwanted company. As soon as she'd pulled out of German Gardens that morning, a black Pontiac had tailed her. So close, at times, she could see in her rearview mirror the young FBI agent behind the wheel. Now the vehicle sat conspicuously across from the theater. Maria had wondered whether the surveillance was meant to send a message, or merely cloddish.

Either way, she'd expected it.

The FBI now made regular rides through German Gardens, spooking many of her neighbors with their efforts to question them and their very presence. Her men had reported that a squad car had remained in front of Einstein's cottage for several days, manned by a young constable.

She wanted to tell them that it constituted a pitifully small surveillance detail. As with the pitiful pair of agents who had appeared at her door, the very lack of manpower was proof that their superiors did not take them seriously. Yet ever since Amos and Weiss had come to poke around, she found that many of her neighbors who had once been proud to be in her presence were now staying away. Even her inner circle at the German Gardens Neighborhood Association, Krieger, Haiden, Lutz, and Kuhn, were making themselves scarce.

It was fine. Soon the day would come when they would boast that they knew Maria Voigt, a heroine of the Reich.

She heard a tremulous voice, but did not look up from her movie magazine. There was a gray blur on the edge of her vision, out in front of the admission booth.

"Twenty cents for a matinee," she said, without looking up.

"I am here to try to interest you in some exceptional newsreels," the voice said, very distinctly, obviously that of a man in late middle age, with a mild German accent. "We have something special. By Walther Frentz."

"We already have a distributor—" she started to say, then stopped. *It was the code—what he was supposed to say when he arrived.*

She looked up and saw what looked like a very ordinary individual. A middle-aged man, much the worse for wear after a day tromping up and down the streets of Yorkville, trying to peddle his newsreels. So, this was *him?*

"It never hurts to look," she said, staring him in the eye.

She quickly summoned Joanne, the perpetually bored local teenager, from the refreshments stand to the ticket booth.

"What if somebody wants popcorn?" she asked, between snaps of her Juicy Fruit stick.

"Tell them to wait," Maria said. "And I told you before: no gum."

Forcing herself to move as slowly as she could, she opened the door for the sweating, pale-faced salesman. He nodded his thanks, then gave her a little bow. In the theatre, she was glad to note, some historical epic about Frederick the Great was blaring away, a battle scene underway.

"Wait until you see what I have, Madam," he said.

She told him to follow her.

Anton knew her at once when he saw her. The fine cut of her jaw, the sensuousness of her face, her figure. How she barely glanced at him at first. This was the woman from the photograph—the woman he had only ever spoken to by phone.

This was Maria Voigt.

A woman born to hate, he thought, *and born to command.*

She led him to a dimly lit stairway. He pretended it was a chore for him to get up each step. Even in her excitement, he could see, she was impatient with him already. *Well, she would have to wait. This role must be played through.*

They arrived at a narrow hall. Maria produced a key, unlocked the door to the manager's office, and ushered him in.

The room was small, adjacent to the projection booth. Barely fitting a desk, file cabinet, and a ratty couch. A black curtain was stretched across a window. Erich Bauer scanned the movie posters that had been tacked on the walls: Leni Riefenstahl's masterpiece, *Olympia,* which documented the 1936 Summer Olympics; *Westfront 1918* with Fritz Kampers; Fritz Lang's *The Testament of Dr. Mabuse.*

"Classics," he purred. "Unlike the filth coming out of Hollywood."

"There's no need for this cover anymore," Maria scolded him.

Erich Bauer bowed his head. "Fine, Madame. A moment, please."

He leaned forward, stretched his muscles, and rubbed at his face.

Almost instantly, the newsreel salesman disappeared, having lived for less than an hour—most of it spent on the East Side IRT. He'd transformed into the Reich's most lethal killer, barely changing anything about his physical disguise, just his whole persona. The eyes sharp, cutting right through her. The shoulders, broad and level.

Maria summoned a smile. "It took you long enough to get here."

He smiled back. This was going to be wonderful.

"Let us get started," he said.

Maria unlocked a safe hidden behind the couch, removed a stack of papers, and spread them on her desk.

"As you know, the theatre is one of several safehouses in Manhattan. There is also one on Long Island, in German Gardens. To contact us, you will call this number—"

"This was all covered in my briefings."

"The Americans are penetrating our networks. I am under surveillance by the FBI—"

"The Pontiac across the street, I noticed it. Amateur surveillance."

"Nonetheless, as a precaution, I have changed the procedures necessary to contact me." She scribbled on a piece of paper. "You will call Bernstein's Sheet Music Company, in Brooklyn."

"A Jewish company?" Gunther asked incredulously.

"We purchased it as a cover. When you call, ask for Carl. The counter-code is 'Carl is with a customer.' To deliver a message or report, ask for Vivaldi's Concerto in D Minor, and we will send instructions. To arrange an emergency meeting, request Mozart's Concerto Number Five. You must report in every day. If there are no developments, simply ask for Wagner's Bridal Chorus. It's quite popular."

German, at least, Anton thought.

Maria Voigt continued. "One more thing. Are you familiar with Beethoven's String Quartet No. 13, Opus 130?"

"Not particularly."

"If anyone mentions it to you, it means you have been exposed and exfiltration is imminent."

"Why that particular piece?"

"It was Beethoven's final composition," Voigt answered matter-of-factly, "before he died."

Gunther sighed. *Always the same way, with amateurs who have decided to play spy. Some elaborate set of rules or codes—*

"No."

"No?" She seemed incredulous.

"This is how it will work," he told her. "I will not contact you every day, revealing the details of my plans. I will not tell you anything at all, in case your wires are tapped, or the FBI has already made a deal with you. They have not, because I circled the block three times before I came here and saw nothing suspicious. But I will not trust that this stays the same."

Her face reddened in anger.

"You arrogant—"

"The one place I will never come is your bungalow colony out in German Gardens, as I am sure it is the one place the American government already has under surveillance."

"You *will* report to me—"

"I will contact you when and only when I need something from you. Or when I want it."

"Those are not the plans—"

"The plans are formulated by a group of game theorists without a day's experience surviving in the field. I do not trust them, or their plans. Or for that matter, you. I operate based on the one thing I *do* trust: my instincts. So here are *my* plans, Frau Voigt."

He fished the ticket from the locker at Grand Central Station from his pocket and handed it to her. "Have someone get my violin and bring it back. A film salesman carrying around a violin would have raised eyebrows. I'll need it when I make contact with Szilard. Within the next few days."

He removed Erich Bauer's jacket.

"Bring me something decent for dinner tonight. I will take one of the rooms down the hall to sleep. On dry land."

He yanked down his tie and began unbuttoning his wrinkled shirt.

"What do you think you're doing," Maria asked.

"Get one of your men to wear this old suit and leave the theater. The person parked across the street knows the basic rule of surveillance: what goes in must come out."

Off came his shirt, revealing arms and stomach, sleek and powerful, like sculpted marble.

He is testing me. He wants me to show weakness. Emotion. It won't work.

He unbuttoned his pants and let them drop. Then his underwear. Completely shedding the skin of the film salesman, Bauer; the refugee, Goldschmidt. Maria remained behind her desk, eyes locked on his face, fighting the impulse to wander down his body, but catching just enough.

"Do you remember what I said about mission planners?" he said.

She nodded.

"Every night I slept naked in my cabin on the *Bremen*. Now that I am here, I've realized they didn't pack nightwear."

"I will find you a robe." she said.

He smiled lasciviously. "Or you can join me."

"I will find you a robe," she repeated.

She drove home in the Willys-Overland, still followed by the Pontiac.

As the evening lights of Manhattan receded in her rearview mirror, she replayed the scene in her office. His body was like a machine, she thought. Built with a plain enough exterior, but underneath, every muscle was compact and powerfully efficient. She was confident she'd passed his little test, and wondered what would have happened if she'd tested *him*—come from behind the desk and stripped off *her* clothing and positioned herself against his body and…

She shook the thoughts from her head and wondered whether to crawl into Krieger's delivery truck later than night and report the Chameleon's behavior. And what good would that do? She imagined the discussions in the dark paneled offices of the Abwehr: *This Americanized woman, incapable of handling her agent. And not just an agent, but our best man!* They would tolerate his misbehavior, even his contempt for their rules, so long as he completed the mission.

And if he failed?

She smiled. Then they'd deny everything and eliminate any

thread connecting him to them, just as he'd done with Erich Bauer. They would let him die, or rot in America.

Somehow, she felt better.

PART IV

MAY–JUN 1939

Chapter Thirty-Nine

"NEVER SEEN A BOAT LIKE THAT. Looks dangerous."

Albert Einstein tried to ignore the critique from the pimple-faced attendant with the severe crewcut at the Little Hog Neck marina. Instead he continued the rhythmic brushing across the hull of his boat, the *Tinef,* studying the varnish as it trailed off the brush and left fine, pale lines.

"Just don't look sea-worthy," the attendant continued.

Einstein swallowed back his annoyance. "And what makes you such an expert, at your young age?"

"I'm sixteen," the attendant shot back. "My family owns this marina. I grew up here. And in all that time I never saw a boat sorrier than yours."

Einstein chuckled. "Looks can be deceiving, young man. Take it from me."

He'd been prepping the *Tinef* for the waters of Long Island since arriving from Princeton. Taking a few hours every few days to sand, repaint, varnish. Content to be doing something physical, something *useful* for himself. Loving how the Valspar varnish soaked into the wood, the excess splattering over his hands and his raggedy work clothes. The marina, he was pleased to see, was no more than a sandy plot along the harbor with a few flimsy, weather-beaten docks, twelve boat slips, and a shack where one could purchase live worms, soda, and sandwiches all stored in the same grungy ice box. Surely no one would bother him here.

Well, except for Constable Krupski who'd been recently following him around like a little puppy dog. Watching him work; baking in the black uniform, the stiff black necktie, the scuffed boots that rode almost to his knees. Always quiet, but always…there.

Now, under a bright afternoon sun, he'd finally completed his preparations. He stood back, letting the brush drip paint on his bare feet, and inspected his work. The metal gudgeons and pintles that fastened the rudder were corroded, but in working order. The single row of keel bolts was tight enough, but needed to be replaced. The cedar wood hull was scratched and chafed, abraded by years of neglect and several collisions. Still, he decided, it would do for the placid bays of the North Fork. *Like a lake,* he had thought.

The attendant stepped up close. "That keel. It looks sawed in half."

"*Yes,*" Einstein huffed. "Better for sailing for the Carnegie Lake. Down in Princeton."

"Well…I don't know nothing 'bout no lake in Princeton. But the bays 'round here, they can get rough. You're going to need stability."

Albert Einstein was known for a certain stubbornness about his theories of physics—a "blockheadedness" some said. This was nothing compared to his views in other areas of life, especially sailing. He thanked the pimple-faced young man and told him he would return the next day for his maiden voyage.

He returned to the Jeep, Constable Krupski in tow.

The next afternoon was perfect for sailing: a high blue sky and a gentle breeze. He had hustled out of the cottage, but not quietly enough to evade the notice of Mrs. Dukas.

"Take your lifejacket!" she called out from the kitchen table, where she was working.

"Yes, of course," he said, walking right by where it was propped against a wall in the front hall.

He was about to step onto the porch when he remembered that Officer Krupski was posted outside.

Not today, he thought. *Today I need time alone.*

He snuck out the back, circled the house, and took the trail down the steep, wooded hill to the marina.

The day was every bit as beautiful as promised. The breeze whisking the *Tinef* east, to the very tip of Long Island. Einstein managed the rudder with one hand and wiggled the other against the hull, refreshed by a gentle spray of cool water. He passed the low-slung expanse of foliage on Robins Island. Then Shelter Island, massive and misshapen, as if splattered across the bay. In its folds nestled manor homes and more modest cottages, summer resorts, yacht clubs, a post office, a school—a hidden little community. Then busy Greenport Harbor, where the *Tinef* bounced in the wakes of the fishing and recreational boats buzzing about.

His eyes caught a lonely seagull riding the breeze, and he smiled sadly as he recalled the day that he and Elsa had finally left for America—and the day that they had arrived. Elsa had pointed out the gulls to make him feel better.

Now, above him, there was only a velvety line of cumulus clouds, drifting across a deep blue sky. All around him, only tranquil waters.

Reluctantly, he decided that this was a sign to take the *Tinef* back in. He began a tacking maneuver, turning the boat around by moving the nose across the wind in opposite forty-five-degree angles. He probed the tiller to find the point where the sail would catch the wind. But the *Tinef* was stubborn, and the sail remained still. After ten minutes, he decided to wait for more favorable winds to carry him back. He stretched his legs forward and stared at the sky. Oblivious to the current as it continued to carry him east of Greenport Harbor, between the diverging coasts of the north and south forks; rocking gently with the boat's motion, as if soothed in a mother's arms.

Time, he thought. So different when he was staring into the reaches of the universe or cradled in a body of water. Time in these places had its own cadence. Here, it was measured by the natural rhythm of waves against the hull and the slow drift of clouds instead of the mechanical, insistent ticking of clocks.

The heavens and the water, he thought. *Among the earliest creations of God. Eternal. Omnipotent. Materially unspoiled by man's inventions.* When technology had ravaged everything else, Einstein was certain, there would still be a sky and the oceans of the Earth.

He fell asleep.

At 3 p.m., Mrs. Dukas headed to the police car parked outside and rapped on the window. "Why aren't you with Professor Einstein?" she asked.

Krupski, in the front seat with his dime store detective novel, blinked back at her. "Isn't he inside the house?"

"No. He went for a sail. Hours ago."

Krupski turned ashen.

Mrs. Dukas sighed. "Don't worry. This has happened before. Do you happen to have a boat?"

Krupski grabbed the radio microphone and called into headquarters. Chief Murphy banged a meaty fist on a desk when he heard Krupski's report. He promised to fire or demote the boy— at the very least assign him to clean the toilets in the jail. As soon as he located Albert Einstein.

He called out to everyone in the station: "Find me a boat. Fast. In fact, get a bunch of boats."

Then he called the FBI New York office.

"How the hell could you let this happen?" Harry Weiss yelped into the phone, moments later.

"Relax. Einstein's assistant told us he did this all the time in Princeton. Snuck away to go sailing. We're going out now to find him."

"We're coming."

"It'll take you hours to get here. Just relax."

Harry slammed down the phone. Across the room, James asked what the matter was.

"Albert Einstein has disappeared on the waters off the North

Fork, and the local police want me to relax."

James Amos bolted from his chair, after Harry.

The sound of a boat horn jolted Einstein from his nap. A rickety wooden skiff was speeding towards him on a collision course, Evinrude propellers growling in the water. He could make out a solitary figure crouching at the tiller.

The professor waved frantically for him to stop.

The boat closed in.

Einstein tried to stand, but lost his footing in the rocking boat, and lunged to grab the mast. His muscular arms twitched as he braced for impact.

At the last moment, the engine of the skiff fell silent, and the boat glided towards him. The pilot was the marina assistant with the crewcut and the pimples, now gawking at Einstein.

He shrieked, "Professor, the whole town's looking for you!"

"I had a slight problem tacking," Einstein explained.

"I'll tow you to the marina."

"Where am I now?"

The boy pointed a thumb behind him. "You drifted past Greenport. Headed straight to Orient Point. Might'a drowned right there, at Plum Gut."

Einstein shook his head like a remorseful child.

"No life jacket either, I see."

"I find them uncomfortable."

As the attendant threw a coil of rope to the scientist, he thought, *Maybe you ain't that smart after all.*

Chief Phineas Murphy was waiting impatiently at the Little Hog Neck Marina when the skiff gurgled in, towing the *Tinef*. Einstein looking decidedly sheepish, as he heard the marina attendant announce for everyone to hear, "I warned him: keel was sawed half off."

"Goddamn," Murphy muttered.

"Coulda ended up in Plum Gut," the attendant added.

Murphy shook his head and thought, *there oughta be a goddamn law against inexperienced amateurs sailing these goddamn waters.*

Several hours later, Harry Weiss and James Amos pulled up to Einstein's cottage. Chief Murphy's car, a boxy Plymouth with a green hood, white roof and trunk, and a yawning metal front grille sat outside, along with Krupski's radio car. They found Murphy on the porch, squeezed into a rocking chair, clutching a bottle of Jameson's which had been dispatched from headquarters.

"He's fine," Murphy growled. "Me? Not really. Not only do we have to protect Einstein from the Nazis, we have to protect Einstein from Einstein!"

Mrs. Dukas appeared at the front door and invited them in.

Harry had seen Albert Einstein in countless FBI files, newspapers, magazines, books, and even newsreels. But there he was, sitting at the kitchen table, smoking a pipe. He was surprised to note just how tawny and sinewy his arms and legs were already. For a man who had just turned sixty, Weiss thought, he had the build of an athlete. *And the head of a rock?*

Einstein studied them, then smiled at James. "We meet again, Agent Amos."

James introduced Harry and said, "We drove out to make sure you're alright."

Einstein frowned. "Just a slight issue tacking."

"He's lucky," Murphy cut in. "We found him approaching Orient Point. Headed smack to the middle of goddamn—"

"Plum Gut. *Jaa*, I heard," Einstein said, sounding annoyed.

"Plum Gut?"

"It's hell," Murphy explained. "Just off Orient Point, where Peconic Bay meets the Long Island Sound. You've got shoals extending off the point, a reef that can slice right through your hull, a nasty chop. We fish a lot of experienced sailors out of Plum Gut every year. Not for the faint of heart, or—" He looked sternly at the professor. "—geniuses without a life jacket."

Mrs. Dukas chimed in, directing a stern "*tsk-tsk-tsk*" at Einstein.

"Have you forgotten what happened in Princeton?"

"What happened in Princeton?" Harry asked.

"The Princeton Yacht Club wanted to ban Dr. Einstein from sailing on the lake," Dukas explained. "They said it was too dangerous for him. They had grown weary after so many rescue efforts."

"A complete exaggeration on their part," the Professor retorted.

At that moment there was a distinct popping sound outside the cottage. "What the hell is that?" Harry barked. James had stepped towards Einstein.

There was another gunshot. A third.

"Relax," Murphy said. "It's someone hunting."

"*Hunting*?" Weiss said, incredulous. "For what?"

"The only things they threaten are the ducks."

Harry and James were invited by Einstein to join him on the porch. Einstein sat back in a rocker and filled his pipe. Murphy took a moment to gaze out to the harbor where the North Fork sky again performed its magic, a radiant canvas of blue, pink, orange, and gold.

Harry ignored the view, focusing instead on a newspaper that lay across a small end table next to the rocker. That day's edition of the *Long Island Press* had been opened to an article about a German ocean liner, the SS *Saint Louis*, which was crossing the Atlantic with nearly one thousand German-Jewish refugees seeking sanctuary in Havana.

Einstein noticed Harry's focus on the newspaper. "Another flock of gulls, seeking a place to land."

Harry nodded with a soft, sad grunt.

Amos said, "Professor, I must reiterate the danger you're in here."

Einstein drew again on the pipe. A plume of smoke drifted across the porch and out the screen windows.

"Actually, I am quite aware," Einstein said. "That's why I've decided to stay."

"I don't understand," Harry said.

Einstein rocked back on the chair, nursing the pipe, seeming to stare beyond Harry at the harbor below. "In England, and Belgium, and that day when we met in New York, the Nazis wanted to kill me only because I was an outspoken Jew. Now they have a more sinister motivation."

"Which is?"

Einstein rested his pipe in a tray.

"The German government has been racing to develop an atomic bomb that could, theoretically, destroy large areas. But the science has not been entirely proven. You see, you'd have to split the nuclei of heavy atoms, like uranium or plutonium, which would release more neutrons, which then strike other nuclei, creating a chain reaction. But many questions remain—"

"Professor, I was miserable at science in school," Harry interrupted. "How is this relevant to your safety?"

"I am coming to that. As I said, there are still significant problems. Is it feasible to generate enough energy to be weaponized? Even if so, is it possible to design a bomb that is not too heavy for transport? Whoever finds those answers has the potential of acquiring an unprecedented weapon of mass destruction."

"Which is why," Amos realized out loud, "the Nazis want to somehow haul you back to Germany. They think you have those answers."

"They give me far too much credit. The hard truth is, I don't know that I have anything to contribute to physics anymore. Few do, at sixty," he said, as if he found each word distasteful.

Amos said, "I'm sure that's not true—"

"And certainly not for this bomb," Einstein cut him off. "I wouldn't have much desire to build it if I could. To spend my whole life trying to pry out and explain the secrets of the universe, only to be known mostly as the man who killed untold thousands, maybe millions with this weapon? No, let others do it. Younger men, in their labs in New York, Chicago, California. I believe they are getting closer. And if they prove the ungodly hypothesis, then I will convey a warning to President Roosevelt. I am told he will listen to me."

"But while they're experimenting," Harry said, "Adolf Hitler is coming for you. Which is why you need to leave."

"No," Einstein said adamantly. "On the contrary: it is why I must remain. Don't you see?"

Both agents shook their heads.

"For as long as I am the principal target here, my colleagues are less vulnerable to threat in their laboratories. Their research goes on ignored, and this could buy them invaluable time."

"So, you believe you're misdirecting the Nazis?" Harry asked incredulously.

"Call it a loose form of Heisenberg's laws of uncertainty. The more one knows about the location of a particle, the less they can know about momentum, and vice versa. If I am a target here, they cannot measure the momentum of research elsewhere."

"I don't know about Heisenberg's law," Harry said. "But I do know about the law of averages. You're entirely exposed here, at the ass end of the earth. You can achieve the same goal under our protection elsewhere. We can bundle you up."

Einstein gave a humorless laugh, then rubbed his hand over his face. "It's an interesting choice: being kidnapped by the Nazis or the FBI. No thank you, Agent Weiss. I did not come to America to live in an elegant concentration camp. I came to enjoy my freedom."

"But the risk—"

"I have studied this place. It is on high ground, approachable by only one road. With a view of everything around me, all the way to the harbor. If it's more isolated than Princeton, it will be much easier for us to see what's coming. And should they come, I trust that you will not be far away. I will be the bait. You spear the sharks."

It was Harry's turn to rub a hand over his face.

"In addition," Einstein said, "I have my very own secret weapon."

"A gun?" Harry asked.

"Worse…Mrs. Dukas," he winked.

James chuckled. "She seems formidable. But we're not taking any chances. No more skipping out on your protection. Understood?"

"I swear it," Einstein said, holding up one hand in mock solemnity.

Harry smiled. "Does it strike you how funny this is, us both being Jews?" he asked.

Einstein looked perplexed. "How do you mean?"

Harry pointed at the newspaper headline. "I mean trying our damnedest to protect democracy, when so many people don't even want us here? When they've done *their* damnedest to keep us out— and after all these other countries threw us out."

"But here, perhaps, we have come at last to a country where everyone has as much of a right to it as almost anyone else," Einstein said slowly, after a long pause. "Or at least, the chance to fight for it. Yes, there is hatred. But we are as much American as any of them."

"Don't tell that to anyone down in Yaphank," Weiss said, rising to go.

Amos stood as well. "Honestly, Professor, I didn't give you enough credit. I had assumed you were in denial about the threat."

Einstein picked up his pipe. For the second time in two days, he said, "Appearances can be deceiving."

Chapter Forty

ANTON GUNTHER SPENT HIS FIRST night back in America sleeping comfortably in the back room of the New Europe Theater. He awoke precisely at seven o'clock on Friday, dressed without shaving or showering. His clothing—Max's clothing—had been left in a crumpled pile on a chair in the corner of the room, stained and wrinkled. Ordinarily, the unwashed stench might have offended him. But now he'd returned to Max Goldschmidt's sensibilities. Seeing the world through the dark, sad eyes; walking with a stooped shuffle; accustomed to the stink of his world.

He felt a lingering temptation to contact Maria Voigt before he left. To enjoy the pure body of an Aryan woman before plunging back into the detritus of Goldschmidt's life. He was certain she wouldn't resist the invitation. She'd feigned disinterest on his first night at the theater, he thought, when he'd undressed in front of her. But he was an expert at reading barely detectable clues: the hungry parting of her lips, the too-heavy focus of her eyes on his, fighting the gravitational pull downward.

He put it out of his mind. He was now Max Goldschmidt, with no room for Anton Gunther. There could be no intermingling of the two, no trace of Gunther's shades on his chameleon skin—not even the leftover scent of Maria Voigt's perfume on his flesh. He'd have to seek satisfaction elsewhere, as Max. He'd heard about Rosie Hertz, who'd built a Jewish prostitution ring on the Lower East side many years before. It had been closed down but surely, he thought, the Jews were still operating brothels somewhere. It wouldn't be so bad. He remembered Rebecca Schoenwald, the communist leader he'd bedded and slain in Berlin. Yes, a Jewess, but the sex wasn't at all unpleasant. Part of the role, yes, but not exactly acting.

He slipped the large envelope containing Zwick's folded sheet music into an inside pocket of his jacket and picked up his violin case and valise.

He was Max again, and would be for another few weeks, if everything went as expected. Then he'd step off America's filthy shores for the second time in his life. Only this time he'd accomplish his mission, even if it was no longer to kill Einstein, but to return him to Germany.

Across the street from the theater, a woman stood at the open window of a black Pontiac, asking the not-so-undercover FBI agent for directions. The distraction worked: Goldschmidt was able to slip out of the theater on 79th Street, walk quickly to 1st Avenue, and head several blocks south, where he hailed a cab. The taxi crawled through rush hour traffic, cutting across Central Park, where the lush green lawns and towering trees reminded Max of Berlin's Tiergarten. They headed north on Broadway, past office and apartment buildings, coffee shops, barbers and shoe repair shops, banks, and then into a canyon of brick stone buildings on the campus of Columbia University. The cab pulled over at West 119th Street. Max paid the driver $1.35, plus a tip of twenty-five cents, and walked to the brown brick Pupin Hall.

It was 9:45, his watch said. His briefings indicated that Szilard typically arrived by 9:00.

He entered the lobby, sniffed the sharp ammonia on the black and white floor, and crossed to an elevator. The doors slid open, and he pressed a button for the 8th Floor.

"Another experiment in fission, Dr. Szilard? We have done so many."

Leo Szilard scowled at his assistant, Jaworsky. "Science is a hypothesis subjected to repeated testing and demanding an identical outcome. Einstein will only be convinced when the evidence is not only irrefutable but repetitive."

Then he sneezed.

His allergies were raging, but he refused to slow down. Since their experiment in March, other scientists around the world had plunged into the mystery of uranium fission and a potential chain reaction. They were like a stirred-up ant heap, Szilard thought. The Germans. The British. But still, the American government dawdled. As if the separation of an ocean could protect them from destruction. As if a bomb couldn't be delivered anywhere.

Someone tapped lightly at the front door. A colleague, Szilard assumed, curious about his latest experiments. He told Jaworski to shoo away the intruder, then sighed heavily as he shuffled towards the laboratory.

He returned to his calculations, and heard a soft voice announce, "My name is Max Goldschmidt. I was sent by Professor Reinhard Zwick."

Szilard spun towards the door, mouth widening at the sight of the haggard visitor clutching a battered valise and violin case, as if perceiving an apparition. "My God! You know Zwick? I have heard nothing from him." Without waiting for an answer, he rushed to the door, took Max by the arm, and hurried him to a chair.

"I was Professor Zwick's assistant. Before the Gestapo killed him."

Szilard brought his hands to his face. "My God! What happened?"

"I was running an errand. Trying to mail this to you." He pulled the composition from his pocket.

By the time he finished telling his story, so well-rehearsed at Quenszee, he was in the Pupin faculty lounge, surrounded not only by Szilard and Zinn, but also by Wigner, Fermi, Rabi, and half a dozen other top scientists Gunther recognized from his briefing books. An American phrase came to mind: *Like shooting fish in a barrel.*

"The Professor had returned from a meeting at the Chancellery.

He gave me the music and told me it was urgent that I mail it immediately to you, and that you would personally bring it to Einstein. But the Reichspost was closed by the time I arrived. That was the last time I saw him."

Szilard exhaled anxiously, then unfolded the sheet music on his cluttered desk, next to a half-finished sandwich from that day's lunch. He furrowed his brow.

"But why to me, rather than Einstein?"

"He believed that anything sent directly to Einstein would be intercepted."

Szilard ran his eyes across each of the eighteen pages, searching futilely for some sign, some message buried within the scrawl.

As he studied them, Rabi asked Max gently, "Did the underground leave you with any kind of papers? A visa, maybe? A passport?"

Max fidgeted with his hat.

"Just enough to get into America." His voice tightened, pleading. "Please don't tell anyone. I will be sent back. You have no idea what they are doing to Jews over there now!"

Szilard placed his hands on Max's shoulders and offered a reassuring smile.

"You are safe here. Where are you staying?"

Max shrugged. "I know no one in New York. I have very little money."

"I will arrange for you to stay in the King's Crown hotel, where I live. Just down on 116th Street—very reasonable. No questions asked, I assure you. But first, let me call Einstein. Then I will introduce you to my colleagues."

He picked up the phone. Max looked up at him, batting his soulful, frightened eyes gratefully. Thinking, *it can't be this easy.*

Albert Einstein was frustrated.

He was in the living room of the cottage laboring through a

Paganini violin solo, a challenge both musically and technically. The piece required agility, a synchronized ballet of fingers, wrist, and elbow. The violin had to sing, but to Einstein, it was protesting. His fingers grasped for the notes, blocking the strings so they couldn't vibrate properly. His transitions were too slow—almost cloddish, he thought.

He was almost relieved when he heard the phone ring.

"Hallooooh," he bellowed into the phone.

His relief dissipated when he heard Szilard's hoarse voice.

"Professor? I have an urgent matter."

What now?

"You won't believe this, but—"

Einstein didn't. Szilard spun breathlessly through the arrival of Zwick's longtime assistant, along with the latest update of *Two Scientists Debate*. Zwick's last wish that the man—Goldschmidt was his name, Max Goldschmidt—bring the score to Szilard, who would convey it to Einstein. The theory, breathlessly whispered by Szilard, was that Zwick was secretly trying to tell them something about the Nazis' progress on an atomic bomb. The urgency of sending the message to Einstein at once, in the care of the assistant—did he mention that Goldschmidt was a Jewish refugee from Germany? This Goldschmidt, this escapee from Hitler, could be on a train to Long Island that very afternoon.

"Calm down, Szilard. The Nazis are not going to produce an atomic bomb over the weekend—and if they do, it's too late anyway. I will be sailing this weekend. Please have Zwick's assistant come on Monday. Mrs. Dukas will take care of the details."

Szilard sneezed once again.

Chapter Forty-One

ON TREE-LINED 116TH STREET, just off the Columbia University campus, was the King's Crown Hotel. It was stately, with a beige brick facade and half-circle pediments above each window. It attracted a significant number of European guests, including Leo Szilard and Enrico Fermi, who were known to debate atomic physics when they bumped into each other in the lobby.

After the meeting in Pupin Hall, Max was personally escorted by Szilard to the hotel. The Professor reserved a room for Max on the second floor, instructing the desk clerk to put the bill on his own monthly account.

"How can I ever repay you?" Max asked, looking up at his savior with his big Max cow eyes.

"No need to even think about that," Szilard assured him. "Gerhardt Zwick was a great friend and a great colleague. It's the least we can do. Now let's get you some clothing. You can't be walking around New York looking like a Jewish refugee from Berlin."

But I must.

Szilard turned to the clerk. "Please have his bags brought to his room."

The desk clerk pressed a desktop call bell. A bellboy in a red uniform and matching red cap marched to retrieve the baggage.

"No. I will take them." Max smiled, reaching down to grab the bags.

"Max, you're in America. I assure you, your belongings will be safe." Szilard wagged his fingers and added, "Come."

Goldschmidt looked anxiously as the bellboy scurried towards an elevator, arms weighed down by so many hidden secrets.

Max let Szilard take him over to the College Shop on West 113th Street for some new American clothes, including an inexpensive suit and a set of pajamas, and then to the barbershop to trim his hair. This was the most difficult part of playing Max, he knew. Here in America, among friends, there was no excuse for poverty—but he figured it would be easy enough to get his brand-new clothes stained and rumpled, his new American haircut disheveled. Whatever it took to gain Einstein's sympathy.

That night, he'd settled in Room 224 at the King's Crown Hotel. The room was drab and dim, with a single grime-caked window looking out on a narrow airshaft between the hotel and the next building. Not six feet away was…a brick wall. He wondered if Szilard's room, three floors above, was just as awful.

But where he was on West 116th Street was a broad avenue, sweeping downhill to Riverside Drive and then to what looked to be a wholly refurbished park, full of trees and winding paths, with the full sweep of the Hudson beyond it. He had been in worse.

There were weeks of work still to do, determining just how far along the Americans were on a bomb. Ferreting out who the driving genius was behind it. Working his way into the trust of Albert Einstein.

An operational possibility ran through his head, as it often did in such missions. So many of the scientists he'd just met in Pupin Hall were listed in his Abwehr briefing materials as essential to America's atomic research. How easy it would be to assassinate them in a single gathering, decapitating the American brain trust and setting back the American program by years. He itched at the thought. But he quickly reminded himself, it would surely complicate the mission objective to abduct Einstein.

He'd keep it under consideration. Strategic and tactical flexibility were always advantages.

Max unpacked the few items of clothing he'd brought, then took a careful inventory of his supplies, including his Sauer pistol, Leica camera, and pen-syringe. All in good order. His cash and documents were carefully folded in a secret pocket inside the valise, which he locked and slid under the bed.

He entered the bathroom and stared at himself in a small oval mirror above a sink stained with blotches of yellow and brown. The sallow Jewish refugee stared back. Weary. Anxious. Oppressed. Somewhere deep underneath lurked Anton Gunther, who had knocked on the door to an impregnable America, and watched it open politely.

Chapter Forty-Two

AS SOON AS HARRY WEISS pulled into the beach at Orient Point, he felt that familiar tightening of his throat, the stabbing above his eyes. Harry desperately wanted to be anywhere else, but the call from Chief Murphy earlier that Sunday morning was urgent.

He'd been eating his Saturday breakfast in his one-bedroom at the Stuyvesant Apartments in Lower Manhattan when the phone rang. Murphy's voice practically barked through the static. "Can you come out here?"

"What's happening?"

"I'll tell you when I see you. How long?"

"I'd have to take a train, but—"

"Get on the train."

"To where, exactly?"

"Meet me at the Long Island Railroad station in Greenport."

It was an eternal train ride from Manhattan to the railroad's eastern terminus in Greenport. To help pass the time, Harry had brought several newspapers, including *The Daily News*, the *New York Herald Tribune*, and *The New York Times*. Each had a feature story about a certain boat. The *Saint Louis* was scheduled to arrive in Cuba in six days, but there were reports that the Cuban people were demanding that it be turned away. According to the articles, negotiations were underway with several Western European governments to accept the passengers rather than return them to Nazi Germany. They would be safe, the articles suggested.

Harry knew better. *What Jew could be safe on the same continent as Hitler? As soon as he invades those countries, they'll be arrested, imprisoned...or worse.*

He spent the rest of the ride relaxing his mind, shaking off the anger.

Finally the train pulled into the station, squatting by the side of a congested harbor, in the small downtown of a village named Greenport. Harry's nose wrinkled at the fetid odors of fish, oil, mechanic's grease, and beer. He walked past a tangle of docks crowded with ramshackle fishing and oyster boats, and several old schooners. A car horn clamored from a parking area, sounding like a goose.

Chief Murphy was beckoning from his radio car. Harry noticed a fishing rod hanging from an open rear window.

They trundled through Greenport and turned east.

"Where are we going?" Harry asked.

"I figured if I told you on the phone, you'd hang up. And I wouldn't blame you. We're going to meet a friend of mine."

"Who?"

"His name's Billy Tuthill. Bit of a recluse. Owns a fishing shack on the beach. He called headquarters this morning. Claims he spotted a German sub off the coast. Claims an invasion is taking place. I took a look myself but didn't see anything. Then I remembered you and Amos asked to be notified of anything unusual."

"Why didn't you call Agent Amos?" asked Harry.

"It's Sunday. He strikes me as the religious type."

They drove along a narrow, rough road that soon became a single dirt track with tire marks. Harry sensed the land narrowing, the waters on opposite sides closing in on them.

"Where exactly is this fishing shack?" Harry asked, in as casual a voice as he could muster under the circumstances.

"At the end of the world," said Murphy.

Half an hour later, they parked at Orient Point. Murphy hung a pair of Zeiss binoculars around his neck and said, "Follow me." Harry swallowed his anxiety and followed the chief as he hobbled, occasionally grunting uncomfortably.

Harry was wary of beaches, but this place was unforgiving. Unworldly, actually. An arrowhead stretch of gravel, pulverized shells, and deformed twists of driftwood, sanded smooth by the tides. It came to a jagged tip, like a spear defending against the eternal pounding of the surf. Piles of black boulders stood about haphazardly in the surf, as if they had been planted there. The only vegetation was confined to an elevated ridge behind them: a knobby, oily spine of oak trees and pitch pine, and low-growth red cedars that rose from a carpet of beachgrass kinked by the unrelenting winds.

"It's called Orient for a reason," Murphy shouted against the wind. "It's the easternmost point of the North Fork. The British used it to conduct raids on Connecticut. Legend has it that Benedict Arnold had a headquarters in the village."

"Even then the place was crawling with spies, huh?" Harry asked.

"And more. There's a rumor that Captain Kidd buried treasure somewhere nearby. You can hide pretty well here."

They arrived at a path that climbed to a lonely gray shack on the wooded ridge, sheltered from the howling wind. On the porch sat a man dressed in denim overalls stained with the remains of gutted fish. A mangy gray beard plunged to his chest. He was barefoot, wielding nails like talons. An open bottle of cheap Bacardi rum rested on his lap.

Murphy introduced Harry to Billy Tuthill and asked him to report on what he'd seen.

"German submarine. Off the coast." Harry noticed he was toothless.

"Did you see any markings?" Harry asked.

"Nope. But this ain't the first time. Seen those subs comin' up and goin' back down. Like whales. 'Cept there ain't any whales in the bays." He took a swig from the bottle.

"Did you see any kind of raft? Anything that might be transporting someone to the beach?"

"No, they just kind of sail along the coast. Spyin' on our

defenses. Which ain't much.'"

"If you didn't see any markings, how do you know it was German?"

The man squinted at Harry. "You read the news at all? War's comin'. They're plannin' an attack."

"But—"

"I tell you it was a German sub," Tuthill barked. "I know what I seen."

"I don't doubt that you saw something," Harry replied. "It's just that—"

"Let's take a look," Murphy interrupted, tugging Harry gently away.

They trudged along the buff. Harry noticed a small pile of discarded cigarette butts, tangled fishing line, and beer bottles. Thirty yards away, the North Fork jutted out into the Atlantic. Like a harpoon, he thought. Just to the east, at the land's end, he could see a mostly flat, wooded island, deposited there like a morainal afterthought. In between it and the end of the North Fork, he could glimpse two converging currents of water slap and smash continually at each other, throwing up dozens of whitecaps.

"What's that out there?" he asked Murphy.

"Plum Island. There was a fort there. To protect us from a naval invasion in the Spanish-American War. And between the island and here is the Plum Gut. See that lighthouse? It warns mariners about the Gut. Been there since the 1860s. Don't always work, though."

"That's where we almost lost the world's greatest scientist?"

"It's no joke," Murphy growled. "The currents are fast, and they run right into each other. Our department recovers too many bodies here every year."

Harry suddenly felt unsteady. He sensed the surf rising over the boulders, consuming the beach, wrapping around his legs.

"You okay?" Murphy was asking. "You look sick."

Weiss nodded unconvincingly. *The smell of saltwater and blood, the pounding of waves, the ocean washing over him, suffocating him.*

Murphy folded his arms. "Look, Tuthill sounds crazy. But it ain't just him. We get calls from other boaters, fishermen."

"If they are subs, they could be our own. The Groton submarine base is just across the Long Island Sound. Did you ever call the Navy?"

"Called 'em once. Told me they'd get back to me. Never heard a thing."

Harry didn't doubt it.

"I fought the Germans," Murphy continued. "They're tenacious people. Wouldn't put it past them to be conducting surveillance. You wanna to take a closer look?" He offered his binoculars.

Harry demurred. "I should get back the city."

"What's the rush? You're in paradise. I got a rod in my car. You wanna fish?"

All Harry wanted to do was plant his feet on asphalt. "I'll take a rain check."

Murphy stared hard at him. "You gotta conquer your fears, Agent Weiss. When I went to Europe, I was so scared that at times I wet my pants. But at Belleau Woods, when it was all on the line, I did what had to be done. Even took this goddam bullet. And I'd take it again. For my country."

"I'm fine," Harry stammered.

"No, you're not. You're petrified. Fishing connects you to the water, Weiss. When you reach understanding with the water, then you'll be fine."

Harry was unconvinced.

"Suit yourself," said Murphy. "I don't mind fishing alone. Why don't I get you back to the train, then I'll come back and salvage what I can of the afternoon. It's Sunday. My day off."

Chapter Forty-Three

THE CHAMELEON WOKE BEFORE dawn on Monday morning. Months of reading, studying, training, planning, and practicing would culminate in the one moment, later that day, when he and Albert Einstein would finally make eye contact. The entire mission depended on the first impression that Max Goldschmidt made on Albert Einstein—on his ability to seduce him.

Everything had to be perfect.

Max combed his hair, flattening it against his scalp with water from the bathroom faucet. Szilard would not be too impressed, but it was best that he looked as much like a bedraggled refugee as possible. He knotted his puckered black tie against the frayed collar of his shirt, then carefully tied the flimsy laces of his shoes. With a measure of delight, he inspected the slight tear of the toe box from the sole of the right shoe. The smallest enhancements, he thought, made his character more believable. The hint of a dilapidated shoe, the jagged fingernails, the unwashed pants.

Veracity lay in the details.

He carefully buried his Sauer in a concealed pocket in his coat, stuffing and flattening the area with tissues to avoid detection. On the desk near his bed was the envelope containing Zwick's composition. He folded it into his outside pocket, checked himself in the mirror, and—as was his practice—affixed a thin, almost invisible strip of tape to the frame of the door to his room.

He and Szilard had planned to leave the King's Crown together, no later than seven o'clock. Max found the Hungarian in the lobby, slumped in an oversized chair, hacking into an already soggy handkerchief. He was pale, his eyes swollen red.

"Professor, are you feeling well?" Max asked.

"No Max. I'm quite unwell, actually." His voice sounded like a saw cutting through wood. "I thought it was my spring fever. Now I believe it's the flu."

"Can you travel in this condition?" Max asked, wondering whether his first meeting with Albert Einstein had just been derailed.

Szilard shook his head dejectedly. "Einstein gets impatient with my various ailments."

"Do you intend to cancel our appointment. Professor?"

After a wipe of his nose, Szilard said, "We have wasted enough time already. I'm afraid you will have to go alone. I will write you instructions for your transportation. Don't forget Zwick's music."

Max Goldschmidt kneaded his hands and mumbled, "I will do my best, Professor."

The 116th Street subway station was airless and smelled of cleaning fluids. It was not quite summer, but already he found the city uncomfortably hot—almost tropical, as he had been warned. The No. 1 train barreled in, thunderous, with lights flickering from inside. *So different from the charming U-Bahn in Berlin*, he thought. *Loud and graceless, like everything else in America.* Even this early the car was already crowded, and it was all he could do to grab onto a leather strap hanging from the metal bar. Everyone was shoved together, lurching and swaying with the subway car, white and brown and black and yellow—all these *mischlinge,* in the country of *mischlinge.* Most were sweating already, the smell of body odor appalling, the only ventilation some small upper windows and big, lugubrious metal fans that slowly pushed the dank, heavy air about.

His fellow passengers rarely made eye contact, he noticed. They buried their faces in books or magazines or, mostly, newspapers, which they folded into fantastic shapes of all kinds so that they could maneuver them with one hand while still clutching onto their strap.

The men turned first to the sports, perusing the ball scores, or the boxing and racing results from the weekend. The women seemed to prefer advice columnists and feature stories. Almost none of them evinced much interest in the headlines about Europe.

This is not a breed of people willing to cross an ocean— again—to protect peoples they care nothing about, he told himself. *No wonder their politicians favor isolation.*

He took the West Side IRT down to Pennsylvania Station, which he had to admit was something else entirely: easily the grandest train shed he had ever been in. He transferred to the Long Island Railroad there, a train that crept through black and dingy tunnels under Manhattan and the East River before bursting aboveground in a suburban borough called Queens, then speeding on east. Goldschmidt watched the farms and hamlets whisk by: Jamaica, Mineola, Hicksville, Farmingdale, Ronkonkoma, Yaphank. When he was studying his maps back at Quenzsee, the names had sounded so exotic. Now the towns they passed through seemed to him the essence of banality: every train station the same utilitarian brown brick with a gray slate roof, every Main Street that whizzed by lined with five-and-dimes, movie theaters, bars, drug stores. Nothing like the ancient, meticulously cleaned and groomed towns around Jüterborg, or anywhere else in the Reich.

He felt reassured after leaving Penn Station. This was a country devoid of elegance and grace, and almost pathetically open to infiltration.

Two and a half hours later, the train arrived in Greenport. Three bright yellow taxis idled on a nearby curb. He slipped into one and pretended to stumble over the name of his destination, though in fact he had memorized it three months ago, back in Germany.

"Doc Moore's home, if you please."

"Where?"

"The cottage owned by Doctor Moore." Max pulled out a slip of paper to show the driver, reading "116 Grove Road, Little Hog Neck."

"Oh, you mean the Einstein place."

"Yes, please," he said meekly, his confusion genuine. *Could the great man's security really be that porous?*

They pulled away from the station, and almost immediately Max noticed the driver's habit of darting his eyes from the road to the rearview mirror, as if examining his passenger. He wore a leather jacket and chomped on a soggy, unlit cigar.

Finally, the driver asked, "You Jewish?"

Max interpreted the tone as conversational and not prosecutorial. He answered bravely, "I am. And you?"

"Me, no. Nothing against 'em, though."

Max noticed the faint hint of a German accent, and asked, "May I ask, sir, where are you from?"

The driver's eyes settled on him in the mirror, and the high ridge of his cheek bounced as he chewed on the cigar.

"Frankfurt am Main," the driver declared. "But I came before the war and I'm no fan of Hitler!"

Max had another reason to find offense in America: Germans driving Jews and apologizing for being German.

They rumbled west, the scenery consistent with the briefings the Chameleon had received at Quenzsee. The narrow country road stretched past sprawling fields, offering occasional flashes of the glittering Peconic Bay. Five miles west of Greenport, they came upon downtown Southold. The camera that was his mind clicked on Rothman's Department Store, the high school, the bank, the public library—all familiar from the photographs he'd studied. They continued another four miles until they turned left on Skunk Lane—*A name possible only in America*, he thought—then rumbled south towards the beach. Max noticed children scampering on three large boulders, and counted a dozen sailboats gliding in the bay. The taxi veered away from the beach onto the bumpy, one-lane incline called Grove Road.

Goldschmidt did not allow the proximity to his target to excite him. Exuberance led to error, after all. He succumbed to emotion only in the final breaths—literally—of a mission.

As the taxi approached, he saw a police radio car parked by the side of the road, and frowned. It was the first evidence of any real protection for Einstein, though it was hardly prepossessing: a single patrol car with a gawky young man who looked little older than a teenager slumped in the passenger seat, reading.

I could kill him before he turned to the next page, Max thought.

The taxi slowed to a halt, and his Jew-pandering compatriot from Frankfurt rolled down the window.

"Got a visitor for Einstein," he told the policeman, whose name tag read "KRUPSKI," Max could see.

"How are you today?" the boy cop said, peering in the window and tipping his cap, and sounding to Max more like a member of the local tourist board than a policeman.

"I am fine, thank you," Max said carefully. "My name is Max Goldschmidt. G-o-l—"

The boy cop looked at a crumpled piece of paper he had pulled from his pocket and nodded.

"I already have you on Mrs. Dukas' list, sir. You may proceed. Give my regards to Dr. Einstein."

Max nodded as humbly and gratefully as he could manage and slumped back into his seat. He wanted to laugh. *It was now clear to him: his greatest mission was also going to be his easiest.* He wondered if he should make some sort of animal sacrifice to the spy gods. But he knew that, chances were, he would.

The taxi left him at the summit of the hill with a cheery, obsequious goodbye from the cabbie, even though he left him a mere nickel tip. Max would have liked to have strangled the man. Instead he did his due diligence, surveying his surroundings. Einstein's property was removed from any main road by the long, winding approach. The forested hill that descended to the harbor offered a fast route to a waiting boat, if necessary. Only a few houses sat nearby, tucked far back on overgrown, wooded lots. He scanned the harbor, his eyes resting on a small island, just two miles out in the bay. *Robins,* he recalled from the maps. *An easy swim*, he thought.

The sound of a gunshot broke the silence.

He nearly ducked and ran for the cover of the house, his hand digging reflexively into the pocket where he had his pistol. There was a second pop, then a squawk of panicked birds rose into the sky.

"Hunters," he heard a woman's throaty voice say from across the lawn.

Standing on the house's small porch, smoking a cigarette, was a neat woman with a large nose and short brown hair parted to one side. He recognized her at once from his briefings: Helen Dukas. She looked to be all business, but with the haughty command of a movie star. When the time came, Max thought, he would likely have to kill her first.

"Come inside. I'm afraid Dr. Einstein isn't here at the moment."

The pitted, unkept front lawn reminded him of photographs he had seen of minefields from the Great War. He minced across it and made a small bow.

"Professor Szilard sent me. I was under the impression I would be meeting with Professor Einstein."

"Impressions are worthless when they compete with a decent wind. He decided to go sailing. If he's not back in an hour, they will get him."

"They?" Max asked.

"Anybody in town with a boat," Mrs. Dukas told him with what sounded like a combination of amusement and exasperation. "Meanwhile, you may wait in his office. It shouldn't be too long. God willing."

Einstein's vacation office had faded striped wallpaper and a scuffed wood-plank floor, both of which the sea and the salt air had done their normal job on. Two white-curtained windows overlooked the harbor. Two others, at the opposite end of the room, faced a rear yard with freshly blooming tulip poplars. The warped plank floor was crowded with cartons of books and papers in various states of disarray. An ancient desk was swamped by piles of books, journal articles, scribbled notes, and a large jar of pipe tobacco.

The mess was daunting. But it was an opportunity beyond measure.

Goldschmidt worked efficiently. Quietly. Keeping an ear open for any approaching sound from outside the office, particularly the staccato beat of Mrs. Dukas' low-heeled, sensible shoes.

He pulled out his Leica camera and went first to a portable blackboard filled with chalk equations and erasure streaks. The figures were meaningless to him, but there was supposed to be an expert now implanted at the German consulate in New York who would look over anything Max could get him at once. The tiny Leica clicked quietly away.

When he was through with the blackboard, he quickly scanned the room and decided on orders of priority and procedure. Next was every paper on Einstein's desk, including several letters from Leo Szilard, all quickly taken from their envelopes, refolded and reinserted exactly as they had been. *Click.* Next the unpacked cartons, one item after another, which felt as though they would never end. *Click.* Next the books crammed into the shelves: their titles, along with any papers of interest that might be jammed in between their pages. *Click.*

He slowly, almost silently, opened each of seven drawers: office supplies, stationery, more articles torn from newspapers and science journals, strewn pipes and tangled pipe cleaners. At least there was little to photograph there. *Still no Einstein.* He thanked the spy gods for this gift, too—access to so much invaluable intelligence. All while Mrs. Dukas nervously paced the kitchen, waiting for the great man's return. It confirmed something just as vital for him as well: he, Max Goldschmidt, was under no suspicion whatsoever. He had completely convinced Szilard and the other great scientists back at Columbia. *This would make everything easier.*

He heard a car being driven very badly up the hill outside,

followed by the sound of tortured gears and a squeal of brakes. Max stuffed the Leica back into its inner jacket pocket and peered out the front window. A quick glance in a hand mirror, the pushing up of a cowlick in his hair, and the Chameleon walked down the hall, waiting for an introduction to the man he intended to deliver back to Germany within the next few days.

The countless photographs in grainy, two-dimensional shades of black and white came to life. The electric thatch of white hair, the long pipe extending from under a bushy white mustache, the heavy, creased eyelids, the rumpled attire. But now, standing within seven feet of Einstein, Max caught surprising details that the cameras hadn't. His sturdy chest and sinewy arms. A build seemingly taller than the official measurements of five feet and nine inches. Also, Einstein was grinning ecstatically.

"I don't know which was more of an adventure, Helen, the *Tinef* or the Jeep. The speedometer is broken."

"Then how did you know how fast you were driving?" she asked.

"Slower than the speed of light, I assure you."

He turned his gaze to Max and brought a hand to his forehead to signify his forgetfulness.

"*Aaach*, our visitor! Why didn't you remind me, Helen?"

"I did, Doctor. Last evening. And again this morning. Dr. Einstein, this is Max Goldschmidt."

Einstein stretched his hand. Max reached to clasp it. The scientist's fingers were thick and calloused, the nails unmanicured, the grip confident.

"I was expecting you to be accompanied by the great Szilard. Another one of his colds, eh?"

Einstein smiled benignly at him.

Max spoke shyly, deferentially.

"It is an honor, Professor Einstein. Professor Zwick talked of you so often."

Einstein's smile faded at once, and he nodded.

"The poor man. A tragic loss."

Max pulled the folded and stained composition from his pocket and offered it to Einstein.

"Here is the music he told me to bring to you, sir."

Einstein looked touched, glancing down at the musical score, then back up at Max.

"Come, Goldschmidt. We will take a look."

He ushered Max back into his office—completely unaware, Max was glad to see, that anything had been so much as touched. Instead, he plopped down in his desk chair and lit a pipe. Fulsome bursts of smoke drifted to the ceiling with every puff, and the aroma of burnt cedar enveloped Max, who sat across from the Professor watching with hidden intensity as he studied the sheet music. The crevices seemed to deepen across his forehead and his eyes narrowed. He dug his index finger beneath his wiry hair and scratched at his scalp. Finally, Einstein looked up at his guest.

"What did Zwick tell you about this piece when he gave it to you?"

"Only that it was urgent you receive it. Personally."

"Nothing else?"

"No. What do you make of it, Professor?"

Einstein took another long puff on his pipe.

"If he was trying to tell me something, there is nothing obvious. It requires further study." He placed the score on a tall pile of papers at the corner of his desk, like a needle tossed into a haystack.

"He was quite proud of the piece," Max said, prodding him as cautiously as he could. "I would often play it with him."

Einstein beamed at his guest.

"You know music?"

"I taught violin at the Talmud Torah School."

"You teach the fiddle?" Einstein asked, sitting up in his chair and leaning across the desk.

"My students were only children, Professor."

"Elsa used to say that sometimes I played like a child. Perhaps, if you have the time, you will practice with me?"

It was almost too easy. He was playing the world's most brilliant man like his fiddle.

"It would be an honor."

"How about this evening? I am expecting a guest for a small recital. Mr. Rothman. He owns the store downtown. Would you join us?"

"But there is only one train back to New York."

"You can stay here tonight. We will eat supper and then play the fiddle! You and I have much to discuss. In particular, our great commonality."

"The violin?"

"No, Herr Goldschmidt," Einstein said between furious puffs. "You and I share something else. We are both refugees from Hitler. We were both in the same boat, and America, it seems, is our life raft."

The Chameleon thought to himself, *yours will sink before long.*

Chapter Forty-Four

DAVID ROTHMAN GUIDED HIS BRIGHT blue Plymouth Business Coupe down Skunk Lane, towards the bay. His fingers were wrapped tightly around the steering wheel; his stomach tugged and a slight sheen of perspiration gathered on his cheeks.

Nerves.

Rothman's customers liked to say he could sell ice to an Eskimo. He could chat about anything to anyone, bestowing a sense of familiarity, comfort. But that night was entirely different. That night was his violin debut with the great Albert Einstein.

Even dressing for the occasion had been a challenge. After all, he'd thought to himself as he'd peered into his narrow bedroom closet, what does one wear for a customer who was last seen shoeless, with a rope tied around his waist? He decided on a brown suit and polka-dot tie clipped to one of his latest products: a Cotton Crinkle Crepe ironless white shirt.

His selection of music had also been unnerving. Einstein had mentioned that he was an amateur, but Rothman considered the description entirely subjective. Now, rounding the bend along the beach and rumbling up towards the cottage, he glanced at the sheet music next to him. The Pleyel duets were the simplest; a bit harder, the Mazas duets; and, if Einstein preferred a bit of a challenge, the *Bach Double Concerto.*

He pulled onto the bluff. He exhaled a deep, calming breath and went to the front door with the sheet music in one hand and his violin in the other.

He heard Einstein's scales, drifting flawlessly from the parlor.

Oh boy, he thought.

Mrs. Dukas greeted him on the porch with a terse, "You're late."

Inside, the little house was already redolent of Einstein's tobacco. "I'm sorry. It sounds like he's started without me."

She shooed him down the hall.

Max sat in a corner of an overstuffed sofa that smelled of mothballs, hands folded on his lap. The room was haphazardly furnished with more sofas, upholstered chairs, and tables—books scattered all over. But it was softly illuminated by a pair of Tiffany lamps and the glow of the setting sun through the front windows.

Einstein stood in front of a large stone fireplace, practicing his scales. It wasn't lost on Max that he could kill the professor at any time of his choosing. That moment, the next day. The weekend. But the mission still required time, patience. The goal was to learn what Einstein and the others knew about American research on a bomb, then abduct him.

His thoughts were interrupted by approaching footsteps, and the sudden appearance of David Rothman. Max stood respectfully and silently took measure of him, remembering the name from the store in town. Rothman was quite affable, he thought, but at the same time anxious and sweating heavily. *A typical little Jew peddler.*

Einstein lowered his violin, shook his guest's hand, and introduced Max, who leapt up and extended his arm.

"A fellow refugee from Herr Hitler," Einstein reported.

"Welcome to America!" Rothman said, exuberant, pumping away at Max's hand and squeezing his shoulder. The grasp seemed to discomfit Max—he backed away. David wondered whether that simple act—a salesman's friendly grip of his arm—had triggered some anxiety. *God only knows what he's been through,* he thought sympathetically.

Einstein asked Rothman what music he'd brought.

"A composition by Pleyel," Rothman replied.

The professor frowned. "*Ach*, this is trivial."

"How about Jacques Fereol Mazas?"

"This, too, is trivial."

Max could see Rothman stiffen, as if slapped by Einstein's rejection of his selections.

"Bach's Concerto for Two Violins in D Minor?" he stammered.

"The Double Concerto? This is better."

Relieved, David opened his violin case and positioned the bow and instrument. Max sat back on the couch, refolding his hands and watching carefully.

They began playing. Einstein took the first part, Rothman the second. Every one of Einstein's notes landed precisely. But Rothman was fumbling. Einstein smiled graciously and they started again. Sixteen measures later, another stumble by Rothman.

"I'm a little nervous," Rothman admitted. "Playing with such a great man."

"I am not a great violinist," Einstein said gently. "Let us try again."

This time, Rothman made it halfway through, his nervous grip on the bow producing a harsh tremolo.

"It's no use." he admitted.

"Perhaps another time," Einstein said with unmistakable disappointment. He turned to his guest. "How about you, Max?"

"I haven't played that piece in many years," he demurred.

"Life is like riding a bicycle, Max," Einstein told him. "To keep your balance, you must keep moving. Will you lend Max your instrument, Mr. Rothman?"

"Of course!" he said and handed them over at once—though Max could see in his eyes that it only humiliated him all the more.

Max cradled Rothman's violin and bow. He remembered the practice sessions at Quenzsee, and the advice of his teacher there: to maintain his cover, he would have to play proficiently, but not flawlessly. He began strumming—lively, lyrical notes that beckoned Einstein to follow. The two violins soon entered a spirited conversation, a statement by one, an imitative counterpoint by the other. The notes flitted across the parlor, then danced out the screened windows and into the warm dusk. Einstein beamed at Max, who reciprocated with a contented smile. The two men, through their instruments, had fallen into a synchronous state.

Then a rhythmic cascade to that final sonorous note when they pulled their bows across the A string. They lowered the violins. A mantle clock tapped steadily, the only sound in the room. Einstein broke the stillness: "You say you are out of practice, Max?" Then laughed heartily.

Max mopped the sweat from his own face with a dirty handkerchief, trying to look shyly pleased. Satisfied that he'd twisted another coil in the rope that would pull Einstein closer.

The professor suggested coffee on the porch. Max heard a chorus of chirping frogs, buzzing insects, clicking cicadas; his nose tingled at the sharp scent of grass and harbor air. The professor took a weathered rocking chair, shooed away some flies with the back of his hands, and lit a pipe. Max studied the flame illuminating the deep crevices along his worn flesh, and the swelling folds under his heavy eyes. Einstein rocked gently, the chair groaning in protest.

"So Professor, how are you finding our neck of the woods?" Rothman asked Einstein.

"It is a beautiful part of the world. Especially now, when I can sail almost every day."

Rothman turned to Max. "And how are conditions in Europe? Do you think there will be a war?"

Max exhibited discomfort with the question. "I don't know politics."

"Of course," Rothman said. "But one thing I have never been able to understand is how it was possible for a man like Hitler—a nincompoop, an uneducated buffoon—to take over the leadership of Germany, the most educated nation in the world."

Einstein answered the question: "At first, everyone thought the

Nazis were just more street thugs. Like so many after the war, they were angry about our defeat, and the worthless money, and how everything was thrown into chaos."

"It was a hard time," Max added sadly.

"We thought it would all go away. And nobody understood just what Hitler was. You know, they say he calls himself a sleepwalker, never putting a foot wrong. He seems like that sometimes—like he has an extra sense. Yes, my dear Rothman, we thought he was a buffoon, a clown. We laughed at him. Until one day we discovered that when we laughed, our faces were slapped."

"I saw it," Max added. "Stormtroopers on the streets. Beating and arresting innocent people. With the approval of the government." He shuddered.

"Now you are here, Goldschmidt," said Einstein. "You are safe."

They fell quiet against the chirp of frogs and the dance of fireflies on the bluff.

David Rothman kept studying Max. He had been a salesman all his adult life and the art of salesmanship, he believed, was reading the unspoken clues of a customer. You followed the direction of their eyes. If they really desired a product their eyes would return to it again and again, no matter what it cost. Hands were also a clue: gnarled, dirt-stained fingers belonged to farmers and fishermen on tight budgets. Smooth, manicured fingers indicated a vacationer with disposable cash. You steered farmers to the cheap tabletop radios, shifted the tourists over to the premium walnut console with the built-in phonograph, fourteen-inch Dynapower Speaker, and Drift-Proof station settings. Top of its class.

You read the clues and made the sale.

There was something about this man. Inconsistencies. David Rothman tried to sort them out as he sat on the porch. Max was unable to see him clearly, he knew, from where he was sitting.

Rothman's face was hidden in the shadows, away from the meager porch light bulb.

Goldschmidt's haggard, ashen face…also hinted at firm cheekbones and a proud jawline. His wrinkled suit drooped on his slender frame, but when David had grasped Max's upper arm he instantly felt well-toned muscle, before Max reflexively turned away. His forlorn eyes were usually cast downward, but seemed to keep Einstein in their peripheral vision. Like a customer who feigned disinterest in a particular product, but couldn't quite keep his eyes off it.

And the way he played the Double Concerto! David Rothman prided himself on his ear for music. The Double Concerto was technically challenging. But Max's performance seemed well-practiced, even though he claimed not to have played it in years.

"Tell me, Max, when did you arrive in America?" Rothman asked.

"This month," Max answered.

Einstein chuckled softly.

"It must have been difficult to leave your family," said Rothman. "I can't imagine such a thing."

"I have no one. My mother died when I was a child. My father was killed by the Gestapo."

"I'm sorry," said Rothman.

There was an awkward silence on the porch. David broke the quiet again, the same way he might refer casually back to the item the customer was still looking at.

"Well, thank God you were able to get out. I was under the impression that it's practically impossible for Jews to leave Germany."

"Unfortunately, it is much easier for Jews to leave Nazi Germany than to get into America," Einstein noted. "Last year President Roosevelt organized a meeting in Evian, France, to decide where the Jewish refugees from Germany and Austria should go. Herr Hitler said he was ready to put all such 'criminals'—all the Jews—on luxury ships to any country that would accept them."

"Have you read about the *Saint Louis*, professor?" asked Rothman.

"Of course. Those poor people. And our own government will slam the door, even to them."

"What ship did you come on?" Rothman asked.

Chameleon fought to control his rising dislike for the nosey Jew. "The *Bremen*. Through the help of the underground. Professor Einstein knows what I mean."

Einstein nodded. "There are ways. If you know the right people and have the resources. Zwick enjoyed both."

David Rothman smiled, and Max smiled back. Both sensed the other's distaste.

A little later, after Rothman had left, Helen Dukas went about the living room of the cottage picking up glasses, ashtrays, and the small plates there.

"Mrs. Dukas, if you don't mind, could you make up the guest bedroom? Mr. Goldschmidt will be staying over with us tonight."

"Yes, you already told me that, Professor. His room is ready," Helen told him, in a voice just testy enough to convey that he was pushing her limits.

"Thank you, Mrs. Dukas," Einstein said formally, then turned and winked at Max, and they snuck into his office. He picked up another much cheaper violin that Max had noticed earlier. He pulled up two hard-backed chairs and a music stand next, and motioned for Max to have a seat next to him. The pages of *Two Scientists Debate* rested on the slightly angled platform.

"I cannot thank you enough for bringing Professor Zwick's copy all the way from Germany," Einstein told him. "That was a prodigious feat. Now let us see what we have. Please take the first part."

They began to play. The same piece that Max had played so often with his old employer, Gerhardt Zwick—enough, even, to make the Chameleon feel nostalgic about his evenings with the man. It was an amateur composition, obviously, but still sweet, earnest. Max braced himself not to give any indication of what he had discovered weeks earlier, playing at Quenzsee with Heydrich. Then it came: a stumble by Einstein on a particular note. He muttered under his breath, and continued playing, another stumble. He turned to Max and said, "Poor old Zwick. So many errors."

They continued through several more stumbles by Einstein. At the end Einstein set the violin on his lap, his eyes scanning the pages quizzically while a clock ticked on a mantle.

"What is wrong, Professor?" asked Max.

"Poor Zwick," Einstein repeated. "I have lost my partner."

"Me too," whispered Max Goldschmidt.

Chapter Forty-Five

MAX AWOKE EARLY ON TUESDAY and peered out a window. The sky was a threatening gray, and a harsh bay breeze ruffled the surrounding trees. He found Einstein at the kitchen table, already engrossed in the day's newspaper.

"Good morning," Max offered.

Einstein peered over the top of his paper and grumbled, "Actually, there is nothing good about it, Goldschmidt."

The Chameleon retained his smile, but wondered whether somehow, overnight, Einstein had picked up on something that had shaken his confidence in him.

"May I ask why, Professor?"

"The weather is horrible. There will be no sailing today."

He smiled at Max then, but went back to his paper. Mrs. Dukas entered to announce that she would call a taxi to return Max to the train station at Greenport, but not before breakfast. Max accepted the offer, trying to find ways to stall as much as possible—to become another fixture in the Einstein household, just as he had in Zwick's. But all his efforts at conversation, with either of them, seemed to fall flat. Mrs. Dukas served him some palatable eggs, bacon, and hash browns, but said nothing before leaving the kitchen again. The coffee she put before them was so insipid that he grimaced.

Einstein chuckled.

"*Ja,* American coffee. Tasteless."

"One of my chores was to make Professor Zwick coffee every morning," Max said sadly. "Strong and black, the way he liked it. I also cleaned his office, ran his errands, brought him his books. Who performs these chores for you, if I may ask?"

Still focused on the paper, Einstein asked, "Are you asking for a job, Goldschmidt?"

"I must find a way of supporting myself in America. While I study."

"Study?"

"I would like to become an American citizen one day."

"Mrs. Dukas handles all of my chores, Goldschmidt. But I can refer you to one of the refugee agencies in New York."

"I understand," Max said, though the disappointment in his voice made it clear that he did not. *Always the sad sack, Max Goldschmidt.*

"Don't worry, Max, we will see each other again. Perhaps a sail, one day. Now I have some matters to work on. And given the weather, I think I'll play the fiddle."

For a fleeting moment Max considered shooting both Einstein and Mrs. Dukas on the spot, then sorting through the scientist's papers at his leisure. The temptation had grown since he'd arrived the day before. *No.* His mission was to return Einstein alive, not mounted to a wall trophy.

He made his obsequious goodbyes to Einstein, and especially to Mrs. Dukas.

Einstein offered to wait with him on the porch. "Even in miserable weather, the view should not be missed."

They stepped out, and Max gazed on the harbor that stretched below, just beyond a wooded hill.

"It reminds me of where I used to sail on Scharfe Lake, Professor."

Einstein chuckled nostalgically. "Or Caputh. Where I sailed my Tummler. Did you do much sailing?"

"Quite a lot."

Perfect.

"Where did you learn?"

"I took lessons at the Westphal Marina."

Einstein smiled. "I remember it well. When? Perhaps we saw each other there."

"1935, Professor. While working for Herr Doctor Zwick."

Einstein puffed at his pipe for a few moments. An approaching taxi groaned in the distance.

"I have an idea, Goldschmidt. On the thirtieth of this month, the Americans will observe a national holiday. Decoration Day. Quite strange, actually—they honor their war dead with loud parades and barbeques. Perhaps you will return for a sail?"

"Really, Professor?"

"Why not?" Einstein grinned. "Here comes your taxi. I'm going inside to pass the time with my fiddle. We will see each other again in less than two weeks."

Max trudged across the scrubby yard, taking stock of his good fortune. Brushing a hand across the Sauer pistol, the Lecia camera full of the images from Einstein's office, still in the sealed inner pocket of his coat. All there. Gazing at the cozy harbor spilling into Peconic Bay, satisfied that everything conformed to the maps and photographs he'd studied at Quenzsee. The ribbons of beach, a treelined elevation in the distance, which he recalled was Robins Island.

His escape route stretched out before him. There were so many bolt holes—all unguarded by the United States Navy and Coast Guard. He carefully went over all of what he had learned, and all of the possible obstacles before him.

Most importantly, he'd been invited back. Nothing seemed suspicious about Einstein's invitation.

Yes, he had established that the musical notation he had so carefully transported from Germany contained nothing of value— just the faltering ear of a doddering old man.

Yes, this lonely stretch of Long Island would be perfect for exfiltration.

But what of the others? The policemen poking around, he was sure, he could take care of. And then there was David Rothman, from last night. *Why the questions?*

He settled into the rear seat of the taxi. It would take him to Greenport, and begin his long, lonely trip back to Manhattan.

The last thing he heard was Einstein playing *Two Scientists Debate.*

After the train pulled into Pennsylvania Station, Max found a payphone and dialed Bernstein's Sheet Music Company. He asked for Carl, and when told the counter-code, "Carl is with a customer," requested a copy of Vivaldi's Concerto in D Minor.

"Where shall we deliver?" he was asked.

He gave the address of the King's Crown, and the very precise time of 9:15.

"Not a minute sooner or later," he demanded.

The knock on his door came at exactly the correct time. Still, as a precaution, Max took his Sauer to the door and opened it a crack. In front of him was a young deliveryman, dressed in white. He passed the sheet music to Max and whispered, "And you have something to return?"

Max closed and locked the door, walked to his desk, removed the sheet music from its paperback and inserted the Leica film cannister. He'd extracted it earlier, in the pitch-black bathroom, using his jacket as a film changing bag.

It was the rare Quenzsee instruction that he'd found useful.

He changed, crawled into bed, and dreamed of home.

Chapter Forty-Six

IT HAD BEEN AN EXCRUCIATING several days for Maria Voigt. On Friday evening she'd returned to the New Europe Theater, along with her Afus radio, which had been concealed as film equipment. The next day she'd received a coded message from Chameleon, relayed by Bernstein's Music Company, indicating that he'd expected to make initial contact with Albert Einstein the following Monday. Now it was Tuesday evening, and she'd heard nothing. She didn't know whether he'd actually met Einstein, or for that matter whether he was still in Little Hog Neck, back in Manhattan, or in FBI custody somewhere. Maria was as in the dark as the theater itself.

Finally, at seven o'clock that evening, as patrons filed in to view the German language drama *Detours to Happiness*, the intercom in her second-floor office buzzed with news. A delivery of movie posters had arrived. Could she come down and fetch them?

The posters were rolled into six cardboard tubes. Maria carried them to the office and carefully unsealed each one. The posters slid out easily. In one tube, however, a poster was wrapped around a thin envelope. Inside the envelope were miniature photographs from Albert Einstein's cottage, and a brief message from Chameleon:

Returning to uncle's on 30/5. Need ride.

She could barely contain a smile. She grabbed a magnifying glass from the top drawer of her desk and studied each image. Exquisite images of Einstein's books, files, furniture, the layout of his office.

Maria rushed to the projection room. It was dark, except for the brilliant column of light plunging from the projector, through a small glass window, and onto the huge screen. She unlocked the door to the equipment closet, rifled through shelves of old projectors and film cannisters, and found the case storing the Afus. She would transmit the news to Berlin. She heard cheering. It wasn't an audience, but her fantasy of the response at the Abwehr when her message was received.

Less than an hour later her message was decoded for Helmut Swan, who indeed let out a triumphant cheer, and ordered a car to take him immediately to the office of Reinhard Heydrich.

General Becker of the Reich Research Council was not happy. Reinhard Heydrich had been slicing through him for nearly an hour already, detailing Becker's every failure as head of munitions for the *Wehrmacht*. Demanding to know why one factory after another was falling grievously short of its production quotas. There were good reasons for that, he knew, but nearly all of them had to do with the incompetent party loyalists who had been put in charge of one critical sector after another. Since he couldn't say that, he kept his mouth shut.

"But sir," the general finally said, his voice pleading. "We are at peace!"

Heydrich's lips snapped into a thin, furious line.

"Peace through strength, Becker. Once we move on Poland, the rest of the world must view us as omnipotent. Otherwise, we invite them to declare war on us. Where is our bomb?"

Becker sighed and shook his head.

"A lot of fertile ideas. But no working design for a possible bomb. Yet."

"Without results, fertile ideas are just shit, Becker."

Heydrich's adjutant appeared in the door of his office at the Reich Security building.

"Helmut Swan has arrived, sir."

"Good, send him in," Heydrich said, slamming shut the sleek

black portfolio that contained his munitions briefing. "You are dismissed, Becker."

The general saluted and stood up to leave.

"Becker..." Heydrich called him back as he headed for the door. "Tell your scientists the Fuhrer is growing impatient. Failure will bring consequences. The same applies to you. That is all."

Heydrich liked Swan much better. He was operational, detailed, meticulous in his planning. And, like a puppy dog, eager for his superior's approval. Indeed, he even seemed to be salivating when he walked in.

"I have good news. Chameleon has made initial contact with Einstein."

"And?"

"And they are meeting again, on the thirtieth of this month."

Heydrich's lips curled back. The whippet hound, on the scent. "That's two weeks."

"*Jawohl*, Direktor. Which means—"

"We must dispatch Einstein's ride. Is it ready?"

"Yes sir, in Wilhelmshaven. Our finest man."

"Who?" asked Heydrich

"Kapitänleutnant Hans Fischer. U-boat 37. Best in the Kriegsmarine."

"He is familiar with Long Island?"

"He's a ferryman. Part of the surveillance fleet that has been moving up and down America's east coast. He could sail right up New York Harbor and put a torpedo up the skirt of the Statue of Liberty, if you ordered him to."

Heydrich didn't smile. "I read a report about these patrols. Hard to believe, actually. The Americans seem to have no concern for their Atlantic defenses. There are no batteries to speak of. No gun-works or naval patrols. Their Coast Guard spends most of its time rescuing fishermen and gentlemen boaters. They are not looking for us."

"An important factor in our plan, sir. The element of surprise."

"The boat is...capable, Swan?"

"It is the first of the IXA line, built for long distance work. It can reach eighteen knots on the surface, and over seven submerged. Its range is ten thousand, five hundred nautical miles, and the voyage from Wilhelmshaven to Long Island is about four thousand. Depending on weather and other factors, it will be off the coast of Long Island a day early."

Heydrich pulled a map of Long Island from a desk drawer and unfolded it. He held a magnifying glass over the extreme tip of the mass, which he'd already circled in red. There, Maria Voigt had found a tiny fishing shack where Chameleon would remain with Einstein until the U-boat arrived.

He sat back in his leather chair, relishing the moment. "Very good, Swan. Send a final order: no radio contact unless critical. Even the crew is not to know the mission until they see Einstein himself on that boat."

"*Jawohl*." Swan turned away, then looked back, taking advantage of Heydrich's good humor. "Sir?"

"Yes."

"It must have been quite difficult. For Chameleon. To be in Einstein's presence and restrain himself from killing him on the spot."

"He knows the mission. We must keep Einstein alive. And for that, we need time."

"That takes great discipline sir."

"You may go, Swan."

Chapter Forty-Seven

TIME, THE CHAMELEON KNEW, was both ally and adversary to any mission. So he put it to good use the two weeks before he departed for Germany—with a brief stop to pick up Albert Einstein. With so much of the university vacated for the summer, Leo Szilard was able to find him a menial part-time summer job at Pupin Hall. The work reminded him of his days with Professor Zwick at the Friedrich Wilhelm University: dusting the shelves, sweeping the floors, fetching tea.

Murdering Zwick.

He sensed that something was developing in the labs. Szilard and Walther Zinn, and their assistants, were always talking furtively about something—or calling Einstein for consultations in more frantic, hushed conversations. They filled piles of notepads, always locking them away when they left the office and carting them home at night. Of course, when he could, Max jimmied open the drawers and photographed the documents with his Leica camera.

They were even more careful about the small, mysterious laboratory next to their offices, where Eugene Wigner often came over to confer with them. A Jew from Hungary, according to Max's briefings. Rail thin, with a monastic band of black hair encircling the back of his head. He came to the office as if there for a funeral: a solemn, even grim, man casting his dark eyes across the room at the tiny lab with the locked door, as if frightened of what it might contain. He and Szilard would nod at one another and disappear behind its door, clinching their privacy with the clack of the lock.

There were other laboratories, other locked offices, doors, and desks throughout Pupin, he began to understand. It was a dark, looming building full of twisting, maze-like hallways. So many of the other physicists working there were always locking doors behind them.

Max was even warned, personally, that he was not to enter certain rooms with warning signs in red block letters on the doors. He did not think that the locks would prove much of a hindrance. But by the locked doors were almost always stationed actual people—invariably large, brawny young men from what he was told was the university's renowned football team. The intense security, one graduate assistant had confided in him, was not so much about national security as it was about securing patents—or a Nobel Prize.

Whatever the reason, it was maddening. Max seriously considered whether he might rig up a silencer for his Sauer and move floor by floor through Pupin, killing everyone who might be working on the bomb project. It could be possible to pull it off before anyone knew what was going on.

He put these thoughts—fantasies, perhaps—out of his mind.

There was one temptation that he could not purge: his sacred triad of seduction, intimacy, and confession. The luring of the target, followed by that long, futile breath after he'd revealed his own truth.

At one point he considered riding the subway to the Lower East Side, where the Jewish flesh trade thrived and the police were paid off to look the other way. But the risk was too high: the murder of even a Jewish prostitute might bring attention, questions, investigations.

There was one possibility.

On Wednesday afternoon—five days before he was to sail with Einstein—he called Bernstein's Music Company.

Mozart needed a meeting.

Voigt arrived at seven that night. She'd dressed plainly: a navy-blue polka-dot coat dress with a button front, and white Sears catalogue slip-on sandals.

Max locked the door behind her and took a seat at the edge of the bed.

"You signaled you had to see me. What's the emergency?" Maria asked, although Max believed she already knew.

He replied, unconvincingly, "A last-minute urgency. I wish to review the final plans for Einstein's extraction."

"When we first met you insisted you didn't trust our plans."

"Trust," Max repeated, rising from the bed. He took several steps towards Maria, using his right hand to block the faint outline of a knife he'd tucked in his pocket. "Next Monday I will be putting my life in your hands, Fraulein. How do I know I can trust you?"

"All you have to know is that Berlin trusts me."

Max took another step closer. "And do you trust me, Fraulein?"

"I trust you not to betray Heydrich. Or the Fuhrer for that matter. And to accomplish this mission for the good of the German nation. Now tell me exactly what I am doing here."

"Why is it you never married?" he asked.

She didn't flinch.

"You have had men, yes?" Max asked.

Maria conveyed a condescending smile. "If you're asking me to make love to you, the answer is no. Not the way you look now—"

"As the Jew, Max Goldschmidt?"

"As any Jew."

"You desire an Aryan. Pure."

"It depends."

"Shall we play a little game about trust?" he asked.

Max was close enough to tower over her. He smelled a delicate lilac perfume on her neck; his eyes wandered down the neckline to the top button of her dress. He undid the button, pausing to see if she would step back or demand that he stop.

She only smirked, a willing participant in his game.

He continued loosening each button, revealing a pearl silk crepe chemise.

He pulled her gently against him, maneuvering her to the bed, as if dancing. He lowered her gently to the mattress, hiked the chemise above her hips. She reached out to unbutton his pants, but he stopped her.

"Let me," he whispered as he brought his pants to his knees, where his knife would be within arm's reach at just the right moment.

Max was gone. Anton was making love to Maria; to Rebecca Schoenwald, the Jewish communist in Berlin; the ravishing British woman in the shadow of the Jerusalem church; even the boy Alois in the woods near Salzburg. He'd stalked, seduced, raped, terrorized. It always heightened his own ecstatic final movements—his fingers clamped around their necks, the slice of a blade against their carnal flesh. As he rocked back and forth, he tasted, smelled, saw them all; heard the primitive sounds of pleasure and pain under him; felt their heavy breaths and their mortal flesh against his own, so that they were all one. He grinded, faster and faster, waiting for his prey's grunts and moans to reach that inevitable, ecstatic cry. And when Maria's body crumpled under him, satiated and exhausted, he knew it was his turn.

"Enough," she panted, trying to roll away.

Max pressed harder against her, pinning her to the mattress. He quickly pulled out his knife and brought it gently against the soft spot in her neck.

Now. Tell her. Tell her.

"What are you doing?" she demanded.

"I am not Max Goldschmidt," he began his breathless confession.

She remained silent, staring back at him coldly.

"My name is—"

"Anton Gunther," she snapped. "You are an agent of the Abwehr. A loyal German who will one day get himself killed with this bizarre ritual. Control yourself."

Maria thrust her knee against his groin, sending him tumbling off of her. She grabbed the knife and pointed it at his own neck.

"I'll hold my report to Heydrich until after you finish your mission," she said, pulling herself up while maintaining her grip on the knife.

"I—I wasn't going to hurt you. It's just my little game...I was..." His words trailed off.

"Your game is pitiful," she snapped. She rose from the bed, buttoned her dress, and marched out of the room.

Maria Voigt returned to her office in the New Europe convinced of two things.

Chameleon was ill enough to imperil the mission.

And once he and Einstein were sailing for Germany, she would warn Heydrich that Anton could never be in the field again.

Chapter Forty-Eight

THE NEXT DAY, FRIDAY, the bells chimed above the door at Rothman's Department Store. David Rothman looked up from the cash register and saw Chief Phineas Murphy hobble in. Rothman knew that Murphy was resistant to sales pressure. You had to ease him into a sale with finesse. So he offered a cheerful "Good morning, Chief!" and resumed his business, positioning himself to keep Murphy in the corner of his eye. The Chief was admiring a display of brand-new fishing rods. He'd pulled out a Saranac, balanced the handle in his right palm, and squinted along the eyelids to the tip. He hinted at a relaxed smile, which Rothman knew was exactly the right time to engage.

"That's a beauty you got right there, Chief. Three-piece, split bamboo. Cork grip. Stainless steel guide."

"I'm just browsing."

David Rothman wasn't a man who discouraged easily. Or at all. Earlier that morning, he'd sold a vacationing woman a Forstmann's winter coat collared with Prince Edward Island silver fox—no matter that it was the end of June.

"Take your time. Going fishing this weekend?"

Murphy's smile vanished as he returned the rod to the display. "You kidding? It's Decoration Day weekend. Parades, traffic, drunk tourists."

Rothman felt a sale slipping away and began reeling it back in.

"You work too hard, Chief. Me? We're closing for Decoration Day on Tuesday, so my wife and I are making it a long weekend. In one of those Catskill resorts. Let me give you a nice discount on that rod, and we'll go fishing together when I get back. I was thinking of asking Dr. Einstein to come out with me anyway. Next weekend."

Murphy looked up from the display. "You two are friends?" he asked, surprised.

"Good friends. Had me up to Doc Moore's cottage to play a little violin. With another fella from Germany. I was no good, though."

"From Germany?"

"Yeah, just arrived. Jewish refugee. Einstein is very close to them. I read they all have an open invitation, which makes sense, right? Him being a refugee himself, and all?"

"You remember the name of the guy?"

Rothman scratched his chin. "Do I ever forget a name? Max Goldschmidt."

Murphy took out his patrol pad and scribbled the name. He'd check with Officer Krupski to see if the name was on Mrs. Dukas' list that day.

"When did you meet him?"

"Ten days ago or so."

"Did he say when he arrived in the country?"

Rothman thought for a moment. "Said he'd just come. On the *Bremen*."

Murphy jotted in the pad.

"Notice anything about him? Anything that stood out?"

"Aww, I'd say he was a nice enough guy. I guess."

"You guess."

Rothman hesitated. He shook his head slowly and kneaded the back of his neck with a hand.

"I don't wanna put anyone down. And maybe I was just sore because of how much better he played the fiddle. But there was something that didn't quite fit. Not sure I can explain it. I have a good sense of these things. Almost a sixth sense sort of thing. People tell me—"

"What about him seemed out of place?" Murphy asked impatiently.

"Well, for one, it was the ship he came on, the *Bremen*. I've been reading those newspaper articles about that other ship, the *Saint Louis?* All those Jews may be turned back to Europe by the Cuban government. And they can't come here because they don't have visas. How'd *he* get here? There are quotas, you know."

"Did he say how he did it?"

"Mentioned the underground. Einstein, too."

"Anything else?" asked Murphy, pencil against his pad.

Rothman contemplated the question, scrunching his mouth and rolling his eyes in search of a definitive answer.

"I don't know. I mean, I can read a cool customer. But he seemed, well, *cold*, actually. Like he was thinking everything through."

Rothman proceeded to describe Max as if he were detailing the specs of a piece of merchandise.

"Mid-thirties. Five feet, ten inches. About one hundred and sixty pounds. Sloppy hair. Dark, heavy eyes. Wore a wrinkled-up old suit, and a shoe with a slight separation between the sole and toe box—shoe made in Europe, as far as I could tell. Quality materials. Just beaten up is all."

"Anything else?"

"Like I say, he put me to shame on the violin. Wasn't one of my best nights. Oh, and he was in much better condition than he looked!"

"What do you mean?"

"I got a feel of his arm, which he didn't like. But it was muscle, through an' through. I never felt a stronger arm on a lobsterman, which is saying something."

Murphy returned the pad to his pocket.

"Sounds like nothing to worry about."

Rothman scratched his head. "Who said anything about worrying? Is something going on?"

"Nuthin!'" growled Murphy. He took another look at the rod, then turned towards the door.

Rothman asked again about fishing that weekend.

The only response was the jingling of the bell.

The Chief returned to headquarters, hobbled to the police radio, pulled the microphone stalk to his face, and turned a dial. The speaker hissed and zizzed, like waves of insects on the beach.

"Calling Officer Krupski," Murphy announced.

"Krupski here."

"You at the Einstein cottage?"

"Yes sir."

"You remember a Jewish-looking guy going up to the house? By the name of Max Goldschmidt?"

Static crackled.

"Yeah, sounds familiar. But if you want to check, I keep all of Mrs. Dukas' lists of approved guests in my desk. Top drawer."

Murphy hoisted himself up, labored down the hall and into the shared workspace of his deputies. Two overhead fans whirled uselessly in the stifling room. He rifled through Krupski's desk and found the page with Goldschmidt's name written in Mrs. Dukas' precise lead-pencil handwriting, each letter clear and thought out.

He returned to his office, worked himself into his chair, and dialed the FBI.

Chapter Forty-Nine

IT WAS LATE FRIDAY afternoon, and many FBI employees had left early for the weekend. James was immersed in the manifest of the SS *Berlin*, the ship that had arrived in New York the day before. Searching, line by line, for…At that point, he wasn't sure what. The lists were eye-straining: fifteen columns across, as many as thirty rows from top to bottom, crammed with names, genders, ages, occupations, nationalities, spoken languages, places of birth, passport numbers, permanent addresses, and more. Across the office, Harry was stretched back in his chair, rubbing his bleary eyes.

The sudden ringing telephone broke a despairing silence. James answered.

"It's Chief Murphy. Out in Southold."

"Yes, sir."

"Look, I'm certain this is nothing, but I just spoke with a local merchant. He told me about a visit…" He read through his notes, including Mrs. Dukas' written approval of Goldschmidt's visit.

"Did he say what ship he came in on?"

Murphy answered, "The *Bremen*."

James recorded the information in a pad. "Einstein is known to welcome refugees. But thanks for being alert. And keep an eye out, will you please?"

"I told ya' nothing gets by me."

James punched a button on his intercom and called out for Agent Crowley, who picked up instantly.

"Have you checked the manifests from a ship named *Bremen*?" James asked.

"Yes sir. Makes two round trip voyages each month. None of

the manifests I looked at showed anything unusual."

"When was it last in port?"

"Lemme check the timetable…"

Amos heard Crowley humming a nondescript tune as he shuffled through papers. Then: "Let's see here… arrived in New York on May 11th and sailed back on May 13th. It's due back here…this Monday, actually. As I said, sir, I reviewed the manifest for the May 11th arrival, but nothing—"

"Check them again. Look for a passenger by the name of Max Goldschmidt. If the name isn't on the May manifest, check the April manifests."

"You think Goldschmidt is our man?"

"Possibly."

"Which means he arrived recently."

"Which means," Harry interjected from behind his desk, "that we have a possible lead that requires research and not guesswork."

Agent Crowley loosened the knot of his tie and began digging through the piles of passenger manifests on his gray metal desk. He recovered the documents from the *Bremen's* voyage in early May. They were segregated by class: over eight hundred entries in first class, five hundred in second class, three hundred in tourist class, six hundred in third class.

All in all, over two thousand passengers plus nine hundred crew on each voyage.

He started with the list of third-class passengers, assuming it was category for a refugee. He ran his fingers slowly down the names beginning with the letter G, but there was no one named Max Goldschmidt.

He continued through the other passenger classes, periodically rubbing his eyes and massaging his temples.

Then pulled the manifests for April…March…February.

Two hours later, he gathered the manifests, pushed back his chair, and headed towards the small office in a corner of the seventh floor. He positioned himself near the door, clutching the passenger lists against his chest. Amos noticed a loose strand of blond hair drooping above his eye, a sheen of perspiration across his forehead.

"If there was a Max Goldschmidt aboard, his name was either entered incorrectly on the manifest or he cleared immigration under a different name," Crowley declared.

"It's a red flag alright," said Harry, "but where does it point?"

James asked to see the manifests. His eyes flicked across the pages, the thousands of names that would need to be looked into in the tedious, nearly impossible task of locating a phantom.

"We're going to need some help," he said. "I'll get authorization for a few more agents. Also, Crowley, you said the *Bremen* arrives Monday?"

"Yes sir."

"Fine. You'll meet her then."

"Yes sir…and what do I do when she arrives?"

Harry asked, "Any idea, Crowley, who knows everything there is to know about the passengers and crew of every ship going to or from Germany?"

"I assume the captain."

"Nope. The Ortsgruppenleiter."

"The who?"

"Yeah, exactly what I thought when I learned about it. It was during one of our early investigations, around the time we realized we were practically blind to Berlin's operations here. We identified a guy on the SS *Bismark*, placed there by the Gestapo to enforce Party discipline and loyalty. His decisions couldn't be questioned by anyone on board, including the captain. A source told us that he had knowledge of German intel assets being ferried back and forth."

"He cooperated?"

"He told us to go to hell," James muttered under his breath.

Harry continued. "They're trained not to cooperate. But a good interview is like inspecting a worn sweater—you might find a loose thread somewhere."

"So I'm going to interrogate a Gestapo agent?" Crowley croaked.

"Agent Weiss will accompany you," James said.

Harry shook his head adamantly.

"I'll be supervising the investigation of thousands of names, Harry. Besides, we know how German crews react to people like me boarding their ships. They've been known to spit on black luggage porters on the quay."

Weiss suppressed an audible expression of blasphemy.

"Besides," Amos said, "how often will you have the joy of interrogating a Nazi thug?"

Harry thought for a few moments. "Well," he conceded, "when you put it those terms..."

James dismissed Agent Crowley, reached for his telephone, and dialed.

He heard crackling transmission of electrical signals traveling from the network of wires between New York City and Little Hog Neck. He remembered the old phone that Theodore Roosevelt had installed in Sagamore Hill.

"Hallooooh?" Albert Einstein crooned into the phone.

"Professor Einstein, this is Agent Amos. From the—"

"*Ja,* I know who you work for. How have you been, since our last meeting at—what was it your partner called my home? The 'ass-end of the earth'?"

James shot an annoyed glance across the room at Harry, who was already scribbling notes from one of the manifests.

"Sir, I'm calling about a visitor you had several weeks ago. Max Goldschmidt."

The conversation—debate, as far as James was concerned—lasted three minutes. James laid out the doubts about Goldschmidt, and Einstein reminded him that the FBI always seemed to harbor doubts about Jewish refugees, including Einstein himself.

"Did someone send Goldschmidt to you?"

There was a brief pause before Einstein said, "I prefer not to say."

"Why?"

"Because there is no crime in arranging for me to meet refugees from Hitler. And I have no intention of subjecting my friends to Mr. Hoover's paranoia."

"We are just trying to keep you safe, Professor."

Einstein politely thanked him for his usual concern, wished him a good weekend, and hung up abruptly.

Amos sighed. Then dialed another number.

Moments later, Chief Murphy's voice broke through the static.

"Thanks for that lead on Max Goldschmidt," Amos said. "Turns out the name doesn't appear on any recent ship's manifest. We're actively investigating it."

Murphy grunted. "I don't get why Roosevelt lets those kraut ships come here in the first place. Right under our goddam noses."

James ignored the slur. "Will you follow up with Rothman? Get every detail you can about this Goldschmidt?"

Murphy agreed.

"One more request," James asked. "Einstein is not taking the threat seriously. Can you station more men at the cottage?"

"More *men*? I don't exactly have Pershing's Army here. Got two squad cars and five unarmed constables. Plus Decoration Day is coming up. Parades, traffic control, drunks."

"Can you call other police departments in the area?"

"They all have their own parades. And those that don't will be at Camp Siegfried, getting drunk themselves."

"Chief, until we track down this Goldschmidt, and any other leads that may arise, Einstein remains under credible threat."

Murphy's grumble came across loud and clear, despite the static. "I'll take care of it. Go up to Little Hog Neck myself. Christ, I took on the Germans at Belleau Woods."

"Be careful. This guy could be extremely dangerous."

"Belleau Woods was no fucking picnic."

Chapter Fifty

EARLY THE NEXT MORNING, FRIDAY, Chief Murphy hobbled once again into Rothman's Department Store. He found a teenage girl behind the cash register, casually flipping through the pages of a movie magazine. She wore a plaid skirt, a puff sleeve blouse, and a heavy application of red lipstick. She introduced herself as Alice.

Murphy silently rebuked himself for forgetting Rothman's plans to visit the Catskills that weekend.

"I need to contact Rothman. Did he leave a number?"

Alice dutifully led him to a small office at the back of the store. Shelves were cluttered with merchandise about to be displayed, returned, or on layaway. A wall calendar featuring the Manhattan skyline was tacked to the wall in front of Rothman's desk. A black metal Bell telephone sat next to a closed ledger. Alice opened the top drawer and found the number that Rothman had recorded before leaving.

Murphy dialed.

"Concord Hotel. How may I direct your call?" an operator answered.

Murphy asked for Rothman's room.

The phone rang, unanswered.

He left a message with the operator, then left the store—but not before briefly admiring the display of fishing rods.

In the FBI office on Foley Square, the weekend unfolded with a broad sweep for a person going by the name of Max Goldschmidt. The search was aided by a combination of FBI efficiency, access to field offices, and J. Edgar Hoover's expansive effort to keep tabs on the American people. Goldschmidt's name and description had exploded off the Bureau's teletype machines in its many field offices, with agents combing through still more files and fanning out to question the usual informants in homes, restaurants, cafes, pool halls, German-American clubs, and the German hotels in Yorkville. All weekend Amos, Weiss, and Crowley, with the help of an additional three agents, read reports and fielded phone calls about Max Goldschmidt—with not much to show for it.

The agents carefully picked their way through the manifests, as if mining for gold. Every name was transcribed and cross-checked against existing FBI files as well as publicly available records.

A total of three Max Goldschmidts had been identified in the files of various FBI offices in the Northeast. One was a reliable informant in a labor racketeering investigation. The second was a rabbi at a synagogue in the Bronx, whose sermons extolling communism had attracted the Bureau's interest. The third Max Goldschmidt had once killed a man, which seemed an intriguing lead until it was revealed that he would have found it almost impossible to be aboard the *Bremen* while also in a cell at Sing Sing Prison, which he'd occupied for nearly twenty years.

In Philadelphia, an informant reported the arrival of a suspicious looking man, loosely fitting the description of Max Goldschmidt and speaking with a distinct German accent. Further investigation revealed that the subject was Amish.

Telephone calls were made, homes visited.

"Were you aboard the SS *Bremen* when it sailed from Germany to New York?"

"What was the purpose of your visit to Germany?"

"Did you happen to see or hear anything unusual on the *Bremen*?"

"Do you recall a passenger going by the name Max Goldschmidt? Fitting this description?"

Not a single person had noticed, observed, or recalled anyone resembling the FBI artists' sketch that had waved uselessly under their noses.

"Guess it was a cruise for amnesia patients," Harry thought aloud.

They worked their led pencils to stubs. Their ears turned pink from the telephone handsets that seemed glued to their heads. And the more they dug, the more they plowed, poked, prodded in a search for Max Goldschmidt, the further away he seemed.

Chapter Fifty-One

ON MONDAY AFTERNOON, HARRY WEISS walked unsteadily along the quay at the 92nd Street Pier, towards the SS *Bremen*, struggling not to reveal his anxiety to Agent Crowley. He swallowed hard against his nausea and showed his FBI badge to the cop on duty. Ever since a bunch of radical merchant seaman—a bunch of Izzy Greenbaum's—had stormed that same ship in 1935, trying to tear down the swastika mounted in its bowsprit, there had at least been some security assigned to ships, however perfunctory.

The *Bremen* had arrived an hour earlier, and the celebrations had already commenced. A band was playing gay German tunes on the A Deck, passengers were throwing confetti and drinking champagne. Harry led Crowley past the bustling porters and disembarked passengers and up a gangway. He peered down at the water and felt suddenly lightheaded. He managed to find the purser who, as trained, took him directly to the office of Captain Adolf Ahrens. It was a large, imperious office, with oak-paneled walls and gold-framed oil paintings of all the ships of the Norddeutscher line—and one, of course, of Adolf Hitler. Ahrens himself proved to be a gentlemanly white-haired man, with a mustache and a cleft chin. He even stood and circled his desk to shake hands with his visitors.

"And how may we be of service to our FBI friends today?"

"Captain, I'd like to speak to one of your crew. Your Ortsgruppenleiter."

Ahrens smiled politely. He'd been through this ritual before, and wielded that courtly, well-practiced smile as a first line of defense. "For what reason, may I ask?"

"We're investigating a discrepancy in your manifests. A

passenger whose name was not properly recorded."

"Agent Weiss, you may criticize the German people for many things: the stormtroopers, the Leader, the weather. But never our record keeping. I will personally check everything."

"That would be fine," Harry said. "While you do that, call in your Ortsgruppenleiter."

Ahrens smiled again. "I'll see if he is on board. He may have already taken his furlough. The crew loves New York City. Times Square, the World's Fair—"

"We'll wait," Harry interrupted, fighting the queasiness at the prospect of another minute on the harbor.

"Let's begin with the records in question," Ahrens responded. "Exactly which trip concerns you?"

Crowley provided the dates, triggering an involuntary clenching of Ahren's lips.

"Is there a problem?" asked Harry.

"You won't be able to speak with the Ortsgruppenleiter assigned to those particular voyages."

"And why is that?" asked Harry, crossing his arms.

"He's dead."

Weiss and Crowley returned to the Foley Building and found Amos behind his desk. For the first time, Harry noticed that his partner looked beleaguered—a slightly loosened tie, vacant eyes, the usually meticulous piles of notes and reports now scattered across his desk.

"Anything worthwhile?" James asked.

"More questions than answers. Now we have one ghost passenger and one dead Nazi."

Harry summarized the meeting with Ahrens. The manifests confirmed no passenger named Max Goldschmidt. The Captain's log noted that assistant waiter Frederick Frank had disappeared, presumed to have fallen overboard, and likely drunk. There were no witnesses.

"The enforcer of Nazi discipline just...gets drunk and falls overboard?" Amos asked skeptically.

"Oh, I'm sure he went overboard. Just not on his own."

"And you think our guy is somehow connected? It just doesn't make sense. If he's a Nazi spy, the Ortsgruppenleiter would have been under orders to get him here safely. To help him."

"Maybe he ended up knowing too much. This wouldn't be the first time one German spy agency tried keeping a secret from another."

"It could also be a coincidence," Crowley stated.

"Coincidence," Harry responded, "is God's way of remaining anonymous."

Amos' eyebrows lifted in surprise. "That's unusually profound, Agent Weiss."

"Einstein said it. I read it one of his books."

Chapter Fifty-Two

DAVID ROTHMAN FINALLY REACHED Chief Murphy, late Monday afternoon. He attributed the delay to his wife's heavy itinerary. "Boating, archery, hiking, Milton Berle, and enough food to choke a horse. I can't speak for more than a minute. The line for dinner gets long—"

"We checked on Goldschmidt," Murphy interrupted. "I need more details." He was in his office, leaning back in his chair. A fan thumped from a corner of the room. A stack of reports on his desk summarized the busy weekend of traffic tickets, drunkenness, and one arrest for disorderly conduct in Southold. There was also the list of assignments for the town parade on Tuesday.

"I knew it!" Rothman chirped. "Sized him up right away, didn't I? What's he suspected of?"

"Just a routine investigation," Murphy replied, knowing Rothman saw through his lie. "Was there anything you noticed that you might not have told me?"

"Nah, I gave you a pretty good lowdown."

"Think, Rothman. He stated that he'd recently arrived on the *Bremen*. But what about his movements since then? Did he say where he'd gone after arriving in New York? Family? Friends?"

"Nope...Although..."

There was a slight pause, a crinkle of static.

"Now that you mention it..."

The name spilled from James Amos' phone moments later, sounding vaguely familiar to him. At his desk, Harry Weiss was stabbing the remains of a cigar into his ash tray. It was the third he'd smoked since returning from the *Bremen*, hours ago.

James wrote the name on a pad and called in Crowley. "Get me a telephone number and address for this guy," he ordered, passing Crowley the note.

"Good lead?" Harry asked.

"Could be," James replied. "Could be the break we need."

"Tell me."

"A friend of Einstein's. Named Leo Szilard."

The telephone rang several times in the cluttered lab at Pupin Hall, but Leo Szilard tried to ignore it. He was at his blackboard, jabbing at an equation. He'd imagined his counterparts, in Germany, standing at similar blackboards, dashing off similar equations, in a mad race of chalk against chalk.

The ringing persisted, forcing him to his desk. He grabbed the phone with white-caked fingers and answered hurriedly. "This is Szilard. Who is this?"

"Good afternoon, Professor. This is Agent James Amos. Of the FBI."

Szilard's throat tightened. *What have I done?*

"I understand you've had some contact with a man by the name of Max Goldschmidt."

"My God, has Max done something wrong?" Szilard rasped.

"I just have a few questions—"

"He's just a refugee. From Hitler."

"Why don't you tell me what you know about him."

A brief interview confirmed that Max Goldschmidt had arrived in Szilard's lab on the twelfth of May, carrying a musical composition for Albert Einstein. He had delivered the materials to Einstein two days later and was invited, by Einstein himself, to return on Decoration Day.

"Tomorrow," James confirmed.

"Yes. But you can speak with him in person. I gave him a room in the King's Crown Hotel."

"What's the address?"

Szilard responded.

James Amos didn't even say goodbye before terminating the call.

The lobby of the King's Crown was modest, with a chest-high front desk, a wall cubby for room keys and mail, and several haphazardly arranged fabric chairs. At the end of a narrow hallway was a rear dining room, famous for lively debates among the hotel's European guests. A small elevator rattled up and down, adjacent to a dimly lit stairway that seemed more reliable.

At six o'clock the desk clerk, a young man with slick-backed blond hair and flushed cheeks, was stunned by the sudden appearance of three uniformed police and two agents of the FBI. The police hurried to the dining room to guard rear exits, triggering excitement from dinner guests. Harry and James took the stairs to the second floor.

They found the door to Room 203, just off the stairway landing. Harry banged against it, announcing, "Federal agents. Open up."

There was no response.

"Open up!" he repeated, banging again for emphasis.

James ran back down the steps, reappearing moments later with the hotel passkey.

The agents scanned the dim corridor to make sure no one was in a potential line of fire, then drew their pistols. Harry inserted the key, turned it, and pushed the door open.

Room 203 was empty.

In fact, it was immaculate.

There was no visible trace that anyone had occupied the room. The bed was made, the bathroom sparkling, the closets cleared of luggage. A single table lamp had been left on.

Harry shrieked, "It's the goddam wrong room!"

"The clerk just confirmed this was the one," James responded.

"He told me no one had checked out."

They looked helplessly at each other.

"How did he know?" Harry asked.

"I don't know," James shook his head. "But we obviously spooked him. I'll call Murphy to make sure Einstein's secure. You look around here."

James hurried to the lobby. Harry went to work inspecting the room for any hint of Max Goldschmidt, searching for any items that could be brought to the Bureau's forensic labs for analysis. He went to the desk and pulled delicately on the single drawer. Inside, he found stationery with the King's Crown letterhead. He reminded himself to have it analyzed for any impressions left by a writing utensil. There was also a Gideon Bible. He noticed the narrow edge of a document barely peeking from the middle pages, like a bookmark.

"Why would a Jewish refugee, or someone posing as one, be reading a Gentile bible?" he asked himself.

He turned the pages to the document, which had been tucked into the book of Matthew.

"Jesus," he exclaimed.

Harry carefully held up the document. It was a Long Island Railroad timetable. Circled in light pencil was the column of trains to Yaphank.

Chapter Fifty-Three

HARRY AND JAMES REMAINED at the King's Crown late into the evening interviewing Szilard, other guests, and staff to find out when Max Goldschmidt left. It was the desk clerk who recalled seeing him earlier that day, entering the lobby and picking up his room key after taking a walk.

"What time was that?" James asked.

"Just after the start of my shift. About one o'clock."

Harry checked the railroad timetable, establishing that only one train had left for Yaphank that day, well before Max could have been on it. The next departure wasn't scheduled until the next morning, Tuesday.

"Did he mention where he'd been on his walk? Who he'd met with?" asked James.

"He wasn't very talkative. Mostly kept to himself," answered the clerk.

After completing the interviews, they ordered two black coffees in the dining room. By then the guests had drifted upstairs. Empty tables were cleared and refreshed with clean white linens for Tuesday's breakfast service. The oak floor had been mopped and dried, leaving a stinging scent of vinegar.

"Did you speak to Murphy?" Harry asked James.

"He told me he's got Einstein buttoned up tight in the cottage. Although we both agreed that it's now less likely Goldschmidt will show up there."

Harry stared despondently at his coffee. "It's like he's playing us," he muttered. "You know—now you see me, now you don't."

"We're closing in on him," said James. "We'll have agents all over Pennsylvania Station before the morning train to Yaphank tomorrow."

Harry shook his head. "The more I think about it, the less sense it makes. He's too smart to sanitize his room and carelessly leave a train schedule behind. And why would he head to Yaphank?"

"Safe place with a network that can support his exfiltration. We'll send agents to the cruise terminals first thing tomorrow."

Harry was unconvinced. "Could be any number of ports. German ships berth in Hoboken, New Orleans, even Nova Scotia. Or he could have arranged pick up at a local airstrip somewhere, just to get him out of range. This guy is wily, James. He got away once before. Left Bobby dead."

Amos sighed as he remembered the bullet that pierced Roosevelt's chest. The final rattling of his lungs at Sagamore Hill years later. The constant doubt about whether the bullet Amos couldn't stop had somehow contributed to Roosevelt's death.

They drank in silence, each man focused on his own resolve.

"If he's now trying to make it out of the country, at least Einstein is in less danger," James reasoned.

"True. But the idea that he could walk in and out a second time…"

James looked at his watch. "What are we waiting for?"

"I was hoping you'd say that. You drive."

At exactly midnight, Maria Voigt sat in her home on Hitler Street, dreading the message she was about to transmit to Berlin on the Afus radio. She'd been smoking for hours, leaving a mess of butts and ash overflowing onto her desk. A wicked headache pounded just above her eyes.

She'd already drafted several versions of her dispatch. But every time her hand approached the keypad, she stopped, puffed hard on a cigarette, and scrawled a rewrite. There was simply no way of explaining the unfathomable news: Chameleon's exfiltration from the King's Crown had gone catastrophically wrong. He'd simply vanished. She'd lost Berlin's most valuable agent.

It had been hours since she'd received the news, and no matter how many times she'd considered the sequence of events, she couldn't understand how Berlin's brilliantly constructed plans and contingency plans had fallen apart.

At about four that afternoon, she'd received the gut-wrenching news that Max Goldschmidt's cover had been blown. The captain of the *Bremen* had complied with procedure and dutifully reported the visit by Agents Weiss and Crowley to the German Consulate. Exactly according to plan, the Gestapo overseer at the Consulate immediately notified the Abwehr via coded transmission. Admiral Swan rushed the dispatch directly to Heydrich. Heydrich could have ignored or downplayed the unfortunate development and ordered the mission to proceed nonetheless. But plans were plans, and Berlin simply could not afford risking the arrest and interrogation of the legendary Chameleon.

Heydrich reluctantly ordered the exfiltration of Anton Gunther.

Now a new set of plans superseded the old ones.

The first elements had worked as planned. Gunther had received a call in his room at the King's Crown Hotel at five o'clock, indicating that Beethoven's Fifth Symphony was ready for pickup—the prearranged code alerting him to exfiltrate. Peering out his window, he spotted the seafood delivery truck idling in the narrow alley behind the hotel. Two men from German Gardens sat in the front seat: Krieger and his neighbor Lutz, the court clerk.

According to Lutz' subsequent report, the two men waited exactly twenty minutes for Chameleon to exit the rear door and load into the van. When he failed to appear, Krieger ordered him to investigate. Lutz snuck through a rear entrance, climbed the stairs to the second floor, and knocked on the door to Chameleon's room. He called out his name, knocked again. He stood there for ten minutes, confused and anxious, before finally returning to the alley.

By that time, the delivery van was gone. Lutz ran five blocks until he found a pay telephone.

Since then, Maria hadn't heard from Chameleon. She'd waited as long as possible to advise Berlin. She was required to report the status of the exfiltration at exactly midnight.

According to plan.

She needed time for the Chameleon to reveal himself, or to locate him on her own, or to construct a convincing explanation for his disappearance.

Actually, she decided, *she needed a miracle.*

She tapped the keypad slowly: "Unexpected development. Require 24 hours. Stand by."

The dream, again. Albert Einstein in the Swiss patent office…the ghostly form of Elsa, trying to warn him…the piles of indecipherable formulas, equations, notes on his desk, keeping her away.

He woke up and fumbled to turn on the small lamp on his nightstand. His old friend, Sigmund Freud, believed that dreams were picture puzzles—the trick was recalling the pieces before they vanished like a popped bubble. He reached for the notebook and pencil he always kept near his pillow.

But the harder he tried to summon each image, the quicker they flitted away.

He swung his legs out of bed and walked to the window. Outside he could make out a police car, illuminated by a waning gibbous moon peeking from behind a thin blanket of clouds.

Earlier Chief Murphy had called and reported the latest news about Max Goldschmidt. Einstein still found it almost impossible to believe. He'd made a conscious decision to position himself in this remote area, far from where the work on the atom bomb was being done. He'd assumed that if a threat emerged it would be in the form he recognized: the bungling *Fehme* assassins in Belgium, the brownshirt stormtroopers in Berlin. Easily spotted because their cold, hateful eyes revealed them instantly.

But Max? A poor refugee with permanently heavy eyes and stooped shoulders, bearing the full weight of Hitler's assault against the Jews?

It couldn't be.

He was up the rest of the night, and into the dawn. He wondered whether Max would show up for Decoration Day.

The Yaphank Motor Court was a concentration of ramshackle cottages on a lonely road several miles from the village. Harry and James pulled in at three o'clock that morning, lured by a blinking neon sign, missing several letters. The twin bed's covers reeked of decades of tobacco smoke, sweat, and sex; the mattresses held the consistency of wafer paper; and the bathroom faucet dripped murky well water into a stained sink. James removed his suit jacket and tie, and stood quietly at the room's only window, illuminated by the flashing neon.

He's out there, he thought. *I can feel it.*

Chapter Fifty-Four

FORTY MILES EAST, A LIFELESS BODY was sprawled on the hard dirt floor of a fishing shack, sliced in a thin, straight line from lower neck to chest. Sitting on a wobbly chair nearby was Krieger, still in the white uniform of a seafood delivery man. He was in sharp pain, his right arm shattered and bleeding from a bullet wound.

Still, he was alive. For how long, he couldn't know.

Guarding the front door was another man. Dressed as a Jew.

The Chameleon.

Kreiger had fully cooperated ever since the Chameleon had appeared out of nowhere in the King's Crown alley, threw his valise in the back of the truck, and took the passenger seat. A change in plans, he'd announced. It would all be explained. Drive to the very end of Long Island.

"The plan is for Lutz and me to take you to Yaphank. You'll wait there until we are ready to transport you to your rendezvous with the boat—"

Chameleon pointed a gun at Krieger's head and repeated, "Drive."

Krieger concluded that he was in no position to argue further. It was as if Chameleon had a roadmap in his mind, directing him across Long Island, through backroads that wound their way east, away from populated areas, past secluded, dark farmhouses.

It wasn't until one o'clock that morning that they'd pulled into Orient Point Beach. Chameleon ordered him out of the car, still at gunpoint, and they trudged through the wind-lashed brush until they reached a shack. The waves roared against the beach. Every once in a while, he turned to the crashing waves as if searching for someone.

A dim light illuminated the front door of the shack. Krieger made out a lone figure, pointing a shotgun in the direction of the beach. "Show yourselves!" the man yelped.

Chameleon pushed Kreiger forward.

The man wheeled his double-pump Remington on them. "Are you Germans? You come off one of those subs?"

Billy Tuthill's words were slurred, as if he was half asleep and half drunk.

"Sir, do you have a telephone?" Chameleon asked politely, from behind Kreiger.

"I got one. Why?"

Chameleon stepped closer, into the light. "I'm a Jew, as you can see. I found this man coming off a raft. Look at him. He's a Nazi. Please, call the police."

Tuthill eyed them skeptically.

Krieger watched as Chameleon lunged at Tuthill, trying to grab his shotgun, which fired aimlessly. The bullet struck Krieger's arm, sending him to the ground in pain. When he looked up, Chameleon was on top of Tuthill, bringing down a knife.

Billy Tuthill flopped like a fish.

In the hours since, the dawn had spread across Orient Point, revealing the wooded bluff, a stretch of rock-strewn beach, and gray water indistinctly meeting a gray slate sky. Krieger remained on a wobbly chair, just a few feet from Tuthill's body. The shack had the stench of death, and it took some time for Krieger to realize it wasn't Tuthill, but the countless fish that had been gutted in the room, entrails tossed and mixed in with the dirt. Chameleon had just returned from one of his walks—wandering the bluff, standing on a high point, sweeping the horizon with binoculars.

"What now?" Krieger asked, shakily.

Chameleon studied him for a moment.

"I am a good and loyal German," Krieger declared. "I swear that I will support you. Your secrets are safe with me. No one will know how you changed the mission. Not even Maria Voigt. It would be an honor to serve you."

Chameleon turned to Kreiger.

"Do you want to live?" he asked. "Or do you want to die like that man?" He pointed to Tuthill's body. The face was chalk white, already a ghost.

"What do you want me to do?"

"Help me get this body where it belongs. Then I will set you free."

They dragged Billy Tuthill's corpse down the bluff, across the rocky beach to Plum Gut. The waves churned violently, as if protesting his death.

They tossed the body and watched as the waves consumed him.

Chameleon turned to Krieger and said, "My name is Anton Gunther," as he raised his knife.

PART V

DECORATION DAY

Chapter Fifty-Five

IT WAS DECORATION DAY, 1939, and radio forecasts reported inclement weather with possible clearing in early afternoon. Albert Einstein rocked back and forth on his porch, suppressing his irritation.

He'd been looking forward to the holiday. Although he wasn't yet a U.S. citizen, he felt strongly that America should honor the sacrifices of its soldiers. They'd put down slavery in their Civil War and made the world safe for democracy in the Great War. Democracy, imperfect as it was, should be trumpeted around the world, drowning out Hitler's mad-dog frothing. Despite the FBI's concern, he'd planned to attend the official parade in Southold, followed by a long afternoon sail on the bay.

But now the sky beyond the bluff looked ominous. When Mrs. Dukas reminded him that Max Goldschmidt was due to join him for a sail, Einstein feigned ambivalence. "Unless the weather keeps him away."

Just across the front yard the young constable, Krupski, was patrolling as if guarding Fort Knox. Like the omnipresent guards in Belgium, his head jerking warily back and forth, as if every mosquito was an incoming threat.

"Constable!" Einstein called out. "Do you enjoy the fiddle?"

Krupski's voice sounded from the distance. "Yes, Professor."

"I need an audience. Come in and I will play a concert."

They walked into the parlor, which was dark that dreary morning. Einstein positioned the violin on his shoulder and began playing.

He came to that first sloppy note.

There would be parades that day, held in rain or shine, in remote villages and large cities across America. The usual, red, white, and blue bunting was draped, and Old Glories were unfurled. Marching bands thumped and trumpeted *The Stars and Stripes Forever*, followed by floats with costumed Uncle Sams and Lady Liberties.

On that day of the year, America wasn't a collection of communities but one giant, collegial neighborhood with a Main Street stretching from the end of Long Island to the Pacific coast, connecting citizens to their war dead.

Except for the tiny village of Yaphank, where the observances offered a starkly different view of the future, and Main Street took a dark detour from the rest of the country. Where the patriotic bunting reflected the patriotism of another nation—another order—far away, and everyone wore the uniforms of that foreign place, sang its songs, and spoke its language.

Harry and James stared out the front windshield of the Oldsmobile, waiting for the arrival of the morning train from Manhattan to Yaphank. The one-room station was white clapboard, with an open gable roof that extended into a narrow overhang. It was south of Camp Siegfried, about a fifteen-minute walk.

At exactly nine-fifty a behemoth steam locomotive lumbered in, pulling four wooden cars. Harry grabbed his Brownie camera and waited for the passengers to exit, hoping that somehow he'd spot and record Max Goldschmidt.

They flooded out of the cars—hundreds of them. Appearing just like Harry, carrying along their Brownies and their new home-movie cameras, the wives and kids hauling along picnic baskets and thermoses. Wearing their red and black swastika armbands and waving their swastika pennants, like they might a Yale pennant at the big game against Princeton. Some men were dressed as Nazi stormtroopers. Harry recognized them as the *Ordnungsdienst*—

OD—the security forces from the big Bund rally at Madison Square Garden.

Harry's stomach dropped. "Shit."

James stood quietly next to him, stunned by the hordes of fresh scrubbed, gleaming white, perfectly American citizens as they began their march to a Nazi camp.

"He could be any one of these people," Harry added. "We're back to a needle in a haystack."

"We need to question Voigt."

"I'll go," Harry insisted. "You kind of stick out like sore thumb in this crowd."

"You're not much better, Harry. Be careful. And keep your eyes open for anyone who looks suspicious."

"Are you kidding?" Harry asked.

Despite the threatening skies, the traffic had swamped Yaphank. Cars and busses tooled slowly through its downtown from all directions, swastikas fluttering from their windows to create a festive atmosphere.

Harry had vertigo. He bit down on his tongue, trying to fight the panicky sense of suddenly finding himself a stranger in his own land. He followed the crowd north to the camp, past the bank and barbershop and church and school and other familiar landmarks of small-town America—past the small, landscaped, orderly homes of German Gardens. He watched as people snapped their photos and stopped to buy sizzling wiener schnitzel and doughnuts from the vendors.

The feeling of disorientation persisted. As if he were an actor who'd wandered onto the wrong movie set.

The crowd flowed along to the parade grounds with its large brown clubhouse, festooned as well with swastika standards flowing from the roofline. The brass and percussion of German marching songs blared from loudspeakers wired onto field poles. Harry estimated that there were five thousand people on hand filling the parade grounds and muddy beach by the lake. He continued walking until he reached 80 Hitler Street. He was overwhelmed by its ordinariness: the plain shutters, the well-tended patch of green grass, the line of hydrangeas under the kitchen window. The very symbol of the American Dream mocking him, winking, he imagined, from behind the lace-curtained windows.

He knocked on the door.

Maria Voigt answered. She wore a plain, light-blue housecoat. Her face was drawn, her eyes red and sleepless. She gazed at Harry, almost numb to his appearance.

"I'm looking for someone," Harry declared. "Thought he might be here."

"No one is here, Agent Weiss," she answered heavily.

"Then you won't mind if we chat inside?" Harry stepped in, immediately noticing a glass tray on the kitchen table, overflowing with ashes and cigarette butts.

"Long night?" he asked.

She remained silent.

"Where is he?"

"Who?"

"The Nazi agent who was planning to kidnap Albert Einstein."

"We discussed this already. Kimmler's ravings."

"Do you know someone who calls himself Max Goldschmidt?"

She shook her head.

"Heard anything about a Nazi agent trying to escape the United States?"

"No."

He was interrupted by the ringing of a phone on the wall of her kitchen.

"You want me to get that for you?" Harry snarked.

Voigt walked to the phone and picked up the receiver. She listened for a few seconds, nodded her head, and said, "I understand. I will arrange to be there."

She hung up.

"Who was it?" asked Harry.

343

"A reminder that I must go to work later today."

"The New Europe? What's playing?"

"You should know. Your men watch us constantly."

Harry considered arresting her on the spot. But he realized that she still had the potential to lead him to Max Goldschmidt. "I'd stick around, if I were you," Harry said. "I may have more questions."

The sound of snare drums crackled through the air, heralding the precision march of the OD across the grounds. Then came the child campers of Camp Siegfried, parading with their own bands, their own swastika banners. They were greeted with tumultuous applause from parents and grandparents. The boys were arrogant and smirking. The girls looking considerably less happy and pleased with themselves, staring about defensively. The same men and women, Harry considered as he searched the parade grounds, who on other days and in other places appeared as law-abiding citizens.

Back in her kitchen Maria Voigt sat at her table, running the brief, unbelievable phone conversation through her mind: She was impressed that she had remained so calm, not only about the news, but in the very presence of Weiss. It had been that unmistakable voice:

"I have found Mozart's Concerto Number Five."

Thirty miles east, in Southold, a more modest parade was just forming under darkening skies. Spectators stood along empty Main Street, gathering under the maple trees in case of rain. Rothman's was closed for the holiday, but its front window was decorated in patriotic bunting around a large sign announcing:

SALE ON ALL SWIMWEAR!

Mixed in with the crowd, just in front of the two-story brick library, were Albert Einstein and Helen Dukas. They clutched miniature American flags on small wooden sticks, waiting for the procession. Standing immediately behind them was young Constable Krupski, whose earnest eyes worked the crowd for any sign of trouble.

Einstein was still hopeful that skies would clear out and he'd salvage an afternoon sail. He'd enjoyed the neighbors' warm greetings, the requests for autographs, the occasional thrusting of reluctant children towards him for photographs. After a brief delay—the local Congressman was running late—he heard the distant sound of a police siren, followed by the rhythmic drumming of the Southold Volunteer Fire Department Marching Band. The procession finally appeared.

It was led by Chief Murphy, sitting behind the wheel of his squad car as it crept forward, his beefy elbow hanging out the open window. He was followed by the Congressman, along with smiling politicians and the fire department band, by waves of war veterans, high-school twirlers and drum majors, by delegations of Presbyterians, Methodists, Catholics, Universalists, Elks, Freemasons, Shriners, Rotarians, and Kiwanians.

Einstein put the sail out of his mind, waving his miniature flag enthusiastically even as the first drops of rain began to fall and umbrellas popped open. Only when the final group marched by— the Southold 4-H club, accompanied by a flock of nervous sheep— did Einstein agree to Helen Dukas' persistent demands to leave.

Chapter Fifty-Six

CHAMELEON PEERED OUT THE WINDOW of the fishing shack. A light rain drove filthy rivulets down the glass panes. He glanced at his watch—it was nearly two o'clock. He closed his eyes, mentally calculating each step: a twenty-five-minute drive from the Orient beach to Little Hog Neck, a ten-minute hike up the wooded hill to Einstein's Cottage, swiftly entering to kill Dukas and capture Einstein, and a return trip to the shack where he would wait for the U-boat.

For most of that time, the local police would be distracted, guiding traffic at parades across the North Fork.

He'd already packed his essentials in a leather knapsack: a knife, Sauer pistol, folded map, and a pen-syringe of Brallobarbital sedative. Next to the sack was a special weapon delivered to the King's Crown several days earlier: an MP 40, the most advanced submachine gun produced in Germany, courtesy of Maria Voigt.

Overkill, he'd thought. But in a real emergency, he knew it might save his life.

Soon, he thought, he'd be back in Germany. His plan was to return to his farm for several months, having left the persona of Max Goldschmidt dead and buried in the wretched United States.

Several miles east of Orient Point, U-boat 43 surfaced slowly under low gray clouds—more concerned about overturning some passing fishing boat than being detected by America's nonexistent coastal patrols. The U-boat raised its periscope, which caught the vague contours of Long Island in the distance. *Kapitänleutnant* Hans Fischer checked his speed—7.6 knots, submerged—and quickly calculated that he was within range of the pickup.

A simple operation, he thought. *Just slip into the bay like a ship into the tiny end of a bottle, during rough seas, dispatch two men on an inflatable raft to a beach, locate one or more passengers— no one quite knew how many—and slip back out without being noticed, all while avoiding Plum Gut. What could possibly go wrong?*

"Submerge," he ordered, listening with satisfaction to the immediate response of his crew, the clanging of the ship's bells, the barked orders and the men's boots racing up and down the impossibly narrow boat.

"God help us," he said under his breath.

Chapter Fifty-Seven

EINSTEIN WAS HOME AGAIN, sitting on his porch, carefully observing the sky. The clouds were thinning gradually, revealing small patches of blue. The improving weather might allow for a sail after all, he thought.

There was, however, a dark cloud hovering directly in front of the bluff: a Southold police car, Chief Murphy's rotund figure stuffed behind the steering wheel. Einstein had noticed over the past week that Murphy had been rotating shifts with Krupski, which presented a challenge. The Professor could slip by the young constable, or at least negotiate a walk to the beach. But Murphy was like a bull, snorting loudly and stomping his feet when he saw Einstein amble from the front porch.

He checked his watch, estimating at least an hour before the weather cleared sufficiently. Perhaps by then Krupski would relieve the Chief.

To help pass the time, he unpacked his violin and opened the manuscript of *Two Scientists Debate*, again—still unsatisfied with how it had sounded.

The initial bars were familiar, comforting, consistent with the tune that he remembered. Then, a discordant note jumped from the strings. Einstein grimaced. He placed the violin on his lap and narrowed his eyes over the page. There, in the second bar of the second line, Zwick had changed a perfectly placed quarter note with a longer half note, throwing off the rhythm.

He shook his head.

Then, another change in tempo, subtle to the unfamiliar ear, but discernible to the composer himself.

And another error after that.

Mrs. Dukas walked in, drying her hands with a dishtowel.

"Is something wrong, Doctor?"

Einstein set down his instrument.

"This makes no sense, Helen. Zwick's scientific work was always so careful. Punctilious. But his musicality became sloppy. Making unnecessary changes. Careless."

He brought a thumb and index finger to his eyes and rubbed gently.

"Is there something I can do to help?" she asked.

The professor blinked back at her. Then said, "Bring a pencil."

She returned a moment later, pencil in hand. He smiled to himself, thinking that she probably would have been back in just as little time if he had told her to bring a giraffe.

"Now stand here." He pointed to the floor, just next to him. "And follow along."

He began playing from the top. This time, when he hit the first incorrect beat he rested the violin on his lap and circled the note with the pencil. Several bars later, he did so again.

And several bars after that.

At that moment, a different tune was blaring at Camp Siegfried. The *oom-pah* music that had been playing over the loudspeakers came to a sudden stop. In its place, the unofficial anthem of Nazi Germany, *Horst-Wessel-Lied,* played across the Parade Grounds. A fanfare of brass, the rolling of drums. Prompting the visitors to snap to attention, salute the flags and bellow:

Clear the streets for the brown battalions,
Clear the streets for the storm division!
Millions are looking upon the swastika full of hope,
The day of freedom and of bread dawns.

Then a closing prayer by a Lutheran minister, followed by the mass singing of *God Bless America*. All under the approving skies, which had given way to the sun.

Harry Weiss couldn't get the *Horst-Wessel-Lied*, out of his head as he wandered the empty residential streets of German Gardens, lost in his own homeland. He'd failed completely to find any sign of a killer German agent, or where he could possibly be hiding.

He wiped the perspiration from his forehead, his finger lingering on the scar.

A nightmare, he considered, *where the beating of Jews won't be confined to the hidden areas under boardwalks but waged openly, on broad avenues, just like in Germany.*

Harry felt suddenly powerless, overmatched. He remembered Dan Larkins' soft brogue on the night he'd rescued him from the beating at Coney Island, saying, "This is America, lad. Sometimes you have to bend the rules 'till you get justice."

He headed back to Maria Voigt's home, first walking, then breaking into a steady jog, racing past the neat and orderly homes of a new America where stormtroopers ruled. He'd get his own version of justice—interrogate her, turn her house inside-out. No forms seeking permission, no warrant, no court approval. Because, he'd realized, if the rules didn't break they'd continue to protect the strong from the weak.

He intended to break things.

A car approached, blaring its horn, forcing Harry to the side of the road.

James pulled up in the Oldsmobile, rolled down his window, and yelled, "Get in."

"I'm not letting him get away again, James—"

"Get. In." James repeated. "Let's make sure Einstein is safe."

Harry entered the car, breathless, feeling more lost than ever.

Maria observed the vehicle pulling away. She hurried down the hall to her bedroom closet, where she'd stowed her Afus. She set it up quickly and tapped out the glorious news that Chameleon was alive… and would need his ride as planned.

Chapter Fifty-Eight

CHAMELEON STEERED THE FISH DELIVERY truck into a clearing in the woods, halfway up the muddy path to the bluff at Litle Hog Neck. The clearing was exactly as it had appeared in the photographs Chameleon had studied at the Abwehr.

He checked his pockets for the syringe and handgun in the deep pocket of his jacket. He clutched the MP-40 upright, like a sword, and disappeared into the woods. Streams of sunlight fell upon the foliage, highlighting the droplets there. The ground was wet which, though uncomfortable, masked his steps.

The sky was now azure, blue. *The spy gods were beaming*, he thought.

Einstein continued his notes on the sheet music. Like a professor correcting an examination, he trained his eyes on Helen's markings on the score of *Two Scientists Debate*.

"A single error in beat in every line on one page. And Zwick's changes from the original composition are consistent: either a quarter note replacing a half note or a half note replacing a quarter. A total of nine changes in tempo."

"I wouldn't have noticed had you not pointed it out," Helen said.

"Barely discernible changes inserted in a predictable pattern. Disorder within order. Recognizable only to the composers."

His eyes darted across the list of errors. He was certain that Zwick was attempting to make time relative, in each instance deliberately lengthening or shortening it from the original score. *But relative to what?*

He required a cipher. Something that would help him to translate each beat's time change into an alpha-numeric character.

Einstein ran his fingers through his tangle of white hair, blew a loud, frustrated breath, and asked, "What are you trying to tell me, my old friend?"

He collected his notes and shuffled into his study in search of an answer.

He parted the window curtains, noting the still-brightening sky. Strewn across the blackboard were chalk equations for the paper he was writing for *The Annals of Mathematics*—meandering white streams of numbers and symbols that he'd formulated over weeks.

The paper, he decided, *could wait*.

Einstein erased the lower left quadrant of the board, wrapped his fingers around a stick of chalk, and began copying each of the changed beats in the order they appeared in every bar on Zwick's draft of *Two Scientists Debate*.

1- Quarter note to half note.
2- Half to quarter.
3- Half to quarter.
4- Half to quarter.

He pounded the chalk against the board, producing an erratic percussion of clicks and swishes, taps and dabs. An arhythmic yet persistent beat, like the clip-clop of a pony.

What was Zwick trying to do? There was no music in this—it was as though he'd been drumming his fingers against the table, lost in thought. It was as though—

Einstein stepped back suddenly, oblivious to the thick coating of white dust on his fingers and the chalk residue on his blue polo shirt, like fresh snow. The sound—the sound!

"Of course!" he exclaimed out loud.

Einstein had found the cipher. Or rather, he'd heard it.

There was one universally understood code that reduced every letter of the alphabet to audible representations of time: Morse.

Dits and dots.

He examined Zwick's changes again. In the first bar, the lengthening of a quarter note to a half note would be represented by a dash in Morse code, which he scrawled on the board.

The next three incorrect notes were shortened, represented by three dots.

He put it together: "-..."

It translated to the letter B.

Einstein couldn't help but emit a satisfied chuckle.

It occurred to him that the title, *Two Scientists Debate*, could not be more wrong. At the moment, he and Zwick were communing.

He continued.

.   = E

. -- = W

.-   = A

Slowly, the first word formed. He read out loud, "Beware."

He stepped back, confounded. There was no secret that he was once in danger. He'd heard the warnings ever since the Nazis rose to power. In Berlin, Caputh, Belgium. The night of his address at Prince Albert Hall. Before he fled to America.

America. . . where he was safe, he thought.

Anxiously, he continued the laborious decryption, igniting minute explosions of chalk dust with every forceful tap. The clock on the mantle ticked loudly, as if urging him on. Faster, faster.

-- = M

.- = A

-..- = X

Einstein stepped back from the board, his cheeks growing flushed and hot.

Not so much shocked as ashamed.

He'd always been rigidly faithful to a fundamental law of science: a theory doesn't become truth until proven. It is simply a falsifiable hypothesis that must be confirmed through repeated challenge, experimentation, observation. Consistently supported as new evidence emerges.

For too long, he'd ignored the evidence about Max.

He'd made a conscious decision to position himself in this remote area, far from where the work on the atom bomb was being done. He'd assumed that if a threat emerged it would be in the form he'd recognized: the bungling *Fehme* assassins in Belgium, the brownshirt stormtroopers in Berlin. Easily spotted because their cold, hasteful eyes revealed them instantly. But he'd disregarded the repeated evidence that Max Goldschmidt, a Jewish refugee, could do him harm. He'd allowed his own prejudices to blind him to an inconvenient truth.

The truth, cleverly transmitted by his friend, Zwick, was there in a simple formula on Einstein's chalkboard. Confirmed, proven, irrefutable.

Where else have I been wrong?

The chalk fell to the ground, where it cracked into shards.

Chapter Fifty-Nine

IT WAS A SLOW, METHODICAL HIKE through the heavy woods. The MP 40 was light-engineered with stamped steel, rather than machined. The rate of fire was five hundred rounds per minute, the magazine capacity was thirty-two rounds, and the effective range was one hundred yards. The downside was that it was loud, and noise could carry across the harbor and attract the attention of even distant neighbors. The preferred option was another weapon: his Sauer 38H pistol, a small, easily concealed semi-automatic. Deadly at close range, and in a remote and heavily buffered area unlikely to be heard.

He froze every few steps, stretching his neck and swiveling his head to detect signs of danger, sniffing for a disturbance in the air, the crack of a twig, the scent of a human.

Like his moniker.

He crept forward, masking the sound of his breaths in the warm, drying air. A few more yards and he came upon a clearing. Just beyond was Einstein's weedy backyard, and the single telephone pole he'd been looking for. He climbed quickly, took out his pliers, and cut through the cable.

The sun now burned brightly, and Chief Phineas Murphy could no longer stand the stuffiness of his police car. He wrestled himself outside and stood on the bluff, reveling in the gentle breeze that was blowing away the squall. Watching benignly as, far below, a fishing boat gurgled from the marina towards the bay, generating a faint white wake. He took a deep, satisfying breath, savoring the mix of salt and wet leaves on his tongue. He'd found a measure of peace.

Murphy was exhausted from the long holiday weekend. He'd planned to get a good night's sleep that night, awaken before dawn, and go fishing. He could almost feel the brand-new Saranac rod he'd finally bought from Rothman's. He practiced a phantom cast or two as another fishing boat motored out of the harbor.

"Why wait till tomorrow?" he asked himself.

He started toward his squad car, planning to radio Krupski back to the cottage to relieve him. Then he heard the sudden rustling of leaves in the woods. He froze and caught a glimpse of something emerging from the tree line. *A deer*, he thought.

No.

A goddam person. Male, five-ten. Dressed in an old black suit. Foreign appearance.

Max Goldschmidt.

"Put your hands up!" Murphy barked while starting to pull his revolver, which stuck awkwardly in his holster.

Max, the sad, beaten refugee, was now someone else entirely, someone he did not know. He darted behind a tree, leveling the MP 40 on the chief.

"Goddamn, goddamn," Murphy cursed to himself, trying to break for his car, wincing and grunting with every limping step.

Goldschmidt found the performance entertaining: the searing pain etched on Murphy's face, the flailing of his fat arms as he tried running, the tangle of his hobbled leg. In fact, he could have watched it all day. But there was work to do.

He trained the submachine gun on the potbellied police chief, running for his life. He smiled.

Murphy heard the crackle of lightening, incredibly loud. He was confused. The sky had cleared; the storm had passed. He was going to fish.

He felt a sudden fire in his chest and saw the warm stream of blood seeping across his uniform shirt, raining down into a small puddle by his feet. He stepped forward, teetering. Thinking that he should have got down in the first place, thinking that was what he should have done in the Argonne, too. He crashed into the ground.

Max quickly stashed the machine gun under a wet pile of leaves and twigs. Loud as it was, he had only fired a single burst. Maybe they would think it was hunters. He turned toward Einstein's cottage, enjoying how good it felt to kill again. He cradled the Sauer in his jacket pocket, moving fast toward the cottage.

He heard a sudden burst of static from Murphy's car radio. Looking back, he saw that the Chief was alive. Struggling to sit up, gun drawn. Murphy fired several shots, aimlessly into the air, then struggled into the driver's seat of his car. Moaning incoherently.

Max pulled the Sauer from his pocket, ran over to Murphy, and pulled him from the car, leaving a trail of blood across the front seat. He heard the squawking of the radio. "Come in, Chief. We didn't get that. Come in…"

Murphy managed a final act of defiance, grinning back at Max, then rolling away, to face the bay. Knowing, somehow, that his last view of Earth should be what he loved and not what he despised.

Max sent a single bullet into the back of the Chief's head.

His mind raced: even if police headquarters realized there was something wrong, it would still take ten to fifteen minutes for the first squad car to arrive. Almost immediately roadblocks would be set up; his route to Orient, via the potato truck, would be cut off.

He'd have to find another way.

He marched towards the porch, quieting his mind, focusing on his next moves.

Einstein was still poring over his musical notations, barely able to accept the stunning message he had just deciphered—when he heard the first burst of shots. *That did not sound much like hunters*, he thought. Reacting with a speed that surprised even himself, he strode across the room and picked up the phone. There was nothing, no dial tone. He tried jiggling the receiver. *Still nothing.*

He peered out the office window.

"What is it?" Helen asked from the kitchen.

"Hunters," Einstein said. "Stay here," he told Dukas, as calmly as he could. "I will tell them to go somewhere else."

Einstein peered through the window again.

"My God!" he gasped.

He had come to America to find sanctuary. But the Nazi cancer had spread across the ocean, penetrated the borders of America. It now approached the front door of his lonely cottage in an isolated stretch of farms and bays.

He exhaled, a long, quavering breath.

Einstein's mind reeled. Was Szilard safe? The other scientists working on the bomb? Or had their secrets fallen into the hands of the Nazis.

For a moment, he was tempted to run.

If America wasn't safe, where would he run next?

He felt a wave of exhaustion, at all this running, by ship, and train, and plane. And with it, a great anger.

It was time to stop. He could only make so many homes—and he would not leave this one behind.

He hurriedly searched the room for a weapon. Nothing.

Then he realized he had one.

He rushed to the door to meet Max Goldschmidt.

Chapter Sixty

MAX HAD CALCULATED HIS NEXT STEPS as he approached the cottage. But Einstein surprised him, bursting out of the house onto the porch. He looked disheveled, his shirt wrinkled and smeared with chalk—but he always did. Max gave Einstein an excited grin.

"Max! You made it after all!"

Max burrowed his hand into his right jacket pocket and felt for the Sauer. For the moment, he considered simply shooting Einstein. But returning empty-handed to Germany would represent a failed mission. And he would never get closer than he was at that moment. Hie eyes darted to the old jeep in the driveway.

He was interrupted by yet another gift from the spy gods:

"I promised you a sail. Shall we go?" asked Einstein.

Max could hardly believe his good fortune.

Einstein looked up at the sky. "We should hurry though. It's clear now, but another rain may be on its way, and Mrs. Dukas will put her foot down. Come, I'll drive."

"Certainly professor," he said, remembering his Max voice. Gripping the door handle, still wondering if this could all be some sort of ruse.

"Come, come! Before Mrs. Dukas comes out and ruins everything!"

Goldschmidt could see it all now, the plan unfolding in his mind. He would avoid the roads and sail with Einstein to Orient Point. Rendezvous with the U-boat. Force him aboard and scuttle the *Tinef*.

The Americans would assume he'd drowned. The world would mourn. Obituaries would be published, sad speeches made about the tragic loss of such a genius!

But the genius would be rotting in a German prison, his brain milked of its secrets.

The Reich would have its bomb.

Already in the passenger's seat, Einstein turned the key and the engine roared to life.

They sped down to the Horseshoe Cove Marina.

The teenaged marina attendant stepped out of his shack when he saw Einstein and a shabbily dressed companion pull up. Although the rain had passed, the beach remained sodden, and a ridge of flat gray clouds was approaching from the west.

"You ain't going out there, are you?" he asked. "Looks like another storm's coming in. A bad one."

Einstein continued walking, looking pointedly at the attendant.

"My friend Max Goldschmidt and I are going on a quick sail to Orient Point. We will return soon. Come, Max."

They walked onto the flimsy dock. Max saw the *Tinef* bobbing in a tiny slip. A small rain puddle had collected at the center of its narrow sole. The mast looked bent slightly to one side, as if exhausted. But there was no helping it. Einstein boarded first, positioned himself at the tiller, and pointed Max to the rickety bench on the port side.

"Would it be possible, Professor, if I took the tiller? It would remind me of my days sailing Scharfe Lake."

Einstein considered the request for a moment.

"Ah, yes, you mentioned sailing on Scharfe Lake when we first met. But are you certain you can handle the *Tinef*, Max? I have made alterations."

"The boats I sailed were quite like yours."

Einstein squinted curiously, then smiled.

"As you wish, my friend."

The professor worked quickly, untying the *Tinef* from the dock, positioning himself on the starboard bench, and letting the little boat drift away from the marina. The earlier rains had ushered in a strong breeze that soon swept them out of Horseshoe Cove.

It was almost as if he were hurrying to his own death, Max thought, now convinced that Einstein did not suspect a thing.

They looked to be the only ship in the bay. Water splashed hard against the hull, spraying them. They sped past the gnarled, narrow fingers of beach, the secluded stretches of scrub oak and sand, the gray rooftops that peeked out through tree-lined hills, the boathouses and the marinas. Past Robins Island and Shelter Island, which Max recognized from his study of nautical maps at Quenzsee. They sailed straight across Greenport Harbor, which was particularly quiet that morning. Most vessels had been tied to the docks in the ill-boding weather.

Max looked at Einstein, who seemed oblivious, gazing at some seagulls in frenzied flight against the gathering winds.

Chapter Sixty-One

JAMES AMOS PUSHED THE OLDSMOBILE towards the summit of Grove Road, yanking the gear shift back and forth to gain some traction in the mud. Harry sat in the passenger seat. As the cottage came into view, they gasped together.

Several police officers were surrounding Chief Murphy's car. Others seemed to be scrambling aimlessly around the property. Mrs. Dukas stood on the front lawn, arms folded tightly around her. James stomped on the brake. He and Weiss bolted from the car, and found Krupski leaning against Murphy's car, tears streaming down his cheeks.

"Aww, God," Harry moaned when his eyes met Murphy's body, sprawled six feet in front of the vehicle. The Chief's arms were thrust forward; his head turned unnaturally towards the bay.

"Did you call for an ambulance?" Weiss shrieked.

Krupski was frozen.

James crouched at the body, then looked up, fighting the heaviness, fighting a world that was crushing him with its inescapable gravity. "No ambulance, Harry. He didn't make it."

The memory of Roosevelt's attempted assassination overwhelmed him. He was unable to prevent either attack. Nothing but an observer of the aftermath. Useless...

"Where's Einstein?" Harry asked.

Krupski stared vacantly.

"Where. Is. Einstein?" Weiss repeated, now standing within inches of Krupski.

Standing nearby, Mrs. Dukas reported, "He went sailing."

For the second time that afternoon, the pimple-faced marina

attendant observed two men crossing the beach in quickstep. A breeze had kicked in, and another bank of gray clouds was closing in against eroding patches of sun.

Harry asked, "Did you see Albert Einstein?"

"A while ago. Told him not to go out. Told him squall's comin'."

"Was he with anyone?"

"Yeah. Religious looking fella. Jewish, I guess."

Amos and Harry looked at each other. "They happen to tell you their course?" asked Amos.

"The Professor said Orient Point."

"You have a telephone here?"

The attendant nodded.

James rushed into the shack, called headquarters, and reported his status. He requested immediate backup.

He returned to the attendant. "Two more things. You stay in that shack and call the police if you see them returning. The man with Einstein is armed and dangerous."

"Yes sir," the attendant replied, accepting the order as his solemn duty.

"Second, we'll need a boat."

"You can use mine," said the attendant. He led them to the dock.

Before stepping off the beach, Harry peered anxiously into the harbor and beyond it, to the gray, churning bay. He watched the undulation of the dock and felt a similar undulation in the pit of his stomach.

"It's okay if you want to stay behind," James said. "It doesn't matter why."

Harry considered the possibility. He could return to Einstein's cottage. Or Yaphank. Take charge of managing the swarm of agents and police that would surely arrive.

No.

He thought of Bobby Larkins walking into the bear enclosure at the Central Park Zoo to protect a bunch of kids. And Bobby's uncle rescuing Harry from his tormenters at Coney Island.

And Isadore Greenbaum charging the stage at Madison Square Garden, where he didn't have a chance of coming out unscathed.

"Let's go," he said.

"I thought so," James replied.

They stepped gingerly onto the dock. The wooden planks swayed under Harry's feet, forcing him to grab a weather-beaten handrail and ease himself forward, as if tiptoeing at the edge of a cliff. The attendant led them to a slip with a fifteen-foot utility boat outfitted with a rusted ninety-five-horsepower engine. The name "Horseshoe" was sloppily painted on the stern.

Amos sighed. "You have anything faster?"

The attendant shook his head.

"You know how to drive one of these?" Amos asked Harry.

Harry shook his head warily.

Amos frowned. He'd accompanied Colonel Roosevelt on some boat rides, and knew barely enough to make it from the dock at Sagamore Hill to the confines of Oyster Bay. *It will have to do*, he thought as he climbed aboard. Harry followed with all the grace of a stumbling drunk. Amos turned the ignition, and the engine began sputtering. The attendant unfastened the ropes from the cleats and pushed the boat with one foot.

They gurgled out of the harbor into the darkening bay.

The attendant raced to the shack.

Chapter Sixty-Two

AS THE *TINEF* PUSHED TOWARDS Orient Point the bay grew darker, the clouds thicker. A billowing wind swept down, sharpening the whitecaps. A relentless spray of cold water slapped across the deck, soaking both Einstein and Max. Max emitted periodic grunts as he fought the tiller. Soon the rain plunked into the boat as well.

Einstein's mouth was clenched around his unlit pipe, Max saw. He seemed all but mesmerized by the rocking of the boat, the sound of its bow slicing through the water, the snap of the sail as it adjusted to the wind.

Max checked his watch and looked out into the waves. The U-boat should be very near, he thought. If it was, he could beach the *Tinef* at Orient Point, force Einstein off at gunpoint, and await the rendezvous. He imagined the shock of the crew as the infamous Albert Einstein boarded.

And if Einstein resisted?

He'd resolved his worst-case scenario: the next-best thing to Einstein cooperating with Germany's atomic program was preventing his cooperation on an American effort. He'd have to kill him.

He was pleased to see the faint glimmer of a lighthouse in the distance, just beyond Orient Point. Another gust of wind slapped harshly at the *Tinef*, Gunther yanking at the tiller to regain control.

Albert Einstein grabbed the starboard rail. He also saw the approaching lighthouse, checked his watch, and determined that time and distance had run their course. He pulled the pipe from his mouth.

"How much farther do you intend to go, Max?"

"Not far, professor."

Einstein noticed a change in Max's voice. Tighter, more urgent.

"I mean *this game*. Pretending to be who you're not."

Max was startled, but he refused to show it.

"In the back of my mind was a theory, Max. I'd hoped it was wrong. But as a precaution, I did whatever was necessary to draw you away from my colleagues. They were right under your noses in Columbia, conducting their research. But you were focused on me, and I have no expertise on the creation of an atomic bomb. Only stubborn opinions."

Max held fast to the rudder with one hand and, with the other, reached for his Sauer.

Einstein continued, yelling above the howling wind. "You made some mistakes, Max, which helped confirm my theory. For example, the story about learning to sail at Scharfe Lake. At the Westphal Marina, in 1935. How could that be, when Jews were banned from the lake the year before?"

Max was annoyed at his mistake, but thought, *What's the difference? I have him.*

"Still, I thought it might be a simple matter of bad memory. I needed some additional proof of your duplicity. Something empirical. Do you know where it came, of all places?"

Plunging into the winds, the boat keeled harshly to starboard. Einstein wrapped his fingers around the deck railing and hung on.

"Gerhardt Zwick!" he yelled above the tempest, studying Goldschmidt's face for any response. But the younger man's eyes faced the sea, only blinking reflexively against the rain. "He inserted a coded equation in our composition. The very message you delivered, and we played together!"

Goldschmidt was stunned, then infuriated. Not at Zwick or Einstein, but at himself. He had been outwitted by that decrepit old man in Berlin, passing on, somehow, his secret message to Einstein. He tried to fight down his rage, to settle his nerves and concentrate on what he had to do next. His eyes focused past Einstein, urgently scanning for any sign of the U-boat.

A wave crashed against the deck, dousing the two men.

Einstein yelled, "I demand that you tell me who you really are."

Goldschmidt pursed his lips.

"You are not in a position to make any demands, old man!" he screamed above the winds. "I will answer your question. But first, if you knew I was an imposter, why did you invite me to sail?"

Another howl of wind rocked the *Tinef*.

"I heard gunfire, then I saw you approaching the cottage," Einstein shouted.

"But you have hunters—"

"Never sounding like that."

So. The fat, crippled old cop had alerted him with that dying salvo. Anton's rage knew no bounds.

"I had to draw you away from Helen!" Einstein yelled. "So I used time and distance. I lured you far enough away that you could no longer threaten anyone else."

"A selfless act."

"Not entirely. They'll come looking for me. They always do. And I told the marina attendant exactly where we were headed. You've been outwitted, Goldschmidt. By an old man in Berlin..." Einstein savored this final remark. ". . . and a Jew."

Anger ripped through Max Goldschmidt. He pointed the Sauer .38 directly at the professor, his index finger taut against the trigger.

No, he thought. *Not yet.*

The reincarnation of Anton Gunther commenced. His lips curled into a tight smile, as if bolted together on the insides of his cheeks. His eyes were no longer the haunted, weary eyes of a refugee. Now they seemed frosted with hate, vacant of empathy and reason, squinting into the windswept rain. The slumped shoulders now erect, the chin turned up proudly.

Einstein had seen it before. On the streets of Berlin, in the newsreels of rallies and riots.

It was what hate looked like.

"My name is Anton Gunther..."

Chapter Sixty-Three

HARRY WINCED AS THE BOW of the *Horseshoe* plunged into a wave, lifted into the air, and came crashing down, rattling his bones. His clothing was cold and wet and clung to his skin. His fingers were numb from clutching the window above the console. To his right, Amos wrestled with the steering wheel and throttle. The engine responded with throaty protests. Harry was especially concerned about the buildup of water sloshing around the deck and swamping a bilge pump. As a result, the boat had become heavy and sluggish. *Still, it had to be faster than Einstein's sailboat*, he thought.

"Can you go any faster?" he yelled at Amos.

They hit another wave.

Harry held on for his life as the boat defied gravity.

Anton Gunther had finished his confession and studied Albert Einstein's face for a reaction. He was disappointed to see no display of shock: no slack jaw or terrified whimper. Just those curious eyes studying him, as if he were one of Einstein's equations.

"Have you nothing to say, Professor?"

The *Tinef* rocked severely. Einstein eyed the white, thrashing waters of Plum Gut, just ahead.

"You can kill me, Gunther. But you will never survive these waters in the *Tinef*. We will both die. Put down the gun and let me handle her. Only I can save us."

Gunther locked the fingers of one hand on the waggling tiller and kept the Sauer trained on Einstein.

"Rotting in an American jail is worse than death. I am returning to Germany, Herr Professor. You will accompany me to our extraction point."

Einstein shook his head incredulously, then his eyes lit on something beyond Gunther.

"It's too late! Look behind you!"

Gunther swung his head over his shoulder. A flotilla of small boats was racing towards them. Einstein estimated they would converge on the *Tinef* within several minutes.

He turned his eyes forward, to the approaching maelstrom of Plum Gut.

"Enough, Gunther!" Einstein bellowed. "Let me take the tiller before we both drown."

Gunther's mind raced. He had been in tight squeezes like this before. There was always a way out. He just had to find it. *Improvise!*

He jerked at the tiller, fighting the current as it swept the boat closer to Plum Gut. Einstein clenched his fingers around the center cleat as the currents snatched violently at the boat. At least Gunther was forced to drop the Sauer .38 as he wrestled with the tiller. When he did, Einstein saw in his eyes a flash of concern, a sudden revelation of vulnerability. In that moment, he was Max Goldschmidt again. But just as quickly, Gunther returned: cold-blooded, deranged.

Einstein lunged for the gun. Reflexively, Gunther moved to block him, releasing the tiller.

The port side of the *Tinef* keeled violently, dangling Einstein precariously over the surf, clawing at a wobbly cleat. Gunther pinned him at the waist, savoring the futile convulsion of Einstein's muscles, the panicked flailing of limbs. He locked his eyes onto Einstein's— those famously dark and heavy eyes, now bulging in primal fear. He wrapped his fingers around the thick neck and began a controlled squeeze, feeling for the trachea, listening for the first short gasps.

Einstein kicked until his muscles, deprived of oxygen, simply gave out. He saw a sneering, triumphant smile cross his assailant's face, felt his harsh, hot breaths. Then the face blurred and slowly retreated into a darkening fog. Einstein's eyes met the dark sky.

The running was nearly over.

He gazed wondrously at luminous paths crisscrossing the universe, dazzling stretches that would steer him to explanations of life's deepest mysteries. He no longer felt the pain of Gunther's fingers. That seemed like another world: small, distant, petty. He sensed himself floating effortlessly, deeper into the universe. Freed from the gravity of ignorance, the limitations on his own mortal life on Earth.

He had explored that stretch of stars. Timeless. Permanent. Infinite.

Except, he thought, *for one*. A tiny pinpoint of blue, extinguished by its own inhabitants. Plunged into an icy blackness, as if it had never been born. All its achievements, wonders, and advances erased.

No.

His fingers flexed for the main sheet.

And yanked.

The boom responded exactly as he'd thought, swinging hard and cracking against the back of Gunther's skull. A triumph of velocity against mass. Gunther's eyes widened; reflexively, he released his grip on Einstein's neck and brought a hand to the pain. Einstein gasped for air, summoned his strength, and kicked, sending the Gunther sprawling into the cockpit. The Professor pulled himself back into the boat, lunged for the Sauer, and pointed it at Gunther as he grabbed the tiller.

Gunther struggled to sit up.

"I don't want to kill you," bellowed Einstein. The Sauer shuddered in his hand.

"And you won't. Your pacifism won't allow it. That is your weakness." Gunther braced himself on his elbows and slowly lifted himself up, grinning.

Einstein aimed the gun while shaking his head.

Suddenly, an explosion. A big bang, thought Einstein,

thundering across the firmament.

Gunther's eyes froze in confusion. His mouth was agape, sputtering a low, trembling moan. He fell across the cockpit. Blood oozed from his back, mixing with the sloshing pool of rain and bay water, turning it the color of rust.

A boat closed in. A voice called, "Are you alright, professor?"

Einstein dropped the gun. The *Horseshoe* was approaching.

"I didn't shoot him!" Einstein cried back.

From the bow of the *Bay Breeze*, James Amos yelled, "No, I did!"

Einstein shouted, "I must take down the sail." He looked down at Gunther, who was struggling to breathe. "This man is still alive!"

Harry yelled, "Good! We're going to arrest him and arrange for one hell of an execution!"

Einstein rushed to lower the mainsail and jib. They fell to a crumpled mass on the deck, and the mast swayed in the wind. When he turned back, Gunther was struggling, again, to stand.

"Don't move. Help is coming, Max."

Gunther glared at the professor. "My name is Anton Gunther," he wheezed defiantly. Then he lifted himself to his knees and rolled into the tempestuous Plum Gut.

Einstein watched as he was consumed by the waves.

Chapter Sixty-Four

PEERING THROUGH THE PERISCOPE of U-boat 42, *Kapitänleutnant* Hans Fischer felt his stomach tighten, his throat clench. He had caught glimpses of the confused fight in and around the boats. He had seen the man who, he assumed, was the German agent in question miraculously make his way up to Orient Point. The others followed him. None of which would have made any difference to Fass and Greitens, or the rest of his extraction team.

But beyond them he could see a dozen boats, of all kinds, escorting a ridiculous little half-disabled sailboat back to land— sailing close in around her. And beyond that there were at least a dozen more small boats of all kinds: sailboats and fishing and lobster boats, recreational powerboats, harbor rescue vessels, and police boats. They seemed to multiply by the minute. All forming a perimeter around Orient Point and the island near it. All exploring farther out to sea, as if searching for something. *His U-boat?*

A small plane cruised slowly overhead, flying low despite the storm. He could see what looked like a convoy of trucks and cars making their way out to Orient Point, full of men who seemed to be carrying weapons.

It was only a matter of time, Fischer knew, before the U.S. Coast Guard, and maybe even a naval patrol, dispatched from the Groton Submarine Base nearby. He was not going to start a war against a continent.

He summoned the landing party and ordered them to stand down. They were visibly disappointed. *That was all right. They would have their fill of fighting, and soon.*

"Reverse engines," he commanded over his speaking tube.

"Set a new course for Wilhelmshaven."

Kapitänleutnant Fischer returned briefly to his cabin, where he jotted down, then transmitted, a message to Berlin: *Ihr Paket wurde nicht erhalten.*

Your package was not received.

He wanted to add, *and fuck whoever planned this insanity.*

Instead, he had a coffee brought to him in his cabin while he waited for the navigator to bring his charts, and sat drinking it in his chair, alone. Thinking of what he had just seen.

All the little ships of Long Island.

He understood that everything would be harder from now on.

The Orient General Store had the only public telephone in the village. At 6:30 a man rushed in, a pair of binoculars swaying from his neck. It was Lutz, the court clerk, who'd been ordered that afternoon to go fishing at Orient Point. There, he was to observe movements on the beach.

He'd seen enough.

He slammed the booth closed, deposited a nickel, and fumbled with the rotary dial.

"Your package was lost," he groaned at Maria Voigt, dreading what would come next.

All he heard was the crisp click of the terminated call.

The mantle in Einstein's office chimed seven o'clock. Einstein sat on one side of his desk. Facing him were Amos and Weiss. Mrs. Dukas sat on a couch. Einstein's chalk scribbling of Zwick's code was still on the blackboard, untouched from when Einstein fled.

Einstein placed Schubert's Symphony No. 9 on a turntable and lit a pipe.

Amos cleared his throat. "It's a matter of national security, sir. Director Hoover would like to speak to you. Personally."

Einstein shrugged his indifference.

The call lasted only two minutes, Einstein frowning occasionally but mostly puffing smoke from the bowl of his pipe. He hung up, shaking his head.

"What did he say?" asked Mrs. Dukas.

"He will never change," Einstein replied. "He demanded that I keep what happened a secret. The White House believes the American people have had about as much as they can take of Nazi spy operations. They wish to handle it through diplomatic channels."

"And if you don't?"

"It would be seen as a reflection of my patriotism. Which could require scrutiny of my application for citizenship. Helen, I'm afraid that very little has changed since 1932, when Elsa and I applied to emigrate and Hoover forced me to sign a document stating I was not a communist. I made the mistake of allowing him to coerce me then. Now…"

The room fell silent, except for the quiet tick of the clock.

James said, "Some secrets of the universe are better left unknown, professor."

Aaach, was all Einstein could say.

Harry and James had one final stop before returning to Manhattan.

They sped to Camp Siegfried. By now the field was empty, beaten to a muddy pulp by the rain and the thousands of spectators. But the swastika banners still hung from the homes, unruffled by the day's events.

They barreled down Hitler Street, brakes squealing at number 80.

Harry pounded on the door, with no response. He pounded again, until James said, "Hold on." He jiggled the knob; it turned freely.

They entered Maria Voigt's house. Everything was as Harry had last seen it, including the overflowing ash tray on the kitchen table. But Maria Voigt was gone.

"She left the door open intentionally," James muttered.

"Sending us a message. She won."

James shrugged. "But Bobby Larkin's killer lost. And Hitler."

They walked back to the car. Before getting in, they scanned the road. Harry noticed a group of children chasing fireflies across the street. It was an ordinary scene to Harry: kids on a warm spring night, in any neighborhood in America.

"What next?" Harry asked Amos.

"President Roosevelt always had another adventure. So will I. There are still bad guys out there, and I intend to catch them. How about you?" Amos said.

Harry gazed at his mentor and said, "Dunno. I don't think I'm cut out for the Bureau. Too many rules. Too much bureaucracy. Not my thing."

"You're a good agent. Despite your cursing."

Harry opened the car door. Before crouching in, he waved to the girls across the street.

They began waving back, stretching their arms.

Their palms opened to a Hitler salute.

"Let's get back to work," Harry Weiss said.

They drove down Hitler Street.

Postscript

SIX WEEKS LATER, ON JULY 12th, Professor's Szilard and Wigner arrived at Litle Hog Neck. The discussion was conducted in German, punctuated by the urgent tap of chalk on the blackboard and the occasional groan of Einstein's chair as he leaned back and forth. Wigner interjected occasionally. Einstein fired questions at Szilard, who fired answers back. Finally, after examining a rambling equation scrawled by Szilard on the blackboard, Einstein's eyes widened. "I never thought of that."

Szilard and Wigner exchanged glances.

"Do you see it now?" Szilard asked.

Einstein puffed rhythmically on his pipe, then said, "There are always two obstacles to proving a theory in science, Szilard."

The two visitors remained silent.

"The first is the science itself. You have proven to me that you are correct. The atom can create a reaction powerful enough to be weaponized. I suppose 'congratulations' is the wrong word."

"And the second?" asked Szilard.

Einstein sighed glumly; the sad eyes grew heavier. "I accept the potential destructiveness of the atom. I could not accept the potential of human beings to destroy themselves. But now I understand. To save the world, we must show the President of the United States that Hitler has groomed men capable of destroying it."

"And how did you come to that conclusion?"

Einstein leaned back in his chair, exhaling a long plume of smoke. "A sail on the Peconic Bay."

The letter was completed in early August after a series of back-and-forth revisions, which reminded Einstein of his collaboration with Gerhardt Zwick on *Two Scientists Debate*. It would be over two months before Franklin Roosevelt received it, but as soon as the letter was read to him, he ordered a major new federal research project on an atomic bomb.

It would be called the Manhattan Project.

When the letter was finally finished, Einstein walked from his office to the kitchen. Helen sat at the table, editing a speech Einstein was scheduled to give to a refugee organization in New York City.

That August afternoon, pink, cottony clouds stretched across a deep blue sky. Einstein peered out the window, sighed contentedly, and said, "Helen, I think I will take a sail."

"Be careful, professor. Take a life preserver."

He strode down the hall, directly past the dusty orange life jacket propped uselessly against a wall.

He walked onto the porch and gazed at the harbor for a long moment, lost in thought.

Einstein returned inside and grabbed the life jacket.

Then he drove to Horseshoe Cove for a pleasant sail.

He drifted into the bright bay and turned his face into a warm breeze, then sailed passed beaches and coves fronting small towns where American flags flew from homes and storefronts. He waved to the boaters and fishermen who'd helped rescue him on two occasions and smiled gently.

For all of its misery, he thought, *it was a world worth saving.*

Author's Notes

As a member of Congress, I occasionally dabbled in the art of embellishment. The skill came in handy in the writing of *The Einstein Conspiracy*. I openly confess to spinning some facts and compressing some dates on these pages. However, the truth about Albert Einstein's extended 1939 vacation on Long Island is fascinating on its own.

The Einstein-Szilard letter was discussed at Einstein's cottage in Nassau Point (then known as Little Hog Neck) on July 12, 1939. Szilard and Wigner did, in fact, get lost until a local boy showed them to Dr. Moore's cottage on Grove Road. Final revisions to the letter were completed during a telephone call between Einstein and Szilard on August 3rd. However, the letter didn't make its way to FDR until October, when Alexander Sachs read it to the president.

Many of the quotes by Einstein and Szilard were taken from their speeches and writings.

There were two known attempts by the Nazis to assassinate Albert Einstein. However, the professor wasn't Hitler's only target. In 1940, Hitler hatched an outlandish plan to kidnap the Duke and Duchess of Windsor. When that failed, he set his sights on Operation Long Jump, the plot to kidnap FDR, Churchill, and Stalin during a summit in Tehran. (For more on this, read Howard Blum's *Night of the Assassins*).

Clandestine Nazi activities in and around Long Island are well documented. In June 1942, the German submarine U-202 landed at the beach at Amagansett, about one hundred miles east of New York City. Four German saboteurs came ashore with explosives, primers, and incendiaries. They were assigned to sabotage critical American facilities. The plan was discovered and disrupted. Plum

Island, just off Orient Point, was used as an anti-submarine base in World War II.

Einstein's less-than-accomplished sailing prowess is also a matter of local memory. Many residents of the North Fork claimed to have rescued him from the Long Island Sound and Peconic Bay. It is, of course, possible that the residents sought more acclaim than they deserved.

Many of the North Fork locations that appear on these pages remain. Rothman's Department Store, where Albert Einstein shopped, is, as of this writing, an upscale coffee shop adjacent to Einstein Square. The Einstein cottage remains and is a private home overlooking Cutchogue Harbor. Einstein's home on Mercer Avenue in Princeton is as he left it in the final days of his life. He bequeathed it to the Institute of Advanced Science (IAS) with the stipulation that it not be opened to the public as a tourist site, but instead used by faculty and researchers. My thanks to the IAS for letting me take a peek.

Yaphank is a real place with a chilling history of pro-Nazi sympathy. Streets named after Hitler, Goebbels, and Goering were not renamed until 1941. Today, Adolf Hitler Street is Park Street, Goering is Oak Street, and Goebbels is Northside Avenue. German Boulevard remains. It wasn't until 2016 that a Federal Judge approved an agreement that changed the German American Settlement League bylaws to open the community to the public in compliance with federal, state, and local housing laws.

Many of the events I describe on opening night of the 1939 World's Fair did occur, specifically Einstein's shortened speech, the thunderstorm, and the blackout caused when he threw a switch to illuminate the grounds.

German scientists, including Werner Heisenberg, were involved in several attempts to develop an atomic bomb. Heisenberg's actual role, either as collaborator or subverter, is a matter of debate and is addressed in *Heisenberg's War: The Secret History of the German Bomb* by Thomas Powers.

My thanks to two extraordinary authors for their indispensable critiques: Kevin Baker and former Congressman Robert Mrazek. Thanks as well for the brilliant editing skills of James Bock, and the research assistance of Andrew Lorenzen and Amy Folk, of the Southold Museums.

Most of all, to my family. To my wife Cara, who pushed me through those dismal periods when the words did not come, here are the words that count: I love you. You make the universe a much better place.

Steve Israel, is the only U.S. Congressman who ever retired from the House to open an independent bookstore, Theodore's Books in Oyster Bay, NY. He has written two critically acclaimed political satires, *The Global War on Morris* (2014) and *Big Guns* (2018). His essays have appeared in the New York Times, Washington Post, Atlantic Magazine, among others.

www.ingramcontent.com/pod-product-compliance
Lightning Source LLC
Chambersburg PA
CBHW020417030726
47495CB00006B/1546